- IN THE GIANT'S SHADOW BOOK THREE -

THE
VOICE
OF
STONES

PETE A O'DONNELL

The Voice of Stones

Cover image by Miblart

First Printing, 2024

ISBN 978-1-7349090-9-8

Ill-Advised Stories
PO Box 6072 Warwick, RI 02887
www.illadvisedstories.com

Also By

The Curse of Purgatory Cove

In the Giants Shadow
Book 1: The Stars Beyond the Mesa
Book 3The Voice of Stones

And for younger readers:
The Merlin's Visit the Fire Station

Chapter 1

In a binary star system, the sole traveler through the habitable zone was a lonely gas giant. Only its moons and a belt of rock and dust kept it company. It appeared solid at a distance but its borders were made from golden, subtle fumes that reached out into the darkness of space while drifting clouds of vapor and the coarse winds of massive storms danced below. This was Altor.

From above one of its moons, a man watched the planet rise, making a slow ascent over the horizon of the green and blue garden world of Uppsala. Emperor Tamerlane was the only person in his darkened quarters, in the farthest edge of the ring of his command ship, The Revenant.

Behind him, barely touching, were eerie shadows that shunned the light of the rising world. He knew they were there, lurking at the edge of his senses. 'What ghosts are these that haunt me today?' He wondered with the weight of something deadly in his hand. He spoke to the darkness, "Where will you lead me?"

Nothing answered above the sound of his command ship coming to life. Stroking his beard, he examined the thing he held, then he looked up to see the reflection of a handsome man in the glass viewport, a man with light brown skin unmarred by time. The emperor was barely in his forties, but his age was difficult to guess behind his black beard which was streaked with a single hint of white. "To war, I suppose, a reckoning," he said, and the words made him smile.

He looked down again and considered the thing in his hand, a dagger with an elaborate handle, made from an alloy that defied study. The edge was sharp enough that he could've forced it through the armored hull of the ship. It would've penetrated into the vacuum of space if not for the weapon's guard, but its real power wasn't the blade itself but the superstitions it evoked, a fear of gods who promised destruction for the unfaithful.

The walls trembled and quaked as the engines of The Revenant fired, moving the massive vessel out of orbit. Taking his hand from his beard, he braced himself against the window while the force of acceleration pushed him back, compelling him to steady his legs. He lifted the dagger higher, playing with the distant light from Altor as it shone off the blade and danced across its etched surface. Nearly his entire life, since the emperor was a boy, the weapon had been a memento to him, a reminder of his duty. In all that time, he'd never allowed it to taste blood. To his knowledge, it had taken only one life, one that was dear to him.

He crossed his cabin and returned the weapon to its place on the wall where it hung with the point toward the floor. Vengeance for that lost life would have to wait. He had new slights and an entire world to punish first. The soldiers of Tairnish had sworn their fealty, only to betray him when they took his daughter. They thought he was weak. That their time had come, but they didn't know the true war he was fighting and how cautious he had to be.

Even this ship, The Revenant, the most powerful battle cruiser in the system, would mean little in the larger war. From a distance, it looked fragile, like a gently spinning ornament, all curves and linked compartments under shining panels. It was an illusion. In truth, each part of The Revenant bristled with weapons. Every component was capable of fighting on if the rest were damaged. It was an old design and an old ship, having seen combat above Grannus a decade ago and serving in skirmishes all across the system before that. It had weapons that smaller vessels weren't capable of carrying, devices of annihilation that would destroy an enemy's will to fight.

It had been remade since the last great war when Tamerlane had pushed to take the water world Grannus, the last living moon to resist him. He held back then, unwilling to destroy the world completely. He thought of those days, of the lessons learned as he turned away from the window, away from his home. Uppsala had been a prize to every noble family that came before him. He'd taken it while he was still a young man, but it wasn't enough.

The emperor moved across his spartan quarters, which were smaller and barer than what most nobles would willingly accept. Fewer still would put up with the level of g-force on the outer edge of the Revenant's ring. As it spun, it created the illusion of gravity at a greater force than Uppsala, closer to what the Tairnishmen were born into on that heavy moon of theirs. The emperor's soldiers were housed and trained in this ring, allowing no weakness for the men and women who served him.

He thought of the Tairnishmen again and felt his face turn hot. At one time there would've been a place for them in his plans, but their foolish pride had ended that. Even now they were fighting, taking positions that belonged to the emperor, like the construction docks around Tairnish. That wasn't their worst insult, though. 'His daughter? How dare they touch her!'

Going to the hatch on his cabin, resting his hand on the wheel, he glanced back at the shadows, considering their darkness. Then he opened it and stepped out, starting for the center of the vessel, the command spire, a central column that linked all the rings, like a spear aimed toward space with a mass accelerator as its point.

When the emperor stepped into the hall, guards in combat armor fell in beside him along with a woman who had dark skin, a few wrinkles, and scars near her close-cut grey hair. She wore a simple uniform, unmarked with rank. Tamerlane glanced back at her, knowing that the guards were ceremonial, while the woman Ada was far more dangerous. She was one of his oldest and most valuable assets.

As they traveled through the long hallways the guard's magnetic boots made their rigid gait more pronounced. They reached a descender, a small modular booth, barely large enough for the four. The doors closed and they dropped down one of The Revenant's structural spokes, falling away from the outer ring and the force of constant inertia, toward the ship's heart. Eventually, Tamerlane had to turn on his own mags as the slow-building acceleration of The Revenant forced him to the wall while the descender pushed him to the ceiling.

The doors opened to more soldiers waiting outside the command deck. The emperor stepped past the guards while they pounded their chest plates in salute. They stood in front of the most armored, well-protected part of the ship. With a nearly seamless outer wall and a curved surface, the command deck was built to move and rotate, attempting to lessen the effect of combat maneuvers.

It locked in place so the door could open, then a nearly invisible seam widened before them. There was no way to hurry the heavy door as it slid back. The walls were thicker than a bank safe, made from tons of reinforced metal and a webwork of micro-carbon materials. The emperor slipped through with Ada following him, leaving the armored guards behind while the command crew inside stood and saluted. The room was softly lit with display screens lining the walls, monitoring the ship through hundreds of sensors dotting its hull.

The admiral wore a strained expression on his face, bringing himself to his feet against the force of acceleration. "My emperor, there's a message for you from Nalanda station."

The emperor glanced over his shoulder, seeing the door had begun its slow trip back. He waited, not acknowledging the admiral till he felt the floor move, shifting so the downward force gave the illusion that the room was facing the right way. He saw the relief on his admiral's face, but he betrayed nothing of what he thought of it.

"Is it that old monk attempting to apologize for my daughter's kidnapping?" The emperor asked. Tamerlane knew the Kavaris, the order's name for their head monk. He'd spent his time at Nalanda and had been top in all his classes there, surpassing most in combat training as well. He'd thought the monk was ancient back then.

There was a narrow window in which Nalanda and Uppsala lined up for direct communications but there was still a delay because of the distance. Most messages came as burst transmissions bounced off relay stations around Altor. He'd been waiting to hear from Kavaris Dell.

The admiral came closer but before speaking, he glanced at Ada, whose expression didn't change as she watched him. He cleared his throat and lowered his voice. "It's not from the Kavaris. It's an encrypted message, my lord. Also, we've received other news. The Æsir have taken action. Apparently, you were not the only one unhappy with the monk."

The admiral offered a tablet to the emperor with the message pulled up. He scanned it quickly, reading about the trial. He already knew the monks had placed Tara under arrest. The emperor thought of the girl, assuming the next thing he'd hear was that she'd been executed. He'd known her most of her life, but he felt nothing at the thought of her dying. She had a purpose, to keep his daughter out of trouble and she'd failed. Putting the blame on Tara for the poisoning of Grannus hadn't been his idea, but he approved of what his agent had done.

He wasn't often surprised but as he read on, he felt his spine tighten. Kavaris Dell was dead, murdered by an Æesir. That was shocking enough, but that wasn't why his body turned cold. It was the method of the monk's death. Tamerlane thought of his father's throne room, nearly forty years ago. He could never forget the image, the man who raised him pinned to a wall while a massive evil thing loomed in the air in front of him, looking like death with its face a twisted version of a human skull. The Æesir had given the same death to the old monk.

Emperor Tamerlane scrolled through the message, seeing that it was only text. "I want an image of the corpse. I want to see it."

The admiral nodded. "It will be done." Snapping his fingers, he pointed to someone behind a display screen.

Tamerlane took a moment and steadied his nerves before opening the transmission from his agent. It was a more detailed account of what happened. It spoke about Alex, one of the travelers from the void, the one Maeven had taken to. The Æesir had gone out of its way to save him.

'Maybe Maeven had been right in getting so close to the boy? If the Æesir were protecting him, then there must be a reason.' The emperor thought before whispering, "Another of our god's weaknesses." His thoughts went to the dead world.

"What was that, my lord?" the admiral asked.

"Nothing," Tamerlane snapped, unhappy at the intrusion. "How long till we're in attack range of Tairnish?"

"At combat speed, we can be there in 120 hours." The admiral sounded apologetic, but there was nothing he could do about the way their orbits lined up.

The emperor continued to read the agent's report. She had included a plan of action for Maeven's rescue. That's what he loved about Edith. Her mind was always three steps ahead, planning and preparing. Tamerlane would trade a thousand of his men for one of her. He read her plan. It was risky and dangerous, but if there was anyone he could trust to succeed, it was her. He drafted his response and sent it, then he looked at the admiral. "Slow us to standard transit speed."

The admiral did some quick calculations in his head. He knew the way each moon in the system moved. "But, my lord, that'll make it nearly fourteen days before we arrive. The Tairnishmen are attacking the docks now. Our men are being overwhelmed, surely you wish to resupply them?"

"I don't know if I've ever had an admiral thrown out an airlock, but you have me considering it." Tamerlane's eyes stayed down, never leaving the tablet.

The admiral glanced at the woman Ada again. She stared directly at him with eyes that were inhumanly dark. He lowered his head. "I'm sorry, my lord. I didn't mean any offense."

When Tamerlane finally brought his attention from the tablet, he smiled. "Stop groveling." He handed the tablet back and rested his hands on the admiral's shoulders, standing uncomfortably close. "I understand your concern. It's good you're worried about our men and even more importantly about our strategic assets, the docks, the bases, but this is the thing, none of it matters anymore. Tairnish is a corpse that hasn't been buried yet. I only need a little time to rob its grave. So standard transit speed if you please."

"Yes, my lord," the admiral said.

Chapter 2

On the water world Grannus, deep below the ocean's surface two exhausted refugees surrendered to their rescuers. Chris was grateful as he felt Katy's arm slip from his, taken up by another swimmer. They were surrounded by divers who came and took them back toward one of the royal subs. He watched the lights on their suits, moving ahead toward the even brighter pool below a small craft, making a wall of illumination against the blackness of the vast and unending ocean.

The Grannusian Chooth was gone, Chris was almost certain. That creature, who he'd thought was his friend, had vanished into the dark, spread to the currents after his largest part, a nightmarish thing called a Caleth-Gul, had been skewered with a harpoon. Chris was content to be handled and guided, no longer having to use his exhausted arms to swim. He had nothing left but he resisted the urge to close his eyes, afraid all the terrible things he'd seen in the last hour would play again across his thoughts. The memories of a dead crew, Katy being choked, and the eel-like head of Chooth, decimated by a weapon he'd fired, were all waiting for him. He knew they'd play again and again. For a moment he envied Katy for her blindness, that she didn't have to see any of it. Some part of him resented her as he thought of his brother and the others, wishing they'd stayed together, that he'd never come to this world.

A circle of light emanated from the hatch on the sub. The vessel was much like the one Cormack had piloted, that they'd lost near the colony. Hands guided him up and he felt the vials against his skin tucked inside the zipper on his top. He protected them as he was pushed through, feeling the water move around in his awkwardly fitting suit. He would've been content to slump on the floor, but incredibly strong arms lifted him and guided him to a bench. Those arms kept him from falling as he pivoted on his legs, which were held stiff in casts. Katy was already sitting. He was carefully brought down next to her then he felt his mask pulled away.

The man in front of him took off his own mask revealing a scraggly, greying beard. With his brow furrowed, he said, "You must be Chris. Prince Cormack sent me to help you. My name is Cathal."

"Thank you," Chris said as he leaned back on one hand and turned to Katy. "Are you all right?" he asked.

Katy nodded. "I think so."

Chris clutched the antidotes and turned back to the man. "Was the prince angry?

"Just worried," Cathal, said. "That's why he sent me, I'm a friend of the family." Cathal wasn't very tall, but he looked as solid as an anchor and had the bearing of a cage fighter. He started to pull off his wetsuit, exposing a scarred torso and a powerfully packed, lean body as he said, "We're going to get you back to the command ship, where I'm pretty sure you're going to be asked a lot of questions."

Chris nodded, feeling exhaustion overtaking him, but Cathal tapped him on the shoulder. "If you don't mind, I've got one question for you now." Chris struggled to nod, feeling his whole body heavy with exhaustion. Cathal continued, "The Caleth-Gul looked like it was chasing you, like it intended you harm?"

"It definitely did," Chris said.

Cathal bit his lip and nodded. "Okay, I made the right call then. Killing any part of a Grannusian isn't something I like to make a habit of. Most people don't even know what a Caleth-Gul looks like, but during the war, I saw them in action, saw them save people. Not many know how much the Grannusians helped us, using beasts like that and even more astounding life forms. Hell, we don't even know how many Grannusians there are, but when I saw that one following Eir, something felt off, so I acted."

"You mean the war with the people from Uppsala?" Chris asked.

"Yes, with the emperor's people, and pretty much everyone else too." Cathal smiled. "I served Cormack and Naiathne's father then. So, I'm kind of their adopted uncle."

Chris looked at the man and thought about his last encounter with Cormack, how he'd accused him and his people of causing the poisoning. He'd been wrong then and he might be wrong now, but some part of him wanted to trust Cathal. "You made the right call," he said. "That was Chooth, but there was something wrong with him. He was going to kill Eir to stop this from getting out." Chris unzipped his wet suit and pulled the vials out. He looked at them, then offered them to Cathal. "It's the antidote. Eir made it."

The man patted him on the shoulder and pushed his hands back. "Why don't you hold onto them for a bit longer? Keep them safe," he said. "For now, catch your breath. We'll be docking in about twenty minutes, then there's going to be a lot more people asking you questions."

Chris looked at the vials again. He was about to stuff them back in his suit, but he shook his head. "Maybe we should get something a little better to hold them in. Something solid."

Cathal smiled again, revealing a number of broken teeth. "Yeah, agreed," he said as he went to the gear locker. He came back with a hard-sided case and held it open for Chris to put the vials in. He closed it and handed the whole thing back. "Like I said, get some rest.

I'm here if you need anything, okay?" Then Cathal went up to the sub's controls to join the pilot.

Chris felt Katy lean against him and ask, "Do you think we're safe?"

Chris nodded. "Maybe for the first time."

∞

Eir stopped speaking not long after breaching the surface of the launch bay in the royal sub. Even after being transported to the sick ward and being given a small dose of the antidote, she didn't return to herself. The bonds that kept her together as a single entity were failing. There were decisions to be made that involved the sub's captain and doctor, a scientist, and Cathal himself, and all of them wished there were someone from the Grannusian race to speak to, but Grannusians had become scarce. They were in hiding, afraid of the poison but also of what might happen to them while they were in a weakened state.

The debrief for Katy and Chris had been long as Cathal promised, but they weren't done when their story was told. The captain allowed them to join the conversation in the galley about what to do next and the realities they faced. Aside from the launch bays, the galley, where the crew ate, was the largest space on the sub with room for a little over a dozen people, or an entire watch, to sit. Even with half that, the room felt tight to Chris, like everything else on the sub. He was tall for his age, and he'd started to notice many of the people on the water world were on the smaller side. The cabins on the sub were big enough for them, but just barely.

One of the scientists, the one that reported on Eir's condition, had explained that they could only give her so much of the antidote because they needed a sample to recreate it.

"But you have to help her," Katy demanded.

11

"We need to help all of them, all of the Grannusians," Cathal explained in a patient, soft tone. He wasn't a scientist or part of the navy, but everyone seemed to listen to him, even the captain and his command staff.

"If you give it to her and she gets better then she can help you make more," Katy suggested.

"Or we use up everything we have," the subs doctor, a lean older man, pointed out.

Chris was sitting back with his arms crossed, considering Katy. Though she couldn't see, her attention appeared heightened as she turned her head at every comment. It was enough to make him wonder about her motivations, remembering the reason she'd followed Cormack to this world, to find Eir and have the healer fix her eyes. Chris hoped Katy could understand that there were bigger issues at hand.

The scientist added, "Look, there's been very little research into Grannusian biology, at least that I know of. They're not fond of us prying into what makes them tick."

"Can you blame them?" Chris asked, rolling his eyes toward the man.

The sub's doctor lifted an eyebrow and said, "Right now, yes, because we want to help them. But here's the problem, we don't know exactly how the poison works and we don't know what it is that Eir created."

Cathal shook his head. "But we do know that if we give it to her, then it's gone."

The scientist added, "Look I'm not going to say we haven't tried to understand Grannusian biotech. We have. We've tried for centuries and what we've learned is that it's incredibly intricate, more like an art form with biology as the canvas. I've examined the poison and surprisingly it's Grannusian in origin, but only passingly so. Whoever created it took a virus that our neighbors have been treating for years and made a sinister variant. The science was blunt but effective. They may not have even known how bad it would be, though I'm sure they knew it wouldn't be good."

Cathal broke in and said through gritted teeth, "I think we all know who created this. Tamerlane may deny it, but this has his fingerprints all over it."

The scientist nodded, then continued, "Either way, whatever is in those vials that Eir created, if it's an actual cure, it's going to be much more elegant than the problem. Eir built it on past knowledge that I don't have and that I doubt any other human has either."

"What are you saying?" the captain asked.

The scientist sighed. "I have no interest in wasting the sample, but the fact is it'd be better if the Grannusians were the ones who tried recreating it. We're just too damn clumsy to do it ourselves and we'd probably lose most of it in the attempt."

"If only they weren't in hiding," the ship's doctor pointed out.

Everyone took a moment to reflect, then Cathal broke the silence. "There's one place we're sure to find Grannusians who haven't been affected." Everyone, including Chris and Katy, turned to him. "Nalanda station," he said. "I have friends there, including Clio. She was a Grannusian who helped us during the war. Without Eir, she's been their ambassador on the station. Their leader, if that word even fits when it comes to the way they organize themselves."

Chris was sitting next to Katy. He glanced at her again, trying to gauge her reaction, and was surprised to feel her reach over and take his arm. "He's right." she said as she squeezed and leaned into him, "And it's just for now. Saving Eir's people is the most important thing. Plus, we have family we both want to check in on, right?"

Chris was surprised. He smiled as it dawned on him that they weren't as far apart on things as he first thought. "I'm glad to hear you say that."

Eventually, the meeting ended, and they were left alone. The captain and the first mate allowed them to use their quarters to rest for a few hours, though later, they'd be berthed with the crew. Cathal took the time to communicate with Anchor Home and with Cormack, starting the process of getting a shuttle ready for launch. After a few hours when he knocked at their cabin doors, he had other news for them. He'd been given a report about Kavaris Dell and Chris's brother. Chris was upset as he heard that Alex had nearly been executed, but he didn't have long to process it as Cathal next told them about Ben, who was in a coma.

Katy's hand went to her mouth, and she uttered the word, "No."

Neither of them was particularly relaxed after that as the captain made all due speed to Anchor Home. Two days after running from Chooth, Chris and Katy arrived at the city.

Grannus for the most part was a continuous ocean, but Anchor Home was one of the few solid pieces of land that jutted above the waves. It was a true island unlike where most of the humans on the water moon lived. They made their homes on massive floating barges made from the carcasses of dead sea creatures, the Gigas Chelonioidea. They were giant animals with shells that could grow to a half kilometer long. Often their bodies floated after expiring because the beasts would turn in their death throws, pointing their watertight shells towards the ocean floor when they passed, leaving the organic material of their bodies to decay and eventually become fertile soil. The humans of Grannus had made their homes on the ancient bodies for centuries and Anchor Home had a string of the barges surrounding it.

Hundreds were set up as farms to feed the populace, and many more had housings that climbed high, making the false islands look dangerously unstable. In the center of Anchor Home was an unending tower that climbed all the way to orbit. This was the Throat, an organic structure that tethered the Star Blossom. an artificial moon to the world, created by the Grannusians in a long-forgotten time when space exploration still interested them. In the shadow of the Throat was the royal palace, a grand structure with white walls that climbed high, made from a porous stone dredged from the ocean bottom. It was surrounded by turrets and towers with weapon emplacements pointed toward the sky. Of course, it was only possible to see this in the royal sub's monitors as it stayed below the surface till it passed through an underwater lock and entered a bay beneath the palace.

When they were docked, Cathal helped guide Chris and Katy out the main hatch, showing them to the ladder that would bring them down to a pier. It wasn't an easy task getting Chris out as he climbed with one leg in a short cast, while the other was useless and in a much longer support. Each step made his bones ache and everything in the sub bay seemed to be damp and slippery and a little dark despite large floodlights high overhead. While he worked his way down, he noticed cranes moving across the ceiling, going to the submarine's cargo hatch. It lowered down and came back out with a tank full of seawater. Inside was Eir and all her component parts, swimming slowly in a disorganized cloud.

The tank was brought to the pier where a number of scientists along with a figure dressed in a robe, the traditional Grannusian garment for dry land, stood. The hooded figure was back from the others, staying in the shadows.

Chris settled onto a set of crutches, then followed Cathal, who was guiding Katy. From a few steps back Chris watched Cathal gently touch the hooded figure on the shoulder, getting her attention. She turned and followed him to Chris and Katy. "I'm glad you guys aren't dead," she said.

Chris couldn't see her face, but he recognized the voice. Katy did too as she said a bit too loud. "Naiathne!?" Luckily the sound of the machines absorbed her volume.

The room was almost too loud to hear the Naiad, as she reached out and touched Katy's arm. "Shush— I'm not exactly the most welcome person here. I just wanted to check on Eir and you guys. I guess it's as bad as they say. About her, and about Chooth." Her head turned a little inside the hood and Chris could feel her looking at him.

"Hopefully it's not too late to help her . . . maybe Chooth too," Chris said, though there was some hesitancy on the second part as he remembered pulling the trigger that killed the main part of the Chooth's body.

"Chris, you did what you had to," Cathal said. "And you saved your friend, maybe the entire Grannusian race."

"Yeah, we'll see," Chris said. Then he turned back to Naiathne. "Are you coming with us back to Nalanda?"

Naiathne let out a long sigh and even under the hood Chris could feel her rolling her eyes. "Cormack is insisting on it. He wants me there. I guess to be his show creature or something."

"He doesn't want your people to be forgotten," Katy said.

"I know." Naiathne crossed her arms.

"It's a lot easier to do terrible things to a forgotten people. Remember what happened to the miners in the ring around Altor? An entire society was wiped out,

16

hunted to extinction, and no one batted an eye, saying they weren't really human anyway. Our supposed gods didn't lift a finger to stop Tamerlane," Cathal pointed out.

"I get it!" Naiathne's voice became hard. "Look, I'm going. You guys want me to go, so I'm going."

Cathal scratched his beard and his brow drew down as his voice turned into a bit of a growl. "Sorry, I didn't mean to upset you."

Chris looked at the man, whose voice had been kind for the few days he knew him. It was strange to hear him turn cold. Then, even more surprising, he heard Naiathne say, "No, I'm sorry. I'm— look, I'm really sorry."

"It's fine," Cathal said, he reached out and touched Naiathne's arm. "Get yourself back into hiding. I'll find you when it's time, okay? I'm going to bring these guys up to their rooms, so they can get cleaned up. They've got an audience with the queen later."

"Hopefully they survive it," Naiathne said in a lighter tone.

"Hopefully I do too." Cathal smiled, though he didn't sound as sure as usual.

Chapter 3

Ben rubbed his eyes as they slowly opened. His vision cleared and he looked around at the gently curving walls and the dim lights of the medical unit. The last thing he remembered, he and Alex had been on their way to save Maeven. He had no idea how he ended up here.

Sitting up, he felt his head start to pound, and when he touched his scalp, he found bandages wrapping it tight and going down over his ears where they muffled his hearing. Between the quiet and the soft lighting, he felt an eerie sense of remoteness as if he weren't quite awake. He glanced at the rest of himself and wiggled his toes, feeling the simple motion anchor him. 'Nothing looks broken or missing, so that's good,' he thought. Then he asked the empty room, "What happened to me?" Only his voice echoed back off the curved walls to answer him, making the emptiness feel strange and hollow.

Ben vaguely remembered climbing down a rope, then falling, but he wasn't sure why. 'Did I slip? No, I was tied off.' He swung his legs over the side of the bed and got to his feet, then took a moment to steady himself. "Where is everyone?" He looked back behind him and realized that this was the very same bed Alex had been in, not once but twice. Ben leaned against it and breathed. He wished it wasn't so dark.

"Speaking of friends," he said, turning to the open space and peering across the med unit at a shadowy doorway that led to the room they kept Tearmai in. Something was wrong. The clean and organized walls with their smooth surface were interrupted by an opening with wreckage hanging from it. They were the broken shards of hard plastic that had been the door. They dangled from a stone frame; the few remaining pieces of the barrier that'd kept the deranged Drake safely locked away.

Keeping his voice low, Ben felt tingles run down his spine and said, "Glad I wasn't on the other side of that." His eyes never stopped moving, darting over the whole unit, but always coming back to that opening. He felt watched sitting there in the low light. He was afraid the room might not be as empty as it appeared. Ever since that night, weeks ago when Amita and he had seen a ghost, he had avoided being by himself on the station. He looked at the lights and wondered if they were turned down because of the night cycle. If Nalanda was on the dark side of the gas giant when ghosts were most active.

He took a few steps forward, feeling relief as the lights turned on in response. 'Better," he said after another step, going slowly toward Tearmai's room. Reaching out, he touched the shards that still hung there in the doorway, pieces of an engineered material six inches thick that had failed under the extreme stress of Tearmai beating against them. Ben could see the claw marks. He stuck his head in the room and more lights came on automatically. The small space was empty without even a bed for the large Drake.

Ben's eyes went to the far wall, to the scratches that were dug into the stone. They were long, jagged claw marks that tore apart the grey solid surface. It took a moment for Ben to realize they weren't random. Strange words twisted in bizarre patterns, like the ramblings of a madman, and there was an image as well, showing caves and tunnels under a sky full of broken, cloudy mountains. Ben realized he was looking at volcanos with ash and smoke pouring from the craters on their tops. He didn't want to imagine how the Drake had made those darker lines, though he thought maybe Tearmai had used his own blood.

"Man," Ben said as he came closer, seeing something else he recognized. It was deep in the center of one volcano. He touched the white scratches of its sharply pointed lines, knowing the Drake had intended to carve out the diamond vessel, the very thing they'd escaped the destruction of the Earth in. "This is where it came from," Ben said, glancing up at the sky over the volcanoes.

There was something else. Tearmai had carved flames shooting across the clouds, but their shape and form were long and stretched out. It was hard to tell from the crude drawing, but Ben thought he knew what they were, Fire-Golems, free of their shells.

Suddenly he remembered why he'd fallen. He'd been hanging on a rope when one of the golems came straight for him and slashed through his line. He'd liked the creatures, and up until then, he'd thought they were more than just tools, that maybe they were alive. He knew he wasn't being completely reasonable, but he couldn't help feeling anger well up. He tried pushing it down as he did with most things.

He looked at the words below the mountains, trying to make sense of what he saw, but his eyes kept wandering back to the Fire-Golems. "You could've killed me," he said, touching the bandage on his head again.

"That would've been unfortunate. More so for the Golems, I'd think," someone said from outside the door.

Ben jumped, nearly falling over. He grabbed his chest and turned to see a monk standing behind him. She nodded, looking amused at how jittery he was. With her head shaved, it took him a moment to realize it was a woman in the red robe. "It seems your people, the ones who came through the wormhole have been chosen by the Æsir. Once it was us, their humble monks, but now we see that you five are the ones they truly hold in their hearts." She came forward and touched the wall. "Injuring you, it appears, carries a terrible penalty." The

20

monk's voice was soft and pleasant with only the smallest hint of rage beneath.

"Um, right. 'Chosen by the Æsir,' I guess that's a good thing?" Ben said.

"I certainly agree." The monk nodded. Her age was hard to guess. Her posture was rigid, not stooped over by time, and she moved with the sure-footedness of an athlete. Ben noticed scars on the back of her head, similar to the ones Edith had. In fact, there was much about this woman that reminded Ben of the former head of security. The monk was looking at him and he realized he'd been staring at her for far too long. It was a prolonged awkward moment.

"I'm sorry. I have no idea what you're talking about. Should I climb back into bed or something?" Ben finally asked.

"If you wish. The swelling in your skull has gone down. Your recovery has been quick. I would recommend you rest, but you can do that in your quarters as well as you can here. There's combat training out in the cage so I imagine this place will be full soon." The monk motioned to the window, sounding aloof as if she really didn't care. Ben had always felt like a problem to the monks, something they needed to solve. Sure, they didn't like him, but at least they were concerned. He didn't trust this new approach, a vague indifference.

"Should I talk to someone else, someone in charge?" he asked.

The monk leaned in and smiled again as if he'd shared a joke. "Funny enough, I am the one in charge. At least for now. I'm sister Nemain, interim Kavaris. My replacement, or I should say Kavaris Dell's replacement, is on his way."

Ben felt some reluctance to ask. "What happened to Kavaris Dell?"

The monk turned, leaving the room to go back out into the larger medical unit, but she said over her shoulder, "He was stabbed through the heart by the Æesir when he tried to execute your friend. The one that killed one of our monks. One of my brothers."

"Jeez," Ben said, letting his mouth fall open. He watched the monk get further away as her words registered. "Those are like your gods, right? They showed up? Like in person and...um?" he called, but he was answered by silence.

"Okay," he said to himself while nervously tapping his toe as he turned back to the wall. He took one more look at the carvings before following her out. He was full of questions, but as he watched the monk move about the medical unit, her red robe flying out behind her, he got the feeling a follow-up wouldn't be appreciated. Instead, he changed the subject. "Could you tell me what happened to the big guy you were keeping in here, Tearmai?"

Sister Nemain didn't stop moving, as she gathered supplies. She huffed, then said, "He escaped after the Æesir visited. Things were, and still are, a bit disorganized here so we have no idea where the mad Drake is. He's probably wandering the lower levels."

"Oh," Ben said. He was about to say more. He wanted to explain that Alex hadn't murdered anyone. That he didn't have it in him, but if Alex was still keeping it secret, then Ben didn't want to spoil it. It took a moment for this to run through his head, which meant more awkward silence between him and the monk as he watched her move.

She finally turned to him. "There's a change of clothing in that cabinet. Let me know if you need anything else." She pointed quickly, then with a swish she headed down the ramp and out of the medical unit, leaving Ben alone.

"Okay, thanks," he called after her. "I guess I'll just go get dressed." He started towards the clothing. "Maybe find my friends. Who aren't here," he muttered to himself as he took out the neatly folded uniform.

Something made him want to go back and look inside Tearmai's room again, some sense of curiosity that he'd very pointedly been trying to ignore since arriving here. He stood in the doorway and his eyes went to the words again, to those scratch marks. When they'd first arrived at Nalanda station, Fafnir, another Drake, had used the remains of a Lightening Bug to rewire the language center of Ben and his friend's brains. Whatever the standard language was, for the most part, it all sounded like English to them. Written words were translated as well, but without context, things could still fail to make sense, such was the case with Tearmai's carving. Ben read the lines as they twisted in the rock.

'Broken stones- the slave set free- a cataclysm- It's awake- a metamorphosis.' Some of the words repeated in different sizes and a few had been scratched out only to be written again as if Tearmai was trying to figure something out.

"Man, I hope you're all right, big guy," Ben said, thinking of the history he and the Drake shared. Even though it started with him throwing a rock at the creature, he'd really liked Tearmai in the brief time he'd known him. He could even ignore the way the alien had pulled him from quicksand using his mouth. Of course, after that, and after going through the void space, Tearmai had gone insane and nearly killed Ben and Amita. To his knowledge, the large Drake hadn't gotten better and now he was lost somewhere in the station.

Ben shrugged and started to get changed. Right in the middle of the med unit, he pulled the clothing on. He didn't feel silly till it was time to leave, realizing there were still bandages wrapped around his head. He

23

touched them, wondering if he could take them off but the idea that something important might fall out, like his brains, made him hesitate. Leaving the wrappings right where they were, he walked down the ramp, going out into the strange world of Nalanda station.

As the doors opened, he heard a crowd ahead gathered in one of the grand halls, at combat training. The hushed whispering sounded more like a tennis match than the simulated battle the students were forced to compete in. Tara, Amita, and Alex crossed Ben's mind, as he wondered, 'Maybe they're part of this.' He stared at the giant cage in the center of the grand hall, at the two teams, one with green markings and one with red.

Ben recognized a few of the students. They were all from Uppsala so both sides were loyal to the emperor, but they were still fighting hard, trying to recover each other's markers and bring them back to their bases. It looked like the green team was currently in the lead, moving to the high ground on the right side of the field with the red marker in hand. The obstacles had been reset from the last time Ben had seen the cage.

He only watched for a moment, till he confirmed no one he cared about was out there, then his eyes went to the crowd. Everyone wore the same clothing, making it hard to tell one person from the next. He searched the balconies as well, but Alex and Tara weren't on Maeven's or anyone else's, not that he could see anyway.

He wasn't sure what to do, not till he peered at the walkways and saw an unmistakable form. "Tearmai?" Ben whispered but quickly realized this creature was far too large to be his friend.

Still, if he wanted to know anything, then who better to ask than one of the stewards of the Extraracial species. He followed the ramp down to where it connected with the central stairs and climbed toward Fafnir's massive form. The Drake was the oldest known of his species and stood nearly three meters tall with his joints and broad back covered in gnarled barbs. It wasn't easy for him to hide, but he was doing his best not to be noticed, standing back in the shadows, just to the side of a corridor, leaning on his staff.

Fafnir continued to watch the combat field, never looking in Ben's direction or acknowledging his presence. It wasn't till Ben was right next to him that his voice rumbled out from his beak, "You're not dead."

Ben felt the vibrations move through him as he stared up at the massive Drake. "No, I guess I'm just a little banged up. Apparently, I was in a coma. First time for that." Ben smiled nervously, but it didn't matter, the Drake never turned to look at him. He didn't respond at all.

Ben followed Fafnir's eyes and saw he was staring at a corner of the cage, where the combatants were in a particularly vicious fight. He turned and watched as well for a moment, fighting an urge to fidget as he rocked up on his toes and asked, "I didn't think the other races liked watching this stuff?"

Fafnir let out a long deep sigh, then growled, "It's humans trying to kill humans. I can't think of anything I like better."

Ben looked at the large Drake, wondering if he was joking. He stayed quiet for a few moments. Then he stood on his toes a second time and asked, "Um, so, you haven't seen my friends Alex and Amita, or maybe Tara, have you?"

"Tara?" Fafnir's eyes flared open, and his voice boomed as he turned towards him. Ben stumbled back a little, then took a few more steps away as Fafnir's clawed hand reached out and dug into the balcony. Suddenly aware of how alone they were and that everyone's eyes were on the combat field, he debated going further, maybe all the way back to the med bay.

Fafnir answered, "No, I haven't seen her or any of your friends. No one has." He took a long slow breath. "There's a shuttle missing from the station, one of the monk's. The rumor is that Andavarri stole it, that she's taking them to Tairnish to save your emperor's daughter." He pointed his staff at Ben's head.

Ben stared at the broken body of the lightning bug, encased in a lamp hanging from the staff and asked, "Amita is with them? Are you sure?" The question was more for himself, wondering about Amita's obsession to learn Nalanda's secrets. He couldn't imagine her up and leaving. Then he muttered, "And I wouldn't say that he's my emperor. I don't even know that much about the guy."

Fafnir pointed to Maeven's balcony. "You live in his royal domain."

Ben held his hands up. "I suppose. But I didn't pick that. I wasn't really given a choice."

Fafnir snorted as if he thought this was funny. "I don't question the motivation of you humans. You're all incredibly plain to me. None better than the rest, always seeking power and advantage, even you small ones." He turned back to watch the combat. Before Ben could interrupt the silence again, Fafnir added, "What I do question, is the Æesir and their foolish monks. Apparently, they are protecting murderers now such as your friend, Alex."

"Alex didn't kill anyone. He's not like that," Ben blurted out. When he realized what he had said, he covered his mouth.

Fafnir swung back again, looking down at him. A rumbling sound came out of his mouth. It took Ben a minute to realize it was a laugh.

"I shouldn't have said that." Ben's face was red.

"Your friend isn't a killer, but you've found yourself in this world where it's better to be thought of as one. It's almost enough to make me pity him." Fafnir shook his head, then added, "Don't worry. I will keep this silly secret for you. It doesn't matter to me anyway, kill or don't kill as many of the monks as you want. It's your other friend Tara who I wanted to see face justice. She enslaved the Grannusian, Chooth, and used him to poison an entire world, but the Æsir freed her."

"That doesn't sound like something Tara would do," Ben countered. He thought back remembering the tank he'd seen in her room.

"You really don't understand who you've allied yourself with? Who the Tamerlanes are?" Fafnir asked.

"They're that bad?"

"You're all that bad." Fafnir turned from the fighting, toward the corridor. He started walking away.

"Hey, wait!" Ben tried to go after him.

Fafnir called over his shoulder, "Don't follow me, boy. I've had enough of this conversation."

Ben stopped in his tracks and said, "So where am I supposed to go now?"

Fafnir shook his head. "I don't know and I don't care."

∞

Fafnir hadn't gone far when he heard footsteps fall in beside him. He was about to turn and yell, but then a familiar voice said, "You were a bit harsh on the boy."

Fafnir looked down seeing the Ice Carver Regin next to him. "He'll be all right. Apparently, he and his friends are protected by the Æsir."

Regin swung along beside Fafnir, using his four arms to keep up while his long tails draped behind him moving like the coils of a snake. "Yes, apparently, things have changed. If you've come through the void, then it doesn't matter if you're a murderer," Regin said.

Fafnir nodded "Maybe, though the monks have never been known for having clean hands either." He wasn't sure how much of his conversation Regin had listened to.

Regin nodded in agreement. "As I said, things are changing and who knows, maybe it's for the better." Regin paused for a moment before adding, "Maybe it's time we pushed a little."

Fafnir glanced at him, wondering what his friend could mean, but then Regin added in a hushed, excited tone, "I found something. Well, not me. Not really. The girl. The one that the older brother freed, Amita. She found a secret room in the lighthouse, a place the monks haven't had a chance to sanitize."

"Please tell me you haven't gone looking in there. It's forbidden." Fafnir's eyes scanned the hallway to make sure no one else was nearby.

Regin shook his head, then raised his eyebrows with a small smile. "Of course, of course. I wouldn't do anything so foolish. That area is off limits and besides the entrance to the secret room Amita found is walled off again." His smile got bigger, showing sharp canine teeth as he added, "I checked while I wasn't in the lighthouse."

"Testing the monk's resolve now, when they're troubled, is playing a dangerous game," Fafnir warned.

"I know, but I'm not as long-lived as you. I don't have as much time to wait." Regin was still trying to sound light but there was something heavier that crept into his tone.

"Eir is older than me but the two of you, and I think others, started something. Something that brought these people from the void."

"I started nothing. You know how Brash was."

Fafnir opened his palm to his staff and the broken Lighting bug there as he nodded. "Yes, I know how he was. I know how his entire people were . . . To tell you what they meant to us—" Fafnir paused and shook his head. His hands trembled and he cleared his throat with a sound like a low roar. "I can't blame him for acting, not after what happened to them. But I think you knew more about what Brash and Tearmai were up to then you've told me. You knew about that vessel, didn't you?"

"The Diamond ship? No, not really. I gave them whatever aid I could on their journey, trusting in the impudence of youth. Others arranged their transport to Tairnish."

"Tairnish?" Fafnir raised his brow and his hand tightened on his staff. He'd been a slave there once, lifetimes ago.

"Yes, but never mind that now. It's all in the past. I'm far more interested in what that girl found. I think there might be a second entrance to that room. I imagine there'd have to be." Regin scratched his furry chin.

"You want there to be, but you need to be careful, my friend. You know how the monks treat the curious," Fafnir warned.

Regin ignored him and asked, "You were here when Emperor Tamerlane was a student, yes?"

Fafnir sighed. "I was."

"And how was he? What was the young Tamerlane like?"

"Driven."

"And— Please, you've told me this before." Regin rolled one of his hands to keep Fafnir talking.

"Curious, like the girl I suppose. Why?" Fafnir asked.

"Because now he's the most powerful person in the system. And while we can't say he's protected by the Æesir, they've certainly ignored his actions. Perhaps curiosity isn't such a bad thing."

"Perhaps," Fafnir agreed. "But you, my friend, enjoy no protection."

"For now," Regin said. "But who knows what could be in that room."

Chapter 4

The last time Katy had been at the royal palace she and Chris had shared a suite and she'd depended on him to guide her around the space, but she'd been forced to dress herself, out of a sense of modesty. This time they were each given their own room, luxurious quarters that came complete with a servant who stood by and helped her with everything. Clothing was laid out on the soft mattress and the sun shone through the tall windows with a blue and endless ocean outside. Katy couldn't see it, but she felt its warmth on her skin. She expected to feel awkward with a stranger helping her undress and bathe, but with everything she'd been through, she was beyond caring, willing to take any help offered.

She bathed and dried off. Then the woman helped her put on the Grannusian outfit, which was only a thin fabric dress. Katy lay back on the bed, above the covers, as the servant said she'd return in a few hours to help with her hair. Katy considered this for a moment. She used to care about things like hair and make-up, but she hadn't given it any thought in the month or so that they'd been on this side of the wormhole. 'Maybe the girl would do something nice,' she thought as she drifted off to sleep with the sun warming her.

Waking was still a strange feeling. In her dreams, memories of Earth and snippets of Katy's life came back in warm waves of color, as if she'd never lost her sight. They were more vivid than any reminiscence of life before. Waking to absence and darkness were like accelerants, hammering her with what she had lost. She was certain she'd never get used to it. A knock at her door forced her back to full consciousness. It felt like an assault as it dragged her to the surface of a black world. The noise came again, and she sighed before calling, "Come in." She assumed it was her servant from earlier, that her time was up, and that she needed to go meet the queen.

"I was dreaming," she said to the light footsteps that crossed her room.

A voice that was not the servant's answered, "Well I'm sorry to have interrupted then. I hope they were pleasant." It was a man's voice but high and reedy. Katy sat up, suddenly aware of how little her dress covered as she wondered exactly where he was. He sounded closer than the door and why wouldn't he be? After all, she invited him to come in, but the tap on the floor of his steps came from only a few feet away, too far into her personal space for comfort.

She got up, then took a single step forward, keeping one leg back against the bed, to anchor herself to something solid as she asked, "Who are you?" She wondered how rude she sounded. As she sensed him, smelt his breath and the salty odor of his skin, she realized how little she cared.

"My name is Darien Altain. I wanted to introduce myself as we will be spending quite a bit of time in each other's lives." His voice came from above her, making her realize he was tall.

"Is that right?" Katy asked.

"Oh, yes. I will be traveling with you back to Nalanda station where I will be taking over the role of the Kavaris, the head monk. In fact, if you wish, you may call me Kavaris Altain now, that way perhaps I will get used to it." He laughed a little. The sound unpleasant, filled with forced warmth.

"Okay," Katy said, sliding around the side of the bed, till she felt its corner, purposely putting it between them.

"Well, go ahead," he encouraged her. He came no closer, but he didn't leave either. "It would be an honor you see, as you and your friends appear to be blessed by the Æesir."

"We are?" Katy felt the sun coming through the window on her back. Knowing that going any further could be dangerous, she stopped.

"Oh yes. Why else would the Æesir save your companion Alex, whom we know to have killed one of our holy brothers?"

"I heard about that."

"Everyone has heard about that," he assured her. "But I'm curious. You've been a bit busy so what do you think happened?"

"I heard the Æesir showed up and saved him," Katy said. Altain didn't add anything and to fill the awkward silence between them, Katy continued, "Look, Alex really isn't the murdering type." Although as she thought of Chris's all too serious brother who had gone up against the hunter back on Earth and who'd driven himself so hard to get to his mother, she had to wonder if there was anything Alex wasn't capable of if he thought it was necessary.

"Well, who knows," Altain dismissed her opinion. "Of course, there was more to it. The Æesir who killed Kavaris Dell left instructions. They told the other monks to protect you and your companions. I wonder why. I can only assume that you are some part of their plan."

Katy could sense that this wasn't just some idle statement. That this man was here for information. "And you want to know what it is?" she asked.

"Don't you?"

Getting tired of being on the back step, Katy's answer came quicker than she meant. "Who says I don't?"

Silence met her again from the other side of the room. Finally, the man cleared his throat and said, "Yes, well. It appears you have other company. I believe your servant is here to get you ready for the queen. It was a pleasure to meet you." He was quiet again for a long pause, then he asked. "Perhaps you could say it once."

"What's that?"

"My title. While you and your people are blessed, I'm soon to be the headmaster of Nalanda. You'll still have to refer to me by my proper designation when we get there. It's important for decorum that the other students know who is in charge. Why don't you give it a try?"

"Okay, you're the Kavaris. Is that what you want to hear?" Katy asked.

"No, it's what I want you to say. It means teacher and master. I think there will be much I can do to educate you and your friends. For now, good day, Katy. I will see you in the queen's throne room."

Katy heard his footsteps recede and sat on the bed, wishing Chris was still there with her.

∞

Across the hall, Chris was thinking about Katy as well, when he heard a knock at the door. He opened it to the smiling face of Cormack with Cathal standing behind him. "Thank goodness you're in one piece," Cormack said, darting in and giving Chris a hug that nearly knocked him off his crutches.

"I'm good, I'm good," Chris said as he gave the prince a clumsy pat on the shoulder. Chris wasn't really a hugger, maybe with his mother but not with other men. The Johnsons just weren't that way. When Cormack stepped back, Chris added, "Hey, um, I'm sorry about, you know, how everything went down. I kind of went crazy on the drilling platform."

"Yeah, you did," Cormack said with a big smile. "I can't believe you jumped like that. I mean you're a terrible swimmer."

Chris tapped his cast. "I did pretty good down there, even with these stupid things on."

Cormack pointed to Cathal, who nodded. "Yeah, I heard. Word is you're kind of a hero."

Chris shrugged. "I'm just happy Katy and I are still alive."

Cormack's smile got even bigger. "Yeah, we're going to go get her next." He raised his eyebrows twice, indicating something.

"What?" Chris asked.

"I don't know. You tell me. I mean you risked a lot to follow her." Cormack shrugged.

"Man, we're just friends. All right?" Chris felt his face flush.

"Okay," Cormack said, holding up his hands. "Well, let's go get your friend then."

Chris looked at Cathal and asked, "Are all princes like this?"

"No, to my knowledge Cormack is unique," Cathal said, turning and heading across the hall to Katy's door. Chris swung on his crutches as he followed.

When Cathal knocked, the servant opened the door, then stepped out of the way and called to Katy, who was further back. "Your friend is here along with Prince Cormack."

Katy came forward, stumbling a little and using the bed for support. When she went to cross the room, the servant offered her hand and helped her to Cathal, who reached out, asking, "May I?"

Katy took the offered arm, then turned at a touch on her shoulder. "It's so good to see you," Cormack said.

"And where have you been hiding?" Katy asked. She reached over and embraced the prince.

Cormack looked over her shoulder, back at Chris. "Oh, you know, royal stuff."

Chris didn't realize that he was staring at them, specifically her. She was always beautiful, but the servant had taken her time heightening the subtle curl in Katy's hair, letting it fall over her shoulders. He didn't know much about makeup, but it seemed like her lips were brighter and that the 'whiteness of her eyes had been accentuated with eyeliner. His mouth hung open till he noticed Cormack looking back at him with a smirk. Chris felt the blood rush to his face again and he clenched his teeth before saying, "I guess we should be going, right? Which way was it?"

Cathal shared a smile with Cormack, shaking his head. "We're going down this hall. There's a lift at the end that will take us to the lower levels. I'll lead the way." Cathal passed by Chris with Katy still on his arm.

"Are you alright?" Katy asked as she went by.

"I'm good," Chris said a bit louder than he meant to, then added, "How about you?"

She let out a long breath as if wondering about what she wanted to say. "I've been better. I just met the new headmaster, the guy that's going to be in charge of us." She shook her head. "I think we're going to miss the old one. This guy gives me the creeps."

Cathal sounded surprised as he asked, "Kavaris Altain visited you? He must've been feeling a bit impatient."

"Do you know him?" Katy asked.

"Once, yes, a long time ago, before he found the faith, he was a commander in Anchor Home's defense force."

"Really?" Katy raised her eyebrows.

"So, he served under you," Cormack asked, then explained to the others. "Cathal was my father's general, in charge of everyone. He was the one who turned the emperor around. They still call him the hero of Anchor Home."

Now it was Cathal's turn to blush. He rubbed his face. "I only kept him at bay. We had a lot of help. We wouldn't have stood a chance without the Grannusians and their creations. Without the Seabhac protecting us from above. But, yes, I was in charge of Altain and many others."

Cormack started to ask, "Was he one of the ones who—"

Cathal finished for the prince. "Didn't care for how I was promoted or how young I was. Yes, but that was pretty much everyone." The bearded man bit his lip and added, "They had old ways of doing things, but I was your father's friend and I had new ideas that he thought would work, including asking the Grannusians for help. Many weren't fond of that, including Altain. I never sought command and, to be honest, I've never understood those that do. Being in charge is a burden I never wanted." Cathal patted Cormack on the shoulder. "You'll find out someday, young prince."

Cathal guided them to the throne room, which sat deep in the heart of the palace below the surface of the ocean, where a royal reception waited for them, along with the queen. There were over a hundred nobles in attendance dressed in their finest. Queen Daonine Sidhe remained on her throne above it all, inside the mouth of an ancient sea creature with her royal consort Duke Sebastian beside her. The far wall of the room looked out through a crystal barrier on the endless sea, its surface sparkling blue above them as the sun shone through coloring the entire hall in a light both beautiful and eerie, especially to Chris, who had no interest in being underwater again.

The nobility of Grannus were all eager to meet Chris and Katy and seemed equally interested in shaking hands with Cathal and Kavaris Altain, who was already there, making the rounds. That the tall monk had been chosen by the order's council of elders, to head Nalanda, was an important development to the humans of Grannus.

Kavaris Dell had held the post for decades and since he was from Uppsala, it gave credence to the notion that the garden moon was somehow special, that they should rule all the human-inhabited worlds. Electing Kavaris Altain was a seismic shift in the order of things, though in truth no one knew exactly how the council made such decisions.

Like the other monks, Altain had been a soldier once and was touched by the flame of faith on the battlefield, claiming a visitation during the siege of Anchor Home. Though, as is often the case, the witnesses to this event were all dead, and Altain was the only survivor. Recently, in order to replace their ranks, the monks had taken to less dramatic recruitment, but those who were actually touched by the Æesir were still considered the holiest and most likely to lead.

Chris and Katy were brought before the queen, where Katy took a knee while Chris was only capable of nodding. He tried to do it as politely as possible, getting as low as he could. That's when the tall figure of Kavaris Altain dressed in his red robe hurried over. Pushing his way through the nobles, he went directly to Katy, reached down with his lengthy arms, took her by the elbow, and pulled her back to her feet. "Oh, my dear, you're beyond all this royal pomp." The crowd gasped, shocked by how forward the man was, coming between the queen and her audience, even turning his back on her.

Chris watched Katy pull away in surprise, shocked by the hands on her. She attempted to hide her displeasure as the monk touched her shoulder and

37

assured her that she was all right. Kavaris Altain smiled and his eyebrows, which were thick enough to hood his face, lifted high above his pale green eyes as he turned and noticed Chris's expression. "Fear not, young man, for you are the blessed of the Æesir," he said. "All those who came through the void are special to our gods."

Turning his attention back to the queen, Chris saw her sit a little higher and hold her back rigid, while her eyes widened, then closed, and her hands tightened on the arms of her throne. Rage boiled beneath her carefully controlled face as she cleared her throat. "I'm glad to see our young visitors have returned in one piece. You've performed a great service to Grannus in stopping Chooth and in finding Eir."

"Indeed, they have." Kavaris Altain stepped away from the two, but only a little. He remained close enough to make it clear that he was claiming some sort of ownership of both their actions and of them.

The queen looked like she was biting back a harsher comment as she said, "I only wish we'd been able to stop the poisoning sooner. Your efforts won't be forgotten." She turned her attention directly to the monk. "May I introduce you to the new head monk of Nalanda station, Kavaris Altain." The tall man nodded.

"We've actually met," Katy said, though nobody seemed to hear her as Kavaris Altain spoke over her.

"Yes, and I have a vested interest in guiding these young people in the ways of the Æesir. Truly I imagine our gods have great things planned for them. While I take on all the duties of running our fine institute on Nalanda, I will see to it that these two and their fellows will want for nothing, including my attention." He settled his hand on Chris's shoulder.

The queen opened her mouth but took a moment before saying, "I'm sure they will benefit from your guidance." The words sounded forced.

Chris looked at the monk's hand and asked, "So, you're Kavaris Dell's replacement, after um . . . after what happened?"

"You may say it. The Æsir destroyed my predecessor because they were displeased. Kavaris Dell was their faithful servant till the end. If he had known they were angry, he would've taken a knife and ended his life himself."

"That's a hell of a commitment," Katy said, making the queen smile for the first time before quickly relaxing her face to cover the expression.

"Yes, well, it is an honor to serve the Æsir. You must give whatever they ask. Surely as their blessed, if you don't know that now, you will soon."

"Things to look forward to," Katy said. The audience ended soon after with the queen wishing them well and presenting medals for valor. There was food and drink and enough conversation to exhaust the two. When they were finally allowed to leave and return to their quarters, it was a relief. In the morning they'd be departing for Nalanda.

∞

As the sun rose, a convoy of skimmers left the palace, heading for the throat, the tower of white in the center of Anchor Home that reached all the way to the stars. After arriving, Chris swung down the front-loading ramp of the skimmer and looked up, feeling incredibly small in its shadow. Behind the endless tower, the gas giant Altor, pale and distant, filled half the horizon with shades of orange and pink, and against that light was a dark spot. This was the Star Blossom, their destination.

Cormack and Katy were with Chris, along with workers and guards going to relieve those on the station. The wide field around the throat was flat, looking like a single piece of pale bone extending kilometers from the massive column, running out to the edge of the city.

"Is Cathal coming with us?" Chris asked, watching the man climb down from another skimmer. He was surrounded by armored troops and carried the case with the antidote.

"Yes, and he's not going to let that out of his sight till we get there." Cormack nodded.

Another figure was with Cathal, covered in a heavy Grannusian robe that hid her form and her grey skin. Chris couldn't be sure, but he thought this was Naiathne. She was staying close to Cathal as they started for the transport.

"Maybe he can save us from Altain. Keep him from climbing so far up mine and Chris's backside," Katy said as their party followed the soldiers.

Cormack laughed, "Luckily, we'll have a quicker trip back. Dropping into the gravity well of Altor makes the voyage to the station take less time than leaving Nalanda."

"It looks like your mother is coming to see you off." Chris pointed to one of the skimmers where soldiers stepped out and formed into lines while others spread further, taking defensive positions, and covering the distant buildings. Chris watched the queen step down. She had the kind of beauty they made movies about with Asian features and a royal bearing that demanded attention. Her white hair was pulled back behind a crown that glinted with dazzling-colored jewels in the morning sun. Behind her was the royal consort Duke Sebastian and Kavaris Altain. The two men were talking and even laughing as they followed her toward the transport.

As the three groups approached the base of the throat, Altain moved toward the center of them and pronounced, "Truly it is a blessed morning as we return these two," he pointed to Chris and Katy, "to our school and to the protection of our order."

Chris felt everyone turn and look at him and Katy as he nodded and gave a hesitant wave to the gathered workers and soldiers. Then Altain stepped a little further into the crowd calling out again, "But who is this that comes with us?" His long strides took him to the hooded figure, hidden behind Cathal. "I did not think any of the Grannusians traveled with us." He reached over and pulled her hood back revealing Naiathne.

The monk stepped away, feigning shock. "A Naiad? What is this?" He swung toward Cathal.

Everyone stiffened as Duke Sebastian called, "Arrest her." The soldiers immediately brought their weapons to bear and started closing in while Cathal and Cormack stepped closer to Naiathne, putting themselves in harm's way. "Hold on," Cathal shouted with his hands up.

"Yes, stop," the queen added in a softer voice. She'd been standing back a little, but she moved toward the center and toward her daughter. "It's never been said in my kingdom that being a Naiad is illegal. They may live apart from us, but that does not make them criminals."

"Just terrorists on occasion," Sebastian said. "We must at least detain her. Find out why she's here."

"She's here to go to Nalanda, as is her right," Cormack said. "This is my sister. She is of royal blood and as such, she's allowed to be educated at the station."

"Cormack!?" The queen shot him such a look. Then her eyes turned to Cathal. "This is your doing, isn't it?" It was impossible for the queen not to look at her daughter as she stood so close to Cathal, though she did her best to keep her attention only on the old soldier.

Cathal shrugged. "I keep my promises, even to those no longer here."

"And I helped him," Cormack added.

Sebastian walked up and jabbed his finger in the prince's chest. "Then you can pay the penalty this time."

Cormack pushed his hand away as the queen said, "Do not touch my son."

Sebastian looked back at her. As consort, and a man of influence, he enjoyed certain privileges, but he also knew there was a line you didn't cross. Kavaris Altain saw the warning in her eyes and ignored it as he said, "I don't care if she is of royal blood. I won't have this half-human creature on my station. The Æsir forbade genetic tampering. The Naiads shouldn't even exist."

"But we do!" Naiathne's voice was full of anger and sorrow and her black eyes were swollen red near their edges.

Katy quietly listened to the voices erupting with emotion, coming from every side. When she finally had enough, she shouted above them all. "The Æsir want her there!"

Everyone turned towards the blind girl as a hush fell over the crowd. Katy's eyes were pale white, but they still moved, darting side to side as if she were searching for something. Feeling the sudden silence push down on her, she threw her shoulders back and continued, "You said we were 'the blessed of the Æsir,' and I'm telling you they want Naiathne to go to the station. If you want, you can argue with them." Katy wasn't sure where the monk was, so she moved her head like she was looking over the entire crowd.

Everyone stayed quiet, considering her words. For a moment Chris looked like he wanted to ask her what the hell she was doing, but he kept his mouth shut and nodded, pretending he knew exactly what she was talking about.

"How could you know that?" Duke Sebastian confronted her.

"They told me," Katy shot back, turning to where the voice came from.

"The Æesir have not visited this world in quite some time," Kavaris Altain said. Katy could sense him moving closer to her. "How have they delivered this message?"

Katy had found a certain kind of freedom after her accident that night in the desert. The last thing she saw on Earth was a monster intent on killing her. She'd been so afraid, but since that moment, when everything went dark, she'd felt detached, like nothing was that important. She hated the feeling, but it had one benefit, it made her fearless. What could touch her in the dark? She planted her feet and looked up, sensing the monk looming over her. "They're gods. They told me in a dream. You think they have to show up to talk to one of their blessed?"

"They always have in the past," the queen pointed out.

Katy didn't flinch as she continued, "That was before. The Æesir have protected us. I'm telling you I know what they want. Naiathne is a human, not some creature. She's coming with us."

The monk stared at her from under his hooded eyes. After a long moment, he conceded, "Who am I to argue with the blessed?" He didn't sound happy about it and moved away from her while others came closer.

Cormack, Cathal, Chris, and Naiathne herself gathered round, and Naiathne leaned into Katy whispering, "Thanks." Then she and Cathal turned and headed towards the transport, only stopping because the queen approached.

Naiathne and her mother locked eyes for a moment, their faces boiling with so many unsaid words. This was the closest they'd been to each other since Naiathne's birth. After a moment Naiathne sneered, bit her lip, and pulled her hood up, turning away. Chris watched the queen's face, wondering what the woman could be feeling.

She approached him, Cormack, and Katy, leaned in and spoke directly to Katy in a whisper. "You're playing a dangerous game."

"It's not a game. I'm trying to do the right thing," Katy said, still holding her shoulders back.

"If only it were that simple," the queen answered before turning to Cormack and Chris. "Be careful of Kavaris Altain. He will not forgive this." She kissed her son on the cheek. Then she turned as the group started for the transport cart.

Chris was next to Cormack. "Hey, why did your mom automatically blame Cathal for Naiathne. And even before that, she looked like she wanted to tear his head off. Everybody else seems to think he's a great guy."

"More than just a 'great guy.' The fact that our capital is still standing is because of him." Cormack pointed towards the distant palace with its white towers, higher than any of the other buildings. "But my mom doesn't like him because he was the one who snuck Naiathne to Nalanda station the first time. Everyone knows she gave birth to a Naiad, that we have that old genetic coding in our blood. She'd prefer they forget, so bringing Naiathne out into the open, giving her people a voice, it calls too much attention to our genetic flaw. My mother needs the support of the other clan chiefs to rule. I mean she threw her own daughter into the ocean to get it."

Chris looked back at the queen as Cormack continued, "My father and Cathal were closer than brothers. He'd do anything for my sister and me to honor my dad's memory. Even if it means breaking my mother's law and being arrested. She put him in prison after the last time. He's only been out a few days but the first thing he did was answer my call to save you guys.

So, like you said, a 'great guy.'" Cormack paused for a second, then added, "I think the real reason she doesn't like him is he's like you and Katy."

"What do you mean?" Chris looked at the middle-aged man helping Naiathne into the cart.

"He's an idealist, always trying to do the right thing. That's not something someone like my mother can do, not in this world." Chris saw a look come over Cormack's face. He knew someday his friend would be in the same position, that someday Cormack would have to make terrible choices too.

Chapter 5

Between Nalanda station and the moon Tairnish, a world of fire and rock, a small shuttle accelerated, burning like a torch across space. Edith sat at the controls in her dark armor with her faceless helmet on. Tara sat next to her, a helmet on as well with a clear faceplate, which meant Edith felt every time the girl's eyes turned toward her. In the tight space, Tara did everything she could to hide her feelings. She had every right to hate Edith, and Edith didn't care if she did, but she needed to know that Tara wasn't going to let her feelings get in the way of the mission.

"Should we talk about it?" Edith asked as the force of acceleration pushed them both back in their seats while the shuttle steadily gained speed. The increase was carefully controlled, pushing at a force greater than someone would expect while lying on the Earth or falling toward it.

"About what?" Tara asked.

Edith's mask hid her face, but Tara would still know what she was thinking. That was the problem with her, the reason Edith had set her up. Tara was an empath and Edith was formerly a spy. Those things didn't go well together even when they served the same master. Tara was not part of the emperor's inner circle and didn't know about his plans. She was only Maeven's handmaiden, which meant she was expendable, and Edith had needed someone to take the blame for Grannus.

"Really, you're going to play games? It was your damn abilities that got you in trouble in the first place. You knew I was up to something. I couldn't risk you asking questions."

Tara shook her head. "That's why you set me up?"

"I needed to protect my position. Nalanda was too valuable. Of course, now we've stolen this shuttle, so that's pretty much over. I doubt I'll ever step foot on the station again."

"Yeah well, unlike you, I can't just walk away. If we succeed, if Maeven goes back there, I'll be with her and since you put that piece of Chooth in my quarters, I'm hated by every Extraracial on the station. I may not have been thrown out an airlock, but that doesn't mean they're not going to finish me when they can."

"So, go home, back to Uppsala," Edith said.

"I'm not a mercenary. I go where the princess goes or my people get hurt." Tara motioned to the forward window. "Even if it means going to Tairnish." She let out a bitter laugh, then added, "You know I always knew you were working for Maeven's father. She did too."

"I have no doubt. But there's something neither of you were aware of, but it's time you understand," Edith said.

"Yeah? What's that?" Tara asked.

Edith's black helmet turned toward her. "The last war never ended, not for me and not for our emperor, and in the end, his rule will be all that's left." Tara could feel the woman's emotions. She didn't need to see her face to know how serious the mercenary was.

After a moment Edith relaxed a little, turning her attention back to the controls as she said, "Maeven is actually a lot like her father with her little plots and games, but they're child's play compared to what Tamerlane is up to. Even what we did to Grannus isn't very important in the grand scheme of things."

"Poisoning an entire population wasn't important?" Tara asked.

"Try not to sound so judgy. I know you've done some questionable things for your princess too. The name Victor comes to mind."

Tara bit her lip as Edith continued, "During the war, I'd been an unwilling guest of the Grannusians. They treated me well, nursed me back to health, which gave me time to observe them and learn about the enemy. What I did to Chooth was only an experiment. I wanted to see if I could break him and change his loyalties. When I started, I had no idea it would work so well. The emperor came up with the whole poisoning thing, a way to take the Grannusians out of play altogether for what comes next."

"And what comes next?" Tara asked.

"For us?" Edith thought of the transmission she'd received from the emperor letting her know that he wanted her to go ahead with her rescue plan. "Well, we'll be saving a princess of course, and for the Tairnishmen, that's going to be a lot less pleasant, a reckoning you might say." Edith smiled behind her mask, feeling a familiar thrill, happy that she'd be seeing action soon. Her post on Nalanda may have been important, but she wasn't sad to see it end. Spy-craft, sneaking about, and gathering intel, got old quickly.

Maeven had created this situation and now Edith would get to end it. They had a ticking clock, arriving at Tairnish in just under eight days. That's how long she had to get Alex up to speed. Failure wasn't an option. Edith took another look at Tara and was jealous of the girl's ability as she asked, "You're on board now. All the way, right?"

Tara nodded and Edith got up, saying, "Good." She pointed to the controls. "It's on autopilot, but I'd still like you to mind it when I can't."

"Okay," Tara said as Edith pulled herself to the hatch and to a ladder that dropped down to the center of the crew cabin.

Unlike the cockpit, the floor of the cabin was pointed in the direction of their acceleration, creating the illusion of gravity as Edith climbed down. Officially the shuttle belonged to the Kavaris monks. It was kept at Nalanda station for emergencies and was small compared to most vessels that traveled between the moons. The pale white living quarters consisted of a four-meter by four-meter room with a small table in the center and bunks lining the walls. The room was big enough for eight people but felt tight with five.

Before she was near the bottom, Edith heard Andavarri say from her perch, clinging to the curved wall, "I understand why you need me for your little rescue mission, but why is she here?"

The Long-Wolf was pointing a clawed finger at Amita, who was sitting in a bunk reading her school monitor. 'Those weren't supposed to leave the station,' Edith thought. She chased the idea away, reminding herself that her days as an instructor were over and that she'd just stolen a shuttle.

Amita's voice dripped with sarcasm. "I'm here for moral support, to satisfy my curiosity, and because I've always been fond of outings." Andavarri crept closer to the girl's bed, trying to stare her down, but Amita only rolled her eyes and went back to reading.

On the other side of the room, Alex sat with his legs pulled in. He didn't even crack a smile at Amita's comment. He only watched and waited for instruction while looking uncomfortable. No one was going to find this journey very pleasant, except maybe Andavarri since she came from Tairnish. Acclimating to a higher gravity could be unnerving if you'd never done it before, but it was better to do it on the ship than on the moon's surface. It was like being crushed, like a claustrophobic's worse nightmare as invisible forces closed in from all sides, making it hard not only to stand but to even open your lungs and breathe. Their shuttle wasn't even at combat speed. It wasn't set up for that kind of acceleration, but they were still gaining velocity at an uncomfortably high rate, making everyone feel heavy. Edith wanted to make up time, but also, she needed Alex to be ready. For her plan to work she would have to have backup.

Edith said to him, "We're cleared for action, but you're going to need a lot more training than we have time for. Come with me." Alex popped up and started toward her, grimacing only a little.

"Where are you two off to?" Andavarri asked, following behind them.

"To the cargo bay," Edith said. She watched Alex closely, seeing the effort he was putting into every step. All the kid wanted to do was act, but even being in shape and as trained as he was, adding constant force would tire anyone out. Built into Edith's armor were tiny motors that would help her, but she hadn't turned them on yet. She wanted to wait till Tairnish where Alex would have something far more impressive to get him around.

The emperor's forces had been monitoring all movement going to and from Tairnish, and they had a pretty good idea where Maeven was being held. Since the surface of the planet was too hostile to grow most plants, vast structures had been built underground and the Tairnishmen mostly lived there in communes, caves and mines that were repurposed for human habitation. The one Maeven was believed to be in was deep and strongly fortified, a military installation with only one way in; or so the Tairnishmen thought.

"We'll need your Fire-Golems," Edith said to Andavarri.

"Why?" The Long-Wolf's head tilted and when Edith didn't answer, she raced over the walls like a gecko, stopping in front of her. "I've only brought four. They aren't going to be very effective if you're planning some sort of rescue mission."

Edith stood over the hatch to the cargo bay looking up at Andavarri as she sighed, then said, "I need them for training. If your people take a side in this, I want the kid to know how to neutralize them."

"'Neutralize them?' You mean like destroy them?" Amita asked. "Even only having four, wouldn't you be better off using them in the rescue?"

"Not for what I've got planned. Fire-Golems aren't very subtle and they're not a tactical advantage on a world where there's so many of them." Edith had no interest in saying any more or explaining every detail of her plan.

"So, you're worried Andavarri's people will side with the Bogatyr?" Amita asked.

"We don't do sides," Andvarri sneered.

"That's not exactly true," Edith corrected. "They will eventually pick one, but only when it's clear who the winner is."

Andavarri's face broke into a toothy grin. "Do I sense a tone of judgment?" She waved her hand. "You humans, I suppose you expect— what do you call it . . . loyalty. What has that ever gotten you? The way you organize yourselves, it allows you to create so much, but always there are those on the bottom and those on the top, a pecking order I believe it's called. Even among the Bogatyr, where they claim to be equals, there are those that'll climb on the backs of their brothers for a better position. It's impressive, but it's not our way."

"Your way doesn't seem all that different to me," Amita said.

Andavarri turned and bared her teeth a bit wider, stretching her lizard-like face to something less friendly. "But it is different. We are individualists. Our ambitions are always clear because we're always looking after ourselves and don't pretend to be better. It's the only way to be free."

Amita swung her legs over the side. "I suppose you think things are more honest that way, but there's those on the bottom for you too. They're just not Long-Wolves, are they? You've got your Fire-Golems and the Drakes."

"We made the Fire-Golems, they're not alive, and the Drakes were brought to our world by you humans."

"Not this human," Amita said.

Andavarri's tail waved leisurely along the wall as she asked, "What's the difference?"

Amita got to her feet and pointed her finger at herself. "First off, I just got here."

"That doesn't matter." Andavarri dismissed her, rolling her eyes just as Amita had earlier. "And you're not as smart as you claim if you think it does."

Edith's hand was on the hatch in the floor, ready to open it and escape these two and their squabbling, but before she could turn the wheel, there was a noise from the cargo bay. Everyone turned to look at it.

"I was hoping he'd sleep a little longer." Amita came closer to Edith.

"Who?" Andavarri asked above the sound of more banging and metal being rattled. Something was coming towards them.

"We've got another passenger." Edith activated the servos in her armor just in case.

"I'd suggest you try not to upset him," Amita said. "He's been a bit fragile lately."

Andavarri put her hand to her neck, connecting the crystals that let her see through the eyes of the Fire-Golems in the cargo bay. The banging was getting louder, coming closer to the hatch. Amita got up and pushed past Edith, going towards the opening. "Careful," Edith said. She almost reached out to stop Amita from opening it, but she held her hand, curious to see what would happen.

"Andavarri, are your golems awake?" Edith asked.

The Long-Wolf climbed down off the wall, putting her tail and legs on a bunk. "They're coming out of storage now. Give me a minute, controlling four takes a bit of concentration. . ." Andavarri was looking through the eyes of the stone creatures out into the dark storage space. It was a long cylinder twenty times the size of the crew quarters with one flat side for a floor. The shadowy space wasn't very full, with a large object strapped down near the front, taking up a quarter of the room and only a couple of crates secured to the floor near the bottom.

The direction of the ship's acceleration made the flat floor become like a wall covered in a webwork of cavities for strapping cargo down. Andavarri's Golems looked up and saw something using the holes in the floor to climb. The subtle glow from their one eye brightened, shining towards the dark form above them. They followed and started to climb as well, keeping their stone bodies intact, moving without speaking as their rocky joints crunched.

"You brought him?" Andavarri glared, her focus back on the crew quarters, seeing Amita at the hatch. "He's insane— Wait, what are you doing?"

Amita turned the wheel that released the latch, then pulled back, opening the tightly sealed door. She smiled down at the creature on the other side. "Hey, big guy. How'd you sleep?"

Tearmai's head popped up with his blue eyes shining behind his broad beak, searching the room before he answered. "We are away, away from my wall where I carved the truth past the colors?"

53

It took Amita a second to understand that he was asking a question. "Yes, that's true. We're on our way to Tairnish, just like you asked."

Tearmai nodded, then squeezed one long arm up through the opening, forcing his shoulder above the lip. Edith saw Amita shiver a little. She knew the girl was remembering their arrival at Nalanda when she'd nearly been killed by that arm.

"He's going to get stuck," Andavarri protested while everyone watched the large Drake shove his way into the crew quarters. It was going to be much tighter inside once he joined them, and a lot more dangerous if he got angry. "Why would you bring him here?" Andavarri demanded.

Edith wasn't big on second guessing herself, but as she watched the Drake work his way into the room, she wondered if she'd weighed her options correctly. "He's got intelligence that could be useful. According to Amita he's been in the mines near the Bogatyr stronghold where they're keeping Maeven. I think he knows a back way in."

Andavarri shook her head. "He never worked in the mines. He was born in the preserve on Uppsala."

Tearmai focused on the Long-Wolf and growled a little before saying, "We wanted answers."

Amita patted him on the shoulder, then went back to trying to help him through the opening as she said between grunts, "He went there with Brash, before they came to my world. I think that's where they found the diamond ship."

Andavarri shook her head, agitated as she moved around the room, pacing and climbing the walls. "It's just foolishness! There's nothing there, just an old mine. And even if he's been there. Do you really think he's capable of showing you? It's mad. This is your plan? You might as well tell the emperor to mourn his daughter now, or better yet, tell him to start negotiating."

"The emperor has left the negotiating to Tara and he expects you to help her." Edith pointed to the cockpit.

"What?! She's a child," Andavarri shrieked.

"I'm no negotiator and I'll be busy," Edith said as she watched Tearmai struggle. She eventually leaned down and with the servos in the armor, she pulled. Once the Drake was out and on his feet, she asked, "You're going to behave up here, right?"

"I've no violence left. My head, it's still. . ." Tearmai pointed one of his claws at himself while he struggled to come up with a single word. Instead, he said, "I'm tangled in light and color, forever falling, consumed by the ever repeating past, always repeating, always repeating!" He roared those last words. His voice echoed as he collapsed to the floor, sitting on his backside with his knees pulled in, while he stared straight ahead.

"So that's your guide?" Andavarri climbed off the wall and ducked into her own bunk. "Good luck."

Edith went and turned on a screen. It defaulted to an exterior view of the shuttle. After pressing a few buttons on her tablet, she had satellite imagery of Tairnish. She brought the monitor over to Tearmai. "Show us the entrance," she said.

It took him a moment, as he slowly and carefully brought his clawed fingers to the device. Then they all watched as the image changed, tightening and moving. Edith had him pause for a second. She pointed to the screen, at a square of burnt rocky ground with a large dark opening above it. "Under here is the compound where they're holding Maeven." She pointed to the opening. "This is the main entrance. We observed a shuttle land there two days ago. There's a deep trench and we've picked up heavy fortifications inside, armor,

55

anti-aircraft weapons. It'd take a major force to breach it. Go ahead, Tearmai."

The screen moved, going towards the other side of a range of mountains. Tearmai brought it in tighter to a shadowy spot under the ledge of a cliff. It seemed dangerously close to an active volcano that was spewing lava and smoke in the air. "According to Tearmai there's an opening to the cave system. One that hasn't been sealed off."

Andavarri slinked down again, going up to the screen. "You know this place?" she asked Tearmai.

"I went there with my flying friend, before the fall."

Andavarri circled towards Edith. "If you enter here, you won't be coming back out. There's only death in those tunnels."

"And secrets," Tearmai added.

"You want to fill us in? Let us know what's got you so worried?" Edith asked.

For a moment it seemed like the Long-Wolf wanted to tell her something, but then she turned away, back to her bunk. "You know enough, and anything I say isn't going to stop you."

Chapter 6

On Nalanda station, the chaos after the death of Kavaris Dell faded into routine and Ben moved along with it, returning to the Tamerlane domicile and to his room there. He eventually took the bandages off his head, knowing that they'd stayed on longer than they should've. The morning after leaving Fafnir, he'd returned to the medical unit and found a monk who, in between caring for the students hurt in combat, helped unwrap his head.

Ben still couldn't get used to how he was treated by the order. The monks weren't exactly nice. They didn't have that in them, but they were agreeable. The wrap was taken away and he was shown where a small line of stitches had been placed beneath his hairline. Apparently, the wound had been part of the surgery to relieve pressure in his skull.

Ben touched the spot, which suddenly became itchy, and the monk swiped his hand away before he could scratch. "Now, I believe you have classes to attend." He turned, shooing Ben out into the station.

At the Tamerlane domicile, he found the nobles less agreeable. None took the time to tell him outright that he was an uninvited guest. Instead, when he tried getting information from them in the domicile's halls, they'd either ignored him or rolled their eyes and walked away. Still, it was impossible not to hear the rumors about the shuttle, Tara, and Alex.

Ben avoided the common room altogether, but sometimes he would listen just outside the threshold. The area was a gathering spot in the Tamerlane domicile near the balcony with fancy couches and elegant tables, where the older nobility spent their time and shot contemptuous glances at anyone they thought beneath them. Not long ago these same people had hung on Maeven's every word and been courteous to him while he was with Tara, but now they laughed about her, discussing Tara's near execution and what would happen to her if Maeven wasn't recovered. They weighed her chances and even placed bets while wondering if Edith had gone with them. No one had seen the security head since the shuttle left, so they'd started to guess she was still an agent of the emperor. In those conversations, Ben rarely heard anyone mention Amita or Tearmai. He guessed they were beneath their notice, a common theme when it came to Extraracials.

Most of Ben's classes were taught by monks, but a few of his professors were like Regin, non-human. The primary purpose of stewards like Regin and Fafnir was to serve as counselors to the members of their species picked to be students on Nalanda. For humans, coming here was an honor reserved for nobles, but Ben didn't know how the Extraracials were chosen and they didn't seem interested in telling him or talking to him at all, for that matter. He'd tried during one crowded afternoon meal to approach a table of male Ice-Carvers, but they became upset the moment he got too close. Their tails started whipping about like maddened snakes.

"Sorry, sorry," Ben said, hurrying away from the creatures who looked like outraged stuffed animals.

He gave up looking for an empty table in the packed room, put down his tray, and began wrapping his food in a napkin. He was ready to leave the large dining hall, when a purple-skinned creature slithered in front of him.

"Dear me, you seem lost," a voice deep enough to be considered male said. There weren't many Long-Wolves on Nalanda. From what Ben understood there weren't many overall and rather than gathering together like the Ice-Carvers or the Drakes, they tended to spread out, often choosing the humans loyal to the Tamerlanes to sit with.

"Come, join me." The Long-Wolf motioned to where he'd been perched. "I'm Fajalar, Andavarri's replacement." He put his hand out in a human gesture.

Ben took it, feeling the long fingers wrap around his palm. "Nice to meet you, I'm Ben."

"Oh, I know who you are. Everyone knows the chosen of the Æsir. The lost children of the void space."

"Yeah, I guess us coming through was a big deal, and the whole thing with Alex— You know, to tell the truth, I don't know much about it." Ben pointed to the spot on his head. "I was sort of out of commission."

Fajalar guided Ben to a spot near the Tamerlane loyalists. Ben recognized some from the domicile and from combat training. The glances they threw him weren't exactly friendly. "You know what, I think I'm just going to take my food with me, back to my quarters." Ben started walking away.

"They frown on that," Fajalar said, following him.

"They frown on everything around here," Ben said over his shoulder, hurrying to leave. When he noticed Fajalar was still with him, he motioned back with his head toward the Tamerlanes "Those guys were my buddies before, when Alex and Maeven were here— Well maybe not buddies, but they sure seemed to tolerate me a lot better." Ben's shoulders were rolled forward and he didn't notice the way Fajalar was watching him. The way the creature scrutinized his every gesture.

"The nobles of Uppsala are raised differently from you, I think," Fajalar said as they reached the door.

Ben glanced back over his shoulder, looking at the mass of people. Even the humans felt alien to him. "Yeah, I'd say. We don't do the whole royalty thing where I'm from. At least we didn't anymore."

Fajalar tapped his claws together. "That's not what I meant. The people from Uppsala are raised not to show their emotions so blatantly. Where you, you show everything. I think right now, you are sad."

Ben stepped out into the wide, empty hall, still walking away. "No, I'm good. I just... it's just... there's a lot of people in there and I can't say I know any of them."

Fajalar slunk low as he stayed next to Ben. "I don't think you're telling me the truth."

Ben swung back and looked down, feeling a bit like he had a mouthy dog tagging along beside him. "Well, my home and everyone I ever knew are more than likely dead. My sister was here with me for all of a few hours, then ran off with a prince to some other planet. I'm sorry, moon. Then I fell and smashed my head and woke up to find all my friends gone. So yes, I'm sad and this place feels incredibly lonely. This all kind of sucks." Ben motioned to the abandoned corridor with its high strange architecture and shadowy corners like a gothic castle made by something that wasn't quite human.

Fajalar tilted his head. "Loneliness is such a strange concept. My people spend most of our lives alone. We come together for councils, but mostly we live our lives in solitude. Where were you planning to go?"

Ben looked in either direction down the vacant passage with the voices of the student body pouring from the hall behind him. He shrugged "I don't know." He didn't really want to go back to the Tamerlane domicile, so for a moment he thought of just going to his next class, where he could eat his food and sulk for a bit. He was about to start that way when he noticed a dark form step into the hallway just ahead of him. A moment before it had blended into the wall, but now with its broad rocky shoulders it blocked the way. It looked vaguely human, only larger and it had a single glowing eye in the center of its head. Taking a sharp breath, Ben nearly dropped his food as he stood rigid, staring at the Fire-Golem. He looked the other way and noticed another, closing off the opposite direction.

There was a happy lilt in Fajalar's voice. "See? Again your emotions are incredibly clear. For some reason, these Fire-Golems frighten you, terrorize you really."

"You're controlling them?" Ben asked, taking a step back toward the dining hall.

"Yes, of course, I control all of the Golems on the station. As I said I'm Andavarri's replacement."

"Why, why are they there?" Ben asked.

Fajalar stopped ducking down. He stood on his two back legs bringing himself up till he was at least a head taller than Ben. "They're security. They're all over the station."

Ben was staring at the Golem in front of him. At one time he'd been fascinated by the sentries. He'd even tried talking to them, but now he had a different memory of what they were capable of, the way they could hurt you. "But why are these ones here? Why are they coming toward us?"

Fajalar took Ben's arm, the one holding his lunch. "I warned you. You're not supposed to take food from the dining hall."

Ben's mouth dropped open as he turned toward the Long-Wolf, then Fajalar's face broke into a toothy grin. "I'm joking, of course, but I was hoping for a moment to talk to you and I'd rather not be interrupted. Please, over here." He motioned to a corner, not far from the central corridor. Back behind an elaborate pillar was a small nook, just tall enough for Ben to stand in. He got the sense he wasn't being given a choice as he stepped into the space. Fajalar glanced in either direction, then settled in behind Ben, closer than was really comfortable.

His head slipped down and up like a snake's, slowly getting ready to strike. "Now, I'm sure you've heard all about your friend's mission to save Princess Maeven."

"Only the rumors. I really don't know much," Ben interrupted.

Fajalar looked to the ceiling. "That's all anyone has heard. They're on a secret mission, after all?"

"Yeah, I guess." Ben backed up till he felt the wall behind him.

Fajalar showed his teeth again in a broad smile, then shook his head. "Again, your emotions are so obvious. Relax, young man," he said while looking down at his claws. "What I would like to know is if you've seen or heard anything about your other friend, Amita, or that pet Drake of hers."

"Tearmai? I know he's missing. I saw his room in the medical unit. It looked like his door didn't make out so well."

Fajalar rolled his hand. "But you don't know where either of them are?"

Ben thought of the wall and the carvings Tearmai had left behind, then he shook his head and held up his empty hands. "I wish I knew."

Fajalar sighed. "I and many others have started to believe they've gone with the rescue mission, with my predecessor Andavarri. The question is why?"

Ben tapped the side of his head, indicating the wound. "How should I know?"

"Oh, I'm aware, you haven't been around lately, but you did spend time with Tearmai on your home planet and, of course, your little friend was always busy investigating the happenings on this station, digging into places she shouldn't. I wonder, did she find something here, or did he tell her something that made them want to go to my home?"

Ben thought of the carved mural again. It wasn't a secret. He was sure Fajalar had already snuck in and seen it himself. Ben bit his lip, then yelled, "I don't know! No one tells me anything." His voice was louder than he meant it to be.

Fajalar wasn't moved. He stared at Ben for a long time, waiting for him to say more.

Ben went to go around the Long-Wolf, but Fajalar stayed firmly in his way putting his hand against the boy's chest.

Ben glanced down at it. "I'm telling you the truth. You could fill this station with the stuff I don't know."

Fajalar kept the clawed hand there a moment more. Then he took it and tapped his claw against his chin still staring at Ben. "You must be the most obvious human I've ever met. Look at you, terrified. As if you think I'm going to hurt you and you're hiding it under outrage." Fajalar stepped back, motioning for Ben to step out. "I'm sorry. Please don't let me keep you."

Ben let out a long breath and hurried away from the wall, back into the corridor. He saw a few people going out, heading to class, and the Fire-Golems stood back, returning to their places by the wall. Ben wanted to get as far from Fajalar as possible, but before darting off, he turned back to the Long-Wolf and asked, "Everyone's pretty sure Alex and Amita went with the shuttle?"

Fajalar stood at his full height, raised an eyebrow, and stared at Ben before answering, "They haven't been seen since, so I'd say yes." Then he leaned down and lowered his voice. "Either that or something bad happened to them."

"Like what?" Ben asked.

"Ghosts. I understand you have some expertise on them. They've been more active since the Æsir's visit, wandering the halls, appearing from solid rock, seen by so many." Fajalar motioned to the walls. "Maybe your

63

friends were dragged off. The little one, that girl, loved exploring so much. Maybe they finally got her." Again, the toothy grin broke across Fajalar's face.

Ben looked over his shoulder and saw the other students getting further away. He spared a last glance at Fajalar, then turned to run after them, hearing the Long-Wolf snicker a little behind him.

∞

A few days later Fajalar stood in the docking bay and was thinking about Ben as he waited with so many others for the arrival of the shuttle from Grannus. He liked the boy. He was small and easy to intimidate, the perfect human in Fajalar's opinion. The Long-Wolf tilted his head, listening to the human boy above the sound of machines and people pushing his way through the crowd, coming down the steps.

The docking bay was a massively tall room with level upon level climbing high into the bottom of the asteroid that Nalanda station sat inside. It dangled below the hunk of rock opposite the main structure of the school with corridors running through the stone and lifts to bring supplies and people up into the chambers above.

"Excuse me, excuse me," Ben said, making his way to the airlock. Fajalar smiled a little as he slinked closer leaving Fafnir and Regin, the stewards from the other races, back behind the monks who were lined in rows, dressed in a sea of red, waiting for the shuttle to dock.

A female Ice-Carver was there as well, back behind a row of Fire-Golems, stooped forward with her eyes glassy from drugs that kept her docile. She was much larger than the males of her species, over a hundred kilograms, but with as many arms, which were thicker and heavier than the male Ice-Carver's. She was brutish and powerful looking, and her furry tails were shorter, running together, making them look like a single appendage.

There was a lone Grannusian in the crowd as well, hidden below a heavy robe. He assumed it was Clio, the latest steward for their amalgam race. He'd only met her briefly as the Grannusians had remained in seclusion since the poisoning. It was a carefully guarded secret, but rumors still spread that a cure traveled with the new Kavaris.

The dark shape of the shuttle moved past the observation windows on every level, slowly blocking the tangerine glow of Altor. When all the windows were dark, sounds began to echo from the wall. Air-actuated machines cycled and pushed locking anchors out grabbing the shuttle and extending short gangways, then the airlock cycled and opened while the crowd stood in anticipation.

Fajalar watched the first person to come out. He was a short man with a beard, and he was helping the blind girl Katy over the lip of the airlock. Behind Katy, holding her hand, was a girl with grey skin and dark eyes.

"Who are those people?" Fajalar heard Ben ask himself as he stared at the Naiad.

Fajalar recognized Prince Cormack's sister Naiathne, but he'd only heard of Cathal, the hero of Anchor Home. He had his suspicions about what the man was carrying. "They are an interesting development," he hissed next to Ben, who hadn't seen the Long-Wolf creep up behind him. Ben jumped, bringing another toothy grin to Fajalar's face. The boy made a sound that wasn't quite a curse or a prayer as he shook his head and moved forward, pushing closer to his sister.

Fajalar followed, his tail waving contentedly and by the time they got to the steps, Chris was swinging out on his crutches, helped by Cormack.

"What happened to you?" Ben asked, watching Chris labor with each step. Cormack was letting Chris use his shoulder while he held the crutches for him. When they were at the bottom of the stairs, he patted Chris on the shoulder and made sure he was situated before nodding to Ben and stepping toward his people.

Fajalar watched them surround the prince and avoid Naiathne. She stayed close to Katy, who, by the time he turned his attention back to Ben, was pulling her brother into a hug. Fajalar watched the boy resist his sister's embrace a little before relenting. Her hand ran up over his scalp. "What were you thinking?" she demanded.

"You ran off to a different world and you're asking me that?" Ben asked.

Katy nodded but Fajalar couldn't hear how she responded as more people came from the shuttle. Even as noisy as it was becoming, it was impossible not to hear Ben as he turned toward Naiathne and asked, "Is that a shark girl?"

Naiathne stayed close to Katy and answered, "I heard you had brain damage."

Ben nodded. "Only a little," That's when a tall, red-robed figure hurried up to him.

"How wonderful, another of the blessed." Kavaris Altain called as he stepped directly in front of them, blocking Naiathne and bowing. "My dear boy, it's a pleasure to meet another who the Æsir have seen fit to consecrate. I am Kavaris Altain."

"He's Kavaris Dell's replacement," Chris said, then he mouthed the words, be careful, bringing his hand to his face to hide it from the other monks.

"Yes, yes, I will be the new Kavaris and hopefully a friend to you, the blessed, so that we may all serve the Æsir. Kavaris Dell was a great man, but I do hope I can keep from repeating his mistakes." Kavaris Altain bowed.

"Cool," Ben said while stepping a little closer to his friends.

Fajalar took that moment to slide forward, bowing in his own way, much lower than Kavaris Altain had, practically putting his jaw on the floor. "And I hope to be of service to you. I am Fajalar, Andavarri's replacement."

Kavaris Altain looked at the Long-Wolf sharply and raised an eyebrow. "It's believed that your predecessor has gone off, taking property that belonged to my order. Will your people be making amends for this?"

The Long-Wolf nodded as he offered, "Of course. We will provide the order with a replacement shuttle along with payment for the trouble it's caused. Truly, Andavarri should've requested its use, but as you can imagine the pressure the emperor applies to my people is a strong motivator. Especially after our Fire Golems, at the request of Kavaris Dell, aggressively stopped the Tamerlane's guards during the kidnapping. The emperor was displeased, but Andavarri chose duty to your order and to the Æsir."

Kavaris Altain put his hands behind his back, taking a stiff step back. "I'm sure Kavaris Dell had his reasons. However, I'm afraid I agree with the emperor on this. Your Fire Golems make me nervous. I will be addressing their use as security at the station."

"I and my Fire Golems shall serve in any way you deem fit." Fajalar smiled with his face twisting.

"Speaking of security." The monk turned and called, "Cathal, would you come here for a moment." Cathal had been moving through the crowd toward the lone Grannusian. Cormack's people had rushed up to see him and he was politely trying to escape them with the antidote case under his shoulder.

Cathal looked over the heads of the monks and of the well-wishers as Kavaris Altain took a step toward him, going up the stairs back toward the airlock, where the entire crowd could see him. He waved to Cathal again. "Please," he said pointing toward the floor, at the spot next to him."

Cathal took another look at the Grannusian while stepping toward Altain, who explained, "You may go in just a moment, but first —" The monk raised his voice. "May I have everyone's attention?"

The monks of the order hadn't broken rank yet, but this was enough to get Cormack and his people to turn as well. "As our former head of security has departed for the gods know where, it falls to me as the new Kavaris to appoint her successor and I've chosen the greatest warrior of my own world. The hero of Anchor Home, Cathal of clan Sidhe."

Applause broke out from Cormack's people as he turned and thanked the monk. A number of people came forward to congratulate Cathal and pat him on the shoulder, while he nodded and turned back to the monk. He held up the case. "Now, may I?"

Kavaris Altain motioned toward the stairs. "Of course, of course. We must help those poor Grannusians. I know how fond of them you are."

Cathal turned and saw Naiathne standing with Katy, Ben, and Chris by the bottom step. "Would you care to join me?" he suggested as he made his way down.

But before Naiathne could answer, Kavaris Altain called, "Wait one minute," as he pointed to Naiathne. Cathal looked back at the monk, who continued, "I know you have some attachment to Prince Cormack's sister, but I don't think I want her running around my station until she's been inspected. Her people are known to be terrorists. As you've taken on these new responsibilities, searching her falls to you."

Cathal's brow furrowed as he stared at Altain, whose gaze was unwavering as he ordered, "Fulfill your obligations. You serve Nalanda station now."

Cathal turned and went down the last step to Naiathne. "I'm sorry," he said reaching for her bag. She didn't have much. The clothes she owned were on her and the uniforms she wore at the station before had stayed behind in the Sidhe domicile. Cathal finished with the bag, then looked back at Altain. He could see the man expected more.

"I've got to pat you down," Cathal said softly as he moved his hand quickly over Naiathne.

Under her cloak, Naiathne's outfit was loose-fitting, a sort of jumpsuit with beaded straps holding the folds of cloth together. Cathal pressed down and felt something as his hand ran over her back. There was a harness there. "Take it off please," Cathal said.

Naiathne's eyes widened as Cathal motioned with his hand. After a moment, she sighed and slipped one arm back. When her hand came out, she held a small, sheathed blade.

"You see, already she's tried to conceal a weapon." Kavaris Altain said, coming down and taking the knife from Cathal. The monk pulled the blade from its sheath and held it up to Naiathne. It was small, but vicious looking, with a handle made from bone and a jagged, serrated edge. "What were you planning on doing with this?" the monk demanded.

"Nothing," Naiathne shot back.

Cormack came forward. "Every Naiad carries one. It's no different from a diving knife. They're a way to get out of trouble when you're in the deep," the prince said.

"Your sister is not in the deep here. She is on my station and has failed to declare a weapon. Do you know the penalty for such a crime? I should have her sent back to Grannus this very moment," Kavaris Altain shot back.

"You sell swords in the market, right outside the Tamerlane doors," Ben pointed out.

"Yes, but those weapons are accounted for."

Katy followed the voices and stepped right up to the monk. "It was a mistake. She's not in the deep but she is here, on Nalanda station, right where she belongs and where the Æesir want her." She held her head up rigid with her blind eyes turned towards the monk.

The man shook his head. "Very well, but I'm confiscating this." He slammed the knife back into its sheath, then stepped away. "Go deliver your antidote," he said to Cathal as he turned toward the monks collected in front of him, dismissing the new security head with a sneer.

Chapter 7

In the heart of Nalanda station, a forest grew from an ancient stone floor, climbing high in a chamber that'd been excavated and made taller so that the trees could rise and form a canopy far above. They were grown beneath artificial lights on a ceiling that was too distant to be seen clearly. This moody place was the entrance to the Extraracial section, inhabited by the Drakes and their steward Fafnir.

Regin, the Ice-Carver, looked up from the ground, watching his friend and a number of other Drakes climbing down, moving their large bodies through the twisting limbs. Fafnir's size, at over three meters tall, was imposing enough, especially when combined with his broad shoulders, but the fact that the creature could climb, using his claws to draw his massive body down the thick tree trunks seemed to defy logic.

All the inhabitants of Nalanda station were told to attend the evening meal to hear a brief introduction from Kavaris Altain. Regin had no idea what to expect from their new head monk, but he wasn't looking forward to the man's rule.

The chaos after that last visit by the Æesir had given him freedom to move around the station, staying busy while the monks were without their Kavaris. He almost felt bad as he thought of the old man, who'd been executed so cruelly because of that boy, Alex. Nearly a century ago, when Kavaris Dell was only a child, the monk had been one of the first blessed by the gods. Left alive while the rest of his people burned, he became the Æesir's acolyte, announcing what the violent deities expected and guiding a flock of red-robed monks in the enforcement of their laws.

Much was forbidden by the Æesir. They stopped the spread of dangerous technology, things like artificial intelligence, advanced quantum physics, Nanotech, genetic engineering, and the study of any artifacts left behind on Einherjar, the dead moon or in the ring around Altor. All of this, the monks said, was to protect life, to keep people from destroying themselves, but Regin didn't believe that. He thought the Æsir were only worried about one thing, being challenged.

The thick trunks of the trees swayed as Fafnir reached the bottom and dropped onto the ground, making the broken stones shake. Regin looked up at his friend. "I suppose we should hurry. We certainly don't want to be late for our dinner date." Regin cocked his head, motioning back up the long ramp that led to the upper levels.

Fafnir sighed and glanced back at the other Drakes climbing down behind him. They settled among the roots and looked to him for guidance. The Drakes had evolved side by side on a world with the Lightening Bugs, creatures who could enter the thoughts of others. Through the centuries they'd lived in harmony with the glowing lifeforms who gently directed the powerful Drakes, forming a symbiosis that'd only been broken when humans, feeling threatened, wiped the Lightning Bugs out, and enslaved the Drakes.

Before Fafnir could swing forward on his mighty arms, Regin pointed to the Drake's shoulder. "May I? I wouldn't mind passing the time in conversation."

Fafnir nodded and held his hand out allowing Regin to climb up and perch on him. "What of your people?" the Drake asked.

Regin settled in with his tails draped over Fafnir's back, gripping his friend's armored hide while cautious of the boney barbs that covered him. "Oh, I'm sure the other males are already there. They're a nervous bunch, as you know, and are rarely late, unlike you, my friend."

"I go at my own pace. I've met few who can cause me to hurry," Fafnir said walking stooped forward with his staff, which was the size of a small tree trunk.

"I suppose that's something to be admired that you claim a bit of freedom," Regin agreed before adding, "I've certainly enjoyed mine while the monks have been occupied."

Fafnir's eye was close to Regin. He gazed at his friend.

"Yes, I'm still investigating," Regin confessed.

Fafnir pulled ahead of the other Drakes in the long passage from the Extraracial territory and in the quiet, dark space he said, "Your curiosity is dangerous. You need to stop."

Regin threw up one set of his hands. "She darted off to another world. You must want to know why."

The giant shrugged, causing Regin to grip tighter. "Not particularly." Then Fafnir added, "It's not only the monks you need to worry about. There's been twice as many ghost sightings since the Æesir visited. Those phantoms don't care if you're an Ice-Carver or a human."

Regin let out a snort. "They haven't taken anyone yet. In fact, I'm not certain they ever have. The monks probably tell those stories to frighten students."

"I've been here longer than you, my friend, and I assure you they're true," Fafnir warned.

Regin shook his head. "Can't you see? Things are changing."

Fafnir huffed. "If there's one thing, I know to be true, it's that things always change."

"I suppose so, but not like this. The gods are acting strangely."

"They've always been strange," Fafnir pointed out. "Look at where we are. Questioning them isn't allowed, but they built a school here in the ring, in an ancient outpost. A place that inspires curiosity in nearly everyone." The two had had this conversation before, with each other and with Eir of the Grannusians.

Both Fafnir and Eir were alive when the station was found. No one knew if it'd been floating in the gas giant's rings all along, undetected, or if the Æesir had put it here, but a century ago, one of the gods had shot across the sky, through a royal armada that was trying to kill him. Alone, his blazing chariot had dove through the rocks and ice, leaving a path for people to follow.

"It was a strange thing for the gods to do," Regin agreed. "But most religions are a bit odd. Take my world. It may be covered in ice now, but according to sacred texts it was once a garden and my people lived together, not divided the way we are now with the females on the surface and males below, hiding in tunnels and caves, afraid of being murdered during mating."

Regin continued, "Our writings say we were tempted. We sought openings in the sky and it led to our home freezing. Warning against curiosity seems to be the one thing all religions have in common."

"Perhaps," Fafnir said. "My people have no holy writings." He held up his staff showing the broken body of a lightning bug encased in crystal. "Our guides were always with us. Maybe, with them gone, we'll start to draft warnings of our own for those that come after."

"Yes, perhaps we're living in days that will someday be studied and written about," Regin suggested.

Fafnir grumbled, "Or perhaps we're just travelers like everyone else and the flow of time will erase us."

"That's bleak." Regin laughed as they reached the top of the ramp, coming out into a large central corridor. Crowds of people were moving along toward the grand hall. Fafnir stopped and waited for his people to catch up. Following him like ducklings, they were small and quick when compared to him, but they were larger than all the people around them.

Humans and the different races moved into the grand dining hall, filling every spot. Fafnir pointed to a table kept empty for the Drakes, telling his people to sit while he stepped back to the wall. The Drake table was a crowded space given their broad shoulders, but they sat without complaint, squeezing tight together. Everyone was gathered, broken up by race or dynasty.

Regin glanced at his own people, hunched over, anxious, watching everything in the room. They were as far as possible from the females of his species, who were surrounded by Fire-Golems and kept apart at their own table. The females struggled to focus through the haze created by drugs that kept them docile. Regin sighed, feeling profound regret as he considered the state of his race. Then he looked at the monks, saw Kavaris Altain sitting in a simple chair at the head of a table, and asked Fafnir, "Have you met him yet?"

"No, not yet and I'm in no hurry. I've met enough humans for a lifetime."

"Even for a lifetime as long as yours?" Regin joked.

"Most certainly," Fafnir groused while nodding.

Regin pointed to Chris and Ben, sitting at Cormack's table. Katy and Naiathne were there as well. He was impressed by the way they'd changed loyalty, going between the Tamerlanes and the Sidhe, the two most powerful families among the noble houses. He heard that they'd even moved quarters, taking an invitation from Prince Cormack to lodge in the Sidhe domicile. Regin said, "Still, you must find this couple interesting, the ones from the void space."

"Must I?" Fafnir asked.

Regin smiled at his friend's surliness. "I don't see how you couldn't. They're harbingers. I'm certain these young people are at the center of the change that's coming," Regin whispered.

"As I said, things always change. Sometimes they're made better, but it doesn't matter, humans never learn. They remain the same. You think there's a brighter future ahead of us. Believe that if you must, but as long as humanity is the guiding force, our people, yours and mine, will never be free, not truly," Fafnir said aloud and unafraid.

Regin kept his voice low though. "Yes, well, perhaps these ones are here to help us end it. Whether they intend to or not."

Fafnir turned his head to the furry alien, waiting for him to say more, but Regin's attention was on a Long-Wolf that was approaching them. "Hello Fajalar," Regin called.

"Master Regin, Master Fafnir." Fajalar nodded, stepping back against the wall with the two other stewards. "What do you expect from our new head monk?" the Long-Wolf asked.

"More of the same," Fafnir motioned to a stage that had been cobbled together with a few tables. A red ceremonial runner with gold edging had been laid across its surface.

Sister Nemain had seen to all of it and now she sat back in the mass of red robes looking up at Kavaris Altain, who stepped to the podium in the center. "May I have your attention please?" he called.

With practiced discipline, the room went quiet. Kavaris Altain smiled and nodded, letting his eyes wander over the space. "Excellent, I see that the self-control of our student body has not broken since my time here. We may teach a number of subjects at this school, but none is more important than obedience.

"Obedience to your teachers, to your families, and most importantly to your gods and their laws. That is the ultimate lesson I hope you leave here with. If you remain subservient to the Æsir, then the challenges of your life, no matter how terrible, will be less daunting. Look at Grannus. Our world gets tighter and tighter each year, but by the grace of the gods, we are raising islands from the sea. Truly it is a blessed endeavor that we know our gods see as good." The monk looked directly at Naiathne. "We've suffered at the hands of those who believe it is wrong, but the gods do nothing to stop us, proving we are just. This is the kindness of the Æesir. The swiftness of their punishment will always be a guide, telling you when you stray.

"I think of my predecessor Kavaris Dell, who acted beyond what his gods wanted, not seeing that these travelers are to be protected, and also educated. Truly I can think of no one in need of more guidance." He took an uncomfortably long pause while his eyes went to Chris and Ben. He lingered on Katy the longest though.

"But was the near destruction of one of their numbers the worst of Kavaris Dell's crimes? I think not. The gods leave humans in power for a reason. They know our strength and our wisdom, but yet Kavaris Dell allowed Fire-Golems, lifeless rocks controlled by alien hands, to attack a royal house. This will never happen again, not under my watch. Security will be done by the chosen of the gods, by the monks that stand before you, and by soldiers that I pick, including Cathal, the hero of Anchor Home. Do not worry if you are from a house that stood against his people. Cathal is a fair man and kind. Follow the rules of Nalanda station and you will have nothing to fear."

Kavaris Altain looked across the room at Fafnir, Regin, and Fajalar. Regin could feel Fafnir tighten beneath him. The massive muscles flexed, and his fist began to splinter the wood of his cane as it closed.

"To be clear. I hold no ill will towards the other races. The gods have told us they have a place here, for we are all their pupils, but I know that man is their choice to be your benevolent master. Many changes are coming, rules will be established to protect all, to maintain order. I will thank everyone to continue with their obedience and to know that I am the voice of the Æesir here. Their laws live in our order." His eyes passed over the crowd one more time, then he stepped back from the podium as the low murmur of conversation started to fill the room.

Regin looked at the Sidhe table with Ben, Katy and Chris. The red-headed boy still hadn't learned how to keep his voice low. Regin saw him turn to Cormack and say, "Man, this guy is from your world? I thought you people were cooler than that." Ben motioned to the stage. "What a tool?"

"Again, change," Fafnir grumbled as Regin looked at the Long-Wolf Fajalar, who controlled the Fire-Golems. His purple skin had turned darker as his mouth pulled back in a sneer showing his long teeth.

Chapter 8

Amita was constantly tired, but her brain never slowed. She spent a lot of time laying in her bunk, staring at her monitor, reading up on Tairnish and the people who called it home. It was one of the harshest worlds inhabited by humans, rich in minerals and ripe for mining but with radiation storms, heavy gravity, and air that was barely fit to breathe.

A long time ago, the people who formed colonies there had organized themselves into collectives following a political philosophy close to communism. The Bogatyr were only a single faction, but they were the most powerful, dictating policy to the others. Over the centuries there had been alliances with the royalists from Uppsala, but none were more one-sided than the agreement they had with the Tamerlanes. In the beginning, the relationship had been good for the Bogatyr, helping them gain power over the entire world, but since the loss at Grannus, the emperor's military had slowed its growth, leaving Tairnish in an economic slump. The people there had spent the last ten years growing disgruntled. They soured as food and resources became scarce, needing a war to survive.

Amita closed her eyes against the force pressing on her. She knew what Edith was doing, but that didn't mean she had to like it. The mercenary was pushing the shuttle, trying to make up time. Days had passed this way as they continued to accelerate, picking up enough speed to make it feel like they were under higher gravity, similar to what they'd face on Tairnish.

After two days Alex came to Amita's bed with a syringe. "I've got a shot for you."

"What is it?"

Alex looked back over his shoulder at Edith, who rolled her eyes. "It'll help you recover from the acceleration, help your body adapt," he said.

"Some sort of steroid?" Amita asked.

"Yeah, something like that, I guess. Look, I don't know, and you don't have to take it, but you look like you're dying over here. We need you. You've had the most luck getting information out of Tearmai. We need intel if this rescue mission is going to work."

"You know that's not my reason for going? That's not why I brought him?" Amita whispered, while nodding to the Drake. Tearmai didn't fit in any of the bunks so he was stretched out on the floor, taking up a good amount of the free space in the passenger cabin.

Alex looked over his shoulder at Andavarri. "Yeah, I mean I guess I know," he said in a low voice, then he turned. Holding up the syringe, he stared at Amita till she nodded in agreement. Alex pulled up her sleeve and wiped a spot clean with alcohol before sticking the needle into her shoulder.

Amita took a shot each day till she started feeling better and it was less of a chore to move about the cabin. Being more active, Alex took a larger dose, as he spent hours in the cargo bay training with Edith. Everyone could hear them and feel it through the walls, something large on the other side of the hatch shook the entire ship. As Amita got stronger, she became curious. She was about to open the access way when Tara called to her, "Where are you going?"

"I want to see what they're up to," Amita said.

"You don't want to go in while they're working. It's not safe," Tara warned.

Amita almost went anyway. Then Andavarri added, "Your friend would feel terrible if he killed you." That was enough to give Amita pause. Hours passed before Alex returned to the passenger cabin. He'd shaved his head at the beginning of the trip. Amita noticed as he came up that his whole body was sweaty and that there were tiny circles all over his scalp, pressure marks where something had been attached to him. He wore nothing but a pair of athletic shorts. Thank god for good ventilation, Amita thought, imagining the cabin smelling like a locker room.

"What are you doing in there?" she asked him.

"Training," Alex said, sounding about as happy as Amita had ever heard him. "Why? Do you want to see?"

Amita nodded, then Alex turned and called down into the hatch. "Can I show her?"

He must've gotten a yes from Edith because he waved her over. "Be careful climbing down," he said as he moved to the ladder. The cargo bay was long and wide and Edith was all the way at the bottom, checking equipment.

"We'll have to move it to the other side of the bay tomorrow when we start decelerating." Edith called. "We're four days out from Tairnish."

"I suppose that's when my part will begin," someone said from above. She looked up to see Andavarri climbing down after her. "What can I say? I was curious too. I've never seen one of these combat suits up close before. I want to know what took out my Fire-Golems."

As they climbed down, they passed a large object secured to the floor. It looked like a massive clay disk, but it had a door on it. She stopped and peeked inside, seeing a few uncomfortable-looking seats that were fully reclined. One seat was missing and there were bolts and tools scattered about the floor. Amita shook her head, imagining what it'd be like riding in that tight of a space, knowing that a craft like this had to be some sort of lifeboat, a way to get into atmosphere when things went bad. It would be a one-way trip.

They made it to the bottom of the cargo bay where a suit of armor was waiting. 'So that was what was in those crates,' Amita thought. The machine was three meters tall, as large as Fafnir, with a thick, heavily armored core, like a tank with legs and arms. Weapons bristled off it, shoulder-mounted rockets, a large rotary gun on one arm and some sort of torch on the other. The armor had no head to speak of, only a hatch with a very small viewport. 'Things would probably have to go pretty bad before you'd rely on that,' Amita thought seeing a helmet and a suit hanging from a nearby rack.

She noticed broken and smashed pieces of rock on the ground. The remains of the Fire-Golems. Of the four that came with them, only one was left tucked in the corner. It stood as a mute witness to the destruction of the others, its head turned down, seeming to look without eyes at where its fellows had been. There was something else, a white crystalline powder scattered across the floor.

Edith saw her looking. "It's our countermeasure for the Golems. You break the shell, then extinguish the fire inside with a burst round of this stuff. The crystalline structure is very effective at bonding and cooling their plasma form." She held up a small canister and a larger one. "We've got low yield and high yield. One to be fired from a launcher on the suit and one that's a grenade packed with a bit less of an explosion."

"So it kills them?" Amita asked.

"They were never alive," Andavarri pointed out defensively. Then she took the grenade from Edith and examined it. "Despite that, I'm disturbed that the emperor has been developing this technology. We've always enjoyed a mutually beneficial relationship with the Tamerlanes."

"And I would suggest you continue to maintain that relationship. The emperor rewards loyalty. You're soon going to see what he does to the disloyal," Edith said.

Andavarri nodded as she examined the survivor. "Well at least leave me this one. I know your mission is far more dangerous, but I'd still like to have a little security in case things go poorly with the Tairnishmen."

"Fine," Edith said. "We've already proven the countermeasures work."

Andavarri nodded as Alex said to Amita, "I can't show you everything the armor does in here, but I've gotten to mess with some of the weapons. Check this out." He stepped over to two boosters coming out of a large box with two-meter-long wings folded down on either side. "We're going to attach this to the suit. It's a rocket pack. This thing flies."

"That's an overstatement," Edith corrected. "The boosters can rapidly extract you from a hostile area, but they aren't capable of prolonged flight, especially not on Tairnish with its heavier gravity, but they will help control our descent."

"'Falling with style,' you'll be a regular Buzz Lightyear of death," Amita said.

Everyone looked at her. Except for Alex, no one was sure what she meant. He was shaking his head, never having been known for his sense of humor.

"Of all the things I miss, movie references top the list." Amita shrugged.

A few more days passed while Alex trained. Amita was feeling better and she spent much of her time trying to talk to Tearmai, attempting to get information out of him. It was frustrating for both of them. He clearly wanted to show Amita something, something he and Brash had found, but most of his thoughts were still confused. There was another problem too, Andavarri.

Tearmai would shut down whenever she was near, and she was almost always lurking. The shuttle's crew cabin was so small that there was little choice, but Andavarri seemed to be doing it on purpose as well. Amita would get Tearmai on a promising thread about what he and Brash had seen, then Andavarri would slip in next to them. At one point Edith had to threaten to put the Long-Wolf out an airlock if she didn't stop.

Luckily, Tearmai had a very clear recollection of the tunnels beneath Tairnish. While Andavarri was in the cargo hold, Amita got him to draw maps on a monitor. They were a massive web going deeper and deeper and Tearmai was nearly manic as he drew them.

Edith was able to copy the information, uploading it from the monitor before Andavarri returned and Tearmai got upset. He looked at the Long-Wolf and pushed his claws through the screen. Everyone tensed up as he growled, "The slave must be released." Andavarri's skin turned a deeper purple and her eyes tightened to pinpoints as she hissed at the Drake. No one spoke, afraid that Tearmai was going to attack Andavarri, but instead he turned and rolled his upper body into an empty bunk and hid his head.

They had to strap in when the shuttle shifted direction, turning its thrusters towards Tairnish to start the breaking procedure. It would be an equal number of days slowing enough to make orbit around the moon. As they got closer, they started receiving signals with a shorter delay.

It wasn't long before they were contacted by the Bogatyr, demanding to know why the shuttle was approaching. Long range scanners showed that the Nalanda shuttle wasn't the only vessel on that heading. From all over the planetary system warships were moving towards Tairnish. The transponder for the shuttle marked them as noncombatants, belonging to the Kavaris monks. Most of the ships heading towards the volcanic world declared themselves in the service of the emperor, but there had been a rash of mutinies aboard vessels with heavily Tairnish crews. These ships delayed showing their true colors till they were in position to defend the moon.

Communications was Tara's specialty, but she'd hardly spoken through the entire trip, only saying a few words to Alex and Amita and staying quiet whenever Edith was around. Still, when the mercenary came to bring her to the cockpit, she followed Edith up the ladder without hesitation. There were two seats. Tara sat in one while Edith took the other and Andavarri hung from the ladder behind them, her head half in the hatch.

Amita, Alex and Tearmai looked up from the floor. In case things went bad, they all had pressure suits on, even Tearmai. Through the coms in their helmets, they could hear her call into the microphone, "I am Tara of the Blomgren, the people of Northern Uppsala. We serve the Emperor Tamerlane and we are on a diplomatic mission, seeking to negotiate the release of the emperor's daughter, Princess Maeven. We have every reason to believe she has been brought to Tairnish against her will."

Before she could release the transmit switch, Andavarri moved forward, adding, "And I am Andavarri of the Long-Wolves. I am here to oversee these negotiations. I wish to aid you humans, in finding peace before this conflict escalates and risks damaging our home."

Minutes passed while Edith watched for an attack. The shuttle had no countermeasures and very little armor. That's why they were in the suits. If they were fired on by long-range weapons, they'd try to run but as their course was direct for Tairnish, they wouldn't have time to execute a full turn. The shuttle would be pierced and they'd be in vacuum.

More time passed than was created by the delay before a transmission returned. There was no picture, only a deep voice booming through the speakers. "The princess is held hostage against aggression by your emperor. Our people have claimed all the battlements around our moon. We no longer wish to serve a self-named royal upstart. As for your Long-Wolf, we are surprised that any of you would choose to side with the royalist of Uppsala. Your people have pulled back below the surface, becoming scarce, avoiding conflict. Perhaps you'd be wise to join them?"

Tara sat back. She knew which battlements the man was referring to. There was an artificial ring surrounding Tairnish. It was the largest piece of manmade technology in the planetary system. Even the fueling docks around the ice moon Oighear couldn't compare. For generations, this was where the fleets of the royal navies had been built. Most warships and large supply shuttles were assembled in space. Having to lift their massive bulk out of the gravity wells of the different moons wasn't practical.

Tara glanced down at a report from the Tamerlane's soldiers. Edith had been in contact with them through encrypted communications. Tara's eyes quickly scanned the report before she responded. "You've claimed the battlements, but you don't yet hold all of them. The emperor's men still maintain position on over a third of the shipyards," Tara said quickly. She released the transmit switch before Andavarri could butt in again.

The voice came back faster this time. "They won't hold out much longer. Your men are weak. We will consider terms for your surrender of these sections in the interest of preventing unnecessary damage to our docks. We're sending coordinates to you for a safe berth. Be advised that any treachery will result in your immediate destruction."

Tara's voice was sharp as she answered, "Save your threats. The emperor is not concerned with the docks. He is prepared to give generous terms to release them to you, however, his daughter is another matter. The attack on his family is an insult well past reproach. There will

86

be no surrender unless you're willing to negotiate for her safe return."

The Tairnishman on the other side came back. "We will discuss the princess when you arrive."

Edith looked down at the coordinates for their docking berth. "We're adjusting our course for the recommended berth," Tara transmitted.

The Tairnishmen answered, "We look forward to your arrival."

"I bet he does," Edith said to Tara as she took her helmet off. She was setting their new course, looking at data coming in. "I'd like to keep someone up here to watch the sensors. Can you handle the docking procedure?"

Tara's face tightened, seeing the course Edith plugged in. "Why are you taking us that way?"

Edith picked up her monitor and scrolled through till she found another report. It was taken from the spy network that still circled Tairnish, satellites that the Tairnishmen didn't know existed. "This part of the ring was heavily damaged. See here, all the debris falling to the planet? That's our best chance to make entry without being noticed."

"You're not even going to give me a chance to negotiate?" Tara asked.

Edith smiled, she knew what Tara was capable of, knew about her abilities. It wasn't as simple as reading someone's mind, but she could sense people's thoughts and feelings.

Edith glanced at the Long-Wolf, who was too damn close to her, then turned back to Tara. "I do want you to negotiate. Do it all in good faith. Keep them busy, but I promise you they've no interest in releasing Maeven. She's the only card they have to play, their only protection from what they know the emperor will do to them. If they'd been willing to let her go, they wouldn't have taken her to the planet's surface and smuggled her away inside that bunker."

Tara stared at Edith. She could feel the rage coming off her, the lust. She glanced at Andavarri and knew what the emperor had planned. He was going to fall on this world like a hammer.

Chapter 9

Each of the houses at Nalanda had their own domicile, a collection of rooms carved from the rock of the station. They were like embassies protected by guards and governed by the rules of the most senior member. Katy and the others waited in the hall of the Sidhe domicile, listening to Cormack call to his sister through her bedroom door. Naiathne yelled back, "I'm not going!"

"What's her deal?" Ben asked Chris. They were supposed to be on their way to the dining hall for a quick breakfast before starting their day and going to their classes. Cormack had explained that Cathal would be teaching their first one this morning.

"Her feelings about this place are complicated," Katy answered for Chris.

Ben grunted and asked, "Whose aren't?"

"You don't know what she's been through," Katy snapped at her brother. Ben had moved from the Tamerlane domicile to the Sidhe only the day before. None of the royals seemed to care that he'd no longer be rooming with the Tamerlanes. Before they left, Chris and Katy's one night at Nalanda had been spent in the spartan monk's quarters. The rooms Cormack provided were much nicer.

"Come on. Cathal is waiting for us." Cormack pushed the door open.

Katy heard Naiathne grab the open door and stop it as she yelled again, "Just leave me alone. I can't today." Her voice was edged with rage and defiance, but also desperation. Ben didn't comment, but he wasn't exactly silent. Katy could hear his mouth gaping as he made faces at Chris.

"Knock it off," Katy warned. It was only her second day back with Ben.

"I wasn't doing anything," Ben whispered, then turned to Chris. "How'd she know I was doing that?"

"Shush," Chris answered.

Cormack pleaded, "Come on, you can't start this stuff already."

Naiathne said, "Easy for you to say. You don't look like me. Coming here was a mistake. You heard Kavaris Altain last night. These monks are just like everyone else, so I'm staying where it's safe." There was the sound of Naiathne stomping on Cormack's foot. She started closing the door again, but Cormack kept his arm out. His voice got louder. "Safe? I know you went out last night. I wasn't going to say anything but—"

"What! You have spies watching me?" Naiathne interrupted.

"No, not spies. They're called guards. They're at the front door and you know they report to me."

"Of course they do, your highness!" she snarled. After a moment she added, slightly softer, "Look, I just need to clear my head. Please?"

Katy heard Cormack's tone come down as well. "Naiathne, it's not safe to go out after dark. You know that."

"The ghosts don't scare me," Naiathne sounded less assured.

Katy raised her eyebrow, questioning.

"Oh, that's right, you don't know about the ghosts," Ben muttered. "I guess when you run off and spend a few weeks on the ocean, you miss a few things."

"Knock it off Ben," Chris said loud enough to get Cormack and Naiathne's attention.

Naiathne threw her hands up. "All of you, just leave me alone. Tell Cathal I'm sorry, but I'm not coming."

Katy heard the door slam, then Cormack's defeated footsteps headed back to them. "Yeah, so apparently she's not going."

"She's just allowed to skip class?" Chris asked.

Cormack sighed as he answered. "Officially, no. Usually skipping means extending a student's time here at Nalanda. That's not something most families want, but it's not like Naiathne has a place back on our world so she kind of shows up when she wants. Eventually, she might get kicked out. You know, when I leave, but as long as she's here, I can protect her."

"Why are you even doing this? She sounds like she hates you," Ben asked.

"I need people to see her. See that she's human," Cormack answered. "Also, she's my sister, right?"

"Yeah," Ben said, taking Katy's arm.

Katy almost pulled away, but she battled the urge as they started off. She kept one hand out in case Ben became distracted. Behind her, she heard Chris swing his legs forward on his creaky crutches.

"What class is this that you're so excited about anyway?" Katy asked.

Cormack had been delighted, right up until he went to get his sister. A little of that excitement slipped back into his voice. "Well, I talked to Cathal last night for a bit. He's taking over security, but he's also going to be doing the combat training like Edith used to. He's starting out with something cool."

"I'm not in the mood to get punched in the head. I'm just getting over a concussion," Ben complained.

"No, we're not doing hand-to-hand. Cathal is going to let us try something else. We're going outside."

"What?" Chris asked, his eyes going wide.

∞

Cathal was in a long tunnel-like room made of stone, standing at the very end with a coppery metal door, which was closed like an iris behind him. There were at least forty students gathered in front of him listening intently.

91

He looked up at the new arrivals and rolled his eyes to the ceiling in annoyance at their late arrival. Cormack mouthed the word 'sorry,' and Cathal shook his head, still talking. "Keep in mind, the effect of Nalanda's artificial gravity will keep you from flying off the surface of the asteroid, however the further you get from the main structure the less of the effect you'll feel, but that's what I want you to get used to.

Cathal turned and tapped the iris. "We're going a full two clicks away from this door, looking for low-g. Boarding operations are a fact of life in ship-to-ship combat. We're going to be performing exercises to get you used to moving and fighting in thick armor and while it's not directly combat related, you'll be learning how to use tools in gloves like these." He motioned to the bulky suits colored pale grey, mounted along the walls. They were covered in lightweight segments of well-used and dented shielding. Ben went to one and ran his hand over the composite ceramic plates, feeling the little holes along their broken surface.

"Oftentimes," Cathal continued. "The thing that decides a battle is how fast you can get your ship back in working order."

"But there's engineers for that," someone in the front row pointed out.

"And what do you do when those engineers are dead? Do you stop fighting, and allow your enemy to take up a position that'll compromise your whole world?" Cathal's relaxed manner seemed to disappear. The volume of his voice stayed the same, but an edge crept in.

"No, sir," a number of students said.

"We are dependent on machines. You want to win, you make sure those machines keep working, keep you breathing, keep you fighting." He paused, looking over the room with a warrior's intense stare. After a moment he exhaled. "All right, let's start breaking down the suits. They range in size running down the wall from large to small." He pointed with both hands. "Everybody find one. I'll walk you through their operation and how to get in."

Ben and Cormack joined the rush of students going off to find their suits, while Chris stood back with Katy and said, "I'm not sure how this is going to work for us."

"What do you mean?" Cathal asked, coming over to the two.

Chris motioned to his legs. "We're both a bit out of commission."

Cathal put his hands on his hips. "You two swam the length of a royal sub and you're telling me you can't go for a little spacewalk?"

"No, I can walk," Katy said. "But I'm not going to be able to see where I'm going."

"Hasn't stopped you from getting around the station," Cathal pointed out.

"Yeah well, I have to do that," Katy shot back.

"And now you have to do this."

"Or do I?" She tried to stare in the direction of his voice.

When he spoke again, Cathal was closer than she expected. "Katy, I know you think you're going to get better. That Eir might be able to give you back your sight. But what if she can't." She felt a rough hand gently touch the side of her face. Surprisingly she didn't pull back, almost enjoying the sensation. "Are you going to let this stop you from doing anything? I haven't known you for long, but I know you two are tougher than that," Cathal said to her and Chris.

"You're really good at talking people into doing stupid stuff, aren't you?" Katy asked.

"It's called leadership." Cathal chuckled. "Come on, let's get you guys some suits."

It wasn't long before Chris and Cathal realized something. Despite his encouragement and a great deal of effort, space suits weren't made for people with casts on. Chris was already a large guy, but with the width around his legs and an inability to bend his knee, there was no way for him to fit. "I might have to get something custom-made for you," Cathal said. "See if we can take some parts off one of the larger species and cobble something together. Next time of course. I've got to get the rest of the students outside."

"Cobble?" Chris asked as Cathal walked away. Then Chris called behind him, "It's like four maybe five weeks and these things come off. Just saying."

"I think we were safer under the ocean," Katy pointed out. After a while and with help from the others, she'd managed to equip herself. She was becoming skilled at remembering the touch of things. Different buttons might've felt the same to someone with sight, but she noticed every detail and carefully gauged the smallest distances. Her years as an artist helped her make sketches in her mind, paying attention to everything she felt. When they were ready, Ben, Cormack and she moved towards the door, leaving Chris behind. Katy could hear the eager voices of the other students in front of her as they entered the crowd near the airlock, bumping up against each other's heavy suits.

Cathal stepped in front of her. "I have something for you." He put it in her gloved hand. She squeezed tight and felt a thin, narrow stick. It was light and though Katy couldn't see it, painted white. "This should help you navigate," he said. "You move it around in front of you, tapping from side to side. Even through your gloves, you should be able to feel the vibration when it hits something. It'll take a little practice to get used to." She felt him grab her arm and move it for her, showing her how the taps felt, touching the floor just enough to let the vibrations move through her palm.

"There's a cord loop on the end so you don't drop it." Cathal's voice moved away from her, going back to the front of the crowd but he added over his shoulder. "I probably should've given it to you before you were in a spacesuit but if you can use it outside, in here should be easy."

Katy touched the top of the stick, feeling the loop. She passed it over her wrist and tapped it back and forth, taking a few steps as a test. She was so focused on the vibrations that the sound of the iris-like airlock pulling apart startled her. "Pick a partner. We're going out in groups of eight," Cathal called.

Katy heard feet shuffling forward and felt a hand close on her arm. "Are we going to stay together?" Ben asked.

"Sure," Katy said. "Why not?" Given his ADHD, part of her wondered if going with Ben was the best decision. Cormack would probably have been a better choice to guide her.

She'd only been around her brother for a little over a day, but she'd noticed he seemed more focused here than he had been on Earth. He was still Ben, but the strangeness of the place calmed some of his restless nature. She'd heard once that people with Ben's condition needed stimulation to focus. Space suits, aliens, the constant threat of execution, till Ben got used to all of that it seemed like he was going to be more dialed in.

Cathal called, "All right, first group, secure your helmet, check your comms, and step forward into the airlock. I'm coming around to double-check you."

Minutes passed as Katy heard the instructor move around, quickly checking seals. All the other students were told to hold their helmets in front of them, and not

95

to put them on till it was their turn. Cathal didn't want them burning any air till they were outside. Katy felt the weight of her suit. It reminded her of the dive equipment they'd used on Grannus. They'd hiked for hours in those heavy things in the tunnels beneath the sea floor.

She remembered how isolated she'd felt when they'd finally put their helmets on. It wasn't a pleasant memory. She'd had a tether then, dragging her along like a blind, helpless puppy. She squeezed her hand. Now she had a stick. She tapped it on the floor, feeling the vibrations through her glove. She tapped it again, feeling it bang against something a little taller than the floor. "That's my foot," Ben said.

Katy nodded, committing the feeling to memory as she heard the iris slip closed ahead of them, letting the first group leave. Katy kept playing with the stick, getting wider with it. "Tell me what I touch," she said to Ben, focusing on the work and trying to ignore her growing anxiety when the iris door opened again. She heard Cathal go through his checks and the iris close. Another group was gone, and the other students shuffled forward.

Ben let go of Katy's arm as she swept the room, getting further and further from the door. She wasn't sure, but this might've been the first time since she lost her sight that she tried walking on her own, with no rope and no hand to hold. She liked it. Eventually, she felt Ben take hold of her again. "Katy, it's almost our turn."

She'd been listening to that door open and close for almost half an hour. She had a solid idea where it was, so when she turned, she tapped Ben's arm, letting him know he could let go. She swung the stick, tapping and tapping, hearing people move out of her way till she was in front of Cathal. "You're a fast learner," he said.

She felt him take her helmet from under her arm. "Are you ready?" he asked. Katy nodded and the helmet was placed down over her. Everything became muted and quiet. She squeezed the stick all the tighter, feeling as if it was the only solid thing in the world.

Cathal was moving her around a little, checking the seals. When he was done, the comms came on. "Katy, I've got your arm," Ben said.

"Cool," Katy's voice trembled. The iris opened again, vibrating the floor. They started forward. She could feel the sensation of the other students' feet echoing off the deck as they marched.

Ben guided her over the threshold, and she squeezed the stick. There wasn't enough room in the airlock to swing it. The iris closed and a moment later another opened. The last sound she heard outside the suit was air rushing out. After that, all she could sense was an endless quiet space in front of her as she stepped into the vacuum.

Chapter 10

Katy shuffled forward, feeling the weight of the suit, listening to her heartbeat bound in her chest. She'd only taken a few steps outside the airlock when Ben's voice echoed inside her helmet. "How are you doing?" Even through the suit's thick shell, she could feel her brother holding her arm.

"I'm good, just trying to get the hang of this." She brought the stick Cathal gave her down, sensing a smooth surface in front of her as she moved it back and forth. "What am I touching?"

Ben said, "It kind of reminds me of the spot we landed on back when we first got here, a big flat area, like a patio without the lawn chairs. A bunch of the other kids are stepping off it, going out where it's rougher. Actually, out there kind of reminds me of back in the desert, only the ground isn't sand and there's a crazy sky above." He sounded distracted as he stared at the gas giant dominating the sky above. It reflected the light of the distant stars, bathing Nalanda in energy. Only the thick suits protected them, blocking out the harsh radiation and filtering the light so he could see.

Katy had been blind since Arizona so her brother saying the surface looked like a patio made her picture someone's backyard, complete with a grill and picnic table. It made everything less scary. "You can let go of my arm, Ben."

"You sure?"

"I've got to learn to do this for myself, right?" She was trying to push down the anxiety she felt as her own breath flowed back off the inside of the helmet. It was closed off, a bit like being inside a box or a coffin. Moving her arm with the stick made her feel better, even with the suit's added bulk.

Ben released her, stepping away, watching the white stick wave back and forth. Then his sister started walking, one small move at a time. He remained next to her, staying surprisingly quiet as they reached the edge of the platform. Ben had seen all the other students go over the side, jumping down onto the rocky surface. He looked back and saw another group approaching behind them, including Cormack and the instructor Cathal.

Cormack had his own partner, someone from his world, but he remained close to Cathal. They approached Katy and Ben. Cormack's voice sounded through the speaker. "Doing pretty good so far."

Ben watched Cormack jump down. It wasn't far, only a few feet to the ground. He started explaining to Katy as her white stick danced over the side. "We're at a lip. It's a little bit of a jump. I'll get down and—" He didn't get to finish. His sister went to the edge and stepped off, bobbling a little as she landed.

Katy explained, "The suits have gyroscopic devices that help you balance. We'll need them more in a bit when the gravity lessens." She started swinging her stick again.

"Good job Katy," Cathal said softly on a private frequency. Then he opened up the group channel. "It's important to establish orientation when you're working outside. On a cruiser or a shuttle, it's a little easier, because they're not so big. Topside is usually established as the side away from Altor and bottom side is towards the planet, then, of course, you have the nose and the thrusters, which are the bow and stern.

"On an asteroid, it's a little different but for now, we'll use the navy terms and call the main building of Nalanda top side. We'll be moving down, going almost two clicks toward the bottom. The side of the station we exited is towards the stern and the other side, past that tall tower, we'll call the bow." Cathal pointed towards a glass dome, the tip of the lighthouse, the highest point at the station.

"Wow, kind of cool to see it from out here. It's bigger than I thought it'd be," Ben said.

"What's that?" Katy asked.

Cathal paused, not done with his instructions. Ben cleared his throat, "Oh, nothing, I'll tell you about it later."

Cormack shot over the speaker, "Are you two finished? You're interrupting."

Cathal calmly ordered, "Maintain comm discipline. Our destination will be marked off in your heads-up display. Spread yourselves out a bit so you're not banging into each other but stay with your partner. Let's move."

All the students started off, silently going across the rocky surface. They followed the terrain moving toward the destination Cathal marked. "Do you have your display up?" Katy changed channels while testing her stick on the surface. She could tell how rough and uneven the terrain was by the way the bounces came back. Moving slowly, she found that she could keep from tripping if she lifted her legs high enough. It would be more work and she'd be slower than the others, but she'd still reach their destination, as long as Ben could find it.

"I'm working on it," Ben said.

"The control is on your arm. Third one down. Cathal has it preprogrammed so it should come right up."

"Okay, I've got it. This is cool," Ben said looking at the entire surface of the asteroid laid out as a grid inside his helmet. "Speaking of Cathal, is it just me or is Cormack really fanboying out for him?"

"You're still on the open channel. Everyone can hear you," Cormack's voice came in.

"Second button down," Katy said. "The suit-to-suit link is the second button down," Katy shook her head while her face warmed, embarrassed for her brother.

There was a click and then Ben said, "You could've told me earlier."

"And you could've listened when Cathal explained how the controls work," Katy came back, sounding harsher than she meant. Two days, she thought. I've been back with my brother for two days.

"Um, sorry. Let's start walking," Ben was quiet for a moment before he asked, "Am I on the private channel now?"

Katy was trying to focus on the feel of the stick in her hand and on her steps, lifting her legs up to avoid obstacles. She took a breath, forcing the frustration from her voice. "There should be an indicator light inside your helmet."

"The blue one?" Ben asked.

"How should I know?" she snarled. After a moment she said more civilly, "Sorry, I didn't mean to snap." She kept walking. She wasn't sure where the other students were, but she had the feeling that they'd fallen behind.

"It's cool. I'm used to it. Remember I've been hanging with Alex?" Ben laughed a little.

"God, don't tell me he was a jerk the whole time." She put her urge to choke her brother away, suddenly feeling defensive.

"You just have to get through the wall of crankiness to get to know the guy. Alex is cool. Brave like a superhero or something," Ben said.

"And you said Cormack was fanboying?" Katy sensed the artificial gravity starting to fade, but moving the suit was still exhausting. It wasn't only the physical effort, but the mental as well.

"Yeah well, you should've seen Alex fight. He took down one of those big guys. . . wait you were here for

101

that, but he took out more of them in the hangar, though I didn't get to see that. I was dangling from a rope—"

"Hey Ben, we're going the right way, right?" Katy interrupted.

It took Ben a moment to answer. She knew he hadn't been paying attention. This was probably the first time he'd looked at the map since he opened it. "Yes, of course, by the way, how long is a click?"

"Pretty long, I think," Katy answered. She thought back, knowing she'd heard the term before, back on Earth, but she wasn't sure if distance was measured the same here or if the changes the Lightning Bug had made to her head would cover things like that.

"Oh, then we should get moving, we're falling behind," Ben said.

Katy sensed her brother's hand on her shoulder, adjusting her a little. For a moment, Katy felt like a windup toy, one of those ones that could only go in a straight line till someone turned them. "Can you see the others on the map?" she asked.

"Yeah, I think they're the little green dots. It looks like they're half a click away. Those guys are moving fast but I think we can catch up."

"How's that?" Katy asked.

"There's a good size crater in front of us. They're going around it but if we go straight through, we could get in front of them."

"How deep is it?" she asked.

"Give me a second." Ben left his sister's side, hurrying across the rocky surface and going to a spot where the ground turned up into a lip. He peered over at the long dark curve as it dropped into a shadowy bowl. Ben couldn't find the bottom but he could see the other side, where the other students were bouncing along. Their heads looked like tiny pebbles getting smaller. "I don't think it's all that deep," he said, coming back to take Katy's arm.

Katy felt for the edge of the lip with her stick, lifting it higher and higher till she found the top. It was almost shoulder height to her. The artificial gravity was even less here. Katy remembered what Cathal had said about the gyroscopic devices placed throughout her suit, that they could be dialed up. Katy touched the controls on her chest plate, tapping them till the devices were maxed out. She felt the suit grow a little more rigid and a little less responsive, then she crouched down and launched herself into the air to test them. When she came down, she was straight as an arrow.

"Screw it, let's try your shortcut." She grabbed the lip and jumped, pulling herself over like hopping a fence. She came down feeling the ground curve away below her. Giving a quick sweep with her stick she felt a smooth slope rolling down in front of her. "Race you to the bottom," she said bouncing forward, letting the gyros keep her upright.

Ben climbed over a little less gracefully and watched his sister start off. He looked at the dark shadowy distance she was heading into, hesitating only for a moment before saying, "Oh, you're on."

Ben was not nearly as coordinated and his gyros were still at the normal setting, so his descent turned into a tumble. He had to stop and pick himself up. By the time he turned to look for Katy, she was completely gone, deep down in the darkest part of the crater.

"I think I'm at the bottom. It starts going up here," Katy said over the comms. "What direction should I be heading in."

"Hang on, I can't see you," Ben said. "By the way, you won the race."

"Here let me turn on my light." Katy still held her stick. Letting it drop on its tether for a moment, she

103

reached for the arm controls. She had no way to tell if the light was on so she asked, "Can you see me now?"

"Yeah, you're not far. Hey, what's that in front of you?" The inside of the crater was perfectly smooth except for one spot near Katy's boots. Her light was on her helmet. The yellow glow touched a form, a faded red sack, laying on the ground.

Katy closed her hand on her stick, probed and felt it touch something soft. Carefully, she moved her stick around. The object was all soft, except for one spot that seemed to ring with the ting of metal. She bent down and reached out with her gloved hands, not sure what she was handling. There was a sheet of flowing material that might be cloth. She pulled at it and felt resistance, tugging something that was heavy, even in the reduced gravity. She felt its firm but still pliable surface. Her hand suddenly pulled away as the memory of being in the sub on Grannus, swimming through the command deck with Chris, came back to her. She'd felt so many bodies floating in the water. The dead had closed in from every direction.

Katy held her hand to her chest, stepping back, knowing what she'd touched, what was in front of her. Ben reached her as her pulse spiked again, thumping in her ears.

"Holy crap, that's a monk," Ben said. "That's a dead monk!" Katy had moved back so far that she bumped into her brother, knocking them both down.

As she got to her feet, she opened the main channel. "Cathal, Cathal, are you there?"

The soldier's voice came back. "I'm here. You guys lost?"

"No, I mean maybe, I mean . . ."

Ben's voice came over next. Katy could hear the shaking in it. "We found someone. He's dead. It's the new head monk and he's dead," Ben said. Katy could feel him gripping her arm again. This time she wouldn't tell him to let go.

Chapter 11

Above Tairnish, in the shuttle's cargo bay, Amita looked up at Tearmai, who was even larger in his pressure suit, and thought the cone jutting from his helmet covering his beak looked like a plague doctor's. Running his hand over the mask he looked uncomfortable as if he were about to rip the suit off. Edith had already warned him to be careful, explaining how expensive a spacesuit for a Drake was.

Their species never stopped growing, getting larger with every year, making any sort of environmental gear hard to maintain. Normally the armor plating on the Drake's body was protection enough but space was a different matter. Tearmai had already survived a short excursion in hard vacuum once. Even with the protection of a Fire-Golem, the ordeal had nearly killed him. "I think it's a good fit," Amita said as she went to her friend and helped him take the helmet off. "There you go, big guy."

Above them, Edith and Alex were prepping the reentry ship, a round flat disc, for launch. They were strapping the combat suit with its booster pack across the top. Climbing on the pile, Edith was moving the armored arms into position, barely using the servos in her own suit as she hooked heavy fasteners across them. The shuttle was slowing down, making the g force and the illusion of gravity less extreme.

She connected fuel lines and extended the stubby wings of the booster pack while saying to Alex, "I'm going to handle getting us down. No offense, but this isn't something we're going to get a second chance at. This dropship is civilian. It's pretty much made to go down through a clear sky. We're not doing that. We'll be passing through a debris field to hide our signature."

"Is that smart?" Andavarri asked, from her perch on the wall. She'd been watching them work offering snide comments instead of help.

Edith smiled. "Definitely not. But they'll never see us coming." She turned to Tearmai. "You want to check the fit?" She motioned to the dropship's open door.

"You're bringing him with you?" Andavarri asked.

"Maps are great, but a guide is better," Edith pointed out.

Watching the Drake climb in, Amita ducked down and followed him. Ordinarily, the reentry ship had four seats but the back two had been ripped out to make room for Tearmai, leaving two in the front. "Which side do you want?" she popped her head out and asked Alex.

"He can have either," Edith said, "because you're staying here."

Amita yelled, "What! I didn't come on this trip to get left behind. I'm going to the surface."

"You came to gather intel from the Drake and to keep him calm. This is a rescue mission, and you have no place on it," Edith said.

"Alex," Amita stepped closer to him, jutting out her bottom lip.

"You'll be safer here." He moved away from Amita's intense gaze.

She grabbed his arm and forced him to look at her. "You may be off to save the bloody princess but that's not why I came to this rock! Tearmai and Brash were here before they went to Earth. You remember Earth, right? Our home, where everyone you've ever cared about is. Wait, no, that's not right. Your brother's here and maybe your mum, so I suppose it's all hunky-dory for you, but my family—" She pointed her finger at Alex's chest. "I'm not giving up on them."

For a moment it seemed like she was getting through. Then Alex looked at Edith, ready to ask her to reconsider, but Edith shook her head.

Biting her lip, Amita considered her position. Her eyes fell on Tearmai as her only play occurred to her. She turned to Edith. "I'll tell you what. You're going to let me go or I'm going to tell my friend to start breaking stuff, like all your stuff," Amita warned.

"You'll just get him killed," Edith said.

Amita set her feet. She was tiny next to Alex. She tensed like a spring and said, "Or maybe I'll get us all killed? How much of a fight do you think this shuttle could take?" She stepped forward and Tearmai stepped out behind her. "Here's the thing, I don't give a toss."

Edith's face was a mask. She wasn't somebody that got angry, not in a way that anyone could see. Amita stared at her, sensing that the mercenary was calculating her next move. She couldn't know that Edith was debating over putting Tearmai down, executing him quickly. It seemed impossible to Amita but then she saw Edith's hand slip down and rest on her sidearm.

An armor-piercing round would do to a Drake pretty much the same thing it did to everyone else. Amita wondered if this whole argument was about to be over fast, if she'd overplayed her hand, but then Edith smiled and said, "You know what, what's one more?"

Ignoring her shaking hands, the young girl kept her face passive as she said, "Excellent," while nodding and resisting the urge to vomit.

A few hours later Amita was strapped inside the curved walls of the drop ship and second-guessing her decision. At first, it wasn't bad. She heard the large cargo bay doors open, and the atmosphere escape in a single burst. Then Edith fired the thrusters on the combat suit, pushing them up and away from the bay.

The shuttle was moving so slow on its final approach that they were nearing zero-g. Tugs and pushes from the thrusters maneuvered the reentry ship through the doors, like a ferry leaving a dock and quickly changing directions in a channel.

Edith hadn't turned on any of the telemetry screens inside the ship, so Alex and Amita were unaware of their location. They only had an altimeter to measure their descent and the small observation window that looked up from the dropship's curved surface. Amita undid her harness so she could get a closer look. "What are you doing?" Alex asked.

"I just want to see." She watched them move past the doors. For a moment the cloudy skies of Tairnish were below them. In daylight, the world would have had a burnished red color, but they were dropping at night. Below them was mostly blackness but in the distance, Amita could see sparks of fire as wreckage from the ring burned up. Giant hunks of metal were igniting and melting in their path. They looked tiny from so far above, but they'd be getting bigger soon.

The reentry ship leveled off. Amita looked up, catching the edge of the shuttle moving away, then only a moment later she saw the dark shape of the docking ring above, like a pencil line through the stars. They were moving faster than it felt but soon the pull of acceleration couldn't be ignored as it tugged her back. "Get in your damn seat," Alex said. They both felt the same thing, like they were at the top of a roller coaster, ready to fall. Hurrying to get her harness on, Amita finished just in time before the plummet became undeniable.

The acceleration pushed them painfully back into their seats. Tearmai was strapped in as well with a makeshift harness, but he reached up and put his long arms to the ceiling trying to gain some sense of control.

Above the reentry ship, in the battle armor, Edith was wearing a heads-up display secured tightly to her skull. She gave the thrusters a long burst and pushed them down into the moon's gravity well. Her eyes were open and relaxed as the sensors on the outside of the suit gave her a one-hundred-and-eighty-degree view of their flight path. It took training and practice to get used to this, tightening the information into something her eyes could process. There were displays projected inside her helmet and a blink code that let her eyes control them.

The sensors pointed down range, picking targets that were miles away, impossible to see with the naked eye in the dark. As the ship accelerated, those objects started coming at them fast. Edith chose a clear path, putting them on a course that would take them through the debris, and it was all going fine till they hit the atmosphere.

Heat built on the surface of the reentry ship as air currents pushed them all over the sky, trying to twist and turn them. Edith used short bursts and the stubby wings of the combat suit to make subtle changes and hold them steady, but as they approached one large piece of the fallen ring, warnings blared in her ears.

Pushing the flaps down she dove under it and then tried to flatten out again. There was more debris ahead. All Edith could do was pick a course and hope it'd stay clear as the air thickened, making steering even tougher. The air got hotter as well and her sensors started to fail as the atmosphere around the ship was ionized, burning as it turned into plasma. She glanced at the altimeter, watching it count down, then she closed her eyes, accepting that she was blind and that there was nothing left to do, except to hold on.

Inside the reentry ship, Amita looked up at the window seeing flames as the vapor scorched the surface. The shaking was incredible, vibrating through everything. She brought her hand up for a moment and saw her fingers blur. How much could the human body take, she wondered, as they continued to fall.

Another warning went off inside the combat suit. Edith glanced at the altimeter again, they were coming up on five kilometers. She braced herself as she heard several pops below her. The lines and sheets of the parachutes jetted past. There was a sickening tug, slowing them down. Then the parachutes broke away. A heartbeat later another set shot from their storage compartments. Edith had adjusted this set to open as low as possible, but it would still be a five-minute fall to the ground. In that time, they'd be visible to everyone, and they wouldn't be falling like the rest of the debris. In every combat descent she'd ever made, this was her least favorite part, floating in the air, waiting to be taken out. She hated it. Finally, touchdown came as a welcome, if painful, relief.

It wasn't a soft landing. They slammed hard into the rocky surface, skidding and bouncing along the ground as the parachutes collapsed and ripped, then finally tore away. Each of the three hard smacks into the ground felt worse than the one before it. Amita didn't remember passing out, but when she opened her eyes, it was to the sound of Edith's voice. "Hey kid, you still alive?" The reentry ship was at an angle, half-buried in the ground.

Amita looked up at the mercenary standing in the crooked door. Edith's face was hidden behind a dark, burnish-red helmet with multiple lenses attached to it. She looked as alien a creature as any Amita had met with the cloudy, angry sky pushing down behind her. reddish-yellow clouds blended together into a wall of haze as the distant suns started to fill the horizon. Morning was on its way.

Amita nodded, feeling the weight of her own helmet. She'd forgotten that she was in a pressure suit. She touched it. "Can I take this off?"

"I wouldn't. Once you get a breath of fresh air on this world, you'll never forget it. Here—" Edith reached down and touched Amita's helmet. "You're off tank air now. I activated your filters. Believe it or not, there's O2 in this soup but the rest you probably don't want in your lungs."

"And people live here?" Amita asked.

"Now you see why they're so pleasant?" Edith gave Amita a hand getting up and asked. "Alex, you good?"

"I'm good," he called after turning on his own filters. Their voices were only slightly muffled by the helmets. Amita didn't turn to watch him roll out behind her, but she could hear him grunting with effort. Even after a week of high acceleration and with the drugs it was still a strange feeling getting used to the extra pull of gravity. It felt like they were wearing weighted vests.

As Amita got to her feet on the edge of their small crater, she noticed Edith's normally dark armor was now the same burnish red as the surrounding terrain. She looked up at the battle armor where it squatted down, waiting for a pilot. It's color had resurfaced as well to match the terrain. Its grey panels were now a broken pattern that blended in with the rocky, barren landscape. The hatch was open, waiting for Alex to climb in.

Tearmai was the last one to make his way from the escape craft. He squeezed out looking vaguely like he was hatching from a broken egg. He took his helmet off and tossed it to the side, managing to tear his space suit in the effort. Amita watched his beak move in disgust as it pulled in Tairnish's heavy air. His tongue flicked in and out of his mouth as if he were tasting something awful as well.

"What now?" Amita asked.

"Now we've got a hike," Edith said before turning to Alex. "I've already dropped the flight pack. Where we're going, you're not going to be able to use it anyway and I don't want the enemy picking us up if we try bouncing," She was referring to the way the battle armor could cover distances, not actually flying, but with controlled bursts, leaping across the surface. She motioned for Alex to get in the suit. He started for the leg, but then Edith tapped him on the shoulder.

"Sorry, but you're going to have to switch caps." She pointed down to the ground where she'd left the control helmet for the armor. It was covered in sockets for the suit to plug into. Alex nodded and took the pressure suit's helmet off. He tried holding his breath but before he could put on the bulkier control helmet, he got a mouthful of Tairnish.

"Ugh, that is nasty," he said as he pulled the cover down.

It made Amita curious about how bad it could be, but not so much that she was willing to experiment. She watched him start back towards the open hatch, climbing up. "So, we're walking? How far do we have to go?" she asked.

Alex closed the hatch and a moment later the suit stood to its full height, even towering over Tearmai. Edith was looking at a display on the arm of her armor. "If the intel you got from Tearmai is correct, then it looks like we're about forty clicks out from the entrance to the mines, then we'll have to travel underground a bit further."

"Forty clicks? You mean kilometers, right?" That'll take us days," Amita said.

"No, it won't. I've got a ride." Edith went around to the back of the armor. There was a rail on it and a foot pad down below. She climbed up and situated herself in the middle. As big as the machine was, there didn't appear to be enough space for two, or at least, Edith didn't seem to have any interest in making room.

"And how will I be getting there?" Amita asked. Then she felt hands pick her up.

Tearmai swung her back over his shoulder. "Squeeze tight so you don't fall off," he said, guiding her arms around his thick neck. For a moment she was worried she'd choke him, but then she felt the armor plating over his throat and worried less.

Tearmai still wore the bottom half of his pressure suit, which included a thick utility belt that Amita locked her foot into. She looked down at her own belt and noticed a pouch with a tether in it. "Pass this around you," she said. Tearmai did as she asked, then Amita secured it again to her belt before going back to squeezing his neck.

"Tighter," Tearmai warned her. He leaned forward on his two long arms, then swung his legs out like a pendulum. Riding on his back meant Amita went rapidly from being up to being down, again and again, swinging back and forth. It was fun for a few minutes, but the thrill didn't last as they made their way across Tairnish's surface.

Chapter 12

While the reentry vessel and the battle suit fell away, plummeting toward Tairnish, Tara piloted the shuttle to a docking berth. They were in a low orbit just above the Ring, passing over its most damaged areas. The massive structure encircled the world, but it wasn't a single solid piece. Much of it was taken up with a webwork of connecting columns, covered in solar arrays that strung together various construction docks. The shuttle could've flown through it in places, but Tara would never attempt that, not with her limited experience. She kept her hands squeezed on the controls following the course Edith had planned to one of the berths controlled by the Tairnishmen, while Andavarri perched in the copilot's seat and read the sensors. "Your people are buried deep. The Tairnishmen won't find it easy getting them out."

"Good, they're our only leverage." Tara's back was rigid, and she had to keep her voice from shaking. There were calming exercises she could do, deep breathing or meditation, but she didn't have time and both things would've been impossible with the Long-Wolf watching her every move.

The shuttle was no longer accelerating or decelerating, but like the ring itself, it was still moving incredibly fast, orbiting Tairnish at thirty thousand kilometers per hour. Very little thrust was required to maintain this speed as the moon's pull did most of the work, but it was up to Tara and a few automated systems to match the ring's speed exactly. She gently touched the controls, bringing the vessel in for docking. She felt magnetic locks reach out and grab hold of them, then she killed all power to the thrusters, relinquishing any influence over their course to the Tairnishmen as the Rings systems pulled the shuttle in and released an airlock gantry.

"Well now the fun really begins," Andavarri said as she floated in the zero-gravity, coming up from her seat and pulling herself back through the crew quarters and into the cargo bay to the main airlock.

Tara took a moment to finally settle her breathing, slowing it down as best she could before following the Long-Wolf. When she entered the cargo bay, the double hatches were wide open, and four armed soldiers floated through from the other side. They wore full combat armor on their hulking forms and their faces were hidden inside their helmets. Tairnish armor was distinct from other soldiers, not only because of the size of the men beneath, but because of the simple face they sculpted into their helmets with deep-set eyes and broad cheeks. It was a stylized version of the perfect worker, the same in every way as the man next to him, steady, reliable, unemotional, a visage unmoved by passion.

They pushed through the narrow gangway into the cargo space like a herd of bulls with their assault rifles pointed at her. Tara held her hands out as she was turned and forced to the wall and three of the soldiers started to search the vessel.

One of the men moving around the ship found the surviving Fire-Golem and tapped his rifle against its chest, calling. "Does this one have its flame inside?"

"Yes, it's my personal guard," Andavarri said. "Last I checked our people were still allies."

The soldier was quiet for a moment and his suit's emotionless face never left the golem. He was a little shorter than the statue-like creature but significantly wider. It'd be easy to think he was in concentration, examining the Golem as if it were a piece of art, but in truth, he was listening to orders sent through a private comm channel. Finally, he turned and said to Andavarri, "It stays on the ship."

Andavarri rolled her eyes and huffed. "Fine." As she moved across the wall coming closer to Tara, who was still pressed against the bulkhead, she commented, "I suppose we all have to make sacrifices." She waved her tail in small, satisfied circles.

After a few minutes passed, the soldiers returned from their search of the shuttle and the bulky armored men closed in around Tara, making her slight form look even smaller. As her arms were pinned behind her back and placed in restraints, her eyes met Andavarri's, who was content to watch the whole ordeal. Then a hood was dropped over her head, leaving her in darkness with only her hearing and sense of touch.

She felt herself handled by armored gauntlets. Bulky fingers that whirled with the sound of mechanization closed over her shoulders and pulled her along through the gantry. She remained limp as she was moved like freight through the station. There was no talking. The soldiers were silent as could be, but that didn't mean Tara couldn't sense them. She felt their carefully controlled emotions. The anticipation, the anxiousness, and more dominant than any other, the anger toward her and the world she came from.

After going some distance, she heard an airlock open and close behind her. One of the soldiers took her legs and arms and steadied her, stopping her momentum in the center of a room. "Wait here," he said, backing out while Tara was left floating there with the hood still on and the restraints squeezing her arms uncomfortably.

She heard the soldier leave but also sensed his emotions no longer present. "Hello," she called wondering if Andavarri was with her, but no one answered. Below her, she felt her foot touch something solid. She moved her leg back trying to determine what it was. It felt too strange to understand, so she closed her eyes and sent her thoughts inside.

An indeterminable amount of time passed before someone entered the room. She heard him and felt the air move, but she also sensed him, feeling emotions that were carefully controlled, though concern and boiling rage still seeped out. "They sent a child? A child!" he growled. With a harsh jerk the hood was removed, pulling some of her pale hair from its braid.

A massive man with dark purplish skin stood in front of her. His pockmarked and wrinkled face was half hidden behind a startling white beard that made the strange color of his skin pop and look brighter than it actually was. His dark brown eyes were harsh as they searched Tara up and down. He looked past her to the door where Andavarri had followed him in. She moved across the wall, taking up a position high and to the right of Tara.

Glancing down, Tara saw the solid thing below her was a chair and it almost made her laugh. The piece of furniture was supposed to create the illusion she was sitting, but with no weight to put in it, and with her hands still behind her back, it was impossible to even pretend.

She looked around the room's confined space. It was set up as an office with a desk on the only flat surface and a few small windows built into its curved walls. The office was an individual unit that had been attached to the Ring. In fact, much of the massive structure was built from small pieces and larger ones like this.

They'd been packed with cargo at one time, then launched into orbit and retrofitted for their new functions, strung together with hatches on either end so they could add more units, like a chain. This particular unit pointed away from the moon at a right angle to the rest of the Ring, hanging out into space. Its far hatch, the one behind the desk had been replaced with an even larger porthole, looking out on Altor.

It was an impressive view, but Tara's thoughts were focused on Andavarri, wondering where the Long-Wolf had been all this time, what she might've told the Tairnishmen. She kept her eyes on the man though, considering his every move as he made his way behind the desk.

He said, "You've offered to surrender the docks, but I don't believe for a second that Tamerlane would do such a thing. Do you take us for fools?" His voice was calm with only a hint of menace and his eyes were on Andavarri.

Tara ignored everything that happened before and calmly asked, "And you are?"

"I'm First Marshal Yulset, first of the Gullatoch collective. Now answer the question."

'Someone important, aged and experienced, not some underling,' Tara thought as she answered with practiced patience. "It's been ten years since Grannus. The emperor is not looking to go back, and his forces are sufficient to hold everything he wants. Why would he need the docks if he's not building ships?" She turned her shoulders and motioned with her hands showing the restraints. "Is this really necessary?"

The Tairnishman ignored her question. "Sufficient? Nothing is ever sufficient for him." Tara sensed the man's anger beneath sadness and fear. They twisted deep inside him, along with a sense of resolve.

She looked at his hand, laying palm down on the surface of the desk that was too small for him, built for an administrator from Uppsala. He looked uncomfortable, too big for the space, and uneasy in the zero-g. The docks were normally operated by people from her world, not Tairnishmen. They were soldiers and miners and little else. If she had to guess, she'd say this man had done a bit of both.

She considered his skin again. The pigment that gave the Tairnishmen their strange color was a complex organic compound called anthro acertilia plasmid. It'd been adapted from Long-Wolf biology and had very little in common with the naturally occurring pigment, melanin that developed in humans, but its action was much the same, creating a unique hue on the surface.

Tara's pale skin was actually much rarer, nearly unseen in the human race anymore. Even in her northern home on Uppsala, most people had some color to them. Her paleness and crystal-clear blue eyes could be upsetting to some. She wondered how it affected her interrogator.

There were other changes engineered into the Tairnishmen. Ones that went deeper. Tara had heard it time and again, that Tairnishmen weren't really human. They had new organs, enlarged kidneys, and a lymphatic system that worked twice as hard to filter out the particulates in the air of their world. Even with those changes, their lifespan was shorter than the average person's. A sixty-year-old Tairnishman was rare. This man who'd come to negotiate with her was just about the oldest she'd ever seen. He was weathered, with those pale wrinkles running along the cracked and dried surface of his skin.

She looked to the ceiling, giving herself a moment to center her thoughts, then asked, "You've got all the power here. What exactly do you want?"

The old Tairnishman ignored her again, repeating the word, "'Sufficient?' You think we don't know our world? That we're not aware of what he's been doing?"

'Information,' Tara thought, 'that's all he wants.' "I have no idea what you're referring to." She watched the man's hand come up and close in frustration. It was impossible to ignore its size.

"Aside from slowly starving us and weakening us, he's been taking our labor force, moving the Drakes off-world, emptying the mines. He has work for them somewhere else," the old man snarled.

Tara had been on Nalanda, away from the politics of Uppsala for too many years to know what he was talking about, but she wouldn't let her lack of knowledge show. "Moving the Drakes is not a decision by the emperor alone. The Kavaris monks have given time, but they've declared that all the slaves are to be set free."

It was the law, but many noble houses had ignored it or been slow to enact the policy, testing the resolve of the monks and their gods. The monks often created policies they believed aligned with the Æesir's will, but if the gods did nothing to enforce such rules, they had little power.

"Tamerlane does not fear the Æesir. It's the only reason he's done all that he has."

Tara began, "I assure you—"

Andavarri interrupted, "And that rule only applies to newborn Drakes, not the old ones raised in slavery. Those creatures are still property until they're released by their owners."

The Tairnishman nodded to the Long-Wolf while Tara kept her face passive, ignoring Andavarri, not turning to look at her as she pointed out, "They were never yours, only contracted to you. Their disposition is up to their individual owners and their owners reside on Uppsala."

"Either way, they're gone. Not that there was much use for them. Your emperor slows construction and keeps the docks from building for anyone else while raising prices from your garden world. You made us dependent on you, then you pull back, leaving us with nothing."

There was that sadness again. Tairnishmen were such proud people. "I won't deny anything you say, but what you fail to see is that you've been presented with an opportunity. A chance to reclaim your independence. The docks can be yours."

"They are ours!" He slammed his fist on the desk. The action forced him towards the ceiling. He had to grip the desk to steady himself.

Tara watched him, waiting till he'd settled back down. "We both know that isn't true. The emperor's men hold a third of the modules and they're buried deep. You won't be able to get them out without risking serious damage. All we want is the safe return of our people and most importantly the princess. She is the future of his empire. His only child. That is what you are denying him."

"Yes, children. Funny that the emperor would send you, a child yourself, to negotiate for him," the Tairnishman pointed out. She sensed him reach a conclusion, an awareness that Tara knew nothing.

Tara held up her shackled hands again. "This is a negotiation? I couldn't tell."

The man smiled but didn't move as Tara glanced at Andavarri, clinging to the wall, completely free. Their eyes met. Not for the first time Tara wished she could get a read on alien minds.

She explained, "I'm here because I had a head start. Others are coming. The emperor himself, if I understand correctly." She turned back to the Tairnishman.

"Yes, with battleships," the man said.

"To come with less would be foolish," Tara pointed out.

"To come at all is foolish. You see us as brutal a people but I think it needs to be said how important our children are to us. They are the future of my people. We're allowed two, only two per marriage. More than that would stress our resources too far, so we value them greatly. Those children are not raised by their parents alone. They belong to everyone in their commune. I watched an entire generation fight and die for your emperor. I'll allow no more. Not for him. Not anymore. If I must keep his child to protect ours, then so be it."

"Don't overplay your hand. Maeven has one life, you have many to lose," Tara said.

"Now we have yours as well," he pointed out.

Tara laughed. "You can't be serious? I mean nothing to the emperor. That's the only reason he sent me. I'm a tool, but to Maeven, I'm more. You speak of the future, but you refuse to see that you hold it in your hand. Someday she will be empress. I'd think about that as you consider the way you treat her."

The man smiled. "Oh Tara, I'm well aware of who you are. You are Maeven's pet. Her servant. Here pretending like you speak for your emperor."

"She's not pretending." Andavarri dove down off the wall and came up across from the man. "The emperor sent her, but she knows nothing about the Drakes leaving, nothing about what he is up to."

"And you do?" Tara asked.

Andavarri sneered at her and then turned back to the Tairnishman. "I know things are turning. Things beyond what we three in this room can control. Powerful people are moving their pieces. Tara is not wrong. You have an opportunity here. One that will not only affect the future of your people, but mine as well. It's up to you what you do with it."

The man stared at Andavarri, then came around the desk. He pulled himself towards Tara, took her shoulder and turned her around. He removed the restraints, placing them down on the desk. "You may go back to your shuttle for now. Get some rest. We'll continue this conversation tomorrow."

"You brought me here blindfolded. How do I get back?" Tara asked.

"She knows the way." He nodded at Andavarri.

Tara turned to the Long-Wolf, wondering if she believed what she'd told the old man. Did she really think they had a chance or had she changed sides and made a deal with these people? If she had, then Alex and Edith were already dead and Maeven's only chance was gone.

Tara knew the emperor. She knew this negotiation was only a delaying tactic. That when he got here, he'd lay waste to this world with or without his daughter.

Chapter 13

Ben was famished. He'd worked up an appetite out on the surface so he didn't hesitate to pile his plate as high as possible. As he sat down across from his sister, he realized that she hadn't gotten anything yet.

"You going to eat?" he asked.

"I'm not that hungry. Besides it sounds a bit crowded over by the food station." Katy nodded towards the buffet, which was full of people. They all seemed to be talking at the same time. The word was spreading about what they had found outside on the surface.

Looking over his shoulder, Ben saw Chris and Cormack coming towards them. Cormack had Chris's tray. "I could get you something," Ben offered. "Or, I've got a ton of food right here. I think this is sausage." He picked up a piece of meat on his fork and brought it towards her face. "Try a bite."

Katy smelt the sausage a moment before her brother got it to her mouth. She grabbed his wrist and squeezed tight. "Ben, don't try to feed me."

Ben looked at her pale eyes and put up his hands. "Sorry, sorry. I understand. That's a line, but you should eat. Here, take my plate."

"I don't want it," she grumbled, pushing his hand away.

Cormack settled down next to her a moment later. He put one tray in front of Chris and then took a second plate off his own and put it in front of Katy. "I grabbed you some food."

She sighed, then grumbled again, "Thanks."

Cormack was distracted, looking around the room so he didn't notice the tone in her voice. There wasn't much on the prince's plate, a bowl of rice and some sort of meat that he ate steadily like fueling a machine.

Ben looked at his sister. He could tell she was upset but didn't know what to do about it. He wanted her to be all right. He was all right and he'd actually seen the dead guy, and outside of Vyktor, the monk was the first dead body Ben had ever been around. Vyktor was way worse. They'd actually watched that kid die. Suddenly, Ben wasn't hungry as the scene from a few weeks ago came rocketing back to him. The way the big kid had dropped to his knees. The way he'd held his body tight.

Ben stared at his food trying to chase the image away, but it was only replaced by the dead monk as emotion overwhelmed him. 'Maybe I'm not all right,' he thought as he remembered how unreal Kavaris Altain's body had looked, all floppy and pale like he was made of clay. Out on the surface, the monk wasn't wearing a spacesuit, just his bright red robe, which hung on his body like a rumpled bed sheet.

Ben and Katy had waited in that crater for what seemed like forever while Cathal and the other students made their way down to them. Ben remembered Katy warning him not to touch the corpse. 'Why would I want to touch it?' he wondered.

"I'm going to have to talk to my mother," Cormack said interrupting his thoughts. "She's not going to be happy about this."

"Why's that?" Chris asked.

"The old Kavaris had been in charge here for close to a century and he was from Uppsala. His position as head of the order gave credibility to the notion that families from Uppsala should rule everyone. Not that the monks are supposed to be political, but like my mother says, it's all politics. The fact that Altain was our world was a big deal. Speaking for the Æesir is the highest authority someone can claim."

Chris and Cormack both glanced at Katy to see if she'd react. Her face had already been painted with concern, her brows furrowed so it was impossible to tell if she'd heard them. Chris said, "Not that I wanted the guy dead, but I wasn't a fan."

"Apparently, neither was someone else," Cormack agreed before shaking his head and adding, "I feel bad for Cathal. He hasn't been here two days and already he has to solve a murder."

Ben tapped his sister's knee with his leg, finally breaking into her thoughts. "What?" she demanded.

"Nothing, sorry." Ben held up his hands, then turned to the others. "So, you guys think it was definitely a murder?" He thought about the way Cathal had rushed all the students back in, telling Cormack to take the lead.

"How else would he have gotten out that far?" Katy pointed out. "Somebody was getting rid of his body. Probably hoping it would never be found."

"People disappear here. Usually, they blame the ghosts though," Cormack agreed, pushing his tray forward. Chris was getting close to being done too and it didn't seem like Katy had any intention of eating, so Ben hurried to get some food down, not wanting to be hungry later. Then they all got up together. Cormack offered Katy a hand, but she waved it off and took out the stick she'd used outside. Moving it from side to side, she picked up her own plate and headed toward the refuse station.

She came back following the sound of Chris on his crutches, then stayed in his wake going out of the dining hall. She stayed a few steps back so she could use the stick without hitting anyone, swinging it back and forth across the floor.

They headed into a broad well-traveled passageway. The top of Nalanda station was laid out like an imperfect starburst with tunnels and paths that plunged deep into the rocky core of the asteroid. Buttress and battlements followed patterns of their own across the surface but the five grand halls were laid out in a semi-symmetrical pattern, so it wasn't hard to find your way. It was a short walk from the dining hall to the marketplace where the entrance to different royal dormitories waited, set back beneath overhanging balconies.

They were nearly to the open market when Ben caught up to his sister. He'd gotten distracted back in the hall, noticing how a few monks had come in behind them, seeming to look around for someone. He stayed behind Katy watching her use the guide stick as he said, "You're getting pretty good at that."

"I'm trying." She stepped into the next hall as Cormack and Chris cut a straight line across the market, heading for the Sidhe door with its armed guards on either side. Because of the head monk's death, afternoon classes had been dismissed early, making the market busier than usual with students who had nowhere else to go. The teachers and monks were all called to special meetings and the students had been left to their own devices.

Katy stopped in front of Ben and turned her head towards the other side of the hall. "What's going on over there?" She nodded toward a commotion, hearing raised, upset voices in the distance that were louder than the rest of the room.

Ben turned and saw Cathal coming into the market from another direction with a number of monks behind him. That's not what Katy was hearing though. Her ears turned toward the stomping of heavy stone feet. Fire-Golems were approaching, moving through the crowd while people complained. The noble students weren't used to being pushed aside and the rocky, unfeeling machines didn't care about politeness as they marched across the floor. Storming forward, their tall heads of dark rock with a single glowing eye, could be seen like beacons above the masses as they closed in on the Sidhe door.

Cormack turned, saw Cathal, and held up his hand in a friendly way that wasn't returned. The security head reached him, and the Golems closed in, forming a half-circle with the monks. Katy, Chris, Cormack, and Ben were surrounded on all sides with the Sidhe door behind them.

"Is there something I can help you with?" Cormack asked as his guards stepped forward, bringing their staffs down from their shoulders. The guards didn't wear the bulky armor of combat soldiers. Their uniforms appeared more civil, though still tactical with armored vests and helmets. The ends of their weapons came to life as sparks jumped into the air.

Ben had a bad feeling about this. He didn't like the stern set of Cathal's face and the sight of the Golems reminded him of the rescue attempt they'd made for Maeven. He touched the back of his head, then grabbed Katy's arm, trying to pull her to the side, away from the center of the group. Katy tugged back. "Knock it off," she whispered.

Looking at the guards, people from his own world, Cathal turned his attention to Cormack. "We found something." He held an item wrapped in a plastic bag.

"Your sister! Where is she?" One of the monks stepped forward and demanded, interrupting Cathal. Ben recognized the middle-aged woman. It was sister Nemain, who he'd met in the medical unit. She ran the station between Kavaris Dell and Kavaris Altain and apparently with this second death she was back in charge again.

Cathal raised an eyebrow as he glanced at her. Then he turned and refocused on Cormack. "I'd like to speak to Naiathne."

"I haven't seen her since we left this morning, since she refused to go to training. What is that?" Cormack tried reaching to see what was in Cathal's hand but the security head pulled it back, not letting the prince touch it.

"It's evidence," Cathal said, moving the bag so the whole group could see the knife inside. "We found it buried in Kavaris Altain's heart."

Cormack recognized the ornate handle. They all did.

"That's your sister's knife," sister Nemain pointed out.

"But you took it from her. You confiscated it," Chris said.

Cathal nodded, holding his back rigid. "And it was Kavaris Altain's possession before being found at the murder scene. It's just a theory, but I think it might have been stolen." He turned his eyes to Chris with these last words.

"Don't you mean retrieved?" Fajalar the Long-wolf said as he came slinking around the Fire-Golems, weaving through the monks, twisting low till he was just behind Cathal's shoulder.

"You know I can't give her to you," Cormack said. "I know how justice works here. I'm not going to let that happen."

"I just want to talk to her." Cathal motioned to the monks and Fire-Golems. "I didn't want all this."

Sister Nemain pointed her finger at Cormack's chest and pushed even closer. "She murdered one of us, another dead! How much more do you think the Æsir will tolerate? You will drag her out of there and she will face justice, or we will go in and take her."

One of the guards pushed a button on his armor that raised an alarm inside the domicile and the other put himself between Cormack and the monk while Cathal grabbed her arm. "You'd violate every treaty you've

130

made? Violate your own laws? Because that's what you're suggesting," he said.

She shook off Cathal's hand and let out a heavy breath before turning to Fajalar, "Long-Wolf, use your Golems."

Cathal put up his hands, "Don't do it," he ordered Fajalar, who was looking between the monk and the old soldier.

Everyone froze for a heartbeat, staring at Fajalar, waiting to see what he would do. Ben was the only one moving. He grabbed his sister more firmly this time. "No arguing," he said as he pulled her out of the way, back as close to the wall as possible.

Katy pushed against him, violently this time, striking her brother with an open hand and yelling, "Knock it off." But Ben didn't let up, pushing her to safety. Everyone ignored the siblings' fight as sister Nemain started toward the door and into the waiting lance of one of the guards. He didn't hesitate, smashing the back of the weapon into her chest, knocking her to the ground.

That's when the door to the Sidhe domicile opened and a crowd came pouring out. The button the guard had touched set off a rallying cry, bringing out more guards in armor and a number of nobles, some armed with primitive weapons such as knives, and bludgeons. They were forming up behind Cormack, but they barely had time as Fajalar sent the Golems forward.

At the back of the crowd, The Long-Wolf saw the one they'd come for. Naiathne stood just inside the heavy door and Fajalar thought he could end this quickly. She stared with her dark eyes going wide, not sure what was happening, but after answering the call like so many in the Sidhe domain, she'd rushed toward the entrance, not even taking time to arm herself.

Sister Nemain screamed from the floor, "Get her!" Then with surprising agility, she got to her feet and ducked beneath the Sidhe guards whose attention had turned toward the moving mountains, the Fire-Golems. The six creatures came crashing in, unstoppable even with an entire noble house in front of them.

The Fire-Golems' chests were glowing in strange patterns as they moved ahead with their rocky arms swinging out, not just moving bodies out of their way, but striking the Sidhe defenders with enough force to send them flying through the air. One guard was struck so hard that he bounced off the bottom of a balcony nearly four meters above them.

The area in front of the door was like a closing knot, getting tighter and tighter. Chris was crushed back in the press with a dozen others. Then that dozen was swept aside with a single hit from a Fire-Golem. It sent them bowling across the floor, crashing and landing at Ben and Katy's feet.

Katy was shaking at the sound of violence so close. She jumped with the ring of every hit while Ben put himself between her and it, trying to protect his sister with his own body as they were shoved into the wall.

A few of Cormack's people managed to scream battle cries and a few weapons managed to land on the Fire-Golems but it was all pointless. In only a moment the way was clear, and the monks pushed forward to grab Naiathne. They dragged her from the door while Cormack was on the ground with Cathal next to him.

All the prince could do was watch as his sister fought against the red-robed figures. The monks disappeared behind the wall of Fire-Golems, then hurried back through the crowd in the market.

Cormack's eyes met Cathal's and the soldier said, "I'm sorry." But Cormack said nothing, as he watched his sister dragged from the grand hall. Then he looked over his people, pulling themselves up from the floor. A few held broken arms. Some didn't get up at all.

Chapter 14

On the barren surface of Tairnish, Alex was starting to get used to the battle suit when he noticed Tearmai had paused behind him. "We don't have time for this," Edith warned through their short-range comms as he turned around to see what was happening.

They'd only been going for a few minutes, trying to put some distance between them and their crash sight. He watched the tiny form of Amita who'd been the Drake's passenger for about fifteen minutes, hurriedly climbing off his back. Drakes moved by balancing on their long arms and swinging their legs out like a pendulum. That meant being on Tearmai's back wasn't a comfortable experience as Amita was thrown one way then the other continuously.

Rushing to get her helmet off, Amita managed to open the suit before she vomited across the dark red soil. Surprisingly, the contents of her stomach were more pleasant than the volcanic, noxious gases in Tairnish's atmosphere. She took a whiff and quickly got her helmet back on saying, "This place is awful." There was a water pouch attached to the suit and a straw inside her helmet that she drank deeply.

"Bloody hell, I can't spit," she complained as she started back to Tearmai. Alex felt bad as he took a tiny bit of joy in Amita's suffering. Of the five he came through the wormhole with, they seemed to have the prickliest relationship. Almost all of his time here had been spent with Amita and Ben. He only knew Katy from Earth and Chris— well Chris was his brother and it had been weeks since they'd seen each other. So compared to Ben, 'his wingman' as he called himself, Amita wasn't easy to get along with.

Alex thought about Ben and the way he'd grown on him with his unrelenting spunk, being upbeat despite everything that happened. It made him smile, until the image of Ben lying on the ground in front of the airlock, not moving, popped into his head. Even worse was the memory of his wingman laid out with a breathing tube in his throat. He never should've let the kid come along on that half-baked rescue mission.

Alex remembered how after the Æesir saved him from the airlock, he needed time to recover, but a day in the Tamerlane domicile was all he was willing to take before he forced his way to the medical unit. He had gone to see Ben, but his eyes went to Tearmai's broken door first. Edith found him there at Ben's bedside and that's where this plan to save the princess began. Thinking that Amita would've been there at Ben's bedside as well, he'd asked Edith, "Have you seen Amita?"

"I helped her find her friend," Edith pointed back to Tearmai's room. "Can I show you something?" she asked.

When Alex nodded, she led him into the small chamber where the drake had been held and showed him the carvings in the wall. She pointed to the tunnels Tearmai had chipped out at the bottom. "I think it's a map. I cross-referenced these markings with some of the intel we already had in the Tamerlane database and what the Drake made here is a surprisingly accurate rendering of the mines. They come very close to where we believe they're taking Maeven." She held out a monitor and opened a screen that showed Tairnish's surface. "This is the Bogatyr's most fortified location. It's deep underground." She tapped the stone wall. "I think these tunnels may be a back way in."

Alex had stared at the wall, wondering if this was Edith reaching. Then she said, "I have a plan, but I'm going to need your help and we are going to need to move quickly."

"Plan for what?" Alex had asked.

"To get Maeven back," Edith had said.

In that moment a number of things Alex hadn't known started to come together as he realized Edith had motivations and loyalties beyond station security and combat training. Alex remembered looking back at Ben, wishing someone was there with him, then he nodded and agreed, "Tell me what you need." Things got busy from there.

They needed Andavarri's help. When Edith went to her, the Long-Wolf deferred without question, obviously worried about keeping Edith happy. It solidified Alex's understanding of who the mercenary worked for and started him wondering about the plot that led to Tara almost being executed. He wanted to ask Edith about it, but he was frightened of the answer.

Andavarri wasn't a fan of their plan, but she went to work anyway, using the Fire-Golems to load the shuttle with the drop armor. It'd only been a few minutes before their launch when Alex realized Amita was going with them. She was waiting inside the shuttle alongside Tara. Edith hadn't told him about that part. "I need her," she explained.

Edith had leaned into Alex and whispered, "My plan requires someone who can talk to Tearmai. Someone the creature is comfortable with. Don't worry. I'll protect her." But Alex knew what happened the last time they were near Tearmai.

"It's too dangerous," he said immediately, ready to draw a line.

Amita stared at him in that unflinching way of hers. "Too bad it's not up to you. I need to go and before you ask, it's not because of Maeven. I don't give a toss about your princess. There's information on that moon. Tairnish was Brash's last stop before he came to Earth and ran off with your mum. It's worth a look, isn't it?"

"She'll be fine," Edith assured him. To Alex's knowledge the mercenary had never lied to him, but she could be loose with the facts, volunteering only enough information to get what she needed. Not that he expected her to confess all her schemes since she was a secret agent for the emperor. It may have only been a few weeks, but Alex felt like he understood Edith's thinking.

Everything was battle to her. She was constantly assessing, working scenarios, and making plans. Life was a game of chess, and everyone was a piece. Alex wasn't sure what that meant for him, but he knew for certain, Amita was only a pawn, nothing more, and pawns were disposable. Unfortunately, she was a particularly stubborn piece and despite his protest she went with them.

Barely two days after the Æesir visited, and three days after the Tairnishmen left, they were on their way to this hellish place, burning hard and following the large transport that held Maeven prisoner. Edith had shown Alex the footage from the emperor's satellites of a smaller shuttle descending to the planet's surface. They were so close now, but time had never been more important.

Amita was climbing back on Tearmai again, but Edith stopped her, calling, "I'm serious. We really don't have time for this." The mercenary moved over making space on her perch behind the battle armor as she reached down, offering her hand.

Amita looked at it for a moment till Edith ordered, "Just get up here."

"Fine," Amita said, climbing up. Edith put the small girl between her and the armor, not really caring if she were comfortable squeezed under her as the suit took off.

Alex had hours of training inside the battle armor, but he still felt awkward giving up so much control to the automatic systems. He picked a path, and the suit did the rest, making him feel like a puppet inside. He watched Tearmai pull ahead and was jealous of the creature's freedom and his athleticism, wishing he could move as freely across the barren landscape, not trapped inside a metal shell. Alex had to trust Tearmai to guide him as he followed Edith's instructions and kept the suit's sensors on standby. Turning them on would've given him the lay of the land, but Edith didn't want to risk their radar transmissions being detected.

She warned, "The terrain may appear empty, but sensors are hidden everywhere looking for things like us." They were staying as low as possible, hugging the foothills of a mountain range, uncomfortably close to an active volcano. Most of the surface was made of brittle volcanic rock that cracked easily under the battle armor's heavy steps. They moved through the remnants of landslides and navigated massive tumbled-down boulders and broken stones, while running the risk of creating another collapse.

The battle armor traveled well over the broken terrain, with intuitive movements that used complicated algorithms to determine the best path forward, picking each step carefully one nanosecond at a time. The suit was built for action like this, but Tearmai was still better at negotiating the rocks, using his long arms to climb and scurry.

They'd dropped down into a dried-out riverbed, climbing over more rocks. These still showed the signs of flowing water, with rounded, smooth edges, though not a drop of moisture had traveled over them in centuries. A few hearty vines climbed over the stones. They were thorned and gnarly looking, with blood-red bulbs and purple flowers pointed towards the sky, taking what sunlight they could while their roots burrowed deep.

Most of the water on Tairnish ran below the surface, deep in steamy channels or redirected into massive reservoirs that were reinforced in ancient times against the moon's constantly shifting plates and active magma rivers. Tairnish was a heavy world with a dense composition of metals that settled to its burning hot core. Digging was life here, burrowing deep beneath the surface, away from the reflected light and radiation of the gas giant it circled.

Alex wasn't completely dependent on Tearmai for direction. Maps had been downloaded of the desolate landscape and their destination was marked by a red dot, but without the use of radar or a global positioning system, they were left to dead reckoning and Tearmai's memory to find the mine's entrance. It'd been abandoned, being too close to an active volcano.

When Alex told Edith they were about a kilometer away, she ordered, "Go ahead and fire up the short range."

Alex moved through the command screens till he found the tight beam radar, then he sent a signal toward the entrance. It reflected back off the rocky walls of the cliffside the mine was buried in, and the armor's systems created a short, blurry video feed from it.

The radar didn't have a direct line of sight, but it was advanced enough that it could use the mountains themselves to bounce the beam through the canyon. Blobs of green formed in front of Alex's eyes. He could barely make sense of anything. Despite that, he knew they had a problem.

Nothing should've been moving in the feed. He watched one the blobs cross in front of the dark cavern. Then he saw it split in two. Animal life on Tairnish's surface was scarce, mostly small creatures, no bigger than rabbits. Whatever he was picking up was larger than a human, most humans anyway and it was walking. 'Tairnishmen, guards probably,' he thought.

"I painted the entrance. There's something or someone there," Alex said.

"Hold steady while I check the feed," Edith said as Alex brought the armor to a stop and squatted down to lower his profile.

"What's going on?" Amita asked. She'd been squished between Edith's armor and the battle suit for over two hours, attempting to hold on and not complain, afraid the mercenary would leave her behind if she did.

Edith ignored Amita and got down. "You've got two targets." She took her rifle off her shoulder and held it down by her side. The scope was tied to her helmet.

Amita took the opportunity to climb off and stretch. She stepped forward with Edith, peering around the rocks. "I don't see anything."

"And you won't," Edith said before telling Alex, "In the arsenal log is a bullet called a spoiler. Move that to your primary weapons control. When you're ready, paint those targets with the radar again and fire on their center mass."

"I'll be able to hit them from here?" Alex asked.

"It's a smart round, effective at ten kilometers and able to turn corners," Edith explained.

Amita turned from Edith and looked back at Alex, inside the faceless machine. "Wait, you're going to kill them. You don't even know who they are."

"They're obstacles," Edith said. "If we get any closer, they could raise an alarm and this mission will be over. Within an hour you'd get to see what it's like to be a prisoner of the Tairnish or you'll be dead. Trust me, you want to pick the second option."

Alex's thumb came down on a selector built inside his armored glove. He clicked it twice, opening the arsenal screen, and then rolled till he found the spoiler. He'd practiced this a number of times with training safeties on the shuttle. Never once had he felt like this. A cold sweat was dripping down his back as he tried to ignore the shaking in his hand.

Attempting to move with mechanical precision and focus on the task, his thoughts started to intrude as he remembered the night he went to get Amita from her cell. They'd both seen Edith kill a monk. Her face had stayed passive, without anger or sadness and without hesitation. Killing was like turning off a light switch to her.

'Was that how it was for my dad?' Alex asked himself as he activated the radar again, seeing the blurry green image and searching it with his eyes. Nothing was moving on the screen. 'Was he that cold when he did his job? When he had to kill someone?' Alex wondered.

These past few weeks, since they'd passed through the wormhole, he'd tried not to think about his family. Avoiding any thought of what they lost had been easier than he imagined it could be. Maeven had helped with that. He'd put up a wall between himself and his past, but as he searched the radar image, he felt those walls collapsing.

He saw his dad laughing and playing Sam Cooke in the kitchen, dancing with his mom. He remembered the dumb comedies they'd watch, movies from the 80s that were in no way appropriate for kids. But he also remembered the way his father would look at him when he had something important to say, his intense gaze. His dad could use eye contact like a weapon.

'Was killing as easy for him as it was for Edith?' His hands still wouldn't stop shaking. His index finger on the right had become a trigger. If he tugged, it meant a shot and he hadn't found his targets yet. They were still, but only for a moment. One of the green blobs moved. He stared at it and blinked twice locking in a crosshair. Then he looked at the other and did the same thing. He didn't even have to lift his arm. All he had to do was twitch his finger.

'I have them,' he thought. For a moment he wasn't sure if he'd said that out loud. Then he pulled. There was a popping sound near his shoulder. He pulled a second time and another pop followed so fast that it seemed instantaneous to anyone but Alex. A lifetime later two green blobs on the screen collapsed to the ground.

Edith saw it, picking up the feed in her helmet. "Good work. We'll go a little slower from here," she said, starting back to the armor. Alex watched her, giving her enough time to climb on, then he started his armor forward, glad for the first time that it could move on autopilot as he hung in the suit, worried about the awful feeling in his own stomach.

Chapter 15

Feeling Ben's hand on her arm, Katy tried to remain calm and passive in the crush of people heading down Nalanda's ancient alien halls to the trial room. The students were pressed together, shoulder to shoulder moving like a herd, squeezed between unyielding walls. There were hundreds of voices and the smell of showered bodies scrubbed with flowery soaps and sprayed with the perfumes that these nobles seemed to love. It was overpowering in such a tight throng.

Katy tried not to breathe too deeply or think too hard as she drifted away in her head, ambling in the squeeze of humanity. In her mind, she went to a place she'd found all too often, a lonely room inside herself where what she had lost didn't matter. She could hear excited voices discussing what happened the day before at the door to the Sidhe domain. No one seemed to care if they were overheard, as they considered Naiathne's grim fate.

Katy's guide stick was folded and tucked under her arm. It would've been in the way with so many people around. Rubbing the palm of her hand, her fingers lingered on the spot she'd struck Ben with. There was no swelling, but the memory remained. She hadn't hit her brother in years, not since they were little, back when their mom was still around. 'You could get away with stuff like that when you were a kid.'

Ben talked as he guided her, jabbering away at Chris, but she missed most of it, listening to the sound of her friend's crutches on the stone floor instead. Behind Chris's broad shoulders there was a small wake, a safe spot where the crowd wasn't packed as tight. "Do you think she actually did it?" Ben was asking.

"I doubt it. I haven't really known her that long but—" Chris started when Ben interrupted.

"Cause things are different here. Killing people doesn't seem like as big a deal. They do it a lot more than I can honestly say I'm comfortable with."

"She's Cormack's sister and he's a good guy and if he's vouching for her—" Chris tried to explain, but Ben didn't let him finish.

"Yeah, but he never said she didn't do it, and don't forget he was ready for a showdown yesterday too. It was like an old west shootout with rock monsters trashing people."

Katy didn't hear Chris's response as they passed through a doorway. She had to stop to keep from banging into him, feeling the warmth coming off his back, from the effort of using his crutches.

She'd spent so much time with Chris over the last month, but if Katy were honest, she had only the faintest memory of what he looked like, holding onto that first impression back at the research facility. She remembered he had a kind, soft way about him and that he was taller than his brother Alex, broader too, and a lot less edgy.

Even when she argued with him on the shuttle, he did it in an easy voice, never really yelling. Katy smiled and for the first time she missed when it was just the two of them, or the two of them plus Cormack and Naiathne.

Her stomach sank, thinking of her new friend. She had to admit she hadn't known the Naiad for long. She had no idea if Naiathne was capable of murder, but she was still someone Katy cared about and from what she heard of the justice system or lack thereof here on Nalanda, Naiathne didn't have much hope.

Feeling powerless, Katy was trying to keep from acting out again while silently listing her mistakes in her head. She'd run off to an alien world to get her eyes fixed, nearly getting Chris and herself killed. She'd spoken out, claiming to know what these people's gods wanted, and brought Naiathne here, where she was more than likely going to be executed. Then yesterday she'd pushed back at her brother, hit him, when all he was trying to do was protect her.

Ben took Katy's other arm and pulled her a little closer, warning her, "Watch out for the door frame." She could feel how close she'd come to the stone wall, the coolness coming off it. It felt nice.

"Let's see if we can find a seat near the front," Ben said. He'd forgiven her for yesterday. Ben got over things fast, something Katy wished she could do.

"Excuse us, chosen of the Æsir here," Ben called as he guided them to seats.

People from different worlds had unique odors. Cormack's people never completely lost the scent of the sea. Katy sniffed, and knew she was among the Sidhe. "Where's Cormack?" She felt the knees of the person behind her touching her back as she sat down. The stands were curved like a horseshoe, pointed at the center of the room and an airlock with large windows.

"He's standing in the front. They've got a stage and a podium. Cormack's waiting there," Chris explained.

Ben added, "That's where Vyktor was before they sent him out the airlock. It's where your brother and Tara were too."

Chris raised an eyebrow, saying, "Catch me up a bit. Tara was the one who worked for the princess my brother is trying to save, right? The one who probably had Chooth's hub tortured and tried poisoning his entire species, leading to me and Katy almost dying, right?" His voice was low and edgy.

Ben shot back, "She's a friend, okay?" Then his tone softened. "And I don't think she did any of that. . . And if she did, she was forced to. It wasn't her fault."

"Yeah, the Nazis said stuff like that too," Chris's hands tightened on his crutches. "Following orders is never an excuse for doing things you know are wrong. They poisoned an entire species, but it's Naiathne here on trial."

"It's not that easy here, all right? Tara is just trying to survive like everyone else," Ben said.

Chris gave a derisive, "Huh," as he crossed his arms and sat back saying, "There's right and there's wrong."

Katy opened her mouth ready to argue and defend her brother, but there was no time as the room fell silent.

Cathal came through a door behind the stage, wearing armor and a sidearm. He kept his hand close to it while taking a position in front of the crowd, where he could watch the whole room. Then a group of monks entered, surrounding Naiathne. Several stepped onto the stage, taking seats while four others stayed close to the prisoner. Katy could hear the shackles on her friend's feet and hands, jangling as she was forced to march.

"Everyone, take your seats," the woman from the day before, sister Nemain, ordered. She was in the center of the stage where another more elaborate podium waited. It was painted red with gold leaf. This was the place Kavaris Dell had stood before his death, where a dagger had struck and pinned him to the wall. Bloodstains still marked the spot, left as a warning to others. "That includes you, Prince Cormack," Nemain added.

"I'll stand by my sister," Cormack answered.

"You will sit or you will be thrown out of this tribunal. You'll have an opportunity to give testimony later. We have questions for you. Though you are not under arrest, there are things you must answer for."

"Such as violating the treaty under which this place operates," Cormack shot back. "Wait, I'm sorry, that was you when you attempted to storm our doorway." Cormack turned back to the crowd of students, nobles from every house, and all the different Extraracial species. "We were given assurances that our territories would be sovereign. To violate one puts all of our positions in jeopardy. This cannot stand."

A murmur in the crowd became louder, but sister Nemain raised her voice before it went too far. "You were hiding a murderer and the Kavaris order are not on trial here."

"I haven't killed anyone, ever," Naiathne shouted.

"You can plead your innocence after your brother takes his seat." The monk looked at Cathal motioning with her head toward Cormack. The soldier stepped near the prince, took his arm, and guided him back to the stands. No one could hear what passed between them, but Cormack's chin jutted out as rage painted the prince's face.

On stage, the monk's eyes went over the crowd, making certain she had everyone's attention. "We are in a time of transition, a time when the Æsir's actions have been less clear but that does not mean their laws are less sacred, nor that their servants should be at risk, but yet our order has suffered two murders. These deaths weigh more than some common slaughter committed in the name of politics or passion.

"The monks of the Kavaris order are chosen for their wisdom, chosen by the gods. A little is lost from humanity each time one of these philosophers and teachers is snuffed out." She took the murder weapon out and held it in the air. "This is the device that was used to kill Kavaris Altain. It was buried in his back before his corpse was tossed out of an airlock. Does the accused recognize this weapon?" The knife was a hazy silver that picked up the light in the room on its razor-sharp edge. It had a curved blade and its handle was shaped like the head of a sea dragon ending in an open mouth.

Naiathne's shoulders were rigid on the podium where she rested her shackles. She tried to hold herself still but it was impossible to hide the tremble in her voice. "Yes, it's mine but it was taken from me when I arrived here."

The monk leaned forward, relaxing her grip on the weapon as she examined it. "I assume you wanted it back?"

Naiathne stayed quiet while the monk's eyes turned toward her. The bald woman in her red robe demanded, "That was a question. Your answer please."

Naiathne looked from side to side. "It's a . . . No. I mean, yes, eventually. But—"

Sister Nemain interrupted, "Your answer is yes then?"

Before Naiathne could respond, the monk turned away speaking to the head of security "Cathal, you found the weapon on her. Is that correct?"

Katy sat listening to her friend. In the time she'd known the girl, Naiathne had been supremely confident when she was in her own element, under the ocean. When she was scared, like when she was nearly crushed escaping a cavern, she responded with rage, fighting the world. Katy had never heard her like this, cowed by these stupid monks and their fake trial. She wanted to run across the room and help. She wanted to shout at the entire assembly, but instead, she held still, scared she'd mess up again and somehow make things worse.

"Yes, I removed the weapon from her before Kavaris Altain's murder. And I recognize it from even before that," Cathal answered.

Sister Nemain ignored the second part of his response. "After it was confiscated, where was it secured?"

Cathal continued to explain, "It was Naiathne's father's. A gift—"

Sister Nemain didn't let him finish. "Where was it secured?"

Cathal's brow furrowed and his face turned red under his beard. "I'm not sure. Kavaris Altain held on to it. It could've been in his quarters or on his person. My point is that Naiathne would never have left it—"

The monk broke in, reaching a conclusion for him. "In someone she hated. You did hate Kavaris Altain. Didn't you?"

"I—" Naiathne started.

"Yes or no, be honest," the monk said.

Naiathne looked back at Cormack as sister Nemain gave up, asking instead. "Where were you two nights ago? The night Kavaris Altain was killed? I believe that was the night you and your party arrived. The very night Kavaris Altain began his position here."

"I went to the dinner service, then back to the Sidhe domicile." Naiathne's eyes were on the floor.

Sister Nemain leaned a little further over the podium. "And you didn't leave. You were there all through the night."

Katy felt Ben's hand close on her arm. He leaned towards her but before he could say anything, Chris whispered, "Ben, don't." They all remembered Cormack complaining about his sister going out the night before their training.

"I, ah—" Naiathne struggled.

Sister Nemain stopped her. "Before you come up with some ridiculous lie, let me warn you, you were spotted during the night cycle. Isn't that right, Fajalar?" The monk turned to the side of the stage where the Long-Wolf took a few steps forward and sat back on his tail.

He tilted his head and nodded. "She was spotted on three different occasions. Leaving and entering the Sidhe domain and coming and going in the lower levels." He

149

held his hands in the air splaying his long fingers. "My golems are always watching as you know. It is unfortunate that students don't take your order's warnings about going out in the night cycle more seriously. Perhaps we could avoid such tragedies if our students would only listen to your rules." Then Fajalar bowed deeply, turned, and slinked back to his seat.

Sister Nemain waited till the Long-Wolf settled before she asked Naiathne, "Where were you going?"

Naiathne shook her head, upset about something aside from the trial. "I was— I was going to see the Grannusians. I was hoping to talk to someone from my world that wasn't—"

"Human?" The monk finished for her.

Naiathne nodded and a murmur started in the crowd. The young nobles began to whisper turning their suspicions to solid belief. They didn't see a person accused of a crime but a monster in the Naiad with her grey skin and her dark eyes.

The monk let the noise grow for a moment as she looked over her students. "What time was this? And where are the Grannusians you spoke to? Why haven't any come to verify your story?"

Chris turned to look back at the crowd as Ben said, "Don't bother. They've been scarce since the whole thing with Chooth. The only place they go, outside their domain, is the medical unit, and even then, it's only for serious stuff, like my brain damage."

The trial went on while the monk continued questioning Naiathne, having her recount every moment of her night. Then she had Fajalar stand again and go over each instance the Fire-Golems saw her. Sister Nemain pulled at the Naiad's half-remembered story, calling to attention any discrepancies.

Cormack was brought forward for questioning. The prince tried to spar with the monk about the rights of the noble house, the protections they were supposed to be offered, but sister Nemain would not be swayed. Slowly and methodically, over hours she built her case against Naiathne wearing her down till the answers to questions she'd already been asked a dozen times, made no sense.

When the monk announced that they would adjourn to consider a verdict and a punishment, there was no doubt in anyone's mind what it would be. The red robes exited the room through the back door and chaos slowly started to spread. As time passed, little comments turned to snickers, then to laughter and taunting.

Cormack tried to go back to his sister's side where she stood out in front of the audience, her shackles seeming to pull her into the floor, but Cathal stepped forward, stopping him. The two argued there in front of the room.

Katy couldn't hear what they were saying as the clamor of voices near her was too loud. She could only hear the cruelty in the crowd as they laughed and joked about what was going to happen to Naiathne. Even among the Sidhe, there was no loyalty. Only the Extraracials were quiet, huddled further up the stands. This was another type of punishment, Katy thought, making Naiathne stay there, taunted by the voices of the others.

Chris leaned over to her and said, "We need to do something."

Katy bit her lip but didn't answer. "Are you all right?" he asked, squeezing her arm.

She shook her head, fighting back the tears she felt welling up. "No, these people are terrible."

Ben slid out and stood in front of the crowd, yelling, "You guys need to quit it!" But the crowd shouted back at him, telling him to sit down. Someone even threw a shoe at him. As he ducked under it, he called, "You all suck!"

"Just don't, Ben," Chris said, tugging him back to his seat as the monks appeared, walking solemnly back onto the stage. Sister Nemain held up her hands calling, "Silence!"

The crowd died down, then she turned to the accused. "Naiathne of the Sidhe. It is our belief that you snuck out after the night cycle and murdered Kavaris Altain. You will be punished for this crime."

The noise broke out again but only for a moment as the monk raised her hands and turned to Cathal. "Escort the prisoner to the airlock."

"We've got to do something," Katy heard Chris whisper next to her while Cathal stayed still.

The soldier's eyes were staring back at the monk in disbelief. Then he shook his head and looked down at the ground while his hand slowly drifted down to his sidearm. The monk watched him. The curious glint in her eyes turned to something burgeoning on outrage. Everyone seemed to be holding their breath watching Cathal, wondering what he'd do. Naiathne was the daughter of a family he'd served his entire life. The sidearm cleared the holster but before the security head lifted it to point anywhere, a voice broke the silence.

"She didn't do it," someone called.

Katy was shocked to realize it was Chris calling out. She felt his whole body rumble next to her as he used the full force of his deep voice to command attention. Then he stood up and swung forward on his crutches. "You can't punish her, because she didn't do it!"

Sister Nemain's face squeezed tight with indignation as she started, "It's been proven beyond a doubt—"

The monk didn't get to finish as Chris interrupted, "I know she didn't do it because I did. I took that knife and I killed that skinny loudmouth monk. Naiathne wasn't there." Chris leaned on his crutches and shoved his thumb into his chest. "It was me and only me."

152

Everyone in the room stared at him as the murmurs and whispers became louder and louder. Before long there was no silencing the crowd as the room erupted with voices. Katy felt it swell over her as she reached out, trying to find her friend.

Chapter 16

Since they started their trek, there'd never been a time when Amita wasn't aware of Edith behind her. How could she not be? The padding in her suit was mostly for insulation and did little to blunt the edges of the mercenary's armor as it pushed into her. Somehow, after Alex's two muffled shots popped from his war machine and disappeared into the early morning sky, the discomfort of her closeness became worse, almost intimate with the plating of Edith's thighs pushed into Amita's back. It became an almost intolerable burden as she imagined where those bullets ended their flight.

Alex said very little after that, only having the briefest of conversations with Edith as they moved along the last stretch of their journey.

"Hold up." Edith interrupted the silence. "I'm going to take Tearmai and scout ahead." When Alex stopped Edith dropped from his back. She brought her rifle down off her shoulder, ducking as she moved up the hill, staying to one side of the riverbed. The further she got, the more effective her camouflage became at blending into the landscape. Even the rifle was invisible, reflecting the hazy sunlight in broken patterns matching the terrain. Tearmai followed a few steps behind with his light grey hide standing out sharply against the scorched volcanic rocks. It dawned on Amita that Edith may have only brought the Drake along to draw fire.

She wanted to call out and tell Tearmai to come back, but she stayed quiet, knowing he was already too far ahead and that shouting would only increase his risk. All she could do was shake her head and say, "That witch," as she climbed off the battle armor.

Stepping away from Alex, she put her hands on her hips and watched her friend disappear around the bend. The Drake had no comms since taking his helmet off back at the landing site. There was no way to warn him.

154

"Are your sensors picking up anything?" she asked, turning back to Alex.

The battle armor loomed over her. Its only answer was silence. "Oi, Alex, are you in there?" Amita shouted to be heard outside her helmet.

She stared at Alex's suit, debating whether to throw a rock at it, when he finally answered. "The scopes are clear. The only thing I can pick up is Tearmai." His voice had a slight electric tone rumbling from a small speaker. That wasn't why it sounded flat and emotionless though.

"You mean Edith's bait," Amita said.

Alex didn't respond at first. Then finally he said, "We're on a mission. That's her only focus."

"Right, and if any of us get killed, it's just too bad, isn't it? That woman has been on a mission since you met her. You just had no idea what it was." Amita realized that standing there, waiting with Alex, was the first time the two had been alone together since they left Nalanda. Actually, it was the first time since the night Edith killed that monk in the cells. Neither of them ever brought it up, and now, for all she knew, Alex had just killed two more people, pulling a trigger as easy as could be. All for the sake of the mission.

'Well, I've got my own mission,' Amita thought as she wondered what she'd find down in that mine. Tearmai had been loose on the details, but he told her that this was where she'd find answers. When she pushed him too hard, his attention would turn. All he could talk about was a slave that he and Brash had left behind. Specifically, he'd repeat over and over, 'we should've freed the slave.' Amita assumed it had something to do with the Drakes. The mine was no longer active, but the webwork of tunnels beneath the surface was unending, diving deep into the planet. She wondered if maybe, somewhere, another group of Tearmai's people were still held against their will, forced to dig into this awful place. From what she understood, many of the mines on Tairnish were closed down, a byproduct of Emperor Tamerlane's power but that didn't mean there couldn't be a few holdouts, Tairnishmen or nobles who kept their drake servants digging.

At one time the royalty of Uppsala had constantly fought with each other, vying for position. Tamerlane had ended that, taking power there and moving on to other worlds. But when he failed to capture Grannus, it seemed like the fight went out of him. For nearly a decade there had been an unquiet peace, and a place like Tairnish with its shipyards and mines only flourished when there was a war to feed them.

Amita wondered what happened to all the slaves. Apparently she wasn't the only one. When she asked Tearmai if that's why he and Brash had come here, he nodded and said, 'We came for answers.'

'Me too, big guy,' Amita thought as the minutes passed and she felt her anxiety grow, worrying about her friend. She walked ahead a little, trying to peer around the bend. She was startled by a click echoing in her ear. It was Edith opening the comm channel. "We've cleared the mine entrance. Move the armor up."

"Are you getting back on?" Alex asked Amita.

"No, I think I'll walk from here. Just be careful you don't step on me with that metal monstrosity of yours," Amita said as she climbed forward, following the path Edith had taken. The vines and the flowers grew thicker here, scaling the canyon walls, making hand holds.

Alex picked a lower path and quickly outpaced her in his machine. It was camouflaged like Edith, but it was still a giant hunk of metal with a sharp angular profile. She lost track of it for only a few minutes as it marched around the bend.

When she caught up, she noticed the others gathered at the darkened entrance to the mine. The plants were thickest here, clinging to the walls twisting and turning up to the low opening buried in the cliffside, but that's not where Amita's eyes went.

Looking at the battle armor standing still, Amita saw the top hatch open. Alex jumped down. He hit the rocky soil of Tairnish and slowly walked forward, staring down at Tearmai. The Drake was kneeling, his eyes low, looking at two slumped forms. Their skin was grey, standing out, much like his against the dark rocky surface.

Amita came closer, moving carefully over the loose soil, going down, almost to the armor before she realized what they were looking at. Laid out were the bodies of two dead Drakes crumpled among the vines and black stones. Their blood, which looked similar to a human's, painted the soil and dampened a few rocks. It was already drying, becoming dark like the ground.

Amita kept going, though some part of her wanted to stand still and not approach. "They weren't Tairnishmen," she said as she passed Alex, who stood frozen.

"No," Tearmai said. "They were survivors."

He looked up at her, then his eyes, shining with their strange blue color, moved to Alex. The Drake's voice was shockingly clear as his words spat out at a rapid pace, rapid for him anyway. "Brash and I came here seeking knowledge. Not of the void. Well, maybe Brash was—

"For me. It was for them." Tearmai pointed to the corpses. "To find out what was happening to them. The slaves weren't freed. They were disappearing— The emperor is doing something. But these two, they escaped."

He shook his head. "They couldn't be happy here, even free, living in a mine—"

Alex was staring at the bodies. "I'm sorry," he said softly.

Tearmai stood, lifting his hands in the air, indicating something high above them. "We were born to a world of trees, massive trees. Humans cut so many. They took them and our guides. Then they took us." Tearmai's voice stayed low, rumbling with such bass that Amita could feel it in her chest. Her eyes went to Edith, noticing how the mercenary had backed away, giving Tearmai space and how she was holding her rifle slung low on her shoulder, not aimed at the Drake yet, but ready for whatever came next.

Tearmai sat down, flat on his backside touching the other Drakes gently. "You've done the final task Alex, taking the only thing they had left."

Alex was still wearing the control helmet for the armor with its different connections pointing everywhere. He shook his head violently as he backed away from Tearmai, then tore the helmet off and threw it. He was too upset to care about Tairnish's tainted air as he spun around and ran, stumbling as he tried to get as far from the others and the bodies as possible.

"Alex!" Edith called, taking a few steps. She stopped though, watching his frantic escape. When she looked back at the dead Drakes, her face was unreadable, hidden inside her helmet. Observing the whole thing, Amita thought of a number of sharp comments but held her tongue as she stepped next to Tearmai instead and put her hand on his shoulder.

Shaking her head, Edith walked away, going back to the battle armor, inspecting it, trying to fill a few minutes. She checked the sensors and diagnostics, but when she could find nothing else to do, she looked down at Tearmai, watching him lay the Drakes on their backs with their eyes towards the horizon. He and Amita started to bury them, using the tumbled-down rocks. He took up the heavy ones while Amita moved the smaller, building cairns over the bodies. Edith eventually shrugged and came back, silently starting to help.

When there was no more sign of the Drakes, Edith stood up, taking off her helmet. She pursed her lips as she breathed in the foul stench of the planet, scowling while staring in the direction Alex went. "We don't have time for this crap," she grumbled, taking her rifle off her shoulder and putting it down on the ground, out of sight.

Tearmai pulled a few of the thicker vines toward the burial mounds without breaking them. He laid the flowery side up and said, "The plants will dig down and take sustenance from them."

Edith stretched her back and started walking. Over her shoulder, she said to Amita, "Stay alert. Watch that entrance but watch the sky too and tell me if you see anything."

"What's the matter, afraid Alex still has a soul?" Amita grumbled.

Edith turned with one eyebrow standing up sharply. "This was hard. Innocents getting hurt sucks. I get that." She pointed to the mounds. "But you don't see why it was necessary. I don't think you guys get it. We've got something to do, and the clock is ticking. When the emperor shows up, Tairnish is going to become a combat zone. I doubt you have any idea what orbital bombardment looks like, but I guarantee you're not going to want to be up on the surface, down in the mines, or anywhere on this cursed world when it starts." She pointed to the rocky graves. "These guys were already dead. All Alex did was pull the trigger. Wherever the other Drakes are, it's a better place than what this moon is about to become."

"It isn't," Tearmai said.

Edith rolled her eyes and started off towards Alex. Amita was tempted to go listen. To see how the mercenary would get him back on mission. How she would manipulate the young man into doing what she needed.

Till they left Nalanda station, Amita had been too busy trying to understand how they got here, trying to put together the puzzle of where they landed after coming through that wormhole to pay much attention to Edith and Alex's relationship. All that time on the station and she assumed it was Maeven who had her hooks in him.

It wasn't until those few days in the shuttle that she started to see how the mercenary had taken control of Alex Johnson. At his core, he was a student looking for a teacher, guided by love and admiration for a father who probably died back on Earth. Amita understood that.

When Edith offered him direction, it was enough to pull him right in. The harsher her lessons, the more Alex took to it. Amita glanced at the burial mounds and realized that this was just one more class, moving Alex toward what Edith needed him to be.

∞

Edith felt her helmet clipped to her belt, but she resisted the urge to pull it back on, knowing Alex was going to need a face-to-face, and maybe a bit more. Still, the helmet would've been nice, not only because of the volcanic stink of this world, but because the optics in it would've made finding him easier.

Trained since she was a child to track, Edith worried sometimes that she leaned on her tech a bit too much. It wasn't like Alex was trying to hide his trail. It was just a question of time. These people didn't get it. The only thing coming to this planet was death. Her emperor had a plan and it didn't include Tairnish. He had no use for it and Tamerlane wasn't the kind of man to let useless things take up space.

160

Following Alex's footsteps, Edith kept on as the cliff got steeper. She listened, turning her hearing aids to the max. There was rapid breathing coming from behind a boulder up a nearly vertical spot. A rock jutted from the wall at a forty-five-degree angle, nearly thirty meters up. 'He must've been really moving,' she thought, noticing where rocks had tumbled down.

"Damnit," Edith said as she leaned forward and started to climb, knowing he was just out of sight. She thought of calling out, but she was afraid he'd try to go further up or maybe do something worse.

The cliff face quickly became shear, forcing her to her hands and knees, free climbing. When she got her hand on the boulder, she pulled herself up and around to find Alex leaning back against the massive rock in the crook where it met the face. Edith stood over him with one leg higher than the other.

"You think I'm far enough up?" he asked without looking at her.

"For what?" Edith glanced back down. They were a good distance from the ground. She couldn't quite see the mine's entrance, but she could see the vines and the dry riverbed.

His face was locked, as hard as the stone around him, but his cheeks were swollen. He'd been crying but it looked like he'd rubbed the tears away pretty fast. "To get this over with?" he said.

Edith looked down again. "I'm not sure this would do it. You might want to go higher to make sure." She put her hand on her sidearm. "Of course, I could just take care of it for you."

Alex finally turned his head and stared at her. Edith was unwavering for a moment, then she relaxed. "That's not what either of us want though." She took her hand away from the weapon. "You don't want to die. You feel awful and you want that to stop, that's all." Edith looked back down the cliff again.

"I felt that way once too. It wasn't that long ago either. At least it doesn't feel like it was that long ago, but I guess a fair amount of time has passed." Edith looked out over the valley at the Tairnish sky.

She wished she could see the volcano from here, but it wasn't tall enough. It was a flat round thing belching disgusting fumes. Like so many other things, it was pointless. She knew Alex wanted her to keep going, so she did. "Of course, I didn't feel that way because I was weak like you." She looked right at him, seeing the shock play across his face.

"After the war, I was a soldier without a fight. The Fish Heads fixed me up pretty good but there were still parts missing." She touched her ears. "And I had scars, but I don't care about that. In fact, I kind of like them. What I didn't like, was not having a purpose."

She leaned down and stared at him. "Do you have one of those, Alex?"

Alex turned away as he asked, "A purpose—" he started but he didn't get to finish as Edith backhanded him.

"Yeah, a purpose," she said, looking at Alex's mouth bleeding, then looking at his eyes that were intent on her. He started to sit up, pulling his feet in.

'Good,' Edith thought before snarling, "You want to lay up here and feel sorry for yourself, that's fine. You want to throw yourself off this cliff, please do. But when I'm talking to you, you're going to give me your whole attention or a smack in the mouth will be the least of your worries. Now answer my question. Do you have a purpose?" She closed in on him a little and Alex hurried to his feet. He had to put his hand out on the cliff face to keep from falling. The outcropping suddenly felt very small.

She hit him again, slamming her hand into his belly. "Answer me!" She pulled her hand back again. This time aiming for his face.

Alex let the blow come and turned it at the last moment, dropping his arm over it and locking it into his side, pulling Edith in close. She looked him right in the eye and said, "Coward."

His face tightened, then Alex headbutted her, smashed his face right into hers. He shoved her back and for a moment with her head swimming, Edith thought she was going to fall off the cliff.

She steadied herself and looked at him as Alex said, "Yeah, I've got a purpose."

"Good," Edith said. "Because we're not done yet." She unclipped her helmet and pulled it back on, then she started to climb down. She heard him following behind.

∞

Amita looked up. About twenty minutes after she left, Edith was returning with Alex walking next to her. His head was low but his eyes were focused. There was a little blood on Alex's lip. 'So it's violence,' Amita thought while looking at the mercenary.

Alex ignored the cairns, purposefully keeping his eyes away from them as he went to Tearmai and said, "I'm sorry, I didn't know." He barely stopped and he didn't wait to hear what the Drake said in response. Picking up his helmet, he climbed back in the armor. The machine came alive, its weapons coming up to bear. Edith picked up her own equipment and started toward the opening just ahead of the machine.

"Let's move people," she ordered, disappearing into the shadows.

Chapter 17

Regin, the Ice-Carver, made his way to his classroom and saw the empty plastic desks built from packing crates. He was happy for the quiet and the time to think as he sat back, looking at the ceiling. High in the center of the room was a model of their planetary system. All the worlds circling Altor hung on wire arms, but it wasn't to scale. If it had been, the moons around the gas giant would've been too far apart to be contained in a single room and Regin's icy world of Oighear, the furthest away, would've ended up somewhere down the hall.

The students were probably on their way, coming to class after the trial, but Regin had this moment to consider what the human Chris had done. A smile formed on his simian face. No one would know it, but Regin didn't normally like humans. He faked an equable manner, seeming relaxed, the wise little monkey man, while he hid his distaste. Humans were fond of male Ice-Carvers, calling them cute, reminding them of some creature from their distant past and found in the mementos that survived their fall.

Regin had spent a great deal of time with humans on Uppsala, where he'd been educated. If you could call it that. Their fondness for the males of his species meant that Ice-Carvers were often brought to the kingdoms of the forest moon to educate and be companions for young nobles, pets who could explain complex math formulas.

Royalty dominated Uppsala, but no civilization could survive with only nobles populating it, ruling and benefiting from the work of those beneath. The nobility may own all the resources by some divine right, passed down through the conquests of their ancestors, but they still needed a servant class. Indentured farmers and domestic workers, humans, and Drakes who were forced into bondage, earning slave wages, made up most of

Uppsala's population. But there were others as well. A small group in the middle of scientists, soldiers, and artisans carving a niche under the eyes of those born to rule. For these people, Uppsala had schools. Regin had been given the chance to go and learn and become a better educator. These institutes were different from the ancient universities that nobles attended. They did more than produce the next generation of lay about elites.

In those lecture halls, he gained knowledge about human nature that was far more valuable. He understood now that they'd always seek domination over cooperation. If given a choice, they'd flock to a strong leader, no matter how abhorrent, as long as it kept their tribe in a position of power. But the ones who came through the void seemed slightly different. Despite not being born noble, they all had a confidence about them, an air of self-determination that Regin felt akin to, especially the little one Amita. She was curious and purposeful, despite being the smallest of their numbers.

Most Ice-Carvers were too concerned with survival to feel such a sense of purpose. After everything that happened at the trial, it'd fallen to Regin to calm the young and nervous males of his species. They were an anxious race by nature. Regin wondered if that was why his people had such short lives. If they could be docile like the Drakes, perhaps they'd live longer.

Nerves may have contributed, but they weren't the main reason so many male Ice-Carvers died young. It was the pull, that biological urge to further the species that drove them to the surface of their icy moon and to the female Ice-Carvers. Regin shook a little as fear and a thrill coursed through him. He was glad that he'd passed through puberty on a different world where he never experienced that drive to go off, mate, and die.

He wondered if that was why Chris had done what he had. Human courtship was a strange thing, always being active. Chris's brother had certainly shown an incredible amount of stupidity when it came to risking his life for the opposite sex, trying to save Princess Maeven.

Regin shook his head thinking of Ben's words after Chris confessed. He'd overheard the redheaded human say, "Is getting in trouble for killing people a family trait or something?"

After the confession, the monks very well could've decided to throw Chris and Naiathne out the airlock. Regin had seen them do worse, but the monks were too afraid and confused, not sure what their gods wanted anymore. For a century they'd been protected, given free rein to enforce their brutal laws, but after the Æesir's last visit, things were different.

Before, when Eir was still at the station, Regin had many long conversations with her and Fafnir about the gods. They questioned the Æesir's bloody methods, but they all agreed that their mission to keep humanity in check, slowing the constant march toward destruction, was a good thing. Regin's friends had seen the way it was before the Æesir came, when constant war and new and frightening technologies threatened everyone. Things changed then and they were changing now. Regin wondered if it would be for the better.

Students started to shuffle through the door. They were abuzz with the events of the day. Regin ignored most of them till the last three came through, Ben, Katy, and Cormack. The youngest one was guiding his sister. Katy wasn't fighting him, but she didn't look happy either to have his hand on her arm.

Regin listened to Katy complain, "Why are we even going to class? This is stupid. We need to talk to Naiathne and Chris."

Cormack was leading them. He shook his head. "They're not going to let us. Let things calm down and I'll go to Cathal."

Ben placed Katy's hand on a desk and said, "You think he still has a job? I'm pretty sure he was going to plug that monk instead of tossing your sister out an airlock. I can't imagine sister Nemain is too happy with him." Ben glanced at Regin and waved saying, "Howdy."

Regin nodded, then pretended not to eavesdrop as more students filtered in. He watched Katy refuse to sit, stumbling as she made her way to face Cormack. The prince didn't try to help her as she insisted, "We have to find out what Naiathne actually was up to. It's the only way to get Chris out."

Cormack's brow furrowed. "You do believe her, don't you?"

Katy took a moment to answer. "I think I do."

"Well, that's assuring. Look, class is about to start." Cormack grabbed her hands and guided her back to her seat while in a low voice he said, "I hope she didn't do it. But we have to consider the possibility. Naiathne has always been angry."

Katy felt the chair behind her. She sat down and crossed her arms. "Yeah, well, her mom, your mom, tried killing her when she was a baby. I imagine that gives you issues. I'd say she has an excuse."

"To be a killer?" Ben asked in disbelief.

Katy shrugged as Cormack said, "It doesn't matter."

"Really?" Ben asked looking between them.

Cormack studied the sibling then his attention drifted to his own hands. "Everyone is capable of killing when you're pushed far enough. It's a survival instinct, but again, it doesn't matter. She's my sister and she's alive because of Chris. I'll talk to Cathal after class. Okay?"

"If he's not fired or about to be tossed out an airlock himself," Ben muttered.

Cormack's eyes narrowed as he grunted, "Right."

Katy rubbed her palms against the desk, then sat back. "Look, Chris did something really stupid and really brave and he's sitting in a cell for it. There's only one way we're going to be able to help him. We need to find out what actually happened. Even if we don't like the answer."

"I'm not going to let them execute her," Cormack said starting toward his seat.

"I don't want that either," Katy called as she listened to his footsteps get further away.

Regin stood on his desk and called for the class's attention. Orbital mechanics was not an exciting subject, especially after the morning activities, but Regin did his best, teaching the formulas and plotting the courses around the moons that these students would never use. They were nobles after all. They would have pilots and soldiers for this kind of work, but it was still part of the curriculum. After an hour, he watched Ben help Katy as Cormack came back to them.

There was too much noise to hear what they were discussing, but the three left together. Regin thought of Naiathne, who was so angry, much like his friend Fafnir. Then he thought of Fajalar, Andavarri's replacement who controlled every Fire-Golem on the station. Those watchers had nearly damned the Naiad girl. 'Perhaps it's time I talk to the young Long-Wolf,' Regin thought, following his students to the door.

∞

The trial had been hours ago and the small cell with its heavy bars was silent. Staring at a ceiling carved from rock, Chris lay on a hard bench and let his thoughts wander to his brother. 'How long had it been since I saw him in person, or on a screen for that matter? Had he been in this cell?' Chris resisted the urge to look over at his fellow prisoner, but he felt her presence looming in the shadows where she sat against the wall.

When they dragged Chris and Naiathne from the trial room, she'd told him in a low voice, "You shouldn't have done this." But her words didn't have their usual bite. In fact, Chris thought he heard relief in her tone, maybe even gratitude.

At the time he was too shocked by his own actions to be sure. The monk's fear of the Æesir was the only thing that'd kept him alive. Somehow, he hadn't considered that he might end up in a cell right next to Naiathne.

She was quiet in her corner, creating an uncomfortable silence that Chris wasn't willing to break. It grew worse with each slowly passing moment. He'd saved her life, and it wasn't the first time, but he hardly felt like he knew her. 'Maybe she was a killer? Maybe she had done it?' Had he really sacrificed his freedom for someone he didn't trust, for someone that might be guilty? 'Sure, we had our underwater adventure and time together on the shuttle, but do I really know her?' he wondered.

When she finally spoke, it was simply to say, "The night cycle will be starting soon."

Chris glanced over, just able to see her in the shadows. "Does that mean it's going to get even darker and more depressing in here?"

She stood, went to the front of the cell, and leaned against the bars to peer down the hall where two red-robed monks waited. A Fire-Golem was even closer, directly in the entrance like a doorway made from a stone figure. The monks weren't messing around.

She said, "Maybe it'll be better for you. You won't be able to see our accommodations. Me on the other hand, I can see in the dark." Naiathne turned back to him and motioned to her eyes, which were like black mirrors.

"Cool." Chris sounded unsure. After a moment's pause, he added, "I suppose there's not much light under the ocean."

"Sometimes there is, but not always." Naiathne shrugged and turned back to the bars.

"The way I remember it, most of the glowing things down there wanted to eat me," Chris said.

"Only the Circien-Croin," Naiathne said.

"There was a jellyfish too. I may not have been digested, but I was inside it, so it counts." Chris sat up.

He heard Naiathne suppress a laugh. Her shoulders moved while a little sound came from her nose.

"Was that a snort?" he asked.

Naiathne didn't answer but after a moment she said, "You're kind of decent, aren't you? You keep trying to. . . be good, I guess. To help."

Chris shrugged. "I suppose."

"My brother is like that. He's always trying. It's really annoying." Naiathne smiled.

It was Chris's turn to laugh and shake his head. After a moment Naiathne added, "I'm sorry about this. That you're in here." She was struggling. "What you did. . ."

"You mean killing that monk." Chris waved his hand. "He had it coming."

"Right." Naiathne cocked her head, looking at him with those dark eyes. When she looked away, she added, "I didn't do it either. Believe me, I'm not sad he's gone, but that's not something—" She stared at the floor. "I'm not a killer, at least I don't want to be. My people, we just want to be left alone, to be safe. Some of us want to fight, but most just want to live in peace, like the Grannusians."

"You know the first time we met, you pointed a speargun at my face," Chris reminded her.

"Never going to live that down, am I?" She looked back at him. "Look, I'm sorry I did that. It's just the Grannusians mean a lot to my people and when I thought someone hurt them."

Chris shrugged. "Stressful times."

"Yeah, stressful," Naiathne went quiet again. Chris's tone had been light but the memory he'd brought back of their first meeting, when she thought human royals like her brother had poisoned the Grannusians, filled her thoughts. She said she wasn't a killer, but as Chris watched her, he thought he could see her debating. He turned away to try and give her a little privacy. That's when her voice filled the silence again. "This isn't the first time I've gotten in trouble for going out during the night cycle. It was kind of an escape for me, before, when I was here at Nalanda. It's hard for me to be around the Sidhe. My supposed people don't exactly like my kind. If you hadn't noticed."

Her voice was low as she added, "It's just no one got killed before."

Chris was trying to think of what to say. That's when he heard voices, there was some sort of commotion back at the entrance with the monks. "Sounds like the cavalry is on its way," Chris said.

They both recognized their friend's voices, especially Ben's who was yelling, "Do you know who we are!?"

"We're going to run out of room in this cell fast," Naiathne muttered as they both listened to their friends outside. The calvary may have arrived, but Chris didn't think they had much of a chance. The two of them, Naiathne and Chris, stood shoulder to shoulder at the bars and listened. "Doesn't sound like it's going great out there," Chris said.

Chapter 18

Far from the hazy daylight, beneath the surface of Tairnish, Amita felt exhaustion setting in, but she refused to fall back or ride on the battle armor. It wasn't out of some sense of pride. She glanced at the machine, seeing how close it was to the ceiling, and shivered at the thought of getting crushed against the rocky surface that seemed to press down and loom like a living thing. The walls felt like a dark watchful force that complained about their presence each time the armor rubbed and screeched against it, knocking anything loose to the ground. Alex kept the legs in tight, putting the armor into an awkward squat as it lumbered along.

The ancient mine was in rough shape, forcing him to stop more than once and clear fallen stones, making room. Luckily, the main support columns were made of heavy steel girders set twenty meters apart, so they were never far from safety. Still, some of the braces had managed to twist with the world's constant seismic activity.

They followed a rail system running along the floor, one that seemed to go on forever in the dark. Passing several off-shoots, they found large chambers with multiple exits. The chambers housed derelict equipment and rail carts and even had shelters built-in with kitchens and large bunks made for Drakes that were stacked to the ceiling. Amita thought they were only shelving, but the rotted bedding let her know someone had once slept there.

These camps were eerily quiet and felt like they'd been abandoned in a hurry, leaving behind spoiled food for the large rodents that were the primary residents of the tunnels now. The creatures with their distant glowing eyes hid and scurried away from the approaching armor, owning the shadows, and the shadows were everywhere. The only light came from the expedition. Alex's were the brightest. His massive floodlights pointed ahead, making Amita's small headlamp seem pale and weak.

The animals scrambling away weren't actually rodents of course. They'd evolved on this world and developed a different biology, more like the Long-Wolves, only smaller and, if possible, nastier, but they filled the niche in this harsh biosphere that rodents would've on Earth.

By the fifth or sixth camp, Amita felt her curiosity about the ghost stations waning and began wondering again about the people who made this moon and all the others, theirs. According to the records stored at Nalanda station, Tairnish was the first human settlement. Nearly a thousand years ago, people came to this world in numbers large enough to establish colonies and built domed villages that still remained partially intact today.

The few accounts from that time established the idea of communes with a collective system of government, one that had lasted longer than any on Earth. She thought of what Arthur C Clark, the science fiction writer, had said about communism, that it was the most perfect form of government if only people had been ants.

Looking around at the tunnels and knowing that most of the Tairnishmen had chosen to dig into this world, living under its surface, she thought, 'they've taken the 'ant' part a little too literally.'

Working together for survival and sharing resources seemed like a utopian idea. Amita wondered how often in human history it happened. Going back to the days of the caveman, when small groups would venture out to claim more territory, they would be dependent on each other. Humans were social creatures for a reason, because we survived through cooperation. It was only when resources became plentiful that we start thinking of our individual desires.

Tairnish had never become the type of world where individuality mattered. 'But where did these colonists come from?' She only had a theory and very little evidence to support it.

As they marched on, she was glad there was so little conversation. It gave her time to think. Going for hours, they followed behind Tearmai, who moved along at an unerring pace. At each turn and intersection, he'd only pause for a moment to consider. Then he'd hurry forward with his legs swinging in their pendulum way, staying at the very edge of the cone of light created by Alex's armor, always heading down, descending further into the moon.

Amita listened to the sound of her own breathing inside her helmet as they went further and further. Her legs seemed to move of their own accord, like limp instruments on autopilot. She and Edith stayed well within the cone of Alex's light as it bounced along and she tried to ignore the darkness at the edges, the way it seemed to be waiting to push in again.

Edith's armor had turned dark again near the wall, camouflaged for the stone. They reached another way station, an abandoned mining camp like the others, but this one was in even rougher shape, only half built, with walls cracking and crumbling. Massive piles of debris were scattered everywhere. Four tunnels came off it. Tearmai headed towards one, but he stopped when Edith called, "Hold there. We're going to take a break and assess."

Amita didn't like the way stations. They felt too large, even this one, which was smaller than the others, felt like it gave too much room for something to approach from the darkness, some horrible thing to creep forward and grab her. As claustrophobic as the tunnels were, at least it was solid stone around her. This empty space with all its corners and hiding spots seemed like the perfect place for something evil to lurk.

Tearmai cocked his head a little as he watched Edith walk up to the tunnel he'd been approaching. She held her rifle up to it, putting the scope close to her blacked-out helmet. After a moment she turned to Alex and ordered, "Give me a ping down this one and this one." She pointed her hand like a weapon at the one to the right of Tearmai.

The armor came forward, awkwardly making its way around a pile of fallen stone. Nothing seemed to happen. All of the armor's detection devices were carefully shielded and covered. There was no way to tell with the naked eye that they were active, but beneath a small dome on the machine's shoulder, a radar transmitter was spun up, sending a signal bouncing down the tunnel. Alex didn't even have to move to get the other one Edith pointed to. He used lasers as well to further a rendering of what was ahead of them. Then the machine's onboard computer added the data to a three-dimensional map that it'd been building the entire time.

Edith's helmet was linked to the battle armor. She pulled up the map and was quiet for a moment as she slipped her rifle onto her shoulder. A subtle motion dropped her hand to her sidearm. She pulled it from its holster and held it low. Like her rifle, it fired armor-piercing rounds, but its blunt nose had a built-in suppression device that would make the weapon deadly silent, and its small size made it more effective in close quarters. Tearmai was so close that she could hear his slow and steady breathing. She took two steps back, her hand on the pistol as she asked him, "I'm sorry, were your instructions not clear?"

Tearmai stared at her but didn't answer.

"Is there a problem," Amita turned towards Edith's faceless form, a black spot beneath the lights of the drop armor.

Edith's voice was calm and emotionless. "Your friend is taking us away from the target. We should be heading due west, but for the last few hours, he's been purposefully moving us south. We don't have time for these kinds of games."

"No games. We're going where she wanted," Tearmai's voice rumbled out as he pointed to Amita.

Edith's head tilted, looking at the small girl who held her hands up and said, "I'm here looking for answers. That's all. I didn't—"

Alex cut in. His voice came from the armor's speaker as the machine twisted towards Amita. "Did you tell him to take us somewhere other than the settlement?"

"No, of course not. That's what I was trying to explain." Amita covered her eyes with her forearm and squinted as she turned away from the bright floodlights. "I get it. What I'm doing is secondary to your whole rescue the princess thing."

"There are answers this way." Tearmai pointed down the tunnel. He stood at the entrance and took a step back, away from the others. He didn't see that something was happening behind him. No one else noticed either, but there was a faint red glow emanating in that direction, coming up out of the darkness.

"But which way is the Tairnish settlement?" Edith asked.

Silently, Tearmai stepped back to the group and pointed towards the righthand tunnel. He looked annoyed.

"That's where we're going. Understood? Now come on," Edith started off.

Tearmai stayed still. "She won't find what she's looking for there. What my friend and I found. It's suffering. The slave must be set free." His voice was low, and he was looking at the ground.

Amita's eyes were starting to clear after being blinded by Alex's lights. She turned to Tearmai ready to ask him what he meant. Then she noticed the hellish red glow shining from the walls behind him. "What is that?' she asked.

Tearmai glanced over his shoulder. "Bad, very bad," he said, pushing into the group, away from the light.

Amita, always curious, took a step toward it. 'It's getting closer, shining off the wall. No, not off the wall—from the wall,' she thought as the stone began to seep light. Cracks rippled over the tunnel, swelling with energy. She could hear something happening to the rocks. It rumbled and cracked.

Suddenly the stone exploded, blasting out in a crimson cloud. Amita was thrown back as the entire chamber shook. Massive boulders fell from the ceiling while the space shifted and trembled. Through the dust they saw a form take shape. A beast was revealed in the tunnel, glowing red along a hundred cracks in its rocky surface.

It was made from the very wall and shaped vaguely like a Long-Wolf, only larger and with a mane of long stony spears, like stalactites, shining with internal heat. It roared. The noise was answered by a second creature just behind it, then a third. They stood as tall as horses, then crouched down ready to pounce.

Tearmai warned, "They're wild," as he swung out of the way of the first creature, grabbing Amita from where she'd fallen. He pulled her aside, back further into the relative safety of the mining camp. Tearmai put her down behind a pile of debris as two of the creatures came galloping forward, smashing into Alex in his battle armor.

"What are they?" Amita whispered, trying to see what was happening.

Tearmai remained over her protectively as he said, "Fire-Golems, wild ones, free of Long-Wolf control."

Alex planted his back foot and tucked his shoulder in to absorb the hit. The armor reacted, detecting his actions intuitively adapting the suit's movements. The impact shook Alex, pushing him back, but he was still standing. He tried swinging his arm and sweeping the creatures away. One was tossed aside, but the other managed to sink its rocky teeth into the armor plating. The fangs glowed blood red as they burrowed into the suit's forearm.

Alex lifted the arm in the air, smashing at the creature with his other fist. It held tight so he brought his other limb further back, making a flat plane of the fingers and swinging fast, using his palm like a blade to crash into the creature and slice it in half. Pieces tumbled to the ground like a load of fallen bricks.

The first creature, the one that tried to pounce on Tearmai, turned back to Alex. It growled, then sprang toward the biggest threat. Barreling forward it rammed its spikes into the suit's leg. Much of the stone broke away and immediately Alex's systems warned him that he'd been breached. A diagnostic screen screamed about leaking hydraulics.

The upper half of the creature still on his arm pulled its teeth out and fell to the ground where the rock of its lower torso had split apart and started to form more legs.

Edith stepped up with her sidearm and emptied the clip into the downed creature. The armor-piercing rounds pulverized the stone to dust. As the rock fell away, the flame that had animated it rose from its corpse, ready to descend on Alex.

"Countermeasures!" Edith screamed in the middle of reloading.

On the other side of the room, the creature that Alex had tossed got to its feet. Amita peaked out, seeing it had a tail that swung just like a cat's, only blazing hot. Like a burning ember, it painted circles in the air with afterglow. Tearmai tried to force her back down into their hiding spot, but it was too late. The wild Fire-Golem saw them and started to approach. It stalked forward, getting low, ready to lunge.

Tearmai grabbed a massive rock from the pile and stood to his full height. "Run!" he yelled at Amita. She took off in the direction of the tunnel Tearmai had initially been heading.

Tearmai launched the boulder at the beast, breaking away some of the spikes on its back, but not doing much more than making it angry. It opened its mouth to reveal flaming red fangs and started ahead, cornering the Drake.

Across the room the living flame of the other golem, now released, lit the walls with an eerie glow. It had no face but somehow Alex knew it was looking at him as it hovered like a phantom before him. When it surged forward, he fired a canister from a barrel beneath the left arm of the armor. Shooting into the flame it exploded leaving a cloud of white dust in the air. The Fire Golem vanished as if it had never been there. Only the cloud of powder remained, but as soon as that disappeared, the ceiling of the chamber started to shake and began to crumble.

"Move!" Edith called, ducking into the tunnel nearest her. She didn't stop to look back, making sure she gave Alex enough room to escape. He leapt for the same tunnel as tons of stone fell behind him. On the suit's back were small thrusters, nothing as powerful as the pack Edith used to guide their descent to Tairnish but enough for a situation like this, when the suit needed to be moved in a hurry.

The battle armor responded to Alex's gestures, giving him the extra thrust he needed to escape the collapse. He bounced off the ceiling and came down hard on the floor, leaving a trail of hydraulic fluid as he landed like an out-of-control freight train. Behind him, the entrance to the tunnel closed as an avalanche of stone smashed to the ground.

Amita was already running when she heard the canister burst. The sound of the ceiling cracking caused her to pause and look back over her shoulder. As the rocks tumbled, she was swept up into Tearmai's long arm.

The Drake hadn't hesitated. While the countermeasure distracted the Fire-Golems, he moved swiftly, not looking back to see the ceiling fall. He grabbed Amita, and as the debris pelted down on him, he dove tumbling and falling in the dark.

Chapter 19

For hours now Katy had been counting steps. She started it after the trial. As the room erupted, when her brother guided her out. She had wondered how far she needed to go to get away from the discordant voices of excited students. The thought occurred to her that counting was something easy to focus on while caught in the press of people. It gave her relief from thinking about Chris who she was convinced had done the dumbest and bravest thing she could imagine.

It wasn't easy and it took nearly an entire day to get the hang of it. But after one ill-received visit to the cells, then going to her classes, followed by a trip to the Sidhe domain looking for Cathal, she could keep track of each stride while still paying attention to everything else around her.

Somehow, not having her eyes made this easier, forcing her to focus on what she could. She learned to round the numbers up to the tens place, finding it simpler to recall where she left off as she tried to remember every turn while following Ben and Cormack to the dining hall.

With the count still going, her thoughts wandered. 'Chris accused me of being reckless, getting on Cormack's shuttle. Now he does this?' As she said aloud, "You big dummy."

"What was that?" Ben asked.

"Nothing, I was just thinking," Katy said as she remembered their visit to the holding cell. She had to admit they should've done as Cormack asked and waited for Cathal, but the security head had been missing through most of the day, confined with sister Nemain.

The three of them, Cormack, Katy and Ben, had gone together to talk to Chris and Naiathne, but as it turned out, the monks weren't overly thrilled to let anyone meet with two people accused of murder, especially after how it went last time someone visited the cells.

Security had been bolstered since then. Four monks guarded the prisoners and seemed to take pleasure in redirecting Ben when he tried to saunter past them. Katy couldn't have seen the brief skirmish, but she heard robes flutter in the air, followed by a crash, and then her brother yelling, "I give up, I give up!"

Cormack had said, "We're sorry, he won't do it again. I promise. He hasn't been the same since the head injury," as he helped Ben to his feet. He took Katy's arm. "We should go."

"But wait," Katy said pushing his hand away. "We need to talk to them."

"I don't see that happening," Cormack explained.

"Fine." Katy opened her guide stick, then started a long count leaving the cells. They hadn't said much to each other since then. As she walked, she thought of Ben's summary of everything that happened while she and Chris were on Grannus. No one investigated that first monk's death, the one Alex supposedly killed. Ben insisted he hadn't done it, but no one cared. The monks thought they had their killer, so it went no further.

She asked Ben over her shoulder as they approached the dining hall, "You don't think that other monk dying could have anything to do with this one, do you?"

The evening meal was more loosely scheduled than the others and had a festive feel, which may have been brought on by the wine and other heady beverages that the young nobles were allowed to bring, along with the abundance of food offered by the kitchen. Dinner could last for hours, going right up to the beginning of the night cycle.

Realizing his sister couldn't see his shrug, Ben said, "I doubt it."

Katy bounced her stick from side to side, paused, and asked, "Are you sure?"

He shrugged again. "Look, I don't know who killed that first monk. But Maeven had security and whatnot, so maybe one of them sprang Amita. She was going out at night, exploring and Maeven let her, as long as she gave the princess information."

"After the night cycle? That's a terrible idea." Cormack broke in. "Didn't she know about the ghosts?"

Ben threw his hands up. "Know about them? We saw one! Yet she still did it, even after Andavarri warned us they like to grab kids. Seriously, what kind of school is this?" He shook his head again. "But it doesn't matter. What I'm saying is that there was a reason for that killing. To get Amita out. Whoever did it, swore Alex to secrecy."

"There was a reason for this murder too," Katy said. "We just have to figure out what it was. Then we'll know who did it. That's the only way our friends go free."

"My money is on Fafnir. He's got some serious anger issues." Ben hurried to keep up with her.

She nodded. "Any of the Extraracials might have a reason to kill the Kavaris after that speech."

"What do you mean?" Cormack asked.

Ben leaned into Cormack and put a hand on his shoulder. "Seriously, man. You people don't exactly treat them great. You've got this whole thing where you act all superior to the other races."

Cormack opened his mouth to answer, but he tilted his head and looked at Ben's hand. When Ben took the hint and pulled it away, Cormack explained, "My mother always said that in order to rule, sometimes you have to believe you have a right to, otherwise no one else is going to take you seriously. I'm not saying it's right. I doubt myself all the time, but this is what I was born to. Humans are like that too. They have beliefs about their place in the world. It's how we've reached the position we have, at the top of the food chain. It's just how things are."

"But should they be? And how do the Extraracials feel about it?" Katy asked, still tapping her stick side to side. Despite her blindness she was leading the way.

Before Cormack could answer, Ben suggested, "Hey, what about Andavarri's replacement? It sounded like Kavaris Altain was going to dial back the Fire-Golems, maybe even send them packing and let's not forget about your buddy Cathal—"

"Cathal? You think he's the killer? No way!" Cormack cut Ben off.

Katy felt the stick in her hand, that thin shaft Cathal had given her, a small piece of independence, a kindness that she felt bad betraying as she said, "He was the only one we know for sure who had the knife and also had access to the head monk. Not to mention he broke the rules once to bring your sister here." Her count continued as the ramp leveled off. She headed toward the voices echoing from the dining hall, but she wasn't sure how she'd negotiate the crowds once she got there. 'Probably have to rely on the others, like at the trial,' she thought, and her hand squeezed tighter on the stick.

Ben added, "and the head monk was putting him under his thumb." He pushed his own thumb forward as a demonstration.

Cormack rubbed his face and brought his fingers to his chin before shaking his head. "If you knew the man, you wouldn't even suggest—" His voice trembled. "But I'll talk to him, okay?"

"By yourself? No way fanboy," Ben shot at him.

"What's that mean?" Cormack's face scrunched up.

"Look, I hardly know you," Ben said. "You seem like a nice enough guy, but I don't think your eyes are all the way open on this. Your judgment is skewed on account of your man crush."

Cormack stopped in his tracks. "Man-crush? Cathal was my dad's closest friend. He's like an uncle to me." His voice went up an octave higher in shock.

Katy turned back and reached out to touch his arm. "Hey, relax. He didn't mean anything by it. But he's right. You're biased. Admit it."

Cormack took a deep breath. "Fine, you guys can come with me and talk to him."

Katy turned her head a little and listened to the crowd ahead of them. She was hungry but knew that many people would be too much for her. "You guys handle it. I'm going to grab something to eat back at the domicile."

"You're going by yourself?" Ben asked.

"Yeah," Katy said. "Just point me in the right direction."

She didn't see the look that passed between Cormack and Ben, but it was easy to imagine. She started away before they could say anything else, counting in her head as she went.

∞

The Sidhe domicile should've been easy to find since it was off one of the grand halls and they all connected at a central hub. Katy thought she'd found that large innermost room, the 'hub,' with its strange architecture. It was an irregular, elongated heptagon. She'd followed the wall with her hand, believing that she'd eventually hear voices coming from the market, but despite the fact that she'd walked far enough, according to her count, this part of Nalanda was too quiet to be that main intersection.

Taps with the stick echoed off the stone walls and high ceiling. The sound's depth made Katy suspect she was still in one of the large corridors. There were so many halls in Nalanda. 'Did I really think I'd be able to tell one from another?'

She passed a few people but most students were in the dining hall or already in their domiciles. Katy knew her brother and Cormack had been uncomfortable letting her go off by herself and she'd be lying if she didn't say she was starting to worry as well. With a good memory and an even better imagination, Katy believed she'd be able to create a large canvas in her head, like a map. The only problem was that a small mistake could send the entire thing into disarray. A break in the count, a missed turn, other things nearly impossible to determine without her eyes, or without more time than she had here at Nalanda could send her in the wrong direction. She felt a turn and wondered if it was the right one as doubt broke loose like a sudden chill.

'Is this even the central hub?' It felt big enough. 'Or did I go past it? No, I would've felt an opening.' She remained on the wall, swinging her stick back and forth, going wide and away, then took a few steps before she followed the turn. 'This has to be it.' She tried to convince herself and stifled an urge to go back.

'I could step away from the wall and confirm that I'm where I think I am.' Crossing a room without sight was always worrisome, but in a small area, the anxiety lasted only a few heartbeats, in a room this big it could be an eternity. She held her hand to the cold stone a moment more, then finally stepped away counting as she went.

In less time than she expected, she felt her stick make contact. 'I haven't gone far enough, either that or I've gone too far.' Her shoulders dropped as she took a long breath. The entrance she'd found was just another offshoot, one she'd never known was there because she'd had her friends guiding her.

She thought of trying to find Cormack and Ben and imagined what they'd say. 'What choice do I have?' she wondered, ready to turn back and give up. Then she heard voices. They were distant but she thought she recognized one, Regin, her professor. He'd always been helpful and she felt better going to him for aid over Ben and Cormack.

By focusing on his voice, she was able to get a general sense of direction. She followed it, eventually finding another passage. Beyond the entrance, the floor started to drop away.

'This wasn't the way to the cells. The angle is too severe.' Katy kept going, still following the voices. A fresh, pleasant smell drifted up from below as she got the sense that the voices were moving away from her. Not on purpose. They were having a conversation while strolling, but their voices got lower as she came closer, almost as if they could hear the tapping of her stick. Katy wasn't doing anything to hide her presence, but she didn't call out either.

Eventually, the voices went silent. 'Did they turn a corner?' she wondered, finally saying, "Hello, is anyone there?"

She heard the tap of claws on the stone turn towards her. As the clicking approached, a new odor wafted past her that she didn't recognize. It wasn't nearly as pleasant as that fresher smell she'd picked up earlier.

Everyone from Tairnish, both human and Long-Wolf, had a unique odor, but Katy hadn't been back at Nalanda long enough to recognize the aroma of creatures and people from the rocky, volcanic world. She heard the nails stop as the voice of Fajalar oozed out in front of her. "Why, what are you doing here?"

Katy felt like the Long-Wolf was too close, like her personal space was being invaded. "I was trying to find my way back to the Sidhe domicile."

"Well, I'm afraid, you're nowhere near that. In fact, you're much closer to the Extraracial territories. This corridor leads straight to it." His speech slithered in the air.

"So, the Grannusians are down here?" Katy asked, backing up a bit.

In an amused tone Fajalar said, "They are Extraracials, I believe."

"It'd be nice to talk to them," Katy said, less for Fajalar and more to herself, thinking that she was here already. "Was Professor Regin with you? I thought I heard his voice." She wondered if he'd be willing to give her an introduction, to show her the way to the Grannusians.

Her thoughts were interrupted by Fajalar's clawed fingers touching her stick. "Yes, he was here but he broke off, going into the forest. What is this device?" he asked.

"It's a guide stick. It helps me find my way." She pulled it back a little out of his reach. "I'm sorry, did you say forest?"

"Yes, there's an entire parcel of woods not far in front of you. The Grannusians planted it for the Drakes in a space as large as one of the grand halls. I'll be honest I'm not a fan. Plants and trees have little respect for borders. No one would go to such extremes for Long-Wolves, not that we require much. We live a simpler life than most races. We haven't time for plants or decorations."

"I see," Katy said then paused for a moment. "I was hoping the professor would be willing to guide me to the Grannusians."

"I thought you wanted to go back to the Sidhe? And what about this?" She felt the stick lifted from the ground. She had no idea that it was Fajalar's tail wrapped around it.

Katy pulled back again. "I'm sorry. Could you leave that alone?"

"Oh, yes, my apologies. I was only curious. Blind Long-Wolves are almost unheard of. They don't survive very long, you see, or I suppose you don't see." Fajalar snickered at his own joke.

"Maybe I should just go back the way I came," Katy said turning around.

"No, my dear. Regin isn't the only one that can be helpful. I can show you the way." Katy felt Fajalar's clawed fingers close around her wrist and start to gently pull.

Katy followed him. She didn't really have a choice. Tugging her arm back felt like it might be rude, though she was filled with doubt and didn't trust the Long-Wolf.

He said helpfully, "Mind your step down here. There's a trail but it's a bit rough. Those nasty roots have done an incredible amount of damage to the floor. May I ask why you wish to talk to the Grannusians?"

It may have been the smell of pine needles or the softness below her feet that helped her picture it, but Katy sensed the forest looming over her while the Long-Wolf's tail swayed and created a small breeze. "I'm trying to help Naiathne. I want to confirm her story."

High above were lights built to shine in the day cycle and feed the plants. They dimmed as the day faded, creating cool shadows and hidden corners. The trees felt old, their growth rushed by Grannusian biotech, creating thick trunks that stood like pillars in the tall room that served as a massive greenhouse.

Katy tripped a little as Fajalar pulled her along. His hand squeezed tighter on her arm as he helped her stay on her feet, but he didn't slow his pace, which would already be considered sluggish for a Long-Wolf. He didn't turn his head as he commented, "You wish to save the fish girl, how admirable. I should warn you the

Grannusians have not been overly friendly lately. Not that they'd go so far as to be rude, but they have kept themselves locked away. You should also know that the alien territories— I'm sorry the Extraracial territories, are unlike human domiciles. In fact, we're above the Grannusians right now. The roots of these trees take sustenance from their little ocean. Do you know what Professor Regin and I were discussing?"

Katy was caught off guard by the suddenness of the question. "Um, no. I mean I heard you guys talking but I didn't hear what you actually said." She couldn't use her stick because Fajalar was moving so fast. She held it up, high above the ground where it wouldn't catch on the roots.

"We were discussing the other girl that came through the void space, the little one."

"Amita?" Katy asked.

He finally twisted his long neck looking at her. "Yes, that was her name. I wonder where she's gotten to?"

Katy was a little confused by the question. "Everyone told me she went with Alex. That they were trying to save some princess."

Fajalar stopped suddenly. He took both Katy's arms and held her in place. "Quiet, girl. You know that's a secret mission." He whispered but still sounded delighted as he added, "A secret mission that everyone knows about. How do you suppose that'll go?" He paused but not long enough to let Katy answer. "Did you know that before Amita left, she'd been arrested? They found her in the lighthouse."

Katy struggled to keep up with the pace of Fajalar's conversation, the way he jumped into questions. He let go of one of her arms and moved back a bit and waited this time for her to respond. "Um, I knew she was arrested, but I missed some of the details. My brother told me the lighthouse was only for the monks, that she was in trouble for going there."

"Yes, but that wasn't her worse crime, not to the monks anyway. You see she was pulling at strings, tugging away at hidden things. That's very dangerous around here. And do you know what she found?"

"Um, I don't think I got that part." Katy tried to keep her voice from breaking, tried to stay calm, but she was very aware of how alone she was.

"She found a secret room. It'd been walled off. That's what Regin and I were discussing. What do you suppose was in that room? No, never mind, don't answer that question. We're not supposed to discuss such things." Katy felt his clawed fingers close on her arm again and tug her behind him as he added, "Regin was being naughty even talking to me about it. We shouldn't follow his example. We'll ask no questions."

Fajalar went quiet, only warning Katy when there was an obstacle in her way. Before long they were on the other side of the forest. He let go of her arm and said, "There's a hallway in front of you. Go twenty meters and you'll reach the Grannusian's door. Be careful though, the passage has some sort of moss growing on it. It's very slippery and like everything Grannusian, it's alive." His voice became more distant as he finished with, "Good luck to you, or whatever it is you humans say." With a swish of his tail, he left. Katy listened to his claws click, glad that he was gone.

She put her stick on the ground and started moving it across the soft surface. She was on soil for a moment more, then the ground became like a sponge, squishy and damp. As she stepped forward, the moisture seeped through her thin shoes and her feet sunk a little. The stick tapped against the wall of a tunnel. Her hand went up and felt the soft cool surface as she carefully walked forward. A coating of slime built up on her fingertips so she took her hand away.

After a moment the stick tapped on something solid that rang with a hollow sound. Katy stepped forward and felt a hard surface beneath her with small ridges.

Not far in front, the stick banged against a wall. She brought her hand up and felt more of the living moss or whatever it was. Going over it, she found a corner, then went to the other side and felt another. She put it together in her head, realizing she was at a dead end. There was no door just more of that plant, or growth, or whatever it was. 'Fajalar was playing games,' she thought. 'Teasing the blind girl.'

She tapped her stick on the surface beneath her feet and felt the hollow ring again. She tapped it once more. This time harder. It started to move.

Too late, it dawned on Katy that she'd found the door. She was standing on top of it. It opened like an iris with folds of metal moving out from the center, right where she stood.

Suddenly, the floor was gone, and Katy plummeted into a pool of water.

She sunk deep with barely enough time to take a breath. The water closed in, enveloping her, taking her hearing as her hands reached out, searching for anything. Her stick fell away as panic and fear overtook her thoughts. She tried to swim up and found only solid stone above her.

'Where is it! Where's the opening!' she screamed inside her head while her fingers hurried over the ceiling. She couldn't find it. She was lost in the darkness.

Chapter 20

Beneath kilometers of rock, Amita kept her head buried in the crook of Tearmai's arm, her hands pressed against her face plate while the walls shook. When it finally stopped and she lifted her head, the only light was from her helmet, everything else was darkness and slowly drifting dust left over from the collapse. Tearmai had squeezed himself next to one of the braces, the safest spot he could find, though the iron had still twisted and bent beneath the strain of tons of material tumbling down.

There was no sign of the wild Fire-Golems. The burning creatures had been inside the waystation when the countermeasure went off. It hadn't been a large explosion, but it was enough to disturb the compromised ceiling. The expedition had passed collapses often enough to know this entire system of tunnels was overly stressed by Tairnish's shifting geology. The shock wave from the powder grenade had slammed into the cracks and fractures with enough force to cause it to give way.

"Are you okay?" Amita asked Tearmai as she tried to find his face through the dust. After tearing most of his environmental suit off, the Drake had very few lights on him, only the indicators that glowed on his belt. She could barely see those through the cloud. Finally, Tearmai coughed and she found his beak and those blue eyes of his staring up at her.

He squinted, turned away from her light, and answered, "I'm still here."

"Thank you for saving me, again." Amita stepped back.

"Careful. It's still not safe." He reached out and touched her shoulder.

Amita looked at the pile of debris and noticed how close it was and how it completely sealed off the tunnel. "How are we going to get back to the others?"

Tearmai got to his feet and looked. "We're not."

Amita looked up at him, wondering if he was serious. He ignored the look and said, "Answers are this way. Something else is where they're going." He pointed further ahead, down into the dark with a question buried behind his words. Amita knew what he was suggesting. She just didn't know how she felt about it. Then she remembered the radios built into their suits. She quickly turned her attention to the controls on her arm pad, trying to remember how they operated. Edith had warned them not to use the devices, to leave them off, not wanting their signal to be picked up by the Tairnishmen, but surely in a situation like this— Amita searched for the right button then tapped it twice bringing up a list of channels. There was a scan setting. She touched that and heard Alex's voice say, "—the ceiling is unstable."

Amita interrupted. "Um, hello, Alex, are you there?" The two-way radios worked in a duplex mode, so both parties could speak at the same time.

"Yes! I'm trying to reach you," he said.

"So, you're alive I take it?" Amita asked.

It took Alex a moment before he answered, "Thank god, I thought I'd—" his voice faded for a moment. "Yes, I'm alive. Edith is here too. I'm trying to get to you, but it's not going great. Every rock I move just drops more down. I'm half-buried as it is. Luckily, this suit is pretty tough." Amita heard the relief in his voice and the resolve, an absolute desire to save her. A moment before he'd probably been wondering if he'd killed her by setting off that canister.

"Is Tearmai okay?" Alex asked through grunts of effort.

Amita glanced over her shoulder and saw the Drake pat some of the dust from his broad shoulders. He was moving slowly, but that wasn't unusual. Drakes always moved slow, right up until they needed to be fast. "Yes, I think he's okay. He saved me." She watched her friend take a few steps down the tunnel. He turned to look back at her, waiting. Amita brought her attention to the walls and remembered how they'd started to glow before the attack. How those creatures had come from it. Thankfully there was no light now. She gazed at the pile of stone in front of her and wondered.

Alex interrupted her thoughts, "Good thing we brought him then."

"Yeah, good thing." She could hear Alex working. The sounds of the battle armor came through every time he opened the channel with his voice, even when he wasn't talking to her. "I'm not stopping. I'm not leaving them here," he said to someone.

Amita could picture Edith standing back a bit in that black armor of hers, like a shadow. She'd probably already told Alex to stop transmitting. She'd probably warned him about the thing Amita was already aware of, that Alex was risking another collapse by digging, and that those wild Fire-Golems could still be waiting for them.

Those creatures could be moving through the stone right now, ready to roast them. Amita wasn't sure how they traveled, if the Fire-Golems that attacked were waiting in the wall like sentries, or if they could travel through solid stone using their plasma form. She thought of Ben and his fascination with the creatures back on the station and wished she'd pursued a little more knowledge about how they functioned. 'If the Long-Wolves made them, were these ones that broke free, or were they something else? And if they are sentries, what are they guarding?'

She shook her head. None of that mattered because either way they needed to be moving and Alex couldn't risk digging them out, not with how fragile this rock was. They didn't have time to stand here waiting. As Edith kept saying, they had a ticking clock. Amita looked back at Tearmai again. He nodded as Amita said, "Alex, you need to stop. I can only imagine what Edith is telling you, but she's right, isn't she? We need to be moving and we can't risk you bringing down any more of this tunnel."

"I don't want to hear it, Amita. I'm not leaving you alone down here." Alex's voice was strained.

"You're not leaving me. I have Tearmai and he knows these mines quite well. He is our guide after all. He'll find me a way out. It's you I feel bad for."

It took a moment before Alex answered. Amita imagined that Edith was trying to persuade him that she was right. She had no doubt that while the mercenary hadn't said anything, Edith was monitoring every word between the two. "Amita, I don't like this," Alex started.

"I know, but we've got little choice. I trust Tearmai and he says he can get me back to the surface." Tearmai had been watching her the entire time. He raised a single eyebrow and Amita held up her hands.

The comms went quiet again. Finally, Alex's voice came back. "Okay, get to the surface and we'll evac you guys from there," Amita heard him say this and wondered again exactly how that would work. Edith had been vague on her plan to get back to the shuttle after they rescued Maeven. "Just be careful, okay?" Alex pleaded.

"You're asking me to be careful while you're going off to storm some military base? That's a bit mad, isn't it?" Amita pointed out.

"I suppose you're right," Alex agreed. "I'll see you when it's over."

Amita heard the tone in his voice, the fear and concern, and answered, "Yes, when it's over. For now, try to be safe." She wasn't sure she even liked Alex. He was terrible company, bossy, too bloody serious, and his priorities had been bonkers since they arrived on this side of the wormhole, but she knew that what he was doing was far more dangerous than her own mission. She was going somewhere Brash and Tearmai had already been. They'd gone and left so she had a solid chance of doing the same. Alex on the other hand— She might never see him again. The first of the escapees from Earth to not make it back. "Good luck, I hope you get your princess," she said, then turned off her comms, feeling strange, worried about her own coldness.

She motioned down the tunnel and said to Tearmai, "Well, I guess, lead the way," as they went off by the light of her helmet.

∞

Time meant very little underground, but Amita knew it'd been a while since the collapse of the tunnel and the trip hadn't been easy. Not long after leaving the others, the passage had become much smaller and rougher, no longer showing signs of tool work. Tearmai and she were forced to climb over obstacles and squeeze between gaps. It was easy enough for her, but a few times she thought Tearmai would get stuck. He pushed himself into the cracks with a confidence Amita didn't feel as her helmet became a burden, the one part of the suit she couldn't jam into the tighter spots.

Her suit had an impressive battery supply, but it was starting to dwindle. The display on her arm showed that she'd burnt over 50% of her power. As it was their only source of light this was kind of a big deal. She wondered if she should open her helmet. Tearmai seemed to have no trouble breathing the air down here. But there was no point since the filter systems in it functioned

197

automatically. She'd only lose the suit's biometric monitoring and that pulled far less power than her light.

The suit had a water bladder that was nearly drained and an emergency supply built into the cooling system. Reading the temperature in the tunnel she was glad to have it as she wondered how long it'd been since she'd eaten anything. She'd ignored the grumble in her stomach till it vanished, only to return and become a constant ache. 'All this way to starve beneath the surface of an alien moon,' she thought remembering all the times her parents told her she didn't eat enough, that she was too distracted by books and projects or sometimes just talking, telling her parents about whatever little tidbit had caught her interest that day. They'd yell at her, "Amita, eat!" It made her laugh as she pictured them.

'If only you could see me now.' They wouldn't be happy to find her so far from safety. Her thoughts returned to the last night she'd spoken with them, back in the desert. Her father had been so mad. She hated that memory almost as much as she hated the memory of them wandering under Brash's control.

She was tempted to turn the comms back on and ask Alex how he was doing, but she knew that was a terrible idea. She'd tried talking to Tearmai, but he seemed cowed by this place, like the memory of his people's slavery was built into the very rocks. His answers were no longer as strange as they'd once been. Now they were just short.

He did mutter a bit, but his words weren't for her. "We should've done it last time, but Brash was scared. Bondage is never right. Kill it if you must, but to keep it a slave, so much worse. So much worse."

The tunnel began to widen again. Amita looked at the walls and wondered if Drakes had ever come this far. The mines had been neat and organized, but these tunnels felt more organic like natural caves. 'Perhaps they were made by Fire-Golems,' she thought looking at the smooth surface. They certainly weren't carved by water. There wasn't enough on Tairnish.

With her helmet light to the side, Amita noticed a glow in her periphery. She shut her lamp off and gave her eyes a moment to adjust as the soft illumination became brighter, reflecting around a turn ahead of them. The glow was faint and her thoughts went back to those wild Fire-Golems. 'Have we gotten ahead of them? Were there more?' No, this light was different. Those creatures had glowed red, like molten lava. This reminded her more of sunlight.

She kept walking as the glow became brighter. It wasn't really enough to see by, so she turned her lamp back on to watch her footing, taking careful steps, afraid she might have to turn and run.

They turned a corner and Amita stopped in her tracks, feeling Tearmai take her shoulder as her mouth dropped open and she caught her breath. She pushed the air from her lungs and muttered, "Phew, would you look at that," as she tried to take the entire sight in.

They stood on the lip of a massive chamber that spread out before them. It seemed unreal after the closeness of the caves and mines. She looked up and saw the light's origin. It actually was sunlight, but at a great height, far away, shining down into a deep cavern.

The space loomed in front of them, a tall vertical shaft that widened out as it plunged deep into a rounded canyon the size of a city. Amita wasn't sure how to gauge the scale. Then her eyes started to pick up details, windows, and openings lining the stone walls, cliff dwellings like in the American Southwest, only more elaborate and on a much bigger scale. Buildings littered the floor with columns and turrets, towers, and minarets. Sunlight blazed down from far above, pointing like a beam on the center of the canyon city.

'How many Long-Wolves could've lived here?' she wondered, sensing that the place was abandoned. Overwhelming silence filled the air and for as far as she could see, nothing moved. She had a distinct feeling that human hands had never touched this place. As someone who had scoured Nalanda's records, she knew it'd never been mentioned, and she believed it would've been because its existence was in opposition to everything humans knew about Long-Wolves. This place meant that the devout individualists once lived together, that they'd worked toward a single goal.

It was common knowledge that Long-Wolves lived far and wide on massive estates occupied by small family groups and most of the members of those families avoided each other unless it was necessary. Being alone was the Long-Wolf definition of freedom. "Is this where I find my answers," Amita asked Tearmai without turning her head as she took in every detail.

She noticed how the towers seemed to glimmer in the sunlight. Their smooth surfaces came together into something reflective at the top. Amita stared more sharply and realized that these weren't buildings after all, but rockets.

"Some," Tearmai answered with little emotion in his voice.

Amita barely heard him as she realized what she was seeing, the thing that attracted her attention, the light glimmering at the top of the rockets was reflected sunlight. Her eyes widened as it dawned on her that the rockets were all topped with diamonds, like the vessel she and her friends had come through the wormhole in. There were dozens of them, standing at attention, ready to be launched into space.

Chapter 21

Amita and Tearmai didn't linger long on the edge of the secret canyon. She had a thousand questions, but Tearmai had more he wanted to show her below in the strange place. Unfortunately, there weren't many options for getting down.

"How did you find this? For that matter, how did no one else?" Amita asked Tearmai. She was clinging to his back as he climbed down the sheer cliff wall. Her head was turned, looking at the canyon floor below and what she now realized was a spaceport or more accurately a launch base for rockets capped with crystal pods like the vessel that carried her through the void.

Tearmai took his hand away from the wall and pointed towards the light far above. "It's hidden. Camouflaged. Long-Wolves are very good at concealing things. They've practiced for a long time, keeping secrets." Amita knew that the Drake taking one hand away from the wall shouldn't make her nervous, since his other claws were buried deep in the stone and he was an excellent climber, coming from a species evolved to live in trees, but it was such an incredibly long way down that she squeezed a little tighter and turned her eyes to the sky. She kept them there as she held his neck with her feet buried in his belt. Eventually, her curiosity forced her to look down again.

As many questions as she had, she decided it would be best to hold them for the bottom, not wishing to distract her friend. Instead, she stared at those rockets and wondered what purpose the Long-Wolves could have for them. 'Had they explored the wormholes? Were they traversable still? Could she maybe go home?' That last question was tinged with too much hope.

She tried to fight the thrill she felt at the thought, remembering the way the void had expanded and consumed the observatory and the ground where it stood. It was an easy pattern to repeat. So many times, she'd asked herself, 'Was Earth still there? What happened to it? Did the wormhole keep growing, consuming the whole planet?' If it had, she'd assume that Earth would end up here. It was the obvious answer, but to her knowledge, a planet hadn't come bobbing through the void behind them. 'The monks would've had a hard time covering that up.' she thought, 'Or would they?'

Amita considered the size of Altor, the mega-gas giant that all these worlds circled. It dwarfed Jupiter with an atmosphere reaching out twice as wide as that largest planet in her own star system. There could be belts of debris floating around inside Altor's atmosphere. On a scale that big, the remains of her home might be nothing more than dust. She felt a chill run down her spine as she thought of the passage. There was a feeling in that timeless place that she didn't want to remember, a hunger that felt insatiable. Amita tried to chase the feeling from her mind, focusing on the void spaces themselves.

Wormholes were theoretical in physics and though they'd now been confirmed, no one could say for certain how they worked. In fact, Amita realized, she might be considered the human race's foremost expert on them, seeing as how she climbed out of one's arse. She thought of Ben and Katy's father, of Chris and Alex's mom, and wished she could go through their notes. Then her own parents entered her mind, but she pushed their memory away as quickly as it arrived. She needed data, and answers, not to waste another second thinking about what was lost. Finally, here was new information, more pieces to the puzzle. 'Stay focused,' she warned herself.

When they were further down, she could look back and observe the rockets. She hadn't seen much Long-Wolf technology as the creatures were content to let humans build for them and most of the modifications for Nalanda station had been made with human hands.

From what she understood, the Long-Wolves had always maintained a low population, a result of being such isolationists, but according to the records they had industry before humanity arrived, suborbital and orbital vehicles. This must've been what their tech looked like.

On the outside, the rockets were constructed with odd angles, and the materials were reflective, shining with strange hues of color, while the vessel's instrumentation and mechanics remained carefully concealed behind shielding. They built with redundancy and care, using segmented fuel tanks and multiple thrusters, far more powerful than what was required to lift off even from such a heavy moon as Tairnish.

More time passed as Tearmai continued his descent with Amita clinging to him, coming down from a dizzying height. The air was cooler out here in the open than in the mines. Warm gentle breezes moved around the chamber and Amita watched dust clouds circle and spin. Somehow, they always avoid the rockets, repelled by some invisible force. 'Maybe it was a static field meant to keep the mechanics clean,' she thought as they came closer and closer to the giant machines.

They passed a few hollows, those darkened windows carved into the rock. She saw passageways and tunnels going back behind them into a murky labyrinth and felt watched as they passed by, expecting to see eyes peering out following their course. Eventually, Tearmai reached the top of an arch above a much larger opening. The sides of it were carved into elaborate columns, at least four stories tall.

From above the large opening, Amita looked down and saw a platform hanging out into the cavern. The walls of the canyon were a murky red, but the platform was darker, made from grays and blacks and a material that was like nothing else she'd seen on Tairnish.

She thought it might be some kind of metal but it clung to the wall like a parasite. There was something familiar about its construction, the way the panels had an organic feel. She'd seen things like this built into the walls of Nalanda. It was the way the alien part of the station looked, the deep parts that weren't carved from the asteroid. This platform felt more intrusive though. Perhaps it was because it was so different from the walls and the rockets.

Tearmai struggled a bit more here, trying to bash his claws into the smoother surface of the columns. His purchase wasn't great, so he looked down, then started to slide, using his powerful arms and legs to squeeze the column as he attempted to slow himself. A good distance from the bottom, he leapt out toward the center of the platform, coming down on his arms, using his long limbs to absorb the impact.

Amita held tight as Tearmai sat back on his haunches. Shaking off the impact she climbed down moving her jaw a little, feeling like her teeth had been rattled. When her head cleared, she peered about and saw that they were lower than the rockets' crystal top. She could see the diamond vessels by the edge of the platform and immediately started toward them, hurrying across the flat surface to get a better look. Then she realized the platform wasn't all that large and that it had no rail. There was only open space out there.

"It doesn't look like they've used this place in a very, very long time," she said carefully peering over the side. The rockets were massive in comparison to the diamond vessels, going another ten stories down.

"Nearly a millennium, except for once," Tearmai said.

"You and Brash?" Amita asked.

Tearmai nodded. "But they're always ready."

Amita considered her surroundings, trying to take it all in. They'd both been so exhausted in the mines and upset by what happened at the entrance, that she hadn't been pumping Tearmai for information, not like she had on the shuttle. She remembered how grueling the process of getting him to talk had been, especially in the tight quarters of the ship with Andavarri always in the way. Every time Amita started to get details, the Long-Wolf would butt in and break his concentration, causing Tearmai to lock down again.

He certainly seemed more clearheaded than when he first escaped the medical unit and his locked room. The madness improved but remnants lingered, a malaise of confusion that refused to vanish completely. Tairnish may have cowed him, but it also seemed to help clear his head. Amita wondered if perhaps now she could finally get a straight answer from him. "You and Brash were here? This is where your diamond ship came from?"

"Yes, these are the tools of scavengers," Tearmai grumbled as he pointed down at the waiting vessels.

A raspy shrill voice snarled behind them. "You say scavengers like it's a dirty word. Well, at least we're not thieves, unlike you and your friend. We only take from the doomed." Amita heard claws clicking on the stone floor as she leaned around Tearmai to find the source of the voice. A form emerged from the shadows of the opening in the rock wall.

Amita saw a tail and claws and long teeth. "Oh, bloody hell," she complained. The creature was a dead ringer for Andavarri, sneer and all. It took a moment to realize this was a completely different Long-Wolf. Her purple skin was much darker, fading almost to ink black. Only the wrinkles were lighter. They ran like pale fault lines over her entire body and her movements were feeble, taking small steps as she leaned on her tail and a heavy staff.

"You've come back. So where is your flying friend?" the Long-Wolf asked as she looked around, trying to find Brash. "It'd be best if I could kill you both at once. Time saver, you know."

Amita saw that the Long-Wolf's staff was now pointed at them and that it was actually a primitive rifle, wrapped in cloth with a dark barrel sticking out.

"I'm sorry but I've come a bit far to be shot," Amita said.

"That's not really my problem, is it?" The Long-Wolf turned to her, then her suspicious eyes went between the two. "A human and a Drake. That's an odd pair, I think. Is he your pet?"

Amita held her hands in the air, making sure the Long-Wolf knew she wasn't armed. "No, just my friend. He told me I'd find answers here. Tearmai has had a rough go of it. His head isn't exactly right. If you know what I mean? I've been trying to help put it back together."

The Long-Wolf nodded, but her eyes were busy still searching the chamber as if she were afraid Brash would drop from the sky. "And where's the flying one?"

Amita glanced over her shoulder at Tearmai. He was staring rage at this Long-Wolf, but he wasn't offering her any more information. "I've no idea. You know how those Lightening Bugs can be. Tricky little buggers."

"Yes, they certainly are. Well, if he shows up, I'll shoot him too." She placed the rifle's stock on her shoulder, ready to fire.

"Wait!" Amita yelled. It was enough that the creature brought her weapon down a little. She sighed saying, "yes."

Amita continued, "It's just we've come an awfully long way. You see, we're on a secret mission for the emperor."

"Really?" The Long-Wolf had a glint in her eye, then she glanced at Tearmai and asked, "Him too?"

"Oh, yes. He was our guide. We were with a military group on its way to rescue Princess Maeven. The Tairnishmen kidnapped her." She saw the look of confusion in the creature's eyes.

"You know who Princess Maeven is, don't you?" Amita asked as an idea crossed her mind. She knew one thing that Long-Wolves loved more than anything else, information, gossip really. True, they were isolationists by nature, but that only seemed to increase their almost desperate urge for scandalous stories. As a species, they understood the value of knowing things and they treated news like a commodity. Amita rolled her eyes as she pointed out, "Everyone knows who Maeven is."

The Long-Wolf seemed angry and embarrassed as her tail slapped the ground. "Well, I'm afraid I don't. I've been down here a very long time and I don't get much information. Last I heard the emperor was on his way to conquer the water world. If I remember, he did have a daughter back when they were still mining and building ships. I figured the war went well or ended badly since the mines were closed down. They started taking the slaves away, which made my job a bit easier. I didn't have to kill any more Drakes who wandered too far. Ones like him. You know, the curious," she said this last bit with a sneer at Tearmai.

He took a step towards her, and the rifle came up again. "Don't be rash," Amita warned her friend, holding her hand to his chest as if there were any chance she could stop him.

Amita smiled at the Long-Wolf and continued, "Everyone knows about Maeven. She's to take the throne after her father, but now she's been captured. There is so much happening. I think you'll find out soon enough, but you see my friend and I are in the thick of it. We just got a bit lost is all."

"Thick of what exactly," the Long-Wolf asked.

"The rescue mission of course and so much more, political intrigue and whatnot. You see I know why all those slaves have vanished." Amita cocked her hip and looked toward the ceiling. "Why it's been rather quiet down here the past few years, nearly a decade I'd say. Is that correct?"

Without meaning to, the old Long-Wolf was lowering the rifle again, leaning forward. Amita took this as a request to keep going. She'd been consuming every piece of information on her monitor for weeks and could probably teach a history class on the invasion of Grannus. "The emperor lost on the water world. Grannus held him at bay with the help of the true Grannusians and their creations. There were peace treaties and what not, though they're shaky at best. I think everyone assumed the emperor would be back, but he hasn't tried. He hasn't been building ships or re-arming or any such thing either. Quiet as a mouse."

The Long-Wolf quickly digested this information and started to say, "Yes, well. I'm sure the terms of the treaty—"

Amita interrupted, "Please, he's Emperor Tamerlane, everyone knows he's up to something."

"Well, obviously." The Long-Wolf agreed, then she waited for Amita to continue.

She crossed her arms. "I've so much more to tell you, but you see there are things I'm fuzzy on. Like I said, my friend's mind is a bit rattled. He went through the void space without the benefit of a spaceship, so getting information from him has been a chore. There are things I'd like to know. For instance, these." She pointed back at the rockets. "Tell me about them."

The Long-Wolf looked at the rockets, and down at Amita. She stared at her for a long moment before saying, "You're a savvy little human, aren't you?" Amita nodded and the Long-Wolf added, "I wonder if perhaps your people are the worse salvage we've ever claimed."

"Salvage?" Amita asked, confused.

"How soon they forget. Though I suppose it is near on a thousand years now. Things get lost."

Amita tried not to seem eager. She kept her arms crossed and pretended indifference while her heart started beating faster. The Long-Wolf must've been convinced by her mask because she continued on. "Your friend called us scavengers and I suppose in a way that's true. It's a harsh universe and we take what we need to survive, even from the void space. These ships, my ancestors used them when the void spaces opened. They'd plummet down through the very maw of the leviathan looking for bounty."

Thoughts were running through Amita's head as a realization dawned on her. All this time she'd been wondering where the humans on this side came from, when the answer was so obvious. She had no idea how time worked in a wormhole. Science fiction had assumed for years that the transfer was instantaneous, but what if it wasn't.

She ignored the terrible chill the guardian's words evoked and asked, "Did they go to Earth?"

The Long-Wolf sensed her anticipation and smiled a toothy grin. "Earth, that's an old word, isn't it?" She held for a moment longer then added, "Well of course they did, and they brought back so many things."

"Including refugees," Tearmai added.

Amita turned to look at him and realized that she didn't have to come all this way to learn this. Her friend had known all along, and she just hadn't been able to pull the information from him. Tearmai seemed to understand this somehow. "That's not why I came here." He said, "There's more. It's calling to me. The slave is calling."

Amita shook her head "A thousand years," she said without being aware that it was out loud.

"Oh my, I suppose that's a bit of a surprise to you. It was a difficult time for your people. Many of them were quite mad when they arrived. The void spaces tend to do that to most lifeforms. There's not much information about that age. At least not in the human records. Long-Wolves are a bit more careful with our history. Speaking of which, it's your turn, girl. What is the emperor doing with the slaves? Where have they gone?"

Amita was running calculations through her head, thinking about how Brash and Tearmai had come to Earth that night in the desert, how she and her friends had gone through first before the rest of humanity but yet people had been here for a thousand years. Time was such a strange thing. When it was broken down to mathematics it did bizarre things, things that made no logical sense to a person who'd lived their life one day at a time, moving along a single linear axis.

'Why were they the last ones out?' Amita thought while repeating the Long-Wolf's question, "What has the emperor done with the slaves?" She was too distracted, imagining the end of the Earth. Her preoccupation was the only reason the words, "How should I know," slipped out.

"What?" the Long-Wolf demanded.

Amita realized what she'd done and cursed, "Bollocks,"

"You were lying?" The rifle was pointed squarely at Amita's chest now. She saw the Long-Wolf's eyes narrow down the barrel, looking through the sight.

Amita started backing away, going towards the edge of the platform with her hands still in the air as she said quickly, "Well, no, I don't know exactly what the emperor is up to, but I can give you some of my theories, and we are here to save the princess, or at least we landed with that crew. That part is completely true, and I'd be willing to tell you all about it, but you see I haven't been here all that long on this side of the void space as you call it, so I'm just getting up to speed on a few things myself." Amita kept walking as the Long-Wolf followed her. "I arrived in a vessel a bit like the ones on top of those rockets, and I was hoping to learn more about them. Perhaps you'd like to know a thing or two about Earth." Sensing the edge, and the open space behind her, Amita glanced at the ships.

The Long-Wolf snarled, "You tried to trick me." She was so blind with anger and focused on Amita that she all but ignored Tearmai, who hadn't moved at all. He watched her stalk his friend, coming closer to him.

Amita smiled. "I certainly did. But you figured me out. So clever of you." A half step more and the Long-Wolf would've been within Tearmai's reach. As it was, when his clawed arm swept out, the Long-Wolf had just enough time to turn the barrel on him instead. His hand closed over it and the rifle went off. Tearmai roared and brought his other arm down like a club. The Long-Wolf was old and slow, unable to twist away as the force of the blow smashed down hard enough that Amita felt it through the floor. The creature crumpled and Amita came running forward.

She looked at Tearmai's side and saw blood seeping over his hand as he held the wound. The rifle was on the ground next to the crumpled form of the Long-Wolf. "Is she dead?" Amita asked.

"I don't know." Tearmai grunted in a pained voice. "I hope not. It wasn't my intention to kill her. Only to stop her."

"Well, it was her intention to kill us," Amita said, lifting the hand away from Tearmai's side so she could see the wound. She bent down and picked up the rifle trying not to look at the dead Long-Wolf as she inspected the weapon. She opened the breach and saw that it fired chemical shells much like a human weapon. Then she went to the wound again and found the entrance and exit. The bullet had passed clear through Tearmai's side.

"You wouldn't happen to know if you have any vital organs in there, would you?" She pointed to his side.

Tearmai shook his head, no.

"Well let's hope you don't." Amita searched along her belt and found a small patch kit for repairing her suit, complete with glue. She tore off two pieces and stuck them directly to Tearmai's armored hide and held them till the glue dried.

Tearmai stared at the slumped form. "I've never killed anything. Not a bird or a bug. I don't like it."

"I know, but like I said she was going to do it to us. Look, this may not be the time, but I believe there's more you need to fill me in on."

Tearmai nodded. "You're correct." Then he reached down to the unmoving Long-Wolf. She had something around her neck. He lifted it and examined a piece of elaborately carved metal. He pulled it away with a single tug. Without a word of explanation, he started off, going into the large, darkened doorway.

"Where are you going?" Amita called behind him.

"You want answers. Follow, follow. They're in the dark and in the light."

Amita looked back at the Long-Wolf. The creature wasn't moving. She shook her head and said, "You may have been intent on killing me, but at least you'd answer a bloody question." Then she glanced up at Tearmai getting farther away, going off into the dark.

Chapter 22

'Don't breathe!' Katy screamed inside her head as she kicked her legs, but that only brought her closer to the ceiling where solid stone waited.

Her fingers frantically searched for the opening she'd fallen through and when she found the cold metal, she discovered the iris had closed. She felt its folds laying on top of each other, sealed tight. As her hand searched for any way to open it, she brought her face close, hoping a pocket of air had formed but there was nothing. That's when she felt a tug at her leg. Something wrapped around her ankle and pulled. She was dragged down and jerked through the water, feeling the solid door slip from her fingers.

Out of habit, her eyes were closed tight. She brought her hand up to her nose to pinch it against the force of the water flowing across her face. So much had already been forced in that she was now fighting the urge to cough and vomit.

Suddenly, whatever had her, let go and Katy started swimming up again. This time an air pocket was waiting. She burst from the water and found the ceiling still close. Her head crashed into it and pain surged through her skull as she tasted blood in her mouth.

"Slow down," a voice said in the dark. She felt tiny life forms, an entire school of fish and other creatures swim up under her arms and legs. They floated her till she was lying flat with her head out of the water sucking in the air. She coughed and brought her hands to the ceiling, convulsing while her body tried to force water from her. The tiny fish turned her and held her head up, letting her retch. Her throat and nose burned as seawater was expelled with every cough. Katy thought she'd done a good job of holding her breath but in the panic, she must've let more pass than she thought. It all happened so quickly.

The school laid her back as the coughing lessened. Between hacking shakes, she said, "Thank you."

"Why are you here?" the same voice asked again. It was soft and feminine but had a strange trill that let her know she was speaking to a Grannusian.

Katy opened her mouth to speak but found it hard to put her thoughts together, feeling shaken and scared. The ceiling being so close didn't help. She finally managed to get out the words. "I need help."

"You certainly did and still do. You shouldn't be here. No human should," the voice said.

Katy could sense the eel, the largest part of the Grannusian nearby. "I'm sorry. I'm Katy. I've been to your world."

"We know who you are. You're the one that can't see."

She nodded her head. "Yes, I helped your people. My friend Chris and I did."

"We know," the voice said simply before going silent, not adding anything else.

Katy tried to break the awkward silence, "Um, well, Chris is in trouble. He's been arrested, both him and Naiathne. You know her too, right?"

"Yes, we know her." Katy felt some of the creatures around her start to swim away as her legs drifted back down into the water.

She kicked a little, turning in the direction of the voice. "Was she here two nights ago? The night arrived."

The voice hesitated, "Yes, she was."

"When? For how long? You're her only alibi."

"What do you mean?" the voice demanded.

"I'm trying to find the real killer for Kavaris Altain. They've arrested Naiathne for his murder. If you guys say she was here, they've got to let her go." Katy was still

215

coughing and her voice went higher with excitement as it echoed off the ceiling.

"She wasn't here very long. We sent her away. We didn't want her company and we don't really want yours either."

Katy was taken aback. She started again, "Um, okay, but—"

The voice cut in, "It's not that we want to punish you who helped us, or Naiathne for that matter, but this is a time of consideration for us, planning and preparation." The voice faded away for a moment, but Katy could still hear her, floating in the dark. "Understand, we on this station are the only ones not affected by the poisoning. We have responsibilities and little time. Creating more of the antidote is our people's only chance at survival. It falls on us. This attack was against our entire race. Imagine your people being assaulted in such a way. A disease that breaks down who you are. Better to kill us. And the way it was done. Using one of our own, torturing him into it. The cruelty is beyond what we can understand. And why were we attacked? Because we defended ourselves and helped those other humans, the ones we've allowed to live on our world? Perhaps the others are right." The words were sharp and growing more bitter with every sentence.

"I'm very sorry for what your people have been through—" Katy started.

The voice cut her off. "Our numbers are small, and we don't have time for distractions. It's why we sent Naiathne away and why we're sending you now."

Katy felt the fish start to move around her. "It's time for you to hold your breath. When you surface again it will be at the doorway. Please see yourself out."

Katy felt herself being pulled down. The last thing she wanted to do was open her mouth, but she did anyway, screaming, "Wait! You're not alone." The pull

216

from below stopped and she spoke with sea water nearly at her lip line. "Many of your people are alive and well, thanks to the Naiads. They're at the colony, protected."

The voice didn't respond for a moment. Then Katy added, "We brought the antidote back to you here because the humans on Grannus don't know how to get to the colony and we weren't going to tell them, not with how they treat the Naiads. It needs to stay safe. Also, they took the memory from my friends, from Chris and Cormack anyway, but I know where it is, at least its general location. Your people are safe there because of Naiathne and her people. That has to matter.

"Please, they nearly killed her and now my friend Chris is in a cell next to her. He fought so hard to get you this antidote. Please, please help them."

After a moment the voice said, "Do you know who I am?"

"No, I'm sorry," Katy said, not sure why she was apologizing, but she felt herself lifted a bit higher.

"I am Clio, the Grannusian steward. Parts of me once made up Eir. Leaving pieces behind is the way we guide our people. She passed on some of her wisdom this way before going home to investigate the poisoning. You sought her out to heal you, and I think she would have, but some of the beings here on the station that she was friendly with would not have been so kind to you. They are full of hate and they've set things in motion to change the way things are."

"Good," Katy said. "Things need to change."

"They will. Things always change but that's not my point. I'm trying to warn you. You're playing a dangerous game looking for the truth behind this murder." The voice paused. When it spoke again, it said, "I really shouldn't speak of such things but please be careful. You've only this one life. I will go to the monks and confirm Naiathne's story. I don't know if it will help, but I will do it."

"Thank you," Katy said.

"Now take a breath and close your mouth. It's time to go. If only your decency could guard you against what's coming." Katy was dragged through the water again. This time more gently, led by her hand. When she surfaced, she was at the doorway. She reached up and felt the lip. Her hands closed on it and found the slippery surface. Then a push came from below. She was lifted in the air and allowed to drop onto the side of the portal.

Katy got to her feet. Standing, soaking wet, she heard Clio's voice come from the opening in the floor. "I'll go to the monks first thing in the morning, but I'll warn you again, child. Be careful. Help your friends, but then let this go. There are those out there that won't want the truth found. I believe the monk was killed to conceal a secret and secrets can be deadly."

Katy nodded, then asked, "If it's not too much trouble. I fell in with a stick. It's how I get around."

"Reach out your hand," the voice said. Katy did as she was asked, holding her legs rigid, afraid she'd fall in again. She felt the thin stick and took it, then heard the door close beneath her. She tapped the side of the entrance in the floor, then turned away and started counting. She knew there was an entire forest in front of her and that she'd have to find her way through.

∞

The noise in the dining room was dying down as the night cycle closed in. Ben and Cormack were sitting across from each other. Neither had spoken about Katy, but they were worried. It'd been nearly an hour since she insisted on going off on her own. Nalanda station was such a large place. If she got lost it could be a very long time before they found her again. Cormack was getting ready to go check on her when Cathal came in.

Ben watched the head of security go to the serving station to get his evening meal. The staff were wrapping up the food and putting away their carts. They didn't look happy to be bothered by Cathal.

"You need to go easy, Ben," Cormack warned, sensing Ben tighten like a spring.

"What do you mean?"

"Your foot is thumping like a broken propeller."

Ben stopped moving. "No, it's not."

Cormack raised an eyebrow, then turned towards Cathal and put his hand in the air. "Just let me do the talking, all right?" Cathal left the serving station with his tray. He looked exhausted, his shoulders slumped down and his smile gone behind his grizzly beard, but he nodded to Cormack, who waved him over.

Cathal approached their table, leaving a respectable distance. "I'm sorry, my prince, but as I'm part of the staff now, I can't join students. Besides you two should be back in the Sidhe Domicile. It's only minutes before full dark."

"I understand," Cormack said. "I only wish a moment to talk."

Cathal gave a solemn nod but before he could move away, Ben blurted out, "Yeah, we've got some questions for you."

"Excuse me?" Cathal asked.

Ben had both arms out as he leaned across the table and his words poured out of him. "We want to know exactly, I mean when exactly, you gave that knife to the head bald guy. We only ever saw you with it, right? Also, were you really going to throw Naiathne out of an airlock, or were you about to start blasting monks, and if so, which one would you start with? Also—"

"Ben, stop!" Cormack grabbed him by the arm and squeezed. The prince looked around the dining hall to

219

see if anyone had heard Ben's outburst. Luckily it was nearly abandoned.

"What the hell is wrong with him?" Cathal motioned with his tray as his face turned red.

"I'm not sure. But he's going to stop right now." Cormack squeezed Ben's arm again.

"Ouch," Ben said pulling back. "Come on, man. We've got questions. You said so too."

"I'm sorry," Cormack started, but Cathal's attention had already been taken somewhere else.

He dropped his tray on the table. As food spilled out, he started off, saying, "By the depths."

The others hadn't heard the tapping of Katy's cane or seen her coming down the corridor, moving slowly into the dining hall. The passages at Nalanda station were never warm, which made being wet even more unpleasant. She left a trail of water behind her as she shivered and touched the corner of the entrance.

Cathal rushed to her and took her arms. He started rubbing them, trying to make friction. Her uniform was soaked through. "You're freezing. What happened to you?" He asked.

"I went swimming. I wouldn't advise it, and next time I'm bringing a towel," Katy said through chattering teeth.

As Cormack came up behind them, Cathal turned and said, "See if they have something behind the serving station to dry her with. And you," he turned to Ben. "Get your sister something warm. Soup or tea." He guided Katy back to the Sidhe table and sat her down.

"Where were you?" he asked.

Katy turned towards his voice. "I visited the Grannusians and spoke to Clio. She's going to confirm Naiathne's alibi."

"Good thing you didn't toss her out an airlock," Ben said to Cathal as he handed his sister his half-eaten bowl of soup.

Cathal shook his head and said to Katy, "You went into the Extraracial territory? Do you have any idea how dangerous that is?"

Katy motioned to her wet clothing. "I'd say I get the idea."

Cormack handed her a stack of folded dish towels. "That's not what he means. You were lucky you ran into the Grannusians and not the female Ice Carvers."

Cathal nodded in agreement, then asked, "How did you even find your way there?"

"A little bit by accident. Look, it doesn't really matter. You heard me, right? They're going to speak for Naiathne. She has an alibi. They've got to let Chris and her out now, right?"

"Maybe," Cathal said. "The monks are shaken by this murder. They're going to be tyrants till I find the killer." Cathal was moving the towels over her arms as he continued, saying, "I took this position, to bring honor to the Sidhe. I'm no investigator, just a soldier."

"Do you know where the murder happened?" Katy asked. She had taken one of the small towels and was squeezing her hair with it, then wringing the water out.

"I assumed in his quarters. It was after the night cycle. No one goes out after that," Cathal said.

"Sure, they don't." Ben smirked and raised his eyebrow at the head of security.

Cathal ignored Ben and looked at his monitor, at the clock on it. "Speaking of which, the night cycle begins now. You all need to be back in the Sidhe domain." As if on cue, lights throughout the station began to dim. Massive banks far above went out, letting the starlight from outside shine in through the massive windows.

Katy ignored him and asked, "Did you search his quarters? Was there any sign of a struggle?"

Cathal shook his head and grumbled, "Nothing obvious. Now come on." He got up and waved for them to follow him, leaving his food and tray behind.

Ben and Cormack both stood, but Katy stayed where she was. With her eyes on the table, she said, "No blood, furniture knocked over, anything like that? Someone stabbed him with a big knife. That had to make a mess."

Cathal came back to her, taking her arm. "No, there was none of that," he said. When she refused to move, he asked, "Please? We don't want to be out after dark. You've taken enough risks for one day."

Katy got to her feet, reached over, and grabbed another dish towel. She dried her face while Cathal guided her. "Have you considered that he may not have been killed in his quarters?"

"Well, we found him outside. Maybe they killed him there," Ben pointed out.

Katy shook her head and explained, "He was only wearing a robe, so obviously he was in the station, then dragged to an airlock. I doubt whoever did this would want to carry him very far. If we could figure out which airlock he came out of, we might be able to get a better idea where the murder took place."

"I'm pulling up a map of the station," Cormack said looking at his monitor.

Cathal cut him off and said, "Wait. I'll use mine. I've got topographical data for the whole surface of the asteroid, including how far the gravity field extends. We should be able to calculate where he came from based on where he landed." He nodded to Katy and Cormack came over, taking her arm to guide her as they made their way down the corridor. Cormack turned his own monitor around, using the light from the screen to guide them.

There were small bulbs strung along the walls, but they were dim.

"It's fine, I've got it," Katy said as she opened her guide stick and took the lead in the corridor, "Just tell me when I reach the turn," she said as she started the count in her head.

"Yeah, but if they had a spacesuit on, then they could've dragged him," Ben said.

"I doubt it," Cormack said. "Those suits are tough to get on and whoever did this just killed a monk. They were probably in a hurry and used one of the emergency masks. They're inside every airlock, but they don't offer any protection against hard vacuum or radiation. They probably got in there quick, got rid of the body, and hurried off."

"Inside every airlock except for the one you guys use to execute people in," Ben muttered.

Everyone ignored the comment, waiting for Cathal, who was working out the calculations as they walked. His fingers moved quickly over the monitor, using formulas that weren't all that different from the ones in combat, projecting the path of projectiles and shrapnel. Combat in space was all about math, predicting the movement of objects. "I wouldn't discount Ben's theory just yet," Cathal said looking up from his monitor and scratching his beard. "For the body to be that far from the school, even if someone really strong threw him, he'd have to have come from a height. The only place that's even close to tall enough is the lighthouse."

Katy started, "We should go check it out—"

"Nope," Ben cut her off.

"Only the monks are allowed in there," Cormack pointed out as they reached the turn. Katy almost went past it, but Cormack gently touched her shoulder and guided her.

Katy stopped for a moment, looked up, and said, "Seven forty-two, then a left."

"Have you been counting this whole time?" Ben asked.

"Dining hall to domicile hall." Katy nodded.

Cathal was still looking at the monitor, checking his calculations. "I'll have to talk to the monks about getting in the lighthouse tomorrow. If they actually want this murder solved, they'll have to let me in. For now, I want you all back in the Sidhe Domicile."

The boys started off, but Katy stood there for a moment more and asked, "So, if the lighthouse is only for monks, Fafnir wouldn't be able to get in there?"

"Why?" Cathal asked.

Katy seemed reluctant as she said, "Well, you said whoever threw him had to be strong. Ben mentioned that Fafnir was pretty angry even before the new Kavaris arrived and, well, I've heard rumblings. I think it might be worth talking to him."

Cathal looked down at his monitor. "I hadn't considered Fafnir's strength. It might even change some of my calculations. I'll check into it. Talk to him, that is."

"If you do, bring back up," Ben said, coming back to take Katy's arm. "That guy seems like he's itching for a fight."

Cathal nodded, then headed off into the dark as Cormack, Katy, and Ben passed the Sidhe guards and entered the domicile.

Chapter 23

High above Tairnish, Tara was back in the interview room. She was exhausted. It'd been an entire day of negotiating and she felt like she'd gotten nowhere. Mainly because whatever she offered the Tairnishmen meant nothing, but she had to pretend like it did. She was playing for time. They were tracking the emperor's fleet and his command ship, The Revenant. It would be within weapons range in twelve hours.

The Tairnishman across from her was named Rolfe Yulset, first of his commune, the Gullatoch. They didn't hold as high a position of authority as the Bogatyr, Victor's people, but according to him, they'd been given the power to negotiate with the emperor or his proxy. It could've been a lie, but Tara doubted it. The rules that governed Tairnishmen were rigid and inflexible. Their government lacked the instability of the imperial system of Uppsala, where different nobles vied for superiority. Even the emperor wasn't immune to the constant games.

Rolfe Yulset was intelligent, but he wasn't very skilled at deception. Not that he could've lied to Tara. What he wanted was clear, a future for his people. Since the last war and with the peace brought on by the Æesir's strict guidance, the position of the Tairnishmen, warriors and weapon makers, had become tenuous. Victor's death had only been the catalyst for a revolt that had been building for years.

Already Tara had tentatively agreed to give up the construction ring around Tairnish. She'd even offered relief supplies from Uppsala, but now Yulset was demanding more. "What good is this damn dock without the fuel to launch from the surface? Or to seek out resources in the system like those in the rings around Altor?"

"You wish to mine the rings and you wish to use the emperor's fuel depots?" Tara asked raising her pale white eyebrow.

"We wish a contract with the nobles of Oighear. One that no longer goes through the emperor. And the rings of Altor don't belong to the Tamerlanes. They should be free territory for all, at least that's what the people of Grannus say and we agree with them. A people should be able to carve out their own destiny."

Tara snorted. "Our emperor doesn't give a damn about your destiny. What you're asking would give those on Oighear too much independence. The emperor would never allow it and as far as the asteroids in Altor's rings go, all that material belongs to the empire. Any mining that took place there was done by squatters and you remember what happened to them."

Yulset sat back. "Oh, I remember. We wiped them out for Tamerlane. The whole time wondering why we weren't being stopped by the gods. I led men down into those caverns and butchered families of skinny spacers. Of course, I don't know how you can call a people who've lived in a place for generations 'squatters.' Some of those colonies looked more ancient than anything here, but I suppose since they were altered, like me and my people, they don't really count as human."

Tara sensed that he wasn't actually upset. He didn't care all that much about the people he killed, so she chose not to respond.

"Oighear is different though. They're regular people and your empire placed them there. They're loyal to Uppsala, aren't they? Are you telling me you'd lose control by giving them such a small taste of freedom? How fragile is this empire?"

"Controlling the emperor's domain is an act of balance. What you ask would move forces besides yours.

It would put too many things in flux, upsetting the order. Your only concern should be for Tairnish."

Yulset shook his head. "Perhaps I will discuss this with Tamerlane himself when he arrives."

Tara crossed her arms. "Fine. But it won't be in this room. I promise you that. If you want to get anywhere, it will be here with me. Either that, or you can pack your things and make yourself ready to board The Revenant, to speak to the emperor in his own territory. Trust me, this room is much more comfortable for you anyway."

Yulset could sense her threat. "Comfort means very little to a Tairnishman. Do you think it matters to a princess?" He slammed his fist on the table again. This was his favorite move even though it had stopped making Tara flinch a while ago. She could tell it bothered him how unafraid she was.

He sat back and considered a new tactic. "Tell me, Tara. You are young. Do you someday wish to have children?"

Much of the negotiation had been Yulset airing his grievances against the nobles of Uppsala, calling into question their entire, degenerate society. Tara had remained calm through all his blustering, never becoming offended or disagreeing with him.

Andavarri, who had been there for the first few hours, had grown tired of it and left. Yulset had tried time and again to get her to turn against their ways as he pointed out the superiority of his own people, repeating practiced rhetoric. Perhaps that's what he was trying now.

"I haven't really considered it," Tara said. "I suppose it will be required by my family if for no other reason than to continue my line."

"You've no choice?" Yulset asked.

"Very little. There are expectations, or there would be under other circumstances." Tara's gaze went to the floor.

"Please elaborate," Yulset asked.

"My father stood against the emperor. He and a number of rulers from the north banded together. We were the last kingdoms to fall on Uppsala." Tara brought her eyes up as she sighed and asked, "Surely you must know all this?"

"I rarely find myself interested in the politics of your world, but I suppose you're right. I know who your father was."

"Is. You know who my father is. He still lives. Still rules." Tara corrected.

"Under the emperor," Yulset said.

"As are all things on Uppsala." Tara nodded.

"So, who will decide when it's time for you to have children? Your father, your emperor, or your princess."

Tara sat back. "I'm sure I'll be the last to know."

"Because you are a hostage?" He smiled.

"Among many other things, but you see my father rules still because he knows one thing."

"What's that?"

"That you can't fight the will of the emperor. It's like standing against the tide. That's what you've chosen to do here. Take the Ring. Take the supplies I've offered you. Don't ask anymore and return Maeven. It's your only choice."

"No, you're wrong. We've studied you people. We see how your games are played. Maeven will remain just the same as you, a hostage."

Tara shook her head. "The emperor will be here tomorrow."

"Do you think we will be any more willing to budge with a gun to our head?"

"I have no idea, but the gun will be there. I will speak to the emperor tonight and tell him your demands."

Yulset pushed back from the table and motioned towards the open door. "I think tomorrow you will only bring me more threats. I think tomorrow you'll have the emperor's promise to destroy us and at the end of the day we'll still have this Ring and his daughter."

Tara got up and started pulling herself through the zero-g towards the door. "I think tomorrow the emperor is going to surprise you."

"I certainly hope so," Yulset said, clearly not understanding what Tara meant. He was wrong thinking Maeven's life was enough to stall Tamerlane. She knew exactly what the emperor's strategy would be. He wouldn't risk giving these people a lifeline. No matter what terms they came to, he had to crush them to keep them from coming back stronger.

Tara moved down the module hall, using the rungs and open hatches. Behind her and in front were armed guards, bulky Tairnishmen in their combat armor that made the space feel tight.

In the larger construction modules, there was more room, but this was an administration hub, made for the middle management that used to inhabit the ring, built for efficiency, not comfort. A few average-sized people could pass each way without a problem, but two Tairnishmen next to each other, in armor, filled the span between one curved wall and the other. It only widened out when she reached the dock.

They came to the shuttle's airlock and one of the guards opened it for her.

The Tairnishmen stayed outside, taking up positions on either side of the lock. One thing Tara managed to get from Yulset, was having the shuttle declared sovereign territory. Of course, that meant when the exchange of weapons fire returned, the shuttle would be first on the target list.

Tara went through the cargo hold and into the crew quarters. Andavarri was waiting for her, curled on her bunk, looking like a sleeping dog. She glanced up. "Finally, I thought that man would never stop whining."

"They're a proud people," Tara said while thinking of her own father, a servant to the emperor her entire life.

"What do these people have to be proud of?" Andavarri asked. "They're on borrowed land, serving a different world. Now they have the audacity to become bothersome while they commit suicide."

"Are you worried about your people getting caught in the crossfire?" Tara asked. It was an honest question.

Andavarri smiled her toothy grin but didn't answer. "You have a message," she pointed towards the flight deck. "It's from Tamerlane."

Tara nodded and climbed up. She knew he probably wanted an update on the surface but there was nothing to tell. They'd been gone for thirty-two hours, a night and a day. She opened the comms anyway, channeling it through encryption. The delay was only a few minutes. He was getting closer with every minute.

∞

'This doesn't look like a mine anymore,' Alex thought. He'd noticed the way the walls changed, no more tool marks and no supports holding up the ceiling. This made him nervous enough, but after seeing those wild Fire-Golems appear from the rock, he questioned if the tunnels they were in were natural or the result of those creatures. That made him wonder if more might be closing in on them now, tunneling through the stone.

"Do you think I ought to scan the rock for vibrations?" he asked Edith.

She never stopped moving as she shot back, "Why?"

"In case those creatures are following us." Alex watched every wall with suspicion. If they were attacked, he worried that setting off another grenade packed with the countermeasure would bury them beneath miles of rock. The walls felt even tighter as he thought of it and they were already as close as could be for the armor.

Ben had been fascinated by the Golems, certain they were special and it was true. There was more to them than the Long-Wolves had said. Now Alex wished he'd been more curious and had the time to be like Amita, but his focus was keeping his people alive. It'd been his only goal since they arrived at Nalanda. Sure, it'd be great to know what the Fire-Golems were or exactly what happened to them, what brought them here, but that information meant nothing if they were dead.

He thought of Amita and wondered how she was doing. 'Was she my people?' The idea slipped into his head unbidden. He tried to chase it away, but that only brought it further into focus as he wondered what they actually shared. That they'd both come from Earth, was that it?

Their home seemed so far away. Only a few weeks had gone by, but it felt much longer and he'd spent most of that time with Edith and Maeven while Amita had closed herself off on the station. Not that she'd been in her quarters weeping or anything. She'd been trying to find them a way home. It wasn't the first time Alex wondered if she were right, if that would've been a better tactic, but then he remembered her in that cell, locked away for asking questions. What he was doing, carving a place out for them, that was the right move. Even if it meant doing things he didn't want to.

The tunnel walls were tight forcing the armor to crawl as it broke through stone. It was easy work for Alex, less so for Edith, who had her rifle slung on her back while she moved over the dark, strangely smooth tunnel. They were descending, going deeper and deeper into Tairnish.

Edith slid down a sharp decline, then called back to him. "I think we're there." He came over the rise and saw her below with her hands on a flat surface, a type of dark concrete. "This is the outer wall of their commune," she said.

"How thick is it?" he asked from above, clinging to the cave floor like a massive spider.

"Thick," Edith said. "At least a meter or more. The good news is Tairnishmen have no imagination. They build everything pretty much the same so once we're through, we should be able to pick a path relatively quickly. In your files, you'll find ten or twelve standard designs for Tairnish communes. Once we're through. I want you to throw a radar ping, then pick the one that's the closest fit and upload it to my HUD. We're going to split up from there."

Inside the armor Alex nodded, then he said aloud, "Okay. So how are we getting in there?"

Edith moved to the side. "Come down and join me."

Alex moved the armor down with care, trying not to crush her. Near the wall, there was a small void where he was able to turn around and get his legs below him, though it was still an incredibly tight squeeze. He could feel the armor crunching and scratching against the stone and the flat surface of the foundation.

"In your weapons inventory, you should have a plasma torch. I'm going to need you to cut a hole a half meter deep. We'll pack it with those canisters on your back and let them do the rest of the work."

Alex had noticed the cans, but he hadn't asked about them. He was glad they hadn't gotten into a firefight. Then he thought of the drop ship and their flight to the surface, how hot the surface of the armor had gotten. "Those are explosives?" he asked.

"Don't worry they're chemically inert for now. You could put them in an oven and they wouldn't go off, not till we mix them. That's when we need to be careful."

"Sounds fun." Alex didn't feel as assured as he tried to sound.

Edith ran her hand over the wall, then tapped it once. "Here, spark the torch and start cutting." She backed up. Alex looked through the menus on his screen and brought the torch up. It was attached to his left arm. He blinked in an activation code, and it sparked to life. A sensor behind the torch was giving measurements for his cut.

Edith's voice came on a direct channel above the sound of cement being melted. "Listen, our strategy is pretty simple. We blow the wall, then you're going to make your way in a straight line to the hanger bay. There can be no hesitation. You need to eliminate anything that gets in your way. And I mean anything."

Alex kept cutting as he asked, "Anything?"

Edith nodded. "Tairnishmen are all warriors, even their kids are raised to kill. They know how to fire weapons and throw grenades as soon as they can walk. If they come in your target scope, you'll have to pull the trigger and keep moving. If you stop, you're dead. Find the hangar bay. I'm going to want you to make a lot of noise."

"I'm the distraction?" Alex asked, feeling a strange urge to laugh as he tried to ignore the first part of what she said. The idea that anyone would send children to fight seemed unreal. 'It's fine, it's fine,' a voice said in his head. 'They won't be there.'

"You're a three-meter-tall killing machine. Yes, you are the distraction. Leave the other part to me. I'll be going after Maeven while you wake up the whole neighborhood." Edith took the canisters from his back and squatted down. She placed them on the ground and examined them, moving like a mechanic.

Inside the suit, Alex tried to focus on the work, but somewhere in the back of his head it occurred to him that the word 'commune' didn't mean military base, it meant people lived there. He thought about his grandfather for a moment, a man he'd only met a few times before he died of cancer.

He remembered the old man was a soldier like his father, but he hadn't been given a choice about it. Drafted on his eighteenth birthday and sent to Vietnam like so many young African American men, Alex's grandfather had only been a year older than he was now when he saw combat. He had metals on the wall, that he never talked about. His silence was the one thing his father and grandfather shared. They never spoke about the things they saw or did.

'It changed them and it's going to change me,' Alex thought as the sensor registered a half meter. He thought of the old man sitting in the living room of his cramped apartment, hardly ever smiling, radiating a constant surly rage, even around his grandkids, though he did his best to hide it. Alex's dad was lighter, trying to be a good father despite the weight of his work. His dad chose to be a SEAL, but he never saw his father turn humorless or dark about it, not till the day Alex said he wanted to do it as well.

A part of Alex screamed, 'Go! Runaway! You don't have to do this.' It wasn't fear. Alex knew how to control that, how to ride the peak and use it on the wrestling mat or in the dojo. What was telling him to run was the knowledge that he'd never be the same again. 'Maybe I won't survive,' he thought and it felt like a relief as he said aloud, "What are the odds I'm actually going to make it to the hanger bay." He stowed the torch and stepped back away from the burnt hole.

"I'll be honest, the odds of success are pretty low." Edith pointed back up the incline. "Get yourself up there, away from the wall. When this goes off, it's going to be pretty impressive." Alex started climbing. He stopped short and Edith told him to keep going. "Try to get some rock between you and this wall."

She combined the contents making a paste. She pushed it into the hole and placed an electronic fuse in it. Then she took a can and sprayed a liquid that expanded and closed the hole back in. Her voice came over the closed channel, "You're not afraid of dying, are you, Alex?"

Alex was looking up the tunnel, the way they'd come. The thought of climbing further, of going and leaving her behind occurred to him. "No, I'm not afraid," he said after a moment.

"I know you're not. It's the other thing, isn't it? The killing?" She scurried up towards him.

"Yeah," he admitted.

"Look, I need a distraction. That's all. I'm here to retrieve a high-value hostage. That's my mission. Your participation is up to you, but I need you to go through that wall and make a lot of noise. Your survival isn't necessary for my success, but I'd like to see you stay alive. I'd like to see who you're going to become. The emperor is coming and he's going to wipe out all these people. They're already dead. If you run and you get to the surface without a ride, you'll be dead too. So, you decide, Alex. I know you're not afraid of dying. Dying is easy. Being the last one standing, well that's a bit tougher. We save Maeven, get her back to her father and you're going to see a lot of doors open."

Edith stepped back behind the armor and said, "Times up." The explosion was quick, blasting heat and debris deep into the tunnel. Alex felt the force through the armor, like being punched with a tree trunk. The

235

walls continued to shake as the noise died away. Alex turned and watched Edith move down the slope. Her sidearm was out. She glanced back at him once, then disappeared into the hole.

Chapter 24

Leaving the hidden Long-Wolf cavern, Tearmai returned to the dark, getting a head start on Amita, lumbering through the gaping entrance into the blackness beyond. Amita was bending over the body of the dead Long-Wolf, checking to see if the creature was truly gone. She found no sign of life, no chest rise, or air moving past her long sharp teeth. She wondered, 'What would I do if she were alive? Leave her here to suffer? Snuff her out?' The thought made her sick. Perhaps that was why Tearmai was in such a hurry to get away from the body, so he wouldn't be reminded that he too was a killer.

She tried to look at the pale purple corpse with academic distance, not to think of it as someone who had just been talking to her. It was hard not to feel shaken with the vast cavern behind her and the darkness in front and this body, this dead thing growing cold next to her. Something else was bothering her, a tickling at her brain, an uncomfortable sense that even though this Long-Wolf was dead, she and Tearmai weren't alone.

She looked around at all the open windows carved into the rock, climbing high and away, and wondered if there were eyes on her even now looking down. Somehow, she knew they were as empty as the eye sockets on a skull, but the one in front of her, the one Tearmai had moved into with unwavering determination, it wasn't a window, but a door, and something was in there waiting for them.

The dark platform she stood on curved into the entry, its black surface penetrating the rock, bleeding into it, and forming a ring along the edges of the unnatural cavity. The construction reminded her of the understructures of Nalanda, like a living metal had done the work, spreading and infecting the rock wall.

She held the Long-Wolf's rifle with the barrel pointed toward the ground. It was longer and heavier than her. As she stepped forward, she turned the weapon as the guardian had, using it as a staff, wondering how fast she'd be able to bring the unwieldy thing up to bear.

Through her environmental suit, she could feel the hairs on her arms stand up as she crossed the threshold. Past the opening, it was impossible to see, the darkness was so complete with only a little light filtering in from the cavern outside. She could hear Tearmai's footsteps out in front of her. They sounded far away. Something was wrong with her helmet light. She tried to adjust it, tried to make a wider beam.

It was pointless. As soon as she crossed the threshold, her light faded and cut out. She checked her batteries and noticed that the indicators were dark as well. They'd been low before, but now they were unresponsive, dead as could be.

She was shuffling her feet, moving forward reluctantly, breathing rapidly as her face plate started to fog. A few steps in she felt the rifle catch on the floor and by accident, she dropped it losing it in the inky blackness. Her hands went to her helmet and searched for the clasps. The filters cleaning the Tairnish air were automatic, but without the batteries powering the suit, she suddenly became claustrophobic.

Pulling the helmet off, she anticipated the foul stench from the surface, but down here the warmth was far more shocking as she took a breath that felt as if it came from an oven. Luckily, the cooling system in her suit worked automatically, using a gel substance in the lining that maintained her body temp.

Looking around at the blackness she thought, 'Hell is probably this dark,' and immediately regretted it. Amita was not a religious person. Her parents were engineers. Science was their faith. Only the generation before them, her grandparents worried about such things. Her Nani especially loved to warn Amita of Naraka, the darkness, in the Hindu faith. She hated those stories, though she preferred them to the Christian beliefs, because at least there was a possibility of escape, redemption, and rebirth.

'Why am I even thinking about this,' she wondered as she called out into the overwhelming shadows, "Tearmai?"

He grunted but didn't really answer. Still, Amita heard his footsteps turn back toward her. She felt lost in the dark and tried going closer to the wall, nearly falling over broken stones scattered across the floor.

She leaned down, hands out so she wouldn't trip again, and found the surface littered with rocks that were shaped into half-formed limbs and appendages, like busted statues. She felt claws and fingers like a Long-Wolf's. Her hand ran over them and eventually picked one up. She held it for a moment while she called into the dark again, "Tearmai?" She was trying to ignore the way her heart raced.

He didn't even grunt this time, but she could still hear his footsteps. They dragged along the floor back toward her. There was a pressure in the air, a charge of energy that felt more intense near the walls as the cavern became lighter.

A red glow slowly illuminated the space. Amita hadn't realized how close she was to the wall as she peered through the dark, sensing the stone. It emanated a subtle red light seeping from the rock itself as the wall twisted and moved. "Oh, no!" The memory of the wild Fire-Golems returned and Amita tried to scurry back. She tripped, feeling the broken stones below her poke through her suit.

This was the same light, but so much closer, only inches from her face. The red-hot stone took form as molten, long, clawed fingers reached toward her, desperately trying to grasp anything.

"Don't touch it," Tearmai warned. He was closer than she expected, bathed in the hellish light. He pointed to the floor where a piece of heavy metal was fastened. Amita glanced at it for only a moment, but her attention was taken away as those hands came closer. The fingers stretched toward her, clasping, and closing. Then the dark metal bar on the floor pulsed and she felt the pressure increase. It vibrated the air like a discordant note played on a broken instrument and the hands dropped away, tumbling to the floor.

"It keeps them at bay." Tearmai's voice rumbled, sounding frail and hollow.

Amita scurried back and muttered while the light from the walls remained. It bathed everything in a red glow as the rock continued to shift. "What was that?" Tearmai asked her.

Amita didn't know that she'd said anything, that she was muttering like a crazy person. "Nothing," she said, not wanting to tell Tearmai that she was praying. The hands still stretched towards them, dozens of them, but the metal bar pulsed another time and the limbs dropped away once more, crashing with a heavy thump to the floor, either shattering into volcanic pieces or splashing with liquid rock. The process repeated again and again as Amita got to her feet and went to the center of the cavern.

The heat became too much so she pulled her helmet on in the hope of closing her cooling system. In the red glow, she turned to Tearmai and saw the wound weeping from his side. "The patch isn't holding," she said.

"No but— It doesn't matter." Tearmai turned and started off again, taking one pained step after another. "There's more we must do. More you must see."

Amita called after him. "Enough with the mystery. Tell me where we're going."

Tearmai didn't look back. He kept walking, leaving a trail of blood behind as he said, "You'll hear its voice soon. Brash taught it to speak."

Amita clenched her fists in frustration and glanced back at the light in the larger cavern where the rockets waited. Before she followed him, she looked for the rifle. In the red light, she could see it near the wall, but she shook her head, knowing it was pointless. 'What could it do against Fire-Golems?'

She hurried to catch up and stayed close to Tearmai as they followed the glowing walls. "Look, I know you're hurt and that whatever this is down here, that you think I need to see, is very important, but my only concern is getting home. You've done that. You went to Earth. You have to tell me how." She tried holding his arm, but it was so wide around that she couldn't grip it. She had to use both hands and hang on him to slow him down.

Tearmai stopped. His breath was heavy and slow as he answered. "It was Brash's idea. He wanted to go back before this all happened . . . before the genocide."

"Before the incident?" Amita added.

Tearmai nodded. "Yes."

"So, when we came through the wormhole, we didn't just come out in another star system. This is another time. The future. This is where people, my people ended up when the wormhole got out of control."

Tearmai nodded and gently pulled his arm free of her grasp. "Your world has been lost for a long time."

Amita's brain was rushing, thinking about the rockets outside, about Brash, and about the movement of time. "But is it?" she asked.

Tearmai didn't answer as he started ahead again, walking on with heavy resolve.

So many thoughts hurried through Amita's head. She needed time to think and consider, but Tearmai wasn't going to stop. She looked at the ceiling and saw more of the heavy metal rails attached to the rock. They looked like the platform outside, almost organic. Placed roughly every two meters, they ran in a circle down the rounded tunnel. Though the darkness of their surface was nearly complete, so black they absorbed the light of the glowing stone walls. They seemed to throb with energy, vibrating with so much power that Amita could feel it in her skull as an unpleasant buzzing. Below her were heavy black ceramic tiles. She felt them shaking and was certain that the rails ran below them as well, forming a cage, protection against the wild Fire-Golems. It reminded her of something besides Nalanda.

"What about the hunter?" Amita asked. "It came to stop you two, but who sent it?" They'd reached another threshold. It was smaller but still outlined by that strange metal. Tearmai stepped through and Amita followed him, leaving the red-glowing tunnel behind. As she crossed, her helmet light suddenly snapped back on and pointed its beam out into a crystal room, reflecting back off curving walls.

Tearmai kept going, not even glancing up as they entered the tall shining chamber. The walls climbed above them turning in and forming a single peak. It reminded Amita of the inside of the diamond vessel, the one they rode through the wormhole, only on a much larger scale and less organized. Patterns of color danced in her light, pink and blue returning to her in shades she'd never seen before.

In the center of the chamber was an altar made from that black metal, rising above the floor of broken stones dragged in from the outside. Tearmai didn't slow as he made his way toward the dark alloy object that absorbed the light of Amita's helmet with perfect blackness. She didn't like looking at it, preferring to examine the crystal walls instead. They went deep into the cliffside, further than just what she was seeing. She was at the top of something massive that plunged far into the heart of Tairnish.

Crystals grew on the altar, looking like hundreds of melted candles as they clung to its dark surface. Tearmai finally slowed, stalled in frightful expectation before the dark thing. "I know very little about the hunter," he said over his shoulder. "There are rumors and stories from the dead world of such horrible things."

"But you said you were attacked."

There were steps before the altar. He took the first one, keeping his eyes forward. The dark thing was like the top of an anchor with elaborate carvings on its side. As Amita stared, she thought she saw an internal light dance and sway beneath the surface of the crystals that littered it. Another step and Tearmai carefully reached out and touched the altar. When he saw it was safe, he leaned forward a little, searching over it.

"Tearmai, you said you were attacked," Amita called again, trying to keep his attention.

"Yes," he said as his hand came up and ran back over his thick skull. He shook his head a little. "When I was young." He finally, looked at her over his shoulder with one eye. "There is a forest on Uppsala. Once it covered the entire world, aside from the oceans and lakes. It's still there but so much smaller. Humans call what's left the preserve. The monks said it must not be touched, that the Æesir wished it to be protected. It's where I was born. We could hide things there.

Tearmai slowly shook his head from side to side. "Brash was the last of his people, not even born yet. The last we could keep safe. He emerged from his chrysalis and dozens of us, my family, and friends were there to protect him. Some were as big as Fafnir. When the hunter came, he looked like a man. They told me to escape with Brash, get him to the monks.

"I did it with Brash's help. He quickened my thoughts, but my family. . . The hunter went through them. He wouldn't cross into the temple though, even that abomination wouldn't risk the wrath of the Æesir. So, it was the monks who saved us and took us to Nalanda."

Amita touched her chin. "Did the hunter follow you back to Earth to stop Brash, or just to murder him? He's some sort of machine following a program, but who controls the machine?"

Tearmai shrugged. "Does it matter?"

"Of course, it matters. It all matters. I'll have to face him again if I go back—"

Tearmai cut her off. "You passed through the void but didn't see." He banged his chest, breathing deep. "I've seen it laid out repeating again, and again, the broken pieces of failure! It won't work. It never works. Forget the past. Only here matters. Right now."

"How can you say that? You tell me there's a chance to go back in time. To stop all this and you expect me to ignore it."

"I'm telling you there is no chance. I wasn't alone. I followed him through the void."

It took Amita only a second before she called, "Yes, Brash. And he came back here. So, I have to find him. That's what you're telling me?" Amita asked while reaching out as if grasping something.   ·

Tearmai shook his head, then turned and searched the altar. His breathing was becoming more ragged. Finally, he seemed to give up. He chose a piece of crystal from the top and snapped it off. Then he started down the steps intent on handing the piece to Amita. As he went, he held his side and collapsed, tumbling and nearly falling on top of her. Amita went to his side, realizing her friend's wound was worse than she thought.

He looked up at her and placed something in her hand. It was a heavy hunk of metal, still warm from his touch. Amita recognized it as the thing the Long-Wolf guardian had worn around her neck. "What is this?"

Tearmai placed the crystal in her other hand. It still glowed with an internal light. "It's a key." His hand touched her shoulder gently. "Focus on now. This moment. You must free the slave. No one should live this long in chains."

Amita stared at the crystal and felt even more that she wasn't alone. Something was calling to her, asking her for help. Amita's eyes went to the far wall where she saw an opening and a black door sealed tight. It was made from metal like the rails and the anchor, like a tumor in the crystal wall. "You want me to follow it?"

Tearmai nodded.

"What about you?" Amita asked.

"I need to rest. I'll be okay here, but you must go," he said.

Chapter 25

Kilometers from Amita but not nearly as deep, Edith moved without waiting for the rumbling in the foundation of the commune to settle. She pushed her way through the breach that had been smashed into the concrete barricade, then broke left at random, going down a corridor before squeezing tight against the wall where she waited for Alex to follow instructions.

With her sidearm drawn, she activated her hearing aids. It was hard to tell, but Edith was mostly deaf, which came in handy around extremely loud explosions. Her advanced hearing aids linked to her helmet. Placed in her ears after she returned from Grannus, they were better than what most veterans could expect. Edith had earned them by going native and gathering intel on the Grannusians, by bringing something valuable back to her emperor. She thought about that time as she checked her adaptive camouflage, sending a surge of static through its surface to clear the dust, then she checked the armor against the walls.

Her breathing was slow and calm as she waited for the upload from the battle armor. Her suit had sensors too but they weren't as robust as Alex's. She could've used them to paint her immediate surroundings and pick up any approaching forces. The only problem was it would light her up on every security screen in the commune and make her a target.

With practiced patience, she waited while alarms sounded through the commune and strobes glared. The walls were still rumbling, but above that ruckus, she heard the armor push through the breach. 'Good,' she thought as she surveyed every corner.

Two forms approached, adults, not wearing armor. They never saw Edith move as she pointed her weapon and pulled the trigger twice. Muffled shots thumped from the barrel and the bodies collapsed. She changed position as they hit the ground and fired twice more as insurance, checking the next set of corners.

The upload came through as she listened to Alex smash through the wall, making the opening large enough for the battle armor. He sent her the map and data from his scan, then her HUD quickly updated the layout of the structure. Edith glanced back once and saw the battle armor push its way in. The tank on legs was covered in debris as it pulled itself through. It stood half-stooped in the hall and Edith said, "Good luck," before hurrying off, putting distance between herself and Alex.

Busting in a door, she ducked inside and examined the new data. The commune was massive, even larger than Edith expected. She marked the hanger bays and launch pads, stories above. They were a good distance from the main body of the commune too, almost a click to the west, but there were transports nearby. She searched for anything that looked like holding cells and found something near the center of the facility, close to their main security hub, three levels above. The good news was that everyone there would be coming here to stop Alex.

Edith heard a muffled sound. Three slow shots followed by three more. That wasn't Alex. Edith could tell by the sound that the kid hadn't used any of his ordinance yet. Someone else was firing at him. If she had to guess, it was a riot gun or hunting rifle, probably for personal use. It wouldn't do a thing against the armor. She heard slamming and banging as Alex pushed on and broke through bulkheads, but still not firing a single shot.

"You're going to have to pull the trigger eventually," Edith said to herself as she examined the map. She wished she could open comms and tell him, but she didn't want the signal picked up. Alex was on his own.

She searched for points of egress between floors. There were stairs every fifty meters down each hall. That was handy, but right now they'd be flooded with soldiers coming up. There were lifts as well, but she guessed those would be locked down during an emergency.

Knowing the Tairnish, the ventilation systems were alarmed. She came across one spot that probably wasn't being watched and that would give her a clear path to the levels below security. "Well, crap," Edith said, going back into the hall.

She could hear more weapon fire. None of it matched what she knew the battle armor carried. She was scanning, listening to the Tairnish channels. They had Alex pinpointed. There were hundreds of armed guards moving toward him.

If he didn't start fighting, he wasn't going to survive. Finally, she heard the high-pitched whine of the rotary cannon mounted on the battle armor's left arm. It was impossible to pick out individual rounds as they were fired too fast, sounding like a deafening buzz. "About damn time," Edith muttered as she threw her shoulder into another door. It wasn't locked, but she came in fast anyway. Quickly clearing the space with her weapon, she bashed in the stalls of the communal washroom.

Tairnishmen didn't have individual bathrooms in their apartments, at least not the common folks. Higher-ups, administrators, and their families might. At least twenty or thirty people shared a facility like this and this one had the extra benefit of being near a drainpipe.

She'd seen it on the diagram. The returns for the water reclamation system on every level ran into large pipes, then into central drainage tubes that went directly to the commune's reclamation facility on the bottom level. It was a massive area with tall ceilings. The only thing between it and the holding cells were two floors worth of farms. The Tairnish may stack housing tight, but these two essential services claimed far more space, several floors each. Edith thought, 'Not a lot of cover, but probably not a lot of witnesses.'

Edith went straight toward the back wall of the gang shower, holstering her sidearm. She turned her armor's augmented strength to the max and put her fist through the wall. With fast chops along the ceramic tiles, she made a large opening, then pulled the entire wall away.

Inside the dark space, steel floor braces ran one way while pipes came in from every direction meeting below her at a central tube. It came down from the floor above and was two meters around. Edith took her torch from her belt and sparked it to life. She started slicing into the solid surface while outside the walls shook with explosions.

'Rocket-propelled grenades,' she wondered if Alex was firing them or if that were the Tairnishmen. The metal side of the tube fell away and she glanced down inside to see the slimy surface as she sealed her armor. She'd use her suit's limited supply of compressed air as she made her descent.

There was a cable attached to her waist harness and she thought of hooking it around one of the floor supports, but she knew there wasn't enough to get her all the way to the bottom of the commune. Climbing into the opening untethered, she tried to control her descent with her legs and arms pressed against the side.

It didn't work. She slipped a little, then a little more against the damp surface. A few meters down a chuck of something awful broke off under her foot. Rather than trying to stop herself, Edith made the call to close her body tight and let go. She plummeted through the pipe, the armor absorbing most of the impacts against the metal walls.

It didn't take long to fall three stories and splash down at the bottom of the sewer pipe, but the last few meters were like being inside a straw, buried in sewage. The liquid level had risen high, equal to the tank outside.

It forced Edith to swim down to find the exit, but with such tight walls, swimming was nearly impossible. She walked her hands and feet down the last stretch of pipe and pushed against the disgusting surface. She felt her foot touch the lip, then tugged herself down and out into the reclamation tank.

When she surfaced, she was grateful she hadn't wasted the line on her harness. Around her were giant cement walls of a vat with no obvious way out. She was swimming in raw sewage. There were massive propeller blades moving slowly through it, separating liquid from solid. Edith climbed on one of the blades and took a small hook that she tossed towards the walkway above. She felt it grab onto one of the rails, then tugged herself up and over the side.

Glancing back at the vat of waste, she was glad she had the back-up air supply. For a second, she wondered what color her active camo had turned, but she chased the thought away with a smirk, shaking her head as she unshouldered her rifle.

Slowly, using her scope, she scanned the massive industrial space. It was hard to see with so many corners and machines, so she risked a quick ping with her radar, searching for people. She assumed there wouldn't be many security sensors in here. The toxic fumes caused havoc with electronic monitoring. Luckily, none of the workers she found had a clear sightline to her.

On the far side of the room, she saw a large conveyor lift next to a pile of processed waste, fertilizer for the farms. It was a massive industrial machine, going at an angle between the levels with a belt constantly running. 'There's my next ride,' Edith thought as she came down off the walkway.

She checked every corner as she went, moving fast, making up time as she got closer and closer to the security office, even though she was floors below it. She reached the conveyor and saw two men with shovels. They were talking to each other, dressed in coveralls, and wearing respirators.

Edith wasn't sure what they'd done to deserve this job but she felt like she was doing them a favor as she pointed her sidearm. Without hesitation, she pulled the trigger, then with quick strides she approached the fallen bodies. She stopped for only a moment to sit the two large Tairnishmen up, propping them against the side of the machine.

"Napping on the job, really guys?" she said. The gore around their respirators from the two clean head shots didn't bother her in the least. She glanced at the conveyor lift and looked for any nasty surprises inside. The passage was clear. The machine was simple, a constantly running belt in a narrow shaft made to lift fertilizer to the floors above. She jumped on, lying flat as she rode it up to the farm level.

A vast green area passed below her as she stayed on the belt, riding it through to another floor. It climbed above a second farm and ended. The belt turned, flattening for a moment before going back under its runners and traveling to the beginning in a constantly moving circle.

Before the turn she dropped into a hopper that was on a rail high over the farm ground. She peered over the side, down at the acres and acres of plants all in neat rows, going on forever. Sitting on a pile of fertilizer she pulled up the map again. She was now directly below the security office, hanging ten meters in the air above a farm.

There were roof trusses over her, holding up the next floor. Not far across the room, she saw an open stairwell squeezed between two ugly concrete pillars. Edith reached up to the roof truss and gripped it. She brought her legs up and clung there, then hand over hand she started pulling herself across. Her active camo turned gray, blending to the ceiling. Not that she had to worry. Even if she'd fallen, no one would've noticed her because the farm was empty. Alarms buzzed away on distant walls, letting everyone know they were under attack. Normal people would've gone to hide, but Edith knew that wasn't what they were doing. These were Tairnishmen and women. They were all going to the same place, with the same purpose, to kill Alex.

∞

When Alex finally activated his rotary cannon, he meant it to be a warning, but these people refused to take the hint.

Since Edith left, Alex had been attacked by small groups of five to ten rushing him with crude weapons like knives and hammers. Someone even tried smashing a chair over him. Tairnishmen were large and strong, but they were no match for the armor as Alex swept them away. Using the suit's strong arms Alex shoved them back, cramming them and kicking them out of the way as he pushed forward. Unfortunately, everyone he didn't knock unconscious managed to get up and continue attacking him. They squeezed in tight beating on his armor.

Edith had given two simple instructions, 'make some noise and get to the hanger bay.' He looked at the map of the facility and was surprised to see just how far the hangar bay was. Ten levels up and even then, it was nearly a mile away down a long open corridor, more of a highway actually. That would be the worst stretch, he thought, 'wide open terrain where they could use larger weapons against me.'

When bullets started flying, Alex got nervous. He saw an old man with an angry-looking rifle but the blast that hit him was only scattered shot, like a shotgun. The armor didn't even recognize it as dangerous. Alex walked right past him, taking a second to chop down and break the rifle in half. At an intersection, more people came from every direction. Alex opened the rotary cannon. He blasted the ceiling and brought down huge chunks on their heads in an attempt to get them to back off.

It wasn't long after that something worse hit him. Surrounded and still pushing forward, he had people hanging on his armor plating when someone called, "Get out of the way!" A moment later something came rocketing at Alex and hit him square in the chest. There was an explosion and all his visual sensors blinked out for a second, a result of the heat and the light. When the screens cleared, Alex saw that he was surrounded by bodies. He looked down range and saw the next grenade coming.

The battle armor was still incredibly responsive. Alex ducked down a hall and out of the rocket's way as the RPG went flying past him, hitting another group of Tairnishmen. Alex saw the green blob of humanity come apart on his radar, and saw the bodies drop to the ground. 'How many people just died?' he wondered, feeling himself become angry. 'How many more would before he got to the hanger bay?'

"I need to move," Alex said, getting to his feet. He bashed in the wall of an apartment and went through another on the other side in a different hall. Then he did it twice more, coming out in the corridor behind the guys with the RPGs. Four soldiers, all in combat armor, were looking down range, trying to understand where the battle armor had gone.

They turned to Alex in surprise before he smashed into them. His hands were flying as he grabbed each soldier and flung them like dolls. Then he took off running. Alex had a large set of central stairs painted on his heads-up display. It was probably the only space big enough for him to get the suit up. All the other stairs were tight and made from concrete. Alex's radar picked up dozens of people coming down towards him.

The ordinance screen was open, and he was looking for anything nonlethal. It was pointless though. Edith had prepped the armor and she wasn't the kind to pack rubber bullets. There were some flash grenades and a few flares. Alex loaded them into the main cannon and hoped they'd be enough to clear the stairs.

He came around the corner and saw that there wasn't a chance. Waiting for him were soldiers, outfitted in armor with shields set as barricades that they squatted behind. They pointed their rifles and Alex had only a moment to identify them before he was greeted with automatic weapons fire.

High-velocity, armor-piercing rounds ripped into the armor. He felt a few wiz by inside the suit, as holes opened and let the light from outside in. Alex ducked out of the way again and felt a burning sensation in his left arm. One of the rounds had found him. A damage screen appeared. It quickly cycled through an assessment, then focused in on the one shot that passed through the pilot as if the pilot were just another part of the machine. 'That's me,' Alex thought as he felt something fill his shoulder, some sort of coagulant was closing the wound.

He heard more bullets tear through the wall behind him. The high-velocity rounds were turning the concrete to dust. Alex pulled up a firing solution and pointed his arm back at the hallway he'd just escaped. The grenade launcher was full of flash-bangs. He fired five in quick succession and the stream of bullets being shot in his direction slowed.

'Now what,' he thought as he considered his next move. His radar was spun up and he was scanning everything around him looking for some other way out. What he found instead were forces closing in from everywhere. Even going back to the caves wasn't an option.

Those stairs were the only way up and the dozens of soldiers on them were going to be pressing down in a moment. He thought about the civilians he'd fought earlier. They were probably on their way now too, more people that were going to get caught in the crossfire. These were soldiers, he told himself. On the stairs, they were all soldiers. They signed up for this. The rotary cannon was ready to go.

'Now or never. Stay here and die or start really fighting,' Alex thought as he got the suit up off the ground. "Ten stories up, that's all," he said aloud, reloading the launcher with explosive rounds. "Time to go."

There was still smoke in the hallway when Alex stepped out. It blocked his field of vision so he didn't see exactly what he was shooting at, but he was all done hiding. He stormed forward and hoped that a few of these men would be smart enough to get out of his way.

Chapter 26

Morning came to Nalanda station as the gas giant Altor captured the rays of the distant twin stars, shining the light back through large windows above each of the grand halls. The lights of the station, kept low through the night, were brought up as Ben and Katy made their way to the dining hall together.

Ben had already made a plate and sat down, but now he was watching Katy, who had insisted on getting her food herself. His sister moved from one serving dish to another with her tray precariously balanced, while still trying to use her guide stick to find her way.

The chafing dishes and counters were crowded. The young nobles moved with manners and were always polite in their gestures. Many, especially from Uppsala, didn't get up for their own food but were served by lower houses. These students, nobles that weren't much more than servants themselves, didn't complain about the way Katy struggled and got in their way, but they did give her a wide berth, avoiding a collision with the blind girl.

"Should we—" Cormack, who was sitting across from Ben, started to say.

"I wouldn't," Ben cut him off.

The sound of something dropping filled the room as glass hit the floor and shattered. Cormack leaned back, looking over, while Ben stayed right where he was, not even turning his head. "It's not going great over there," Cormack pointed out as people in servant's clothing came over to help clean the mess.

Ben tilted his head. "She was stubborn enough to make it all the way across the station, nearly drown, then make it back to us, and she's already told me a bunch of times not to help her. She's doing a whole independence thing and I'm not about to get my head torn off for it."

Cormack was still looking while Ben added, "She'll probably be nicer to you, but I promise, if you go over to help, it won't be well received."

Cormack pointed out. "She seems different since the trial. Back on Grannus she wasn't so... insistent."

Ben laughed. "Ha, I think you're just meeting the real Katy. You came into her life at a weird time. About as weird as things could get. She's just starting to catch up with everything now. Also, keep in mind, she only went with you to solve a problem." Ben pointed to his eyes. "Now she's trying to learn to live with it and my sister never does anything halfway."

"Yeah, but why's it been since the trial? Why the sudden change? She's been relentless," Cormack said.

"Stubborn, the word is stubborn. I think she decided that it's her job to get Naiathne and Chris out and not much is going to get in her way. You haven't known her that long, but I've known her my entire life. Sometimes Katy is up and sometimes she's down and when she's on something, a project, or whatever, she can be pretty intense. You've got to learn to ride the wave." Ben shrugged with his hands in the air.

Katy came towards them as Ben raised an eyebrow and took a scoop of his porridge. He and Cormack both went suddenly quiet. After giving up on trying to balance a tray, Katy now held a single plate. She bounced her thin stick across the floor and searched for her friends.

The stick contacted the table leg. "How come you guys are so quiet?" She put the plate down, but before either of them could make up an excuse, she moved her head around, perking up her ears. "Actually, how come the whole room is quiet?"

Neither Cormack nor Ben had noticed it, but Katy sensed the hush right away. The brief silence was followed by a growing hum of whispers. Ben looked over and saw five figures moving with ungainly steps into the

257

room. They passed under the tall stone archway, from the shadows of the corridor into the crowded warmth of the dining hall. Covered in cloaks with their hoods up, there was a sound of clinking water bottles coming from them, along with a strange squishing noise at each step.

"Looks like your friends are going to take care of things early." Ben pointed out. He turned to Katy and added, "The Grannusians just showed up. There's a bunch of them too."

The whole room was curious. The Grannusians hadn't been seen since the poisoning of their world. They'd only come out once to receive the antidote from Cathal. Other than that, they'd been in hiding, staying in their own domain.

Ignoring the murmur of curious students, they made their way across the hall to the monk's table. The room was laid out so that the monks sat in the center, separating the space between the students and the different Extraracial species. Their table was no different from anyone else's, long with a simple bench, but sister Nemain had taken the position at the head. Other monks came towards her, but she waved them away as her attention remained indifferent to the disturbance.

Fafnir was sitting with Regin at a table full of young Ice Carvers and Drakes. Regin popped up, curious. Even Fafnir turned at the Grannusian's approach. His face moved only a little, but his eyes widened. When he saw Katy fall in behind the Grannusians his brow dropped low in annoyance as he muttered something to Regin.

Katy had immediately put her plate down, gotten to her feet, and followed the Grannusians as if she were part of their group. It only took a single look from Cormack. With a sigh, Ben got to his feet as well, going after his sister.

Cathal was at the center table with the monks. He stood as the Grannusians approached while sister

Nemain barely glanced up. Her plate of food with some sort of pink meat, nearly as pale as her bald head, held her attention. "Well, this is a surprise," she said.

"We've come to speak for Naiathne. It is our understanding she is being held for the murder of one of your numbers, two nights past." The trilling voice came from under the hood. Katy recognized it from the day before as Clio's.

Sister Nemain was still looking down. "She was out, spotted by the Fire-Golems the night our Kavaris was murdered. No one else was seen after the night cycle, though we have a young man who has confessed to the crime."

"We understand. We've come to tell you that Naiathne was with us. She was in our domain," the hooded figure explained.

Nemain sighed, finally turning her entire attention toward them. "For how long?"

"Longer than she should've been, hours perhaps. She was in pain. Being here, away from her people brings her much discomfort. She wished to be housed in our domain. We told her no. Perhaps we should've let her."

Nemain looked to the ceiling and tilted her head. "The Naiad isn't exactly human. Perhaps she was right to seek you out." She looked back down at her plate and continued to eat. "What time was this?"

"Late, more than halfway through the night cycle. She stayed close to dawn," the Grannusian said.

Sister Nemain leaned towards one of the other monks. She whispered something and the man got up. Then she looked around at the room as if noticing for the first time that all the eyes of the students and teachers were on her and the Grannusians. She turned to Cathal. "You believed the murder occurred sometime near dawn, correct?"

"It's hard to say. Kavaris Altain's body was outside, but the blood had been warm when it froze in the vacuum. It didn't have time to pool, suggesting he hadn't been dead long when he was tossed out."

"So, you're going to let her go, right?" Katy interrupted from where she stood just behind the Grannusians.

Sister Nemain peered around the hooded figures and stared at Katy for a moment. Her cold gaze wouldn't work on the blind girl so she let the chill out in her voice. "I'm considering it." She turned to Clio. "It really would've been better if you'd come to the trial. There is an order to things. Perhaps we could've kept this from being such a debacle."

The Grannusians ignored the comment as the monk who'd gotten up came back with the Long-Wolf Fajalar. Sister Nemain said to him, "The Grannusians claim that Naiathne was in their domain the night of the murder for several hours near dawn. Where was she spotted and at what time?"

Fajalar looked around appearing mildly nervous. He nodded and repeated "'Where was she spotted and the time?'" He tapped his claws against his chin. "Actually . . . it makes more sense that she was in the Extraracial territory." Then he looked pointedly at Cathal. "I mean you still don't know exactly where the Kavaris was murdered, but the girl wasn't really near his quarters."

Cathal turned to Nemain and said in a low voice, "I'm still investigating, trying to find the actual site." He glanced back over his shoulder. "It's something I was hoping to discuss in private."

Sister Nemain laughed without humor. "Yes, private." She looked around the room again. "Imagine."

"So, you'll let her go?" Katy demanded, coming forward.

Sister Nemain shook her head, "Fine, we'll release the girl. Take care of it, Cathal." She turned back to her food.

"And Chris too?" Katy leaned past the robed Grannusians.

Sister Nemain asked, "You mean the murderer who confessed?"

Katy pushed in closer and raised her voice. "He only did that to save Naiathne, to keep you from throwing her out an airlock," Ben reached forward and put his hand on his sister's shoulder, trying to get her to back up, but she twisted away.

"You're saying he's a liar and not a murderer?" Sister Nemain's teeth were clenched and her fists closed on her silverware. She dropped them heavily to the table.

"To save her life—" Katy started.

Sister Nemain pushed her seat back and stood as the bench screeched across the stone floor, cutting Katy off. The monk stormed toward her, pushing past Clio. "You're admitting he gave false testimony before the Æesir. Before the gods." The monk grabbed Katy and pulled her roughly forward till she was so close that Katy could smell the breakfast meat on her breath. "You and your friends seem to think this is some sort of game. That they won't come back and burn you where you stand or destroy us for not serving their will. This is no game!"

Katy who was much smaller than the monk was being held on her tiptoes, nearly off her feet. Katy's voice shook as she answered, "I understand—"

"Do you?" Sister Nemain shouted, full of rage but under the anger was a desperate sort of fear. "I don't think so, but I promise your friend will stay in that cell until you do."

She still held Katy as the word, "But—" escaped from the blind girl's mouth.

261

Sister Nemain released her, but it wasn't done kindly. She tossed Katy away, across the floor, then she took a few steps forward and loomed over her. "Say another word and you will be right next to him, maybe your brother too," she warned as she looked at Ben, whose eyes widened.

"Katy, come on." Ben took her arm and pulled his sister to her feet. He turned her away from the monk.

Katy didn't fight Ben at first, but after a few steps she turned back and shouted to Cathal, "Tell her about the lighthouse." Cormack and Ben wouldn't let her say anything else as they forced her to keep walking, trying to get her away from the enraged monk.

Sister Nemain spun towards Cathal. The soldier sighed and explained, "Yes, that was the thing I wanted to talk about in private."

Sister Nemain clenched her hands, then motioned to the door. "Go to my office," she demanded. She didn't look back at the Grannusians or at the rest of the room as she exited with Cathal.

∞

The day passed with the students going to their classes. Katy had biology, which included a lab portion that took up the entire morning. Ben was with her in the middle of dissecting a Frozen Flower, a beautiful plant from Oighear that survived on the surface of the icy world by thawing out one day out of a hundred.

It adapted to grow in the hunting ground of the female Ice Carvers, taking seed in the corpses of the massive Undell slugs that moved across the icy landscape. Most everything from Oighear was adapted to move slowly and conserve energy, then to attack with speed and ferocity. Even the flowers could be dangerous, attracting those slugs with their bright colors and sweet smell into the open where they would be slaughtered by the female Ice Carvers. The flowers then took sustenance from the slug's corpse. It was a life cycle that played out at a laborious pace right up until the final moments.

The Frozen Flowers were different from Earth flowers with thicker cell walls more effective at storing energy. The stalk was like steel. Ben had to slice it open, avoiding the thorns, with a small, intense torch of blue plasma. He examined the plant through a view screen attached to a microscope while Katy sat back and half-listened to his description.

The instructor was a human, named Akyima, originally from Uppsala but who spent most of his life on Oighear working for one of the corporations that mined there. There was a ring around the frozen world like the one around Tairnish and there were colonies built in the ice that mined the reserves of complex hydrocarbons deep below the surface.

Geologists believed that Oighear had once been a lush world with vast oceans. In fact, a few land masses still stuck out above the frozen wasteland and liquid water remained below the ice, though poisoned with complex chemicals that seeped from deep in the moon where heat radiated from its liquid core of heavy metals.

The same process that created hydrocarbons on Earth, turning dead organic material into complex molecules that could be used for fuel, had happened on Oighear. Time, compression, and oxygen starvation made fossil fuels. Only on the Oighear the decaying life somehow made chemicals, and flowers, that stored energy more effectively, creating fuel that could be compressed for easier storage and that would react in a vessel's engines for a longer time.

The liquids leaking into the ice and the gases mined from the rocks were used to power the ships that traveled between the different moons and to power the energy grid of Uppsala and the space stations that circled above the different worlds and in the belt around Altor. Powerful corporations had grown massive fortunes owning and operating the industries that dug and refined the chemicals. Those corporations were owned by royal families on Uppsala. Their laws protected their rights to the resources and garnished generation after generation with power and influence.

Professor Akyima had no royal blood but he was a man excited by science. His enthusiasm had taken hold in Ben as well, who smiled as he cut the plant with superhot plasma. He barely noticed that they'd been joined at their lab table by another person. Naiathne entered the room, came over and touched Katy's shoulder. "I hear I've got you to thank for my release."

Katy's thoughts had been somewhere else. She hadn't heard Naiathne's steps but the voice of her friend was enough to get her to jump and turn. She made an excited squeak as she reached out and took Naiathne's arms pulling her in tight for a hug. "Whoa, now this is a nice welcome." Naiathne laughed.

Ben startled and nearly dropped his torch. "Wow, they actually let you go?" Ben said.

"One thing about the monks. If they say something, it happens."

"Like opening an airlock and tossing someone out," Ben mentioned.

"Yeah, exactly. Luckily, I had someone out here in my corner." She squeezed Katy's arm and let a quick smile cross her usually stiff or scowling visage.

"Naiathne, I'm happy to have you in my class but perhaps you could catch up with your friends after we're done here." Professor Akyima called from the front of the class. "Ben, would you fill her in on what we're doing."

Ben nodded. "Sure, professor."

"So, this is a frozen flower—" Ben started, but Katy interrupted in a whispered voice.

264

"How's Chris?" she asked as her hand moved down, squeezing Naiathne's.

Naiathne looked at the hand, her normally pale grey skin had turned a little pink as she kept her voice low. "He's okay. I mean he wants out. When he told them that he was lying, the monks just gave him this death stare. I don't think they're going to do anything to him, but I don't think they plan on letting him out anytime soon either."

"We need to find the actual killer. It's the only way he goes free," Katy said.

"Ladies!" Akyima called from the front, hearing their voices.

"Back to the flower," Ben added as Katy went quiet. Naiathne listened to Ben politely. When Katy dropped her hand, she stared at it for a moment more. Then Naiathne touched her own palm feeling the warmth where Katy's had been.

Chapter 27

In the heart of the commune, Edith was unseen as she made her way across the farm floor to the concrete steps. Cautious and silent, she climbed while behind her the farm echoed with emptiness. It was a vast warehouse with concrete walkways and long rows of green plants and golden grains, growing in perfect order. The emergency of Alex's one-man invasion had called away all the farmers and left the place abandoned.

She needed to put the kid out of her thoughts as she tried not to feel guilty about sending him on a suicide mission. They'd never formalized their relationship, so she owed him nothing. She wasn't his First, which was the only loyalty someone in her profession or her culture understood. There were rituals that needed to happen where he would agree to be her student, her Second, and she would choose to take him on and become his mentor. It was the way of her people but those promises had never been made. That meant Alex was nothing to her but another resource.

He'd never be one of the Shaka Tal, though most just called them mercenaries or the people of the southern islands. It was a harsh and rocky part of Uppsala that the nobility never saw as worth conquering, where the temperatures plummeted in the winter and scorched in the summer. That was Edith's home, the place she'd been brought up and trained from the time she could walk.

Edith thought of her own First, a woman past her prime but still incredibly dangerous, a harsh master who had taken her on at the age of five while her parents were both on campaigns. She was cared for by her grandmother, a warrior once herself, who was glad to see her go, not because she didn't love the child, but because she saw the potential in Edith.

Edith came from good stock. Her father was an impressive soldier and her mother, well her mother had a different destiny, but like them, Edith was a natural athlete with a ferocity about her. Her early combat training from her First had given her the mental focus she needed to command a picket ship and its handful of drones without losing her mind. The trick was to see the small, guided weapons as extensions of herself. So many pilots came back with fried neuro-synapses from being jacked into a combat system. They'd return to the islands and never be the same again, shells of themselves.

Her First had taught Edith to see an entire battlefield and to understand that the battle was everywhere. Her name had been Suri, a friend of her grandmother, who thought nothing of taking the young Edith across Uppsala and picking up contracts for assassination or sabotage. Back then there was no Emperor. Tamerlane was still building his power while everyone watched, wondering if the Æesir would stop him. That meant there was plenty of work.

Edith wondered sometimes if Tamerlane knew how long she'd been in his service. That even as a child she was helping Suri pick a winner in the silent war of politics. At fourteen, she was sent into the pilot core. She never saw Suri again though she knew the old woman was still alive back in the southern islands, rusting with age. A weapon without a use. Tamerlane's success had left most assassins without work. When there was only one power, there wasn't much competition, and if you were foolish enough to align yourself with someone against Tamerlane, you didn't last long and neither did your benefactor.

Edith reached a heavy door controlled by a simple combination lock. She didn't bother to decipher the code, checking for alarms instead, then using the power armor to pull the cover away before shoving a thin knife into the latch assembly and manipulating it back.

She didn't open the door right away but stayed low on the stairs and used a microfiber camera to check what was ahead of her. Passing it through the latch, she rotated it slowly and scanned the hallway. Across from the door was a small, severe-looking lobby. There was a counter inside, encased in heavy glass with a single door next to it.

A large Tairnishman stood there, his face lit by the glow of various monitors beneath the countertop. Edith noticed the heavy blast doors at the entrance to the lobby. There was probably a switch near the man that would slam those shut, effectively trapping anyone inside. She wondered if she had enough explosives to destroy the glass.

She shook her head. The lobby didn't offer enough cover for that kind of damage. If the doors closed behind her, even with a focused charge and her armor on, she'd probably get herself killed or knocked unconscious.

She needed to get the Tairnishman to open the door. She wondered how many people were still back behind him in the security office, if they'd all responded to Alex, or if this sentry was the last one. The security hub on her map hadn't appeared overly large. A small armory, a few offices, and a handful of holding cells. Tairnishmen didn't usually keep prisoners for long. They favored banishment, sending criminals out to survive on the surface where no one would give them shelter. A rogue Tairnishmen could never be accepted into a new commune. If they even approached one that wasn't their home, they'd be shot on sight.

Edith stared at the heads-up display in her helmet, at the image of the lobby, wondering how to get the guard out. She thought of the words of her own First, the lessons she'd taught her. 'All war was subterfuge, feints, and tricks,' she'd said. 'Your strategies and training will never be more valuable than the enemy's mistakes.'

'Now how to get this guy to make a mistake?' she asked herself. She only saw one solution and it meant taking her armor off. The camera cable retracted and Edith unclasped and lifted her helmet away, getting to see the world with her own eyes. She sneered a little at the sludge and fertilizer that still clung to the surface of her suit. Then she started to pull off the rest of her gear.

When she was left without a hint of combat equipment, not even her boots, down to the tank top and tights she wore under her gear, she took out a knife and made a small quick slash across her forehead, above her eye. It didn't take long to feel the warm sticky blood drip down her face. She smeared it a little but didn't wipe it away, then she added some of the muck from the outside of her armor to her light brown arms and legs. Edith didn't have much hair to tussle, only what was in her tightly cut mohawk. She did her best to mess it up then carefully tucked the knife into her waistband behind her back.

Edith glanced down at herself. She didn't have the purple skin of a Tairnishman but with the muck, it was hard to tell and while she lacked the broad frame of a woman from Tairnish, she was more muscular than most.

She got to her feet, took a quick look at her pile of equipment, then after a deep breath, with manic energy, she flung the stairway door open. "Help me, help me," she screamed as she ran into the lobby, tripping and falling just out of view of the counter. She landed half on her side and closed her eyes tight, holding perfectly still with an arm draped across her hip.

She lay there listening. What she was most worried about was the guard not being alone, that a team of helpful Tairnishmen were on their way. Her second concern was that he'd close the blast doors before he came to check on her and she'd never get her armor back.

"Hey, hey you," she heard him shout from behind the glass. There was a grunting noise as he tried to peer down but Edith had picked the perfect landing spot. He was only getting a look at her legs and feet. She listened carefully, hearing him step back, followed by the sound of the door opening. He called again, still holding the door. "What are you doing here? What happened?"

Edith didn't make a sound. She heard him take one step, then another, coming closer. She knew he was still holding the door, 'probably holding a firearm too,' she thought. He started to go back, maybe to get more help.

Her eyes popped open and met the guard's. The knife was already in the air and landed squarely in his chest. Edith glanced down and saw the stubby assault rifle in his hand start to come up. He struggled to bring it to bear, but Edith was already on him, springing from the floor and grabbing the barrel. She pushed the weapon down with one hand, grabbed the door with the other, and shoved the knife deeper into his chest with her shoulder. The guard's heavy form slumped down. Edith tried to guide him, but he was so heavy that his body fell with a resounding thump. His limp form kept the entrance open while Edith listened and wondered if anyone else was coming. It was quiet.

She pulled the knife back out and wiped it on his sleeve. "Thanks for holding the door," she said as she ran back to the stairs and grabbed her armor. A moment later she was behind the counter, looking at the monitors as she pulled her armor back on. It didn't take her long to find Alex on the central staircase. He'd made it up a few levels and he was still moving. Edith plugged into a terminal and did a quick data dump of their standard operating procedures.

She didn't bother going deep into the files. Luckily, the emergency evacuation plan was clearly marked. It included the fastest way to the launch pad. When she'd looked at the map Alex had uploaded, built from his scans and their knowledge of Tairnish structures, the launch pad had seemed incredibly far away with open ground and lots of room for people to shoot at you.

She pulled up the feed from the hangar bay and confirmed that what the kid was going into was a meat grinder. Even in the battle armor, he didn't have a chance. Edith squeezed her fist and pulled the rest of the information she needed. 'That's the way Alex is going, not us. Stay on mission,' she told herself as she examined an escape tunnel for the lower levels, including the one she was on. A few select families had made themselves a back door.

Edith plotted the route and was about to shut down the heads-up display, but she looked at Alex's path a second time. There were pillboxes filled with men and weapon emplacements all along the main passage to the launchpad. He wasn't going to get through that. She typed a command into the security system, scheduling a full reboot in eight minutes, it would only give her four minutes of travel time where the cameras in every hall would be out, not much time, but every little bit helped.

Edith got to her feet, had her rifle unslung and held low as she went back into the holding cells. She'd released all the doors from the security desk. Twelve doors opened but only a half dozen people wandered out, most of them looked like they were from Uppsala, probably administrators from the mining operations. At the end was Maeven. Edith pushed her way through the crowd of confused prisoners. "Princess, I'm here to bring you home."

Maeven's long hair was tied back, barely kept and the jumpsuit she wore hung from her like a sack, but her perfect face with its high, soft cheeks, full lips, and large smoky eyes sparkled with a mischievous light that could melt anyone's heart. Edith glanced down at her rifle and thought, 'armed,' in a different way.

"Edith?" Maeven asked only mildly surprised. She couldn't see the mercenary's face behind the black helmet but she recognized the voice.

Edith nodded and Maeven added, "I doubt the monks sent you."

Edith tilted her head. "No, I think the monks were glad to see you go. Your father was less pleased."

If Maeven was surprised to hear that the mercenary worked for her father, she didn't show it. She only nodded and motioned towards the door saying, "Shall we?"

The other prisoners were looking at Edith and Maeven, confused. One of them asked, "What do we do now, princess?"

Maeven looked at Edith, who turned to the man. The mercenary wouldn't let anyone compromise her mission. "I'm only here for her. If any of you try to follow me, I'll put a bullet in your head." The prisoners looked at each other, still confused. Edith's shoulder came up a bit, lifting her rifle, a subtle answer to their question, wondering if she were serious. First one, then another wandered back into their cell. They stood just inside their doors as if that would protect them. "Come on, princess," she said as she took Maeven by the arm.

∞

Alex didn't want to die. Despite the recklessness of youth and the situations he'd put himself in, such as this one, he knew for a fact, he wanted to keep living. More than that, he didn't want to fail. Edith had defined his mission as creating a distraction, but as he made his way up the broad stairs, his priorities had changed. It started and ended with 'Make it to the top.'

The assault team at the bottom of the stairs came for him in armor like Edith's, just bulkier to house the Tairnishmen beneath. It was easy to think of them as ogre's or some other fantasy creature in that armor with their hulking shoulders and strange face plates, a frozen face without eyes.

They'd tried setting up heavy metal barricades at the base of the steps, emplacements that could be moved up by a two-man team. The rounds from Alex's canon bounced off them so he switched to grenades. As bullets thumped into the battle armor's chest plate, ricocheting from the thickest part of his shell, the launchers made short angry fump sounds and lobbed the explosives.

Some of the enemy rounds penetrated into his limbs, clipping him or passing straight through places like his calves. The automatic medical systems tried to keep up, filling the wounds with more sealing coagulant. The bullets burned terribly but only for a second as he felt the wounds stiffen and topical anesthetics pushed into them.

The grenades were set for a short release. They barely bounced on the stairs before blowing them to hell. Smoke and debris followed the yellow flame of rapidly expanding gas as the pressure wave and shrapnel crashed into the shields. Anyone near them didn't survive as the very floor became compromised, holed, and smashed with the steel underneath showing through the steps.

Alex charged through the smoke and fired his small boosters, bouncing up onto the next flight, then to the landing. Each floor had a wide area about eight meters across with an open balcony overlooking the rest of the stairs.

He was no longer seeing the bodies. The fact that the Tairnishmen were in armor helped. Their faces weren't like the people in the hall when the RPG went off. 'What it'd done to them . . . Stop!' Alex screamed silently, 'get up the stairs.' He returned his focus to the mission. 'Keep moving.'

The next group of Tairnishmen weren't ready for him. They hadn't set up barriers, so the rotary cannon proved more effective at cutting through their armor. It spun and whined as Alex forced them to give up ground. Some of the men were pushed back so far that they tumbled over the balcony and dropped several floors to the bottom of the stairwell. He tried to maintain some trigger discipline and not go through all his ammo, but the Tairnishmen kept coming and the canon kept firing releasing thousands of rounds.

Soldiers poured out at every level and tried to get a firing position on him. Alex barely aimed, spraying his weapon like a fire hose as the heads-up display showed the ammo reserve and the count plummeting each time he pulled the trigger.

The Tairnishmen used the corners for cover. Alex pulled up the screen for his rockets and found the attacker's heat signatures. He fired two at every flight, not targeting people, at least not in his head, but only the green blobs of heat signatures that were firing searing white rounds that streaked past his eyes in the display. Alex kept the suit low, following quickly after the explosions.

The soldiers never stopped coming at him, but now Alex was moving. The landings were the worst. He had to clear each clot of soldiers, open a path with explosives, and then keep pushing. The resistance couldn't get organized against the pace of his attacks. At a point, he stopped firing and let the strength of the suit clear his way. He used its heavy arms to sweep the Tairnishmen from the stairs, tossing them over the concrete rails.

Alex fired the boosters in short bursts to spring ahead. When he came down on the soldiers, they'd try to fight but at close range, their numbers worked against them. Six floors went by, then seven, eight, nine, ten. He knew more soldiers were coming up from below and occasionally he'd lob a grenade to cover his rear. He felt his limbs stiffen and the pain from his wounds wash over him as exhaustion set in, but he kept pushing. He came storming out at the top of the stairwell and had only a moment to appreciate his success.

Around him was a large chamber filled with cargo with a vaulted ceiling high above cut into the rock while massive braces supported it against collapse. Alex looked across the room at the entrance to the supply road, the only path he knew of to the launch pad. It was like a highway tunnel through the mountains, a curved archway cut into the rocks. He thought, 'That's where I need to go.'

The threat assessments started blaring, letting Alex know he was surrounded. He only had time for a single breath when something hit him. It wasn't an RPG or any sort of handheld weapon. It was a high-explosive round, fired from a tank made to destroy armor. It impacted just ahead of the battle armor, only a few inches in front of Alex but with enough concussive force to throw him through the air.

A single glancing hit released a shock wave that demolished the top of the stairs and did more damage than all the shots fired below. Somehow Alex had the foresight to pull his limbs in and curl into a ball. Maybe it was something Edith instructed him to do, or maybe it was some fetal instinct, but it was the only thing that kept him in one piece as he was thrown back.

The armor smashed through the balcony on the top level and fell into the open space next to the stairs. The battle armor tumbled, dropping and crashing into the walls, banging against the landings. Alex was only vaguely aware of the fall as he squeezed his eyes tight, his entire body shaken from the explosion above.

When he looked around again, he struggled to remember what happened. He wasn't sure if he'd lost consciousness, but he was still in the armor and somehow, he was looking with his own eyes through a cloud of dust and rubble at the artificial light of the stairwell.

'I'm upside down. Why am I upside down?' he thought. The hole he was looking through was where the left arm of the battle armor had been. Worse than that, the control helmet was cracked in a dozen places leaving him half blinded by the broken faceplate. His ears were ringing and his head pounded as he worked his hands up to get the helmet off. Without the heads-up display, the helmet was pointless anyway.

His eyes stayed on the armhole as he forced the helmet off. There wasn't enough room in the suit for his head and the large helmet so he had to crook his neck to the side at an uncomfortable angle to fit.

Slowly, he realized what had happened. That the blast had thrown him back down the steps. 'But how far?' he wondered as he moved the other arm of the suit and felt it respond. He wanted to turn the whole thing and get back to his feet, but the armor barely responded.

Suddenly, the whole thing moved, making a quick drop as the sound of metal shifting filled Alex's ears. There was a terrifying moment when Alex felt the suit plummet. He felt it in his stomach as it started to fall, sliding down the wall.

He could hear voices calling from nearby and movement above. 'I've got to get out of here,' Alex thought while his hands scurried over the inside, trying to find the emergency release. Edith had him drill blindfolded to locate it just in case he ended up in a situation like this.

She'd also left him a goody bag. He'd memorized the contents but the weapons and other tools for survival wouldn't be nearly enough to get him out above. In his mind, he flashed back to the second before the explosion. He'd seen what was waiting for him up in that chamber. There'd been hundreds of soldiers, mounted weapons emplacements, and more tanks than he could count. 'I can't go that way,' he thought as he found the t-handle and pulled. The top of the drop armor popped open.

He grabbed the bag and released his harness, realizing too late that he wasn't in the best position as he half fell from the armor, slipping out and finding himself dangling above a void. Catching the harness with his foot, he felt the tug at his ankle and the pull on the wounds in his leg. He looked down. There was nothing below him, just an open space full of smoke and destruction. He realized he wasn't completely in the stairwell but hanging half off one of the balconies somewhere near the middle level of the facility. The battle armor was wedged against the wall.

Below him, he heard more voices. He couldn't see through the smoke, but he knew more soldiers were coming up and others were at the bottom of the well trying to get a look at him. They were in armor with HUDs, which meant that while he couldn't see them, he was probably as plain as day, just another green heat signature for target practice.

Alex did a crunch to get himself back up to the lip of the suit as the bullets started flying. He grabbed the front of it and released his foot, then climbed over the dented and beaten chest plate before dropping to the floor. On the landing, he took a moment to breathe, staying low, below the smoke and dust.

The temptation to lay there and recover was overwhelming, but he knew he didn't have time. Pulling open the goody bag, he reached inside and grabbed a knife, then took out a small submachine gun with a suppressor on it. There were goggles with a respirator and a handful of grenades. They functioned like the ones on Nalanda, the ones Ben had grabbed the first time they tried to save Maeven, using powerful magnets to float or attach to objects.

The goggles were more important though. They would protect his eyes and give him access to limited information with another heads-up display. There was no infrared or anything, but the display gave him back his map, which was the most important thing to him right now. He noticed that the data on it had been updated recently, less than ten minutes ago.

He blinked at the information packet and Edith's voice came over the earpiece attached to the goggles. "Alex, I'm violating my own protocol by sending you this. Actually, I'm risking the entire damn mission. . . look, just follow this map. It'll take you to an emergency exit. You did good. Now get yourself out. We won't be able to wait for you, so move fast."

Alex looked at the map. He had no idea how much resistance was between him and the exit, but he was going to try. He took one more thing from the pack as he heard voices closing in from all around him.

Getting to his feet but still staying low, he hurried down the hall, then turned off the main passage and turned again before looking at the thing in his hand, flipping back a cover to reveal a button. He jammed down on it. Inside the armor, a valve opened and two chemicals mixed together. A moment later the walls shook as the suit exploded from the inside. He heard the stairs collapsing like a stack of pancakes, one on top of the other.

'That should buy me some time,' he thought, turning to run but finding his body wasn't capable of it. It was all he could do to get his stiff legs to move as he leaned on the wall and struggled ahead.

Chapter 28

Inside the crystal chamber, Amita's helmet lamp reflected back to her, magnified by the chamber's wall as the beam made dozens of surfaces glow. The only sound was her own breathing and the crunch of volcanic stone under her feet as she stepped away from Tearmai with a crystal in one hand and the key in the other, going toward the black door. The door was like a cancer in the gemstone wall, a dark thing that shoved its way into something beautiful.

'I don't want to go,' Amita thought as she looked back. Her friend Tearmai, whose chest rose slow and regular, lay against the altar. He followed her with his blue eyes and a desperate kind of hope. She still wasn't sure what he wanted from her. 'Free the slave,' he'd said, but as Amita remembered the words in her head, they sounded more like, 'free me.'

It sent a shiver down her back, a feeling like being inside a haunted house with a ghost who'd finally decided to reveal itself. "No," Amita said as she glanced down at the small piece of crystal, tempted to throw it away as far from herself as possible.

She squeezed it instead and looked up at the vaulted ceiling, then back at the door they'd come through, back where the wild Fire-Golems remained in half-molten walls, kept out by a cage of the dark metal. She wondered if they were free behind the door; if this was where the protection of that metal cage ended.

The door was round with a spikey frame that bloomed out and flowed down into the entry. It was marked with a curving pattern that felt like the ridges on a lizard's spine. In her other hand, she held the key. She brought it forward, unsure where to place it or which side was the front. It looked like a squashed E with three prongs that ended at different points.

Her mind went back to the rockets out in the chamber and the possibility of returning home. She was trying to picture how Brash and Tearmai had launched them.

'Were they in some sort of standby mode?' If she were lucky, they might be prepped to fire at a moment's notice. That seemed to be what the guardian had suggested. She considered this as she took one more look at the wounded Drake and thought, 'Brash and Tearmai figured it out after all.' Amita shook her head surprised by her own arrogance. She didn't like feeling so prideful. It was just that all her life she'd been convinced that if a problem could be solved by someone, then she could do it as well, even if that someone was an alien lifeform with psychic powers.

Launching those rockets and going home was the problem she wanted to solve. Not this. Not what Tearmai was asking. 'Go through this door and free . . . What?' She had no idea.

She touched the metal, fighting the urge to turn away. She wanted to see her parents again. She pictured coming out of the wormhole, days before the incident, before they lost control, before the power to the magnetic bubble cracked and the event started to grow. She thought of how she'd convince Dr. Virtanen to shut it down. 'Perhaps seeing two of her would be enough.'

'It won't be that simple,' the thought entered Amita's mind. It didn't feel like it came from her. It'd slipped into her thoughts as something foreign. She slowed her breathing, letting her head empty and calm. Ideas fell away as she focused on the air in her lungs.

'I'm here, waiting for you.' The words entered her mind again uninvited, and Amita knew they weren't her's.

"Who are you?" she demanded as a hot flare of anger ran through her. She took another breath and

281

wondered if the rage was her own or if it'd come from outside. She realized it had to be hers, a flight or fight response to the most intimate of intrusions.

'I'm the one you came to free,' the voice said, 'the slave.'

The words in her head felt like they were hers, similar to the way someone would play a conversation over and over again that had happened in the past or hadn't happened yet. Only these words carried an immediacy with them, entering like alarm bells. It said, 'Open the door. You must come to me.'

'Said the spider to the fly,' Amita thought.

'I won't hurt you. I promise.'

'So, I have no private thoughts?' Amita asked, but before the voice could respond, Amita said aloud, "Again, I only have your word, haven't I?" while looking down at the key.

She held it towards the door and saw three slots open, flowing back like liquid. "Don't think for a moment that this means I trust you," she said as she pushed the key in. The whole entrance moved out from the center of the opening, revealing a tunnel.

'Then why—" the voice started to ask, but Amita cut her off again.

"Because I'm curious," she said as she stepped forward with the light from her helmet guiding her. The tunnel went immediately down with crude steps carved into the stone floor. Even through her environmental suit, she could feel the warmth from the rocks. It made her wonder just how much the suit could handle. It would've been designed to protect her against the hard radiation in outer space. That meant if she were feeling anything through it, it must be scorching.

She noticed that her headlamp wasn't the only light. The tunnel was glowing much like above, only softer. It was the light of the Wild Fire-Golems, just inside the walls. "Will they attack me?" Amita asked the voice in her head.

'I won't let them do anything to you and the deeper you go the more control I have.' the voice answered. For some reason, Amita was convinced it was female. She didn't know why, but some part of it reminded her of her Nani back in London. It was ancient, wise, and incredibly demanding, as a grandmother should be. Perhaps her own mind was filling in those details.

The tunnel had a long wide curve that went deeper and deeper into Tairnish like a corkscrew. To her right she noticed the walls were different. They didn't glow red, but they reflected her helmet lamp like the chamber above. In fact, Amita believed they were part of that room, the outside wall of it, and as she went, the curve of the structure got bigger. She realized that where Tearmai was resting was only the tip of this thing.

She had the sense that the stairs and the tunnel itself hadn't always been there. That perhaps it was only now being formed as she went. Fire-Golems or perhaps something else were at work just ahead of her. She went slow, afraid to step into molten rock, but everything around her seemed solid enough.

Amita said aloud, certain she wasn't only talking to herself. "My friend is very concerned about freeing you, but I'm not certain what that means or what you are."

'I'm alive, like you but I'm much older and I've been held in captivity and taken advantage of in ways you can't imagine,' The voice in her head pleaded.

Amita started with a thought but as soon as she realized the entity would be able to hear it anyway, she said it to the empty tunnel, "Mind you, I'm not calling you a liar. It's only that sometimes, when someone is imprisoned, well there might be a reason for it. I'm not about to wander into the local jail and start breaking people out, am I?"

'Crime is an odd idea. Even right or wrong seems strange to me. but from what I understand for something to be truly evil, there must be intent. Would you agree?'

Amita thought about it and nodded her head. 'Well by that concept I assure you, I've done nothing wrong. I've been here on this world far longer than any of the creatures who claim it as their home, and I've simply lived my life as all things do.'

"How long?" Amita asked.

'I struggle with your concept of time as well. It was the Lightning Bug that taught me how to communicate with you, but their perception of the universe is bizarre even to me. They exist somewhere else, while still being here. Things aren't as linear to them. Perhaps you could show me how your people count.'

Amita didn't need the entity to explain. She understood what it was asking as she moved knowledge forward into her thoughts, describing in her own mind the way days passed with Earth spinning around the sun, the seasons going through their cycles, then she thought of the time frame of man, the rise of empires. She felt the entity say, 'No.' And Amita followed up with thoughts of a longer span, the rise and fall of species, rocks tumbling making rivers and mountains as she considered the passage of millions of years.

'Close, but even then, I'm older, I was born among the stars but I've lived beneath this world for ages. My life cycle is in the billions. I age as a world does."

Amita considered this for a moment. She knew the entity was listening so she grabbed onto the thought that was the strongest and said aloud, "Amazing really that you can even talk to me."

If the voice in her head could've sighed it would've as it said, 'Well, it isn't easy.'

"I won't take offense to that," Amita shot back, noticing something sticking into the tunnel a few steps down from her. She approached it carefully. It looked like the altar in the chamber above but laid on its side, half buried in the wall. 'What is that?' Amita asked in what was meant to be a private thought.

The voice interrupted, "You must use the key here."

"But what is it?" Amita asked again aloud, seeing that the tunnel had changed. The object was to the left. To her right, the crystal wall was broken. Shattered pieces of gemstones were buried in the volcanic rock of the cavern. It looked thousands of years old, like a fossil.

"I'm not certain but the Long-Wolves use them as shackles. There are five of these spikes buried through me. They are the bars to my prison."

Amita took the key and held it near the black anchor. She saw three holes open on the flat surface, just as she had on the door above. "It's so strange. It almost seems like it's alive or was at one time. I don't think it's Long-Wolf technology."

'No, I assure you it's not theirs. Very little is. I don't know where it came from but they buried them in me a long time ago. They control my children through me.'

The word 'children' was a little unclear in Amita's mind. When the entity put the thought out, it felt smudged as if it weren't an accurate description. "I'm sorry, your what?" Amita asked.

She felt the idea pulled from her, then the entity explained. 'You call them Fire-Golems. They are part of me. Not children in the way you'd think, but something different. They come from me and we're connected. Even far away, we still remain part of each other, different but the same.'

Without meaning to, Amita thought of her parents. "That's more like children than you'd think," she said. "So, the ones at the station, the ones that the Long-Wolves brought there, serve against their will?"

"They have no real will. They haven't been alive or free long enough, but when you release these locks, they will start to become independent."

"I see," Amita said holding the key. She was thinking about the wild Fire-Golems who attacked them. They'd been relentless. Then she thought of Ben standing, staring up at the one in the hall that first night they went out exploring. "Will they be like the ones here, as dangerous?" she asked, picturing the creature crushing Ben with its fist.

'I don't know. We are still connected so I may be able to speak to them, but I can't promise anything.'

Amita didn't pull the key back but her hand floated there, remaining closed around it. She looked to the ceiling. "And what will you do?"

The entity answered with words entering Amita's head more intensely than she'd ever felt before, with a mountain of emotion that she could barely stand. 'Continue my life cycle, grow, and become stronger. I will move. Centuries have passed while they've kept me feeble, pinched, and trapped! 'The feeling of claustrophobia nearly suffocated Amita. She placed the key in the lock and pushed it forward, willing to do anything to escape that pain.

Her hand felt frozen on the key as the wall began to shake and the black anchor rippled and moved like it wasn't quite solid. Before her eyes, it folded and twisted, becoming smaller and smaller. She could hear stones inside the wall crumbling as the metal came towards her, pulling back into a single lump of something dark. Finally, it released its grip and Amita jumped back as the lump fell to the floor with a heavy, wet, thud. It continued to shrink till it was only about the size of her arm, with curved surfaces and a strange organic shape.

'Take the key, but do not touch the spike itself. It can be unpredictable when it contacts living things.' Amita stared at it, trying to understand where the key was in the fleshy dark mass. When she found it, it was half buried in the side. She wasn't sure she'd be able to pull it free but as her hand approached, it fell away dropping onto the step.

She hesitated for only a moment, staring at the thing the spike had become, realizing how much it reminded her of the hunter back on Earth. She pushed the key further away from it with her foot before picking it up again.

'Thank you,' the voice said filling Amita with relief.

"Only four more to go." She started down the stairs, glad to be getting further from that first anchor, even though she knew she was going to find others. Somehow the device felt more dangerous when it was collapsed as if it were waiting to fulfill a malicious purpose.

As Amita walked, she considered the entity's words. "When you said you'd grow, that you'd continue your life cycle, what did you mean?"

'As all things do, I will feed and flourish,' the voice answered.

Amita was almost afraid to ask the question, but it was already in her head when she said, "How big will you become?"

"As large as my sustenance will allow."

There were fish, lizards, and snakes that were indeterminate growers, whose size was in theory only limited by their environment. Amita realized that many plants were that way too, moving across a territory until something stopped them. "And what is your sustenance? What exactly do you feed on?"

There was a moment's pause while Amita waited to hear the answer. She could sense the entity's anxiety about responding. Finally, it said, "This world."

"Oh." Amita stopped in her tracks. For a moment she felt detached.

Amita leaned against the wall and pictured it closing in and crushing her while the voice said, "As I grow, I will boil the ground, heating it and breaking it down to its component molecules, then they will become part of me. This world as you see it will be unmade. After, I will enter the next stage of my life cycle."

"But you'll kill every living thing here," Amita said.

"Not right away. It will take a millennium for me to become."

"To become what?" Amita demanded.

'Something amazing.' The voice trembled a little with excitement. It sounded unsure but full of awe.

Amita looked at the key in her hand. "I don't know if I can do this. If I can release you knowing what you're capable of." Amita added, "Please don't kill me for saying that."

'I will not hurt you, no matter what you do. I do not believe I am evil and that would be an evil thing, but I must live and not as this captive.'

Amita felt the wall shake a little. "What are you doing?" she asked feeling the small vibration again. It wasn't much, but while she was surrounded by rock it was enough to make her nervous.

'That isn't me. It came from the sky.'

"What is it?" Amita demanded though she had a feeling she already knew. The clock had run out on Tairnish. The emperor and his fleet were here.

'I believe someone up there is intent on killing every living thing on this planet,' the entity said.

Amita looked at the ceiling, seeing it shake once more and her thoughts went to Tearmai in the crystal chamber. She worried about her friend, then she thought of the diamond-topped rockets. They were so massive that it was difficult to imagine them being fragile, but if this shaking was the emperor bombing the surface and she was feeling it this deep, then those rockets didn't stand a chance and any hope she had for setting things right would be over.

Amita took one step up, wanting to run back there, but she stopped, feeling the entity's misery. She looked down into the dark, wondering how far she had to go. How long it would take her to free all the locks? As she started back on the path going deeper into Tairnish, she felt its relief. The entity's emotions were so strong that it nearly overwhelmed Amita as she continued down, wondering if she were doing the right thing.

Chapter 29

On the surface, the main halls of Nalanda station appeared separate, but beneath the starburst of windows, beneath the ground were tunnels and passages connecting them. In fact, most of the royal domiciles were carved from subsurface chambers and tunnels with no windows or exits. This is how their balconies opened above the combat floor. The grand hall that the massive cage sat in was sunk deep into the ground. Even the medical unit overlooking it was below the surface of the asteroid with the windows above, looking out on Altor but only a few meters above the asteroid's rocky exterior.

Tapping her stick on the stone floor of the Sidhe balcony, Katy leaned against the wall, enjoying the silence in the large chamber as she focused on the way the taps echoed in the open space. The combat cage was out there, or so she was told. She'd heard the practices hours before, loud enough that she didn't need her eyes. She thought, 'Maybe someday, I'll show them what a blind girl with three months of self-defense classes could do. After all, Ben had to participate, why not her?' She clamped her lips together, not wanting to smile. 'Cathal would probably think it was a good idea.'

Then she remembered the way that monk had thrown her to the floor and her smile disappeared as the tapping stopped. She flailed the stick out, feeling the open floor, making sure she was alone. During the bigger battles in the cage, this balcony would be full of noble youths, but at this time everything was quiet and better. No one came out here during the night cycle. What would be the point? But it was perfect for her, dark, deserted, but not isolated, the way she felt in her room.

Her thoughts wandered back to San Diego and the ocean. She'd spent so many hours in the waves, paddling out, then coming off her board to swim in the salty cold water. The sight of the beach and the way the dawn came up over the land, revealing a small community of surfers was home to her and she was grateful she could still go there even if it was only in her head.

The ocean of Grannus had been different, warmer than the Pacific, with a strong smell and a bitter taste. Its movement even felt strange, pulled by a distant gas giant instead of a close-by moon, making the wave intervals longer and deeper. For a moment Katy wondered if she'd only been aware of it because she didn't have her eyes. Maybe, if she could've seen the ocean, it would've just been normal. She'd have to ask Chris . . . if she ever saw him again.

Sister Nemain's harsh voice invaded her thoughts as her fist clenched her stick, squeezing so tight her knuckles hurt. 'That woman is never going to let him go.' Her mind wandered back to the sub, deep beneath that alien ocean. Underwater, her ears had been unreliable, but Chris had always been beside her. He'd been steady like an anchor in the madness. Even when Chooth was choking the life from her, she hadn't been alone. She reached up and touched her neck, feeling the memory on her skin. Down below in the water, pain was the only way she knew what was real, from the pressure in her ears to the stifling heat in those caverns, it had kept her moving

It would be easy to give up now and settle into her new life, but she wasn't going to do that. She was going to save Chris, then they'd work on the other problem. They'd join Amita, wherever she was. From what Ben said, she'd never given up hope, never stopped looking for a way home, and if someone as smart as Amita thought it was possible, who was Katy to surrender?

First Chris though. There only one way she could imagine him going free, solving the murder. Cathal was trying, but he was a war hero, not a detective. The thought, 'And what am I?' crept in. She shook her head chasing it away.

Still upset, it took a moment to notice a scent in the air. She realized she wasn't alone as the colony popped into her mind, and she said, "For someone who gets around mostly by swimming, you walk very quietly."

Naiathne's voice was hushed. "I find the fewer people that notice me the better it is when I'm on dry land." She paused. Katy could hear the Naiad take a deep breath before asking, "Do you mind if I join you?"

Forcing a smile, Katy nodded. "Sure, pull up a seat."

Naiathne looked around. The furniture had been stacked back in a corner so she sat on the floor next to Katy instead. Sliding over a little, Katy gave Naiathne a bit of the wall to lean against. Naiathne was quiet, but there was an air of anticipation in her silence. Out on the balcony was the first time they'd been alone together. She heard her friend's shallow breaths and didn't want to seem unfriendly, so Katy asked, "How's it feel to be free?"

They'd eaten dinner together with everyone at the Sidhe table, Cormack, Ben, and the rest of the clan. Naiathne tried to dote on her, helping Katy fill her tray and Katy had let her, even though it was an annoyance she wouldn't have tolerated from the boys. After the way breakfast had gone, her only concern was to finish the meal with as little drama as possible. They talked then but it was tough to hear in the crowded room and while Naiathne wanted her attention, Katy had been more interested in listening to Cormack, who'd finally spoken to Cathal.

"'How's it feel to be free?'" Naiathne repeated Katy's question and made a short, awkward sound that could've been a laugh. "Well, the view is better, that's for sure," Her hand touched her own neck, running through her soft black hair.

Katy picked up the tone in her voice and could hear her fidgeting. She ignored it as she motioned towards the grand hall. "I wouldn't know of course."

"Oh, I wasn't talking about out there. Besides the lights are out. There are only a few twinkling way over on the other wall. Plus, you can see the dark side of Altor through the window. It glows a bit even during the night cycle. The storms, you know? They're kind of pretty." Naiathne's voice rambled out. She'd been so confident on Grannus, angry, almost shrill, but here on the station, she was a different person. Her self-assurance felt naked and artificial. She was afraid, even more so as she tried to flirt with Katy.

"No, I knew what you meant," Katy said. "Um," she started, and even though she didn't need to, she turned a bit to face Naiathne, sliding over and giving a little more room. "How was Chris? Is he holding up okay?"

Naiathne didn't answer right away. "He's not happy to be in a cell of course. And he's worried about his brother, but I think— well, he's Chris. He's tough to figure. He's got a cast on both his legs and the only thing he can complain about is that he doesn't have anything to read."

"Sounds about right," Katy said.

Naiathne was quiet for a moment. Then she asked, "You care about him?"

"Of course," Katy said. Naiathne was close enough that Katy could feel her back move and her shoulders drop.

"He's hard not to like, I suppose," Naiathne said.

Sensing the disappointment in her friend's voice, Katy reached out to find her hand. Naiathne's skin was cold to the touch, especially at the fingertips, but as Katy touched her palm, she felt it bloom with warmth. 'Is this cruel or kind,' she wondered as she explained, "It's not like that. I think all of us from Earth, we've been through something together. We all understand what we lost. Plus, this place is so strange and the way people see things, it's a different point of view than ours. I think I'm still in culture shock. I don't know if any of us will ever understand this world. The five of us should be together because we get each other."

"The five of you, like as a group. Not as a couple? Because you know, I think Chris has stronger feelings," Naiathne said.

"He has a crush." Katy shrugged. "It happens." She was trying not to sound annoyed. Instead, she was afraid she came off as aloof. She didn't want that either.

Over her life, people wanting more from Katy had happened time and again. She was aware that being pretty had its benefits, getting out of tickets, people buying her gifts, and cutting her slack when she was late to class. She'd be lying if she said she didn't enjoy the attention, sometimes, but she'd found that it also made it hard to open up to anyone since all they ever saw was the surface. Even with her mom, when she hurt herself— When people found out about it, they treated Katy like a wounded thing, but it always came with a catch. They wanted to fix her and more than that they wanted their affection returned.

"But you don't feel the same?" Naiathne couldn't hide the little bit of hope in her voice.

"I don't know. Probably not, but even if I did, you have to understand, with everything going on the idea of worrying about something like that, relationships, boyfriend/girlfriend crap, it's kind of nuts.

"Chris is a friend. I care a lot about him, but he is a friend and that's what I need right now. I think that's what all of us need. He gets that, I hope, but we haven't talked about it— I don't know, maybe we should, but after everything we've been through. . ."

Naiathne didn't say anything as Katy's thoughts faded away. Then she shook her head and said, "I can't believe he tried taking the blame for me. He's lucky they didn't execute him right there."

"Strong, silent, and stupid type, right?" Katy smiled, feeling more warmth than she expected as she thought of Chris's voice. "I need to help him. I need to get him out. I owe him too much to let this go."

"I'll help in any way I can," Naiathne said. "I'll be your friend too." She squeezed Katy's hand. "But I've got to be honest. I, ah—"

"I know," Katy turned to her, having to guess where Naiathne's eyes were. "I'm just not looking for that . . . not right now anyway."

"I get it." Naiathne's voice sounded more confident.

She tried to pull her hand away, but Katy held onto it for a moment more, squeezing back before releasing her grip and saying, "Do I need to tell your brother too?"

"Why?" Naiathne asked.

Katy motioned back to the entrance of the Sidhe domain. "Come on. I may be blind, but it's pretty obvious. Look what he's done for me."

"Katy, I hate to break it to you, but if Cormack gave you anything or was being nice to you, he was probably just being nice. I've never known him to be interested in anyone."

Katy was honestly surprised. "Really?"

Naiathne lowered her voice. "I've never known him to even talk about it. I think it's because he's the heir to the throne. He's going to be told who to marry and he'll be expected to keep the line going and whatnot. I guess he figures it's not worth the effort to care about anyone in that way."

"Or maybe he's just not into girls," Katy suggested.

Naiathne was quiet for a moment as she considered it. "I mean other rulers have been suspected of being that way and it's not unheard of in royal families, but, as I said, lineage is everything, so that sort of thing is frowned on. Our mother would probably toss him in the ocean too if she found out." Katy couldn't see it but Naiathne pointed back at the door as well. "Stuff like this, all the royalty and the power, well, it kind of traps Cormack. He doesn't get to be himself. In a way, I'm the one who's free. In the colony, they don't care who you love. We're just happy when they're not trying to exterminate us."

Katy wasn't sure what to say. All she wanted to do was go home. Leave this place behind and take her friends with her, including Naiathne. She wanted a place where her friend would be safe. She thought of Earth and said, "Our world was sort of like that, centuries like that, but things were changing, getting better, I think. At least where I was from, that kind of hatred was no longer generally accepted. Unfortunately hate still happens. It's like people know the right way to be, that they should accept others for who they are and not what they are, but it seems like human nature to think the worst of those that are different from you. And how do you fix human nature?"

After a moment Katy answered her own question, "You probably start by not calling hatred natural. Not giving it an excuse."

"Things don't ever change here," Naiathne said.

"Not unless you change them," Katy said.

"You sound like you want to lead a revolution?" Naiathne cocked her head and raised an eyebrow.

Katy heard the playful derision in her voice. "Maybe later, but first I have to get Chris out." She shook her head and jammed her hands into the air in frustration. "I Just don't know how to do it. I have no idea what my next move is. According to Cathal, the lighthouse was a bust. There was nothing there. No sign of someone being murdered anyway, but then again, he said they didn't give him much time to look around. They're more worried about their weird alien machines and now Cathal is sworn to secrecy about it."

Katy stopped for a moment remembering the reverence in Cathal's voice as he mentioned the machines in a whisper, then silenced himself. Of course, Ben had gone there before with Amita, and he was more than willing to give a detailed account, but that was from well before the murder. "I really thought we were onto something there. Do you think we can trust Cathal?"

"What do you mean?"

"Well, I think he hated the head monk as much as anyone else and I keep getting this sense that he's dragging his feet as he looks into this."

Naiathne sat back. "I think you're just being impatient. And do you really think he'd take a bunch of students for a hike where he got rid of the body?"

"No, I suppose not, but I can't help feeling like he's hiding something. He seems reluctant to talk to any of the Extraracials. Like he doesn't want it to be one of them."

"That's because he doesn't. On my world, they gave Cathal credit for saving Anchor Home, but he had help, lots of help. He was always outspoken about how he saw things. That the way the royals and people think of themselves is wrong. People are no better than anyone else than any of the Extraracials."

Naiathne got to her feet and wandered over to the edge of the balcony. She turned and leaned back against it as she asked, "In fact, if you really want to know what's going on, you should try talking to Regin. He's one of the smartest beings here. Have you ever had a conversation with him?"

Katy thought about the night she'd followed his voice down into the alien sector when she'd run into

Fajalar. "No, not really. I've been to his class but I haven't talked to him about the murder." Her conversation had been so uncomfortable with the Long-Wolf that she'd nearly put it out of her mind. Coming close to drowning a moment later had helped with that.

"You should. If you want my advice, then I'd say, get his. Regin keeps his eyes open all the time. Fafnir, Andavarri even Eir, before she got sick, paid attention to everything that happened at Nalanda. Most people don't notice the Extraracials. Royal brats are really good at ignoring things they consider beneath them but trust me our professors know a lot more than they let on."

"Okay, so I'll talk to Regin." Katy started to get up, but Naiathne held up her hands.

"Well not now," Naiathne said. "Not during the night cycle."

Even with her eyes bleached and scarred, she was still able to roll them as she cocked her hip. "Everybody is really afraid of that?" she asked.

"Yeah, and you should be too. The ghosts are a real thing," Naiathne said.

"Ben said Amita went out every night while she was here and they never bothered her."

"Yeah, and I used to go out at night too, at least for a little while. But then, one night— Well I saw one."

"Really?"

"There's a reservoir a few levels down, pure clean drinking water, melted ice from one of the asteroids. Sometimes, I— um' would go swimming in it."

"In the drinking water?" Katy's face tightened up.

"Well, yeah, I swam in it. But it's not like I peed in it or something. Anyway, I'd been hearing these strange noises at night, but I ignored them because the water was just too nice. Then one time I came near the surface and saw this thing with all these eyes staring down at me. It had long blades from its arms and it was dancing

298

the point of one just above my head like it was waiting to skewer me. If I'd been a normal person, I would've drowned waiting for it to go away. It was nearly an hour before I could run back here." She laughed nervously. "Honestly, you're the first person I've said anything about it to."

"Why?" Katy asked.

"Because I didn't want Cormack getting all brotherly with me and saying I couldn't go out anymore. But the ghosts aren't even what you need to worry about if you go looking for Regin."

"Are you sure?" Katy asked. "Cause' that sounds pretty horrible to me."

"Yeah, but female Ice-Carvers are worse. The Ice-Carver domain is divided so the males and females hardly ever see each other, but what with being blind you could easily get lost and end up on the wrong side."

Katy felt a little rage flare up inside her and she opened her mouth to say something, but then she remembered her last trip to the Extraracial's territory as Naiathne continued, "During the day the females you see are heavily drugged, but at night they go into a deep sleep cycle. If you ever woke one, well let's just say even Fafnir would have to worry about getting his head ripped off."

"If they're so dangerous, then why are they here?" Katy blurted out, realizing that she was lucky she only took a swim with the Grannusians and that she hadn't followed Regin any further.

"According to the monks the Æsir wanted all the sentient species in the system brought together. I don't know. It's some sort of half-hearted attempt at keeping humans from wiping them all out. And trust me they tried with the female Ice-Carvers. They almost went the way of the Lightning Bugs. The only reason any are left is because they're better at hiding."

"But if they killed all the females—"

Naiathne finished her thought. "It would effectively wipe out their species, yes. So, I guess things do change. The Æesir are vicious and their monks suck but, in a way, I suppose they've made some things better."

"Okay so tomorrow I'll talk to Regin after class," Katy said.

"Don't you mean we'll talk to Regin?" Naiathne asked.

"Oh, no. I have a much more important mission for you. You're going to have to distract Ben. His interview technique leaves a bit to be desired."

"Not very subtle, is he?" Naiathne asked.

Katy shrugged. "Yeah, no, that's not really his style." Naiathne didn't say anything, but Katy felt an urge to point out. "He's got a good heart, but he can be a bit much."

Naiathne said, "He's family, they're always a bit much." Then the two of them went back in, leaving the darkened hall behind.

Chapter 30

Edith felt Maeven tucked behind her as she hustled through the halls, only stopping to clear corners before moving on. She'd told the princess to stay tight and hide behind her armor. Knowing her uniform wouldn't do a thing to stop a bullet, the princess listened to every instruction the mercenary gave her. They were on a clock, and it wasn't only because of the camera blackout Edith had scheduled. She knew her father was on the way and that he had no interest in talking to the Tairnishmen.

An explosion echoed through the halls, shaking the concrete walls. As they ducked, Maeven asked with her voice low and tense, "Did he start?"

Orbital bombardment worked best in clusters, there wouldn't be a single impact. It was probably the charge rigged to the battle armor. "No, that was inside. That might've been Alex," Edith admitted, knowing she was taking a tactical risk.

She glanced back at Maeven to see if his name evoked any sort of response. Maeven was scared, but she cocked her head and asked, "He came with you?"

All this time Edith wondered what the princess wanted from him. Was it simple attraction or did she see value in learning about the void spaces and where the five travelers came from? The first reason was understandable, the second gave insight into the princess. It would let Edith know how much Maeven was like her father.

"Is he going to be joining us?" Maeven asked as they moved again.

The explosion was closer than Edith would've thought, maybe even on the same level. Alex had been higher than that, closer to the top of the commune when she checked the security feed. She thought of the information packet she'd sent and her message, hoping Alex had a chance to open it before setting that charge.

"Probably not," Edith said. "He's the distraction and he's doing a hell of a job."

"Oh." Maeven's eyes dropped to the floor as the little bit of hope she'd held disappeared.

'So maybe it was more than attraction, real affection, even love,' Edith thought. 'I wonder if Alex understands how valuable that is and how dangerous.' She preferred keeping her dealings with nobles businesslike, making herself invaluable for her skill, not caught up in their whims and emotions.

Not long after the explosion the duo came to an area that was grander than the rest. This part of the commune had high ceilings and wide doorways that were set back with barred vestibules in front of private apartments. Edith imagined the original intention was to position security inside the vestibules, protecting the restricted homes of the ruling class, but adornments had crept into each entrance. She peered through the bars and saw soft lighting dangling down, different than the utilitarian illumination in the rest of the commune.

There were elaborate carvings on the stone walls with beautiful scrolling designs as well. Even as spartan as these Tairnish claimed to be, they were still people, and this proved it, the urge to own pretty things was a part of their humanity they couldn't deny. Of course, the second part of that was the urge to laud those things over others.

She motioned with her hand, telling Maeven to stay back as she peered inside the bars. The vestibule was empty. While every other Tairnishmen was on their way to kill Alex, Edith had no doubt these guards had a different destination. They were getting the family they protected to safety.

Edith took out a small torch and started cutting through the lock. Only a moment later the hardware dropped away and she motioned for Maeven to follow her in as the gate swung open.

"These are the homes of the wealthy of Tairnish," she explained.

"I thought they didn't believe in wealth, that everything was shared," Maeven asked snidely. She was trying to sound aloof, but it was impossible to hide the tremble in her voice.

"The ruling families make out a bit better than most," Edith said. "Bigger quarters and more importantly private escape routes to emergency shuttles. It looks like these folks already started that way."

"So, we're stealing their shuttle? That's the plan?" Maeven nodded her head approvingly.

"They'll be easier to take than the combat ships. That's where Alex was heading to, unless—" Edith came to the door. It was disguised to look like wood, but she could tell it was made of something much stronger. Her best chance was the locking mechanism.

She heard Maeven ask, "Unless what?" as she started to cut away the casing.

Edith shook her head, wondering why she'd done it. "I tipped him off. If he's still alive then he's got our location. If he can make it here, he can exit with us, but we can't wait for him." She almost added, 'Since he's probably got about a thousand Tairnishmen trying to kill him.' She turned back to Maeven, wondering if the princess was going to play the royalty card and order her to go back for her boyfriend, but Maeven stayed quiet, nodding and turning to watch the hallway.

Edith kneeled and examined the lock. The casing was off and she could see the mechanism inside. It was weak, which wasn't a good thing. There's no way a simple lock would be the only way they secured this door. There had to be something else on the other side. Edith tapped the solid surface once and made a decision that she didn't like.

"I'm going to have to make some noise," she said taking out a shaped charge and pressing it along the hinge side. She took Maeven's elbow and guided her back into the hall, past the bars, and out into the open. She glanced at the time in her display and knew the camera blackout was over. "When I move, stay right on top of me," she ordered.

Maeven nodded while Edith holstered her silenced sidearm and unstrapped her rifle. No point in being quiet after this. She removed the lengthened barrel and held it low and at the ready as she glanced back once more at the princess. "Cover your ears," she said before pressing the detonator switch. She felt the wall shake behind her and the concussive force pushing into the hall. When it stopped, she tapped Maeven's shoulder and started into the smoke and debris.

∞

Alex was on the floor again, tripping for the second time. His left leg was so stiff that it was tough to stay on his feet as the muscles in his thigh and calf had been torn in the firefight and patched with some sort of hardening substance. The good news was the high-velocity rounds missed his bones. He was still dragging the leg, finding it impossible to run. Any attempt left him like this, face down on the floor.

He heard voices in the hall ahead of him and glanced up, seeing two Tairnishmen approaching. They were dark shadows against the green grid lines painted in his goggle's display. These were the first two people to come across him since collapsing the central staircase, giving him a momentary reprieve that he didn't think would last. They weren't wearing armor but they were carrying firearms. Alex was so small compared to them and covered in dirt and debris that while buried in the corner of the hall, they didn't notice him, giving him a chance to move his weapon forward.

With the submachine gun pointed out, he rested his elbows on the floor and pulled the trigger, feeling it nearly jump out of his hands. He'd never fired a fully automatic weapon before, outside of the armor. Alex tried to control it, hardly able to believe that he could pilot a massive weapons system but struggle with something this small.

At home, his dad had shown him and Chris how to shoot the Sig Sauer they kept in the house, but the sum of his training on this weapon was a quick explanation of how to load it on the shuttle.

He was lucky though, one of the green forms dropped to the ground while the other ducked back around the corner. Alex had no idea how many people were on this floor. but so far, in the few moments after exploding his armor, it'd proven fairly empty. That wouldn't last now that weapons fire was being exchanged.

He heard the other Tairnishman screaming at him and firing with a small pistol. The shots landed above his head, exploding in the wall as he pushed back and scurried to find cover. Without the armor, the acidic smell of gunpowder combined with the concrete dust filled Alex's lungs and made him cough.

He listened to the shots, wondering how many the other man had fired, wondering if a bullet was going to crash into his skull. He sat back, searching Edith's goody bag for one of the grenades.

"What am I doing!?" he demanded, talking to himself as he fell back on his side. It was partially to find cover but also, he could no longer control his body. He trembled with fear, almost like his head was separated from the rest of him and the rest was beginning to revolt.

He pulled one of the little spheres out. He armed the grenade and set it in the air, watching it float a half meter above the floor, then with a hand motion he sent it towards his enemy.

The grenade moved with a single-minded purpose and disappeared around the corner. This wasn't the same as on the station. It wasn't smoke that came pouring out. Instead, it erupted with a deadly charge, a cargo of shrapnel meant to kill. Alex heard it pelt the concrete and felt the pressure wave as warm air moved past him. He took a long breath before getting back to his feet, using the wall to push himself along, dragging his nearly useless leg.

He didn't look down at the first man he shot as he kept his eye on the corner. Coming around the wall he tried to maintain as much cover as possible. The next body waited, looking incredibly real, even with the grid from the goggles painted over it. Alex turned from the man's remains and tried to control his emotions. 'It's nothing, not a person, not anymore, not real, just an obstacle,' he told himself with his attention further down the hall, pointing his weapon that way while trying to hold it steady.

He stepped around the remains, finding them impossible to avoid as he still had to use the wall for balance. 'You're never going to be the same again,' a voice said in Alex's head that he barely recognized as his own.

Reaching the end of the hall, he tried again to control the shaking. 'Were those voices?' he wondered at the next corner, steadying himself to clear his head. He didn't want to do this anymore. He didn't want to shoot anyone else.

'That's not true,' the voice said as he remembered the training in the shuttle, the thrill of moving that armor. He remembered his father standing on a sunny day as an admiral saluted him on a stage. Men in uniform came up to Alex's family, shaking his dad's hand. Trumpets played and flags were flying in the air. All Alex ever wanted was to be a soldier, a sailor, like his dad. He remembered his father's face, then said to himself, "Keep moving."

He pulled the map up, trying to find the route Edith had laid out for him. He wasn't far and by luck, he was on the right level. There'd been a one in ten chance that he'd hit the right landing after being shot by a tank. 'I guess things are going my way.'

That's when he heard another explosion. It came from the direction marked on the map. He dropped to the floor, covering his head. 'How close?' He wasn't sure.

He thought, 'That wasn't for me. They're not trying to blow me up and there was only one other person who'd be making a racket like that.' Alex laughed a little, grateful for the explosion because it confirmed he was going the right way. He also knew it would bring everyone else on this level. He got to his feet and started trying to run again, forcing himself to stay up.

∞

Edith had fought with Tairnishmen during the Grannus campaign. She'd served as their air support taking tiny islands from the scattered clans of that watery moon. The Tairnishmen were good fighters, but Edith didn't like them. They were always ornery, had no sense of humor, and not much respect for women, at least not as fighters. No, Tairnishmen weren't who she would choose to go to war with again.

Their harsh world with its strict rules and respect for only physical strength gave females very little chance to succeed in their military. She remembered the look the infantry soldiers gave her when she climbed down from her drop armor, nodding their heads as if it figured that she'd need such equipment to compete on their level.

As Edith stormed through the door of the apartment, she smiled a little, hoping to see that same look again, but the rooms were empty. Her movements were rapid as she cleared the dwelling, going through the front room into a hall that branched off in three directions, to the bedrooms, the main room, and to a private kitchen, which was the ultimate luxury in a Tairnish commune. The space was large but not nearly as big as what a noble would enjoy on Uppsala. After making certain it was unoccupied, she went back through the short hall and into the main sitting room, where a sunken floor led to a window looking out on a massive, softly lit cavern.

"Was this Vyktor's home?" Maeven asked, following her.

"I doubt it," Edith said. "Tairnish children are raised together. He wouldn't live in a place like this till he was an adult. It might belong to someone related to him though, an aunt or something maybe even his mom, but probably not, there's more than one family with this kind of clout," Edith motioned to the window. "And they're all probably down there getting ready to run."

"His mom? Why do you say that?" Maeven asked.

Edith never let her hand slip from her rifle as she searched the wall for an entrance. It was probably disguised in the paneling. The security briefing hadn't been specific about its location, probably as an extra layer of protection against someone doing what they were trying right now.

The window took up most of the far wall of the room, then there were bookcases on one side and paneling on the other. The entrance was probably hidden in one of those. She searched the floor looking for any breaks in the molding indicating a secret entrance while explaining, "Vyktor's right to sit on the central committee came down through his mom's family. His father has been dead since Grannus, but you know, fallen hero and whatnot, it would've only cemented his spot."

"I've never really understood the way they run things," Maeven said distracted by the window. She peered out trying to see if she could catch a glance of the escaping aristocracy.

"Nobody does. It's all pretty secretive. That way they can say it's fair but in truth, it's not all that different from your own monarchy. Families sit on committees and those organizations run their government. Those seats are supposed to go to the most deserving, smartest or whatever, whoever's leadership would best guide their government, but you know how it is, people don't give up power once they have it."

"You don't approve?" Maeven turned back, perfectly comfortable communicating with Edith's darkened helmet.

"I wouldn't dare to have an opinion about government. That's not my job. I'm a killer, and my work is made easier by keeping my eyes open and observing and by understanding how things function. What are you doing?" Edith watched Maeven wander over to a desk with a terminal.

"I'm going to try and open their network and get an update. I figured if these rooms belong to one of their leaders, they might have access to the security systems, or even be able to tell us when my father will arrive."

Edith didn't think it was a bad idea, but then she heard a sound that let her know their time was up. Heavy boots came stomping towards them. She glanced back as a canister came bouncing into the room. With incredible speed, she kicked it back out.

Her reaction had been lightning-fast, but still, she caught some of the blast as it exploded in the air. It threw her back, slamming her into the window. The force of her body didn't leave a mark on the reinforced glass.

Alerts went off inside her armor as Edith hit the floor and pulled herself out of the line of fire a heartbeat before bullets started pouring in, thumping and tearing apart the walls.

"Find cover!" she screamed to Maeven as she flattened out and brought her rifle up to return fire. She let out a quick burst as she scurried to the side of the doorway where she dialed up the sensors in her armor to see what she was facing. Radar penetrated through the solid walls, revealing four soldiers. Judging by their size, they were probably wearing tactical power armor like hers.

The rounds Edith fired were made to crack armor. If only they could turn corners too, like the spoilers on the battle suit. Luckily her random fire had caused some damage. She saw two men carrying a third back into the kitchen, out of the line of fire. Edith doubted he was down for good, but she could always hope.

One thing she knew for certain was that these guys had backup on the way and they'd be here soon. For right now though she only saw one form moving toward them. She stared at it for a moment and noticed how it was limping, looking like it was about to fall over. "Huh," Edith said, having a pretty good idea who this might be. Her radar picked up something else. Back in the hall, just inside the wall was a void, an opening, and the top of a ladder. She dialed her radar out further, no longer caring if it were detected.

"What the hell," Edith said shrugging as she leaned her head out just a hair to see that the grenade she kicked had blasted away the paneling and revealed a heavy door. Bullets came ripping down at her, forcing her to pull back before her head was blown off.

"So, I found our exit," Edith called over to Maeven, who had climbed under the desk, understanding how vulnerable she was. Maeven looked at her questioningly.

"It's back there." Edith pointed while using the wall to get to her feet. "I'm going to have to rush these guys in a second. When I do, try and get out that way. The door is probably locked, but try it anyway."

"We can hear you," Someone yelled down the hall.

"Oh, okay," Edith called back to them. "Just so you know, I'm going to come down there and kill all four of you in the next minute/minute and half. It might even be quicker than that." Edith checked her weapon. "You might want to think about running," she said as she checked the radar again, watching the blob, holding something dark.

A loud, derisive laugh answered. 'And I thought these guys didn't have a sense of humor,' she wondered as the laugh was cut off by an explosion. The soldiers hadn't expected a grenade to come floating down the hall from behind them. She felt the pressure wave.

Edith didn't hesitate. She came around the corner, keeping the wall to her back as she stormed forward in the fading debris cloud. She had her targets painted. One man only a few meters in front of her was getting to his feet, kneeling forward in a lunge. The force of this second grenade had been enough to knock him down, but his armor kept him alive for the moment.

He was blocking the entire hallway, with each of his reinforced shoulders to a side and barely enough space to bring his weapon up. He saw Edith come through the veil of destruction and with a quick pull of her trigger, she sent three rounds into his center mass, cracking the armor and killing him.

Putting her barrel on his shoulder as he fell, she shot the man behind him who collapsed to the side, slumping down the wall. There was another, not far away still on the ground, getting up to his hands and knees. This soldier had taken most of the blast and was still recovering.

Edith lifted her rifle and let the man in front, the first one she killed, fall. Climbing over his hulking form, she walked down his back in the crowded space, then clambered past the next body.

The third soldier was pulling himself out of the line of fire and attempting to turn to fight, but Edith was faster. Standing awkwardly on the second fallen Tairnishman, she fired and killed him. Then she started looking for number four, the one they pulled out of the hallway in the beginning.

Movement caught her attention at the front door. She pointed her rifle that way but didn't pull the trigger seeing Alex come stumbling into view. "There's another one to the right," Edith said as she checked the radar, seeing the last soldier close in on the boy. Edith placed the butt of her rifle on the ground and launched herself toward him, tackling the soldier before he could grab Alex.

She knew that if the man had managed to get a hold of the boy, the hurt soldier, in a power suit would've been able to crush every bone in Alex's body.

She slammed the man into the wall, then threw him back the way he'd come, into the kitchen. Cabinets along the wall shattered and blew apart from the impact. The soldier pulled his sidearm, but Edith was already on him with her knife in hand. With the hardened blade out, she fell on him and drove her knees forward, thrusting the blade under his helmet, finishing off her last target.

"I warned you guys," she said tapping him on the head before taking the knife back out. She found a kitchen towel hanging above the sink and wiped the blade off as she went back to Alex. "You did good." she pointed down the hall. "Your girlfriend is over there. Go grab her so we can get out of here."

Alex took his goggles off and stared at the mercenary in her black faceless armor. Then his eyes went over the

312

bodies on the floor. Edith had moved so fast that all he could understand were the results.

He felt a shift in reality as he answered, "Yeah, I'll go get Maeven." Then he started to climb over them, thankful they were in hardened shells. Coming into the sitting room his eyes met Maeven's. She was still hiding below the desk. He heard the sound of Edith punching the wall and glanced over his shoulder, seeing her open a secret hatch, then he turned back and waved awkwardly to the princess.

"Hey," he said as he leaned down to offer his hand. Maeven took it and got to her feet. Their eyes met for only a moment before she wrapped her arms around him with more emotion than Alex had ever seen from her. The moment lasted a long time, neither willing to let go till Edith called, "Come on kids. The fights not over yet and we've still got a shuttle to steal."

Chapter 31

Nearly five hundred kilometers above Tairnish, Tara waited at the airlock of her shuttle. She closed her mouth and tried to wipe the shocked look from her face as she listened to the hiss of the doors opening. A breeze touched her, moving her pale hair, while the pressure regulated and she turned away from Andavarri, who a moment before had smiled and confided that the emperor was listening to them. "This is your chance to impress him," Andavarri said, touching a spot behind her ear. "Your master will hear everything you have to say." The door opened to soldiers standing inside the ring dock. These were her escorts to the latest day of negotiations.

Without enough time to question Andavarri, Tara felt her eyes go wide as she forced her attention from the Long-Wolf and tried to compose herself. She knew about the command crystals Andavarri's people used to direct Fire-Golems, surgically implanted beneath their skin. She wondered if Tamerlane had found some way to hijack that transmission or if he'd had Andavarri implanted with a different listening device.

"Are you all right?" one of the guards asked, his voice coming out slightly distorted from behind his armored mask and that strange, almost human face sculpted into his helmet.

"Yes, I'm sorry," Tara said as she pushed herself off the doorway. "Ambassador Andavarri will be joining us."

The guard looked at the purple creature and nodded. "Follow me."

Last night, in his message, the emperor had made it clear to Tara that he wanted the Long-Wolf in the room for the next meeting. Tara had been a little insulted, wondering if his faith in her was waning. Now she knew the truth. He wanted a spy. All this time she'd been wondering if she could trust Andavarri, or if she was playing both sides, but now Tara saw the truth. The Long-Wolf was Tamerlane's through and through. With the Revenant so close, he'd hear everything in real-time, know every word spoken in the room and he'd be able to respond at a moment's notice.

She followed the guards through the airlock and into the corridor. After hours of debate and under constant threat, this was the first time she felt dread in her stomach. Her back rigid, she tracked Andavarri with her peripheral vision, moving easily through the zero-g corridor. The Long-Wolf's tail was waving behind her, like a water moccasin.

Ahead was the small office that had been her home for the past two days during hours of negotiations and interrogation. Andavarri looked as comfortable as ever, while Tara stifled an urge to run back to the shuttle.

One guard took up a position in front of her while the other stayed behind, looking like squat, angry boulders in their armor. They paid little attention to the Long-Wolf, who had officially declared her neutrality and been given free rein over the station. Rifles were stowed on their backs but in those powerful suits, Tara knew they wouldn't need a bullet to kill her. A swipe of the arm, swatting her against a bulkhead, and she'd be dead in an instant. She allowed herself to imagine it and thought, 'it'd be a relief.'

She sensed the guard's feelings. They were barely even considering her. Their minds were rigid and focused, leaning into their training to stuff down their own anxiety, but worry was in the air like blood in the water. Tara could feel it coming from everyone they passed.

In only a few moments the emperor's flagship would finish its deceleration burn and slip into an orbit around Tairnish. He'd been in effective weapons range for a few hours, or at least close enough that the Tairnish could do little to stop him if he decided to start his bombardment.

It was possible to launch ordnance from anywhere in the system, but a missile fired from several moons away was easier to counter. With a projectile fired from orbit, time was no longer your friend and neither was gravity.

When the Revenant took up its position with an entire fleet not far behind, it would mean the sky belonged to Tamerlane. The Tairnishmen controlled only a small defense fleet and they had only a handful of combat pilots with experience. There were defenses on the ring itself, but many of the tactical satellites around it were still code-locked by the emperor's forces. Somewhere, Tara was sure, captured Uppsalan officers were being interrogated, slowly broken to get those codes, but that was a long, arduous process and not one that the blunt Tairnishmen had ever proven effective at.

Their military services had almost always been infantry or artillery. The only advantage they held was in their zero-g combat training with veteran marines experienced at boarding enemy ships.

That's how they'd taken the ring so effectively, but they'd have to get to the emperor's ship to use that advantage, not an easy task given the number of combat drones at his command. Already, the swarm had deployed and surrounded the Revenant like a cloud. The small picket ships with their human pilots controlled the cloud, staying tight to its massive form, protected by rotary cannons that would slice through any boarding craft that approached.

Tara knew this ring would be the emperor's first target, yet here she was walking away from her shuttle, her only escape. The emperor had no interest in taking back anything from Tairnish. She didn't know why, but he was done with the world. He may hope to recover his daughter, but that wasn't his main purpose. The Tairnish had declared themselves his enemy and now he was going to punish them.

The door to the interview room opened and the guards took up positions to the left and right. Rolfe Yulset stood behind the table, his feet firmly planted on the ground, though he had to hold the table to do it as his eyes went to Andavarri. "Well, today should be interesting." He sneered behind his white beard, bright compared to his light purple skin.

Andavarri rolled her clawed fingers. "I assure you I'm only here out of curiosity. Please ignore my presence." She took a spot near the ceiling. Then she added, "I have nothing to add to this conversation."

Rolfe Yulset nodded and looked down at his monitor, saying to Tara, "It appears your emperor has nothing to add either. His flagship has finished its burn and settled into a high orbit just above the ring, but he doesn't seem interested in talking to us. The communications officers on the Revenant made it quite clear that all negotiations are to be done through you, and you alone."

"I'm honored by my emperor's trust." Tara nodded as she entered the room with its curved ceiling. There was no up in the zero-gravity, but the module had a flat floor installed to give them reference.

Yulset stared, considering her, before he asked, "You're what, sixteen? A child. Why? Why would he insist on this? I thought you'd only come for your friend. Gone ahead with some stupid idea that you could save her. I placated you in case I was wrong. Now I see what you really are, an insult."

Tara gave a gentle nod, exhaling slowly. "'An insult—' I disagree," she said simply while thinking, 'And you weren't placating, just probing. You wanted information.'

Yulset could only see her calm face, unmoved by his words. "No? Then please, explain."

Tara looked briefly at Andavarri, who rolled her eyes in response. "Why would the emperor have me negotiate for him? Is that your question?"

Yulset nodded. "Yes."

"There are two possible answers that I can see." She pulled herself across the room, till she was floating above her assigned seat. "The first is that I am the daughter of a king. One, who despite being beholden to an emperor, his servant as you've said before, is still incredibly powerful. The emperor knows that I've been raised since I was a child for diplomacy, raised in his own house as a handmaiden to his heir."

Tara smiled. "Trust me, I couldn't do this work for Maeven if I weren't a skilled diplomat. There aren't many who could handle her."

Yulset didn't share in her smile. She could sense his skepticism overwhelming a glimmer of hope as he asked her to continue, "Be that as it may?"

Tara pretended ignorance for a moment till Yulset motioned with his hand for her to answer. "Oh, the other option. The one I think you suspect is the emperor's real reason for sending me. You think he doesn't care about what happens in this room. That he doesn't care about what happens to you or your people, or to me for that matter. We're spent resources, both you and I, with no actual value left."

"Yes, well, if that's the case, then there's no reason to continue talking. If your emperor believes you aren't worth his notice then it will fall to us to demand his attention."

Tara held up her finger. As she opened her mouth, she knew she was about to take a pointless risk, but she thought of her friend Maeven. She had no idea if Edith's mission would succeed and this might be her last chance to free the princess through diplomacy. "Or, perhaps the truth is somewhere in the middle. Perhaps things are exactly how I've presented them, on both sides of this argument."

She waited to see if she was getting through to him, but Yulset's face was as rigid as stone. She continued, "You've angered the emperor in a way that few have. You talk about getting his attention. Well, I assure you, you've got it. What you do now is up to you, but if you want my suggestion, I would continue talking to me, take the opportunity to get what you can, even if it's only scraps. Then I would do my damndest to make amends and show your value to him."

Yulset was silent considering her words. He lowered his eyes and in a deep voice snarled, "Amends? Value?" His eyebrows furrowed. Rage seeped off him.

Tara broke a little under it, curling away. Not because she was scared but because she knew there was no getting through. She leaned forward anyway. "Yes, settle this, take what you have, give back Maeven, and apologize for your actions. Before this, your people may have served the empire but you always had some level of independence. Perhaps more could be arranged. You need to find a path forward before it's too late."

"We will serve no more!" Yulset was about to slam his fist on the table again but he thought better of it, remembering how it'd gone before. Instead, he stared at her. "This conversation is pointless. Perhaps I could get your emperor to talk to me by sending you back to him through an airlock. Let your icy corpse speak for me."

Tara could sense that this wasn't an idle threat. "He wouldn't care," she said softly.

Yulset's mind was busy, but through the noise, she heard something like sympathy touch his feelings. It made Tara feel even more terrible. She watched his hand go down to his monitor and press a button, a moment later the doors opened. "I've wasted enough time with you. I will take no more advice or assurances from a child. Your emperor sits above us with his bombs ready to drop. With weapons pointed at us and I'm only given you to talk to. Take a few hours. If you have his ear, then tell him that if he wants his daughter treated well, I'll hear from him personally. When he deigns to speak to me, then I will consider coming back here. Till then I'll waste no more time."

"You're making a mistake," Tara said.

Yulset pulled himself down into his chair, then waved dismissively. "It's not my first and it won't be my last. Guards, take her back to the shuttle."

Tara opened her mouth to speak again, but long fingers touched her face, and another hand took her shoulder, turning her away. It was Andavarri dropping from the ceiling and using her momentum to spin Tara toward the door in the zero-g. "Let's be on our way," the Long-Wolf said as her tail swished. The guards stood back making room for the two to exit.

Watching them leave, Yulset glanced down at his monitor at a blinking alert. Tara looked over her shoulder and saw the man's eyes go wide as he received a report from the surface that the commune had been attacked. The report was vague, but Yulset didn't need details to know what was happening.

Only a little while before, beneath Tairnish's surface, Alex had gone through an outer wall and made his way to the stairs. Somewhere far below he was working his way to the top level while Edith was killing a security officer.

Maeven's location wasn't common knowledge among the Tairnish. Only those in charge were privy to it. In the chaos, information was slow to make its way out and only a few down below understood the purpose of the attack but Yulset knew. His eyes came back to the door as he shouted, "Hold her!"

The guards closed in while the old man returned to the report, going over the information again. Yulset saw through what was happening, and suddenly understood why Tara was there. She was the distraction.

Andavarri grabbed hold of a handrail and whispered into the transmitter buried under her skin, "A bit of help please."

Tara's gaze stayed locked on Yulset as she felt a guard take her arm in a death grip. The old man typed a quick message to the surface and pushed himself up from behind his desk. By the time he was done, a siren was wailing in the hallway. The guards looked at each other, unsure what to do or what it was for. They turned to Yulset, who had been too forceful again, driving himself toward the ceiling in his anger, spurred on by the alarm.

The sound was to let them know that something had left the Revenant, a single projectile moving fast. By the time Yulset slowed himself and corrected course, heading towards Tara, his time ran out.

The construction ring orbited Tairnish at five hundred kilometers while the Revenant was nearly twelve hundred above the moon, so the distance between the two was roughly twice the distance between Boston and New York, but the round fired from the Revenant's railgun was moving at four kilometers per second. It took just under three minutes for it to reach them.

Andavarri watched the old Tairnishmen approach and whipped her tail out, touching the controls for the door, slamming the hatch shut. The interview room was a module like everything else, built and attached as an independent piece but dependent on the main structure for air and power. When the projectile hit, it ripped the room from the ring breaking it into a thousand pieces.

The impact rattled the walls, making the main structure quake with the violence of the interview room's sudden removal. For a second the sound of metal and synthetic material being torn away rose above the warning alarms. The guard holding Tara released her and reached out trying to hold onto anything, afraid the walls of the main section would rip apart.

As the shaking settled, the guard took out his sidearm. It dawned on him that the Long-Wolf had been the one to close the door. That she'd known. He turned his weapon on her, ready to put her down if she resisted.

Andavarri held her hands in the air. "After I saved us! This seems like poor manners."

"You creatures. Only a fool would trust you," the man snarled behind his helmet with deep-seated disgust. "You are part of this." He nodded to the door.

The other guard took his weapon out as well. "We need to secure them."

The sirens hadn't stopped as they warned of more incoming projectiles. The Revenant began to fire in earnest with four rail guns sending projectiles at incredible speed toward the wiry structure of the ring. Luckily, for Tara, Andavarri, and the guards, they were no longer the direct target.

The ring was spinning around Tairnish a little faster than the Revenant, bringing the emperor's flagship further along above the military docking bays. Tairnish ships scrambled in response and countermeasures were activated as rotary cannons tried to put enough flack above the ring to stop the incoming rounds. Against drones or missiles, this might have worked, but rail guns relied only on speed and mass. Their devastating power came from momentum alone.

Andavarri slowly drifted against the wall and advised the guard, "If I were you two, I'd be less concerned about us and more worried about getting to safety."

"Quiet," the first guard ordered. He looked to the other for advice. They both knew that prisoners would only be a burden now that the fighting started. The two men nodded their armored heads with their expressionless metal faces. They turned, ready to eliminate Andavarri and Tara.

Tara sensed their thoughts, felt their resolve, and knew there was no point in pleading. She felt frozen. She'd known how dangerous this mission was, but some part of her still struggled with the notion that she was about to die. She closed her eyes, not wanting to see it and barely noticed something twisting around her waist. It was Andavarri's tail.

She waited for the shot, but before either guard could pull their trigger, Tara felt incredible heat. It came rocketing down the hall just as Andavarri's tail finished twisting around her. Tara felt herself pulled back out of the way with a hard tug as she opened her eyes and saw fire.

The light was incredibly bright, and the air turned to boiling vapor as it was consumed by the living flame of a Fire-Golem. It smashed into the two large Tairnishmen, breaking on them like a wave and washing over their armor.

Tara covered her face and curled into a ball to try and block the burning air as the guards fired their weapons. She heard the sound further back as she was pulled along, away from the men. The guns went silent as screaming and scorching echoed through the narrow corridor. The Fire-Golem penetrated the armor of one man while the other tried to fight. There was little he could do against the living plasma and staying there with his companion meant the flames would kill them both at the same time.

Tara glanced back to see the two armored men flailing, banging against the walls of the corridor, then she looked up at Andavarri dragging her along. The Long-Wolf was using the rails hurrying back to their shuttle. Their eyes met and Andavarri shouted, "Care to help?" Tara nodded and felt the tail release her. She floated in the air, carried forward by Andavarri's momentum.

Andavarri didn't wait for her. She moved ahead even faster without Tara as a burden, leaping, and flying along the corridor. "We need to get to the shuttle before it's blown to hell, or they close the blast doors," she called back.

Tara nodded, too shocked by the last few minutes to come up with words, but knowing she had to move. She reached for a handrail and followed the Long-Wolf's lead, tugging herself down the hall. Ahead she heard Andavarri yell, "They already tried closing the emergency doors but luckily, we had help."

Tara looked at the blast doors and saw the stone body of the Fire-Golem wedged there, crushed by the heavy gates, leaving a narrow space. Andavarri flattened herself and squeezed through while Tara was less graceful following her. She could hear the stone form crunching as the doors continued to try and close on the Golem's torso, cutting into the porous volcanic rock.

On the other side, there were no more soldiers. This smaller docking bay was empty while further down the larger military hubs were being shelled and ruined by the rail guns. Though it wasn't being targeted, there was still a feeling of wrongness in the smaller dock attached to their shuttle. It felt like the entire section was out of place, like it was curling further toward the planet below, ready to break away. Tara sensed the structure's movement as it slowly started to fall.

She hurried to the airlock, seeing Andavarri's tail disappear through it. She was pulling herself in as she heard the Fire-Golem return to its body, reanimating it. It creaked as it started to move, trying to pull itself from the closing blast doors. Tara looked back for a moment watching it when she felt Andavarri grab her arm and pull her out of the airlock into the cargo bay.

"What are you doing? Launch the shuttle!" The Long-Wolf ordered as she pushed Tara sending her toward the top of the cargo bay in the direction of the crew quarters and the cockpit. "I'll help our friend aboard."

Before going into the next section, Tara looked back and saw the stony body now cut in half with only its upper torso remaining. It used its stony arms to pull itself through the airlock. It floated in the zero-g of the cargo bay as Andavarri chastised it. "Look at you, you foolish rock, you left half yourself behind."

Tara hurried to the cockpit, through the crew quarters, and into the pilot's seat. Her first and main concern was checking the ship's air pressure. With so much flack flying through space, she wanted to make sure the shuttle was still in one piece. She could see the debris and wreckage out the viewport. Chucks of metal shimmered in the light from the distant stars. Then she saw brighter lights, streams of them, streaking across the vast expanse. That was the Revenant, a dark spot just over the horizon of Tairnish, releasing hell on the ring, devastating the incredible feat of engineering, like a child crumpling up and throwing away a drawing they no longer cared for.

It was a quick procedure to release the docking clamps and set the shuttle floating away from the ring. Tara fired low-energy maneuvering boosters and pushed them off from their section of the ring, setting them adrift. She took a moment then, looking to the pilot's locker where a pressure suit waited. She nodded her head making the decision to get in it, knowing it was her best chance of surviving a trip through a battlefield. In those two minutes, Andavarri made her way next to her. "Stop wasting time, get us out of here."

Tara had the suit half on as she looked back at the creature's long snout. "Sorry, I like breathing." She pulled the helmet down and powered the suit. If they lost pressure, it would activate automatically. She didn't say anything as she heard Andavarri go into the passenger compartment and into her own locker.

Tara started initiating the computer systems and warming up the engines. This was the nerve-racking part, as the shuttle came alive it would show its heat signature and paint her as a target. The shuttle still had a transponder from the Kavaris order. Tara activated it, hoping it would warn both sides away from killing them.

"Strap in," she called and her voice-activated the internal ship's comms. The message went straight to Andavarri's helmet, but she didn't need the Long-Wolf to answer as she felt a long, gloved finger touch her shoulder. Andavarri climbed back in the cockpit and took the co-pilot's seat. She checked the course Tara plotted, taking them to The Revenant.

"Are you mad?" Andavarri asked as she deleted it. The new course she set was longer, all the way back to Nalanda station.

"But—" Tara started.

"There's less chance of anyone shooting at us this way," Andavarri pointed out, shutting Tara's protest down. Tara didn't know if they had enough food stores or fuel for the journey, but she knew the Long-Wolf was right.

She was about to start her burn when there was a loud bang that echoed up through the ship. "What was that?" Andavarri asked.

"I was going to ask you." Tara checked her systems, looking at the cabin pressure to see if they'd been hit. There were no alerts, the engines were hot. All systems were go.

"Something in the cargo bay is banging at the door. I told that damn half-a-golem to secure itself," Andavarri said, looking back through the open hatch and unclipping her seat belt.

Tara put her hand out. "We don't have time." She reached back, dropping the round door into place and turning the securing handle. "We'll lose our window if we don't go now." She pointed to the course Andavarri plotted.

Andavarri tightened her chest straps and said, "I'm sure it's nothing. I'll have a stern talk with it, once we're away." Tara was focused on the controls, but she couldn't ignore the nervous tone in Andavarri's voice. She glanced over and saw her touching her neck, placing one control crystal on another, then shaking her head in frustration. Neither had any idea that things were happening on the world below that had nothing to do with the emperor.

Chapter 32

The far-off thuds of the explosions were almost impossible to hear, but Amita still thought she could feel them vibrate through the stone walls of the narrow passage. She'd used the key four times, closing the dark locks and this was the last stretch to the final one. Her legs felt impossibly heavy, and each descending step was less a conscious effort and more like a controlled wobbly fall. She could sense the dark thing ahead of her, down and around the corner, a grim presence that waited. She wondered if it was alive. If it would start speaking to her as well.

'I don't believe they're capable of that,' the voice in Amita's head answered.

"You don't believe in privacy either, do you?" Amita asked.

'Of course I do. I've been alone for as long as I've existed. I understand privacy completely, but I don't know why your species needs it. You're hardly ever alone. You should be used to others.'

"That's exactly why we need it, certainly inside our own skulls," Amita snapped back.

'I'm sorry, I will try not to intrude.'

Amita shook her head, feeling silly, and thought, 'Here I am getting pissy with an alien consciousness that's older than any living thing on Earth, some scientist I'll make.'

'It's fine, I'm not easily offended,' The voice entered her mind again uninvited.

"You really need to pick your moments," Amita said, finally coming to the lock.

The steps and the tunnel ended, no longer twisting and descending. The black lock hung on the wall like the others, like the head of an anchor, so dark, but somehow shimmering as if it weren't quite solid, more of an oily

328

substance. This was the fifth time she would do this and somehow it was the worst for being last because she'd no longer be able to change her mind. Once this was done, the entity would be free, 'free to become,' as it said.

Amita thought of the Earth. The vast deserts of Arizona, the mountains of Switzerland, and the English countryside. She imagined it all being consumed by this creature that she was about to release. Did she have any right to free something that would do the same to this world? She thought of the bombs falling above. The emperor had no problem scouring Tairnish, clearing it of life. 'Was she like him if she did this?' Then she thought of Tearmai. He'd been so intent on giving this being freedom and she knew why.

To him, there was no crime worse than slavery. Tearmai had never been a slave himself, but his people, nearly all of them had. He'd known freedom and seen the institution from the outside. His entire life he'd watched his species suffer and he would not see it done to another.

Amita pictured scales in her head and tried to weigh what she believed. Societies removed criminals that were dangerous, locking them away, but that's not what this creature was. It simply wanted to live and fulfill its life cycle. Then she thought of the Fire-Golems, made to serve, the way the Long-Wolves claimed to have made them. She hadn't met a Long-Wolf she cared for yet. From individuals to the institutions of their entire society, they seemed intent on taking advantage of others. 'But who am I to be their judge?' Amita thought.

"I wish this decision wasn't mine," she said.

'I understand,' the voice was softer as if slipping away.

Amita thought of the Earth again and the rockets out there waiting for her. Brash had launched one. He'd come to her world. If she could do the same, then theoretically I would've never been here. Things would be different, and she would never have to face this decision.

Amita looked down at the key in her gloved hand. It looked like a child's toy, shaped as an E, made to teach kids their letters but carved from dark rock. She stepped towards the lock and put her hand out, holding the key like an offering. The holes opened to accept it and she turned her hand to place it in. She watched it dissolve and shrink like all the others, falling to the floor. Amita sat on the steps watching, feeling incredible exhaustion overtake her.

'Thank you,' the voice said.

"Yeah, no biggie." Amita felt her shoulders slump forward. She turned and looked up the stairs, back to where Tearmai and the rockets waited. "I have a bit of business up there, but I may have to rest a moment. Catch that ole' second wind."

There was a rumbling as the walls higher than her started to move and a glowing form emerged. Clawed fingers, just like in the chamber above reached out and then arms and a head, then the back legs. A lion-like creature stepped into the stairwell just like the wild Fire-Golems that attacked them in the waystation. Amita stared at its glowing eyes. "So, this is that part," Amita said turning and looking at the ground. "I've got nothing left. If you're intent on murdering me, do it quick."

'I promised I wouldn't hurt you. Trust a little, Amita.' the voice said as the wild fire-golem started down to her. 'This is your ride.'

Amita nodded and tried to sound more confident than she felt while the creature approached. "Excellent. I suppose if you're not going to tear me limb from limb, I'd be happy to get the hell out of here." She stood and dusted her suit off as the fire-golem ducked down on its front paws, presenting its back. Amita took a deep

330

breath, went around to its side, and grabbed one of the spikes coming from its head, careful not to get impaled as she pulled herself up and mounted its back, just behind its shoulders.

"Alrighty," Amita said once she was settled. There were red lines blistering over the entire stone body, growing brighter as it flexed, ready to run, but directly below Amita, the creature was cool enough that she could sit comfortably in her environmental suit.

The tunnel shook. "That's not the bombs, is it?" she asked.

'No,' the voice answered. 'After far too long I'd like to stretch a bit.'

"So, I should be going?" Amita asked.

'Yes, hold tight.' The Fire-Golem turned to face the stairs, then took a leap forward, followed by another, driving itself up. It moved like a cat, pouncing up the stairs with bounding strides at a reckless speed that forced Amita to duck beneath its spikes, feeling the low ceiling pass far too close to her head. Her helmet light shone to the side as she turned away, but she didn't need it to see the creature. The tunnel brightened with a red glow as the walls came to life. Amita squeezed tight, holding on for dear life, not particularly enjoying the speed, or the rough ride. It dawned on her that, while she'd spent far too much time as a passenger on this little adventure, it was still better than walking.

Minutes passed as they barreled up the closing path. She could hear the walls collapse behind her, folding in on themselves with a sound like a massive wave crashing on the shore. To her left were the crystal walls of the chamber where she left Tearmai. As she got higher, she felt the turns of the tunnel becoming wider, then they came to the opening.

At one time this was where the black door had been, but it was gone now. Somehow it had been connected to the anchors. As they shrank so did the strange alien metal in the rest of the caves while the crystal walls remained.

She climbed down from the golem and made her way through the opening to see Tearmai still lying there. The altar was gone, and the smaller crystals littered the floor. Where the raised platform had been, nothing but rubble and debris remained. Outside, Amita could hear the far-off noise of orbital bombardment. As deep underground as the rockets were, the larger chamber that housed them was open to the sky. Amita hoped that didn't make it an attractive target for the emperor.

She had no idea what he was dropping on this world, but he wasn't holding back. Amita could feel the ground trembling beneath her. She wondered if they were nuclear. If she was risking being irradiated by staying here.

'That's not him,' she heard the entity say in her thoughts. Amita looked down at the crystal still clutched in her hand. 'I'm causing the tremors.'

"Could you stop?" Amita asked.

'I don't want to,' the voice said in a way that made Amita believe there was no point in arguing.

She shook her head and went to Tearmai, glad to see his chest rise but feeling her heart break as she watched it shutter and fall again. She felt something sticky on her boots and realized she was standing in a puddle of his blood. It leaked out in a dark mess that was slowly being absorbed by the broken ground. The Fire-Golem followed her into the chamber and its light awakened the crystal walls in a way that Amita's tiny headlamp wasn't capable of.

She turned back to the creature. "Can you help him?"

She heard the entity inside her head, but the voice felt different. 'I know little about your biology.' It echoed like two personalities speaking at the same time.

Amita thought for a moment. 'Your biology.' It seemed such a strange thing to say. Tearmai was so different from her, but they were closer as lifeforms than the Golems. "We need to close the wound. Stop him from bleeding."

Amita could see that the patch on the front of Tearmai still held. The blood was coming from her friend's back. She ducked down trying to look, but the wound was low, near his spine. "Help me roll him," she asked.

With its snout the wild Golem pushed at the Drake's shoulder, lifting him onto his side. Then it steadied him with a paw so Amita could see the angry opening. Dirt and grime had built up around it and the patch had mostly fallen off.

"Hold him there," Amita asked as she checked her suit's water supply, glad to see some left. The closed system had been filtering and recirculating her sweat. She opened a valve on her arm and pressed some of the precious water out onto Tearmai's wound, cleaning the dirt away. Then she shined her helmet light directly into the exit wound. It was larger than the one on the front. That's why the patch hadn't held.

Amita bit her lip and considered her options. She was no trauma surgeon, but her fascination with forensic science had given her some knowledge, just nothing she'd ever acted on. She thought the pile of books she'd consumed, the vivid descriptions that never bothered her, not till now, with flesh and blood bleeding in front of her. 'Solve the problem,' she told herself, knowing that cauterizing the wound was likely the right thing to do.

Amita had some knowledge of Drake physiology. She'd studied it while Tearmai was recuperating from his trip through the void space. Still, the last thing she wanted was to make things worse. Drakes were different from humans, right down to the basic building blocks of life. Their cells were more rigid than a human being's. It was part of what made them so tough.

She had no idea what organs were inside this hole, but they were weeping. The texts on her monitor back at Nalanda were a pale replacement for an actual anatomy class. She knew a Drake's vascular system was different from a person's, with the oxygen-carrying blood more readily available in the plural space of their body. Perhaps this was part of his healing process, Amita wondered.

She glanced towards the exit, knowing her chance of survival was made worse with every passing second. "We need to stop the bleeding in here," She tried to sound confident as she spoke to the entity, knowing it was pointless to pretend while they were connected. Luckily, she didn't have to explain what she wanted. It was plain as could be in her thoughts.

'He won't care for this,' the entity said.

Amita heard a different voice too, quieter than the first one. 'Should I?' it asked. Amita looked at the wild golem and realized that not only was the main life form on this planet sentient, but each of these creatures was capable of thought as well. They were independent beings tied through a link to the mother entity.

"Please," Amita asked, looking at the lion-like face with its broken, glowing lines of stone.

It nodded. Then with one paw firmly planted on Tearmai's shoulder, the Fire-Golem sat back on its haunches and lifted a clawed finger on its other leg. The stony tip stretched a bit, reaching toward the wound. It went from a subtle glow to a blazing radiance that Amita had to turn her eyes away from as it slipped into the wound with a hissing sound. Smoke poured from the hole and the finger went deeper. Tearmai started to move, awakened by the pain.

Amita's first instinct wasn't to stay there and calm him. Instead, she darted to a safe distance, remembering her arrival at Nalanda station, and the way Tearmai had nearly crushed her.

"Careful there. He's not known for waking up happy," Amita called to the Golem as one of Tearmai's mighty arms swung back, throwing an elbow toward the creature. Amita saw the tip of the finger break away, still wedged in Tearmai's back. The drake scurried from the creature and the pain and the heat coming from it.

The Drake rolled again and again, then struggled to his feet, pulling himself into a crouch. She'd seen him do this before when he was getting ready to charge, but this time it was all Tearmai could do to stand as he stared at the Golem.

"We're trying to help you," Amita called, carefully approaching him. Tearmai swung sharply toward her, but his eyes were only mildly enraged, not filled with the madness they'd held after the void.

"Your help hurts," he said reaching back to touch his wound. He grimaced as he tore into it and pulled out the little bit of stone left behind. Tearmai's eyes went to the fiery creature passively standing there, then he asked Amita, "It's done?"

She nodded. "Yes, the slave is free."

"Good." Tearmai looked ready to fall over.

"Do you know what happens next?" Amita asked.

Tearmai shook his head, 'no.'

"I don't either, but I think we should be on our way before things get worse." She held her finger in the air, listening to the far-off explosions, though the constantly trembling ground was more disturbing.

"Is she still in your head?" Tearmai asked, motioning to the crystal in Amita's hand.

"A bit. But she's different now, not as intrusive."

'She's distracted,' that other voice said in Amita's thoughts. She looked at the Fire-Golem, realizing that the creature was speaking clearly to her, its voice stronger than it had been just moments before. Perhaps this was happening with all of the Golems, here and at Nalanda station. This one had always been wild, never a slave. Amita wondered how the others were reacting to their years of servitude.

The tremors in the cavern became more severe and Amita shook her head bringing her thoughts back to the problem at hand, their survival. "Tearmai, before, when you were here. Was it you or Brash who launched one of those rockets?" She pointed to the chamber outside.

"We began together. There was danger, darkness, the hunter was after us. Brash thought he could change things. It followed us here and out there." Tearmai pointed towards the sky. "It was on the rocket, not in the crystal though." Tearmai dropped his head and there was sorrow in his voice. "Brash left me. I told him to. He went into the void to escape. I tried to turn away, but the course was set. There was no turning back."

Amita felt the urge to interrogate him further. She wanted to know every detail of their trip, but she didn't have time. At any moment one of the emperor's bombs could hit the cavern with the crystal rockets or the shaking from the entity could bring the whole place down. Luckily the walls of this chamber seemed sturdy, but she had no wish to be buried inside while the caverns outside collapsed.

Amita grabbed Tearmai's arm. "We need out of here," she said, starting toward the exit. She stopped at the broken wall, looking out. The dark passage no longer had the black rails. It was brighter. She could see the rocks and debris collapsing and the scattered pieces of Fire-Golems shattered on the floor. She could see the end of the cave where they'd met the guardian. Light shone through the openings now. Amita squeezed the crystal in her hand and yelled while thinking about the mother entity. "Do you mind holding off on this bloody shaking!? I helped you. It's only fair you don't kill us!"

Slowly the trembling stopped. 'Go now,' a voice said but Amita had a difficult time telling which part of the entity was speaking, the golem that was with them or the mother again. Amita grabbed Tearmai's arm giving him a hard tug. It wouldn't have moved him at all if he hadn't chosen to follow. She hurried through the cave, coming to the opening where the dark platform had been.

"Bollocks!" Amita cursed as she nearly slipped and fell over the edge. The dark metal had retreated, somehow tied to the anchors like the rails and portals. Tearmai's large hand grabbed her shoulder and steadied her above the sheer drop.

Across the way, the rockets were still standing, but Amita couldn't see any way to get to them, even the closest was far out of reach. "How did you get in them before?"

The rockets were as tall as ten-story buildings with three massive boosters covered by oddly angled shielding below them. Amita guessed that the shielding had some radar-neutralizing effect. "I jumped," Tearmai said while pointing down a bit where wire-thin scaffolding stood, and Amita could just barely see the outline of a hatch.

"You jumped?" Amita asked. It was at least seventy meters from them. Even with Tearmai's strength, it was an impossible feat. She felt the ground begin to shake again. It started slow but she knew that wouldn't last. She could still sense a little of the mother entity's feelings bristling with excitement, like a dog seeing a rabbit. The entity was at the very edge of control. She wanted release. When it really got going, Amita knew these rockets, in fact, this entire chamber wouldn't last long.

Tearmai explained, "Brash helped. He can push with his mind, even something as large as me."

"Well, that's just wonderful for him, innit?" Amita shook her head, then looked back at the cavern, wondering where the Fire-Golem had gone. A plan entered her mind that she immediately wanted to dismiss as stupid, but she couldn't think of anything else to do. "I'm going to need another favor," she called while squeezing the crystal. She pictured what she wanted.

When there wasn't an immediate response, she squeezed the crystal tighter and yelled back at the cave, "Hello, is this thing on?"

'I'm coming,' the voice in her head answered. She was almost positive it was the creature that brought her up out of the caves. Back in the dark, she heard the sound of paws galloping and saw an approaching glow. She immediately regretted the strategy she suggested but it was too late. "Tearmai, would you be kind enough to lift me?" Amita asked. "I believe we're about to get pushed as well."

He glanced over his shoulder and his eyes went wide at the sight of the Fire-Golem barreling towards them. Tearmai had only a moment to pick Amita up and spring from the cave entrance while the golem leapt toward him.

The lion-like creature used its front paws to sweep the Drake up, pulling him forward from the mouth of the cave, out into the larger cavern. The fall looked endless below them with far too much distance to clear. There wasn't enough time for Tearmai to complain as the living flame inside the Golem broke free.

Its stony body dropped away as dead weight, while the being inside continued on, gripping Tearmai in its fiery fingers. Tearmai roared with the heat, but it only lasted a moment as they crashed into the scaffolding. Rolling to protect Amita from the landing, he let his body slam into the side of the rocket.

"I'm sorry." Amita crawled out from the crumpled ball of her friend and touched his face. "It was the only thing I could think of."

Tearmai took a deep breath while laying on his back and watched the Fire-Golem, released from its form. It danced in the air for a moment, then turned and shot straight down following the rocks of its former body, leaving nothing behind except a few spots of light in their eyes. "I think the ones on the station are better at touching, not so hot," Tearmai explained. "They've more practice."

Amita looked down at the fading light. It was too far away to see but she thought she saw the debris of the lion melt into the floor. It made her wonder if they could manipulate any rock or if the were connected to specific stones. "A question for another day," she said as she offered a hand to help Tearmai up.

He got to his feet himself and said, "I never want to travel that way again."

Amita nodded before turning to the hatch. It was barely big enough for Tearmai. "Yes, well, our next ride awaits." She pushed at the opening and climbed inside. "Come on then." She called behind her, "No time to waste."

Tearmai sighed, then followed her.

Chapter 33

The day cycle began on Nalanda station and Katy was early to the dining hall, though Ben and Cormack weren't far behind her. They had orbital mechanics first thing and she intended to go early to talk to Regin. In a hurry to get there quicker, she even accepted help from her brother so she could start eating. Between hurried bites, she told the others her intention.

Before she could finish, Cormack interrupted from across the table asking, "How much longer do you plan to go on with this?"

Katy's mouth fell open as she dropped her fork and asked, "What?"

"Even if he knows something, and he's willing to share it with you, what are you going to do with it?" Cormack crossed his arms.

Katy wished Naiathne was there, but the night owl hadn't gotten out of bed. "I don't know, tell Cathal, maybe." Her voice was laced with sarcasm because she knew it was the only answer Cormack would accept. "You know, because that's been super useful," she added in a mutter.

Cormack shook his head, ignoring her tone. "But what's the point in keeping at this? Chris will officially recant his confession. I'll talk to my mother, and we'll apply political pressure. Kavaris Altain was from our world anyway—"

"But we still won't know who the killer is," Katy interrupted.

Cormack was about to answer her but Ben broke in first. "So what?"

"'So what?'" Katy turned to her brother's voice.

"Yeah, so what?" Ben grumbled as he leaned across the table. "This place is brutal, and Kavaris Altain sucked and even if he didn't, it doesn't matter. These people kill each other over nothing. I mean I worry tossing my trash in the wrong bin will get me thrown out an airlock. I've been to a couple of trials now and I don't know much about justice but I'm pretty sure this isn't how it's supposed to work. It's an eye for an eye and these people don't care whose eye gets taken. We should leave it alone and be glad we've got friends like Cormack to help us. This isn't Scooby-Doo."

"Scooby what?" Cormack asked.

Katy ignored him as she threw her hands up. "You're just scared."

"Of course, I'm scared," he pleaded. "We don't have much left to lose. I don't have much left to lose."

Katy was quiet for a moment. She could hear Ben digging into his plate, aggressively shoveling food into his mouth, trying to keep from becoming more emotional. After a long moment of silence, with only the sound of his fork striking his dish, she reached across the table and took Ben's arm. "Look, I'm just going to talk to him. It's going to be all right. Nothing bad is going to happen, not from just talking." She turned to Cormack. "And if your mom could do something for Chris, that'd be awesome, but I'm going to ask my questions too. Everything will be fine."

Ben shook his head. "I really don't think you've been here long enough to say that."

Katy ignored him and finished her meal, then pushed back from the table. "I'm going to class."

Cormack and Ben looked at each other. "Fine, I'll take you," Ben said going around to the other side of the table to pick up his sister's tray. They said little to each other as they made their way through the hall with Ben gently guiding Katy while she swung her stick back and forth. When they reached the room with its model of the star system hanging from the ceiling, Ben said, "He isn't here. I guess you don't get to ask your questions."

"He's on his way." Katy motioned to the door, hearing the swish of Regin's tails and the click of his nails, though there was a louder sound that nearly covered it, the heavy stomping of Fafnir's steps.

"I wonder if Cathal ever spoke to the big guy," Ben whispered, paying attention, hearing the steps as well now. He peeked out and said, "My money is still on him."

"You really think so?" Katy asked.

"He hates us. Well, maybe not us specifically, but people in general, like all people." Ben backed up as Regin came in. The teacher was less than a meter tall. He swept through the opening with his furry tails billowing behind him, only pausing for a moment to glance at them. "Well, this is a surprise. Most don't hurry to my class."

"We were hoping to ask you some questions." Ben blurted out before letting out a surprised gasp. From across the room, Katy heard her brother jump and hurry away from the door. For a moment she wondered why. Then she realized Fafnir was still at the opening. His breath pushed into the space, like a gust of warm air, rattling in his long snout. Somehow Ben hadn't been aware that the Drake was still outside and just over his shoulder.

Katy heard Fafnir push his way in. "What kind of questions?"

Turning toward the sound of his voice, she looked up but couldn't get herself to speak. She didn't mind talking to Regin. He'd always been kind, but she knew very little about Fafnir, never having a conversation with him, only hearing the wake of his movement when he stomped through a crowd. She heard him struggle at the opening, which was barely big enough for him to fit through.

"I asked, what questions?" he repeated after finally clearing the door. His tone was far from friendly. She sensed him in the space, like standing in front of a mountain, though she couldn't see the way he stayed near his friend, a protective presence above the Ice-Carver.

Katy took a deep breath and refused to be intimidated. "I was told that the stewards of the Extraracials might have seen or heard something about the head monk's death. That you and your people are often ignored by the nobles and the monks. You might have a different view of the happenings around here."

Neither Regin nor Fafnir spoke. Katy couldn't see the glance passing between them, but Ben could. There was an entire conversation in that look. Nervously he said, "You know what, guys. Don't worry about it. My sister thinks she's like an amateur detective or something."

Katy cut him off. "It's because of my friend Chris. I need to find the murderer so we can get him out."

"You think that will matter?" Regin asked.

Katy turned to him. "I hope so."

"From what I understand and from what I know of the monks, they're not going to let anyone go. Even if you find this supposed 'murderer,' your friend gave false testimony. The monks take that kind of thing seriously. They take everything seriously."

"Even if he tells them it wasn't true, and we find the killer?" Katy asked.

Regin shrugged. "I can't say for sure. You do have powerful friends."

"Cormack's people. I knew that was where we should've started." Ben nodded.

Regin laughed. "No, not the Sidhe. I'm referring to the Æsir. The gods these monks worship. In fact, while we're asking questions, perhaps you could shed some light on that. Do you know why they favor you? Why they saved your friend?"

Katy shook her head. "I would tell you if I could, but I don't know anything about them or why they protected Alex."

She could hear Regin, moving behind his desk. "I've always wondered about the Æsir. I've lived my entire life under their rule. Fafnir and my friend Eir remember a time before them, but for me, they've always been a fact of life. You have to study history to see how much their laws and rules, as brutal as they are, have benefited my people and Fafnir's." Regin pointed back. "In this century they've done much to stabilize our worlds, weakening the noble's power, beginning to free the Drakes. Things were heading in a better direction till Tamerlane. He is the biggest anomaly in their rule."

"He's a monster," Fafnir growled, "like his forefathers."

"Yes," Regin agreed. "I was there on Uppsala, a student when he solidified his power. The Æsir never protected him like Alex, they simply didn't show up. Allowing him to do things no other noble had since their arrival. He made war against the other Uppsalan nobles, purged mining colonies in the rings, killing thousands, and, of course, he attacked Grannus, trying to pull all the moons under his power. The Æsir did nothing." Regin's voice was the steady timber of a teacher, sounding if anything slightly amused.

"Now it's believed your friend Alex has gone to work for him, off to save his daughter. Intriguing that those two would end up together. One protected by the Æsir and one ignored by them. That they would be allies is something worth noticing, don't you think?" Regin asked.

"Again, I don't know," Katy said.

Regin added, "But surely these questions are more important than what happened to the monk."

Katy wasn't sure what to say, but Ben spoke up, "Well, I can explain the Alex thing. Not why the Æesir saved him, but why he's off to save the princess. It's pretty obvious. It's not for the emperor at all, he's just really into Maeven. I mean, have you seen her?"

Regin laughed. "You're right, that is obvious, and I suppose it makes sense. Still, I think ignoring the Æesir connection is a mistake." He tapped his long fingernails on the desk, looking at the ceiling in thought. "Your other friend, Amita, was looking into things the monks would've killed her for. My friends, the older stewards like Fafnir, told me the emperor was much like her when he was a student. Insatiably curious. Searching in places he shouldn't, secret rooms and whatnot."

Fafnir nodded, agreeing. "He liked to go out at night, against the monk's commands. Strange things started to happen while he was here."

"Like what?" Ben asked.

Fafnir glared in annoyance, not wanting to answer Ben, but Regin urged him on. "Please, we're just talking."

"It was the ghosts. They started taking people," Fafnir explained. "They'd been sighted for years but taking people had been a rumor, nothing more to my knowledge. When Tamerlane was here, they became aggressive. There was even talk of sending the students home."

"Perhaps he found something, and they didn't like it," Regin proposed.

"Or perhaps he was behind it," Fafnir snarled.

"Whoa, like he was controlling the ghosts," Ben asked.

Fafnir's lip curled showing his teeth as he said, "It's been speculated."

Katy began, "This is all very interesting, but—"

"The murder," Regin interrupted, finishing her thought. "You are tenacious, aren't you? Well, I'm sorry I have little help for you. I have no idea who killed the monk. What about you, Fafnir?"

Fafnir shook his head and added, "There are too many possibilities to count."

"Yes, in fact, If I were attempting to solve this crime, I would stop looking for the motive. There are, as my friend said, too many. I would look for who felt safe enough to do it in the first place. Who doesn't feel they will be punished for the crime?" Regin looked at Ben. "Perhaps others are protected like your group, the ones who came through the void space?"

Katy followed his logic and wondered, "But who?"

"I don't know, You're the investigator," Regin pointed out, then turned towards the door, where voices echoed from the hall. "Now it appears that the rest of my class is trying to get in but Fafnir, my friend, you're a bit in the way."

Fafnir grumbled as he turned back to the exit. He said nothing to Regin, Ben or Katy, but Katy could hear his footsteps resounding on the ground and feel the movement of the air change as he pushed through the opening and back into the crowd of waiting students. They moved back out of his way, then started to filter in.

Cormack was one of them along with Naiathne, who had finally gotten out of bed. He came over to Katy's desk just as she sat down and leaned over, apologizing, "Look, I'm sorry. I'm not trying to get in your way. I just don't want you to get hurt pursuing this."

"It's fine," Katy said in a distracted voice. Her head was running, thinking about everything Regin had said. She had a theory and again she wished Amita were here.

"Did you learn anything," Cormack asked.

"I don't know," Katy said. "Maybe."

∞

Katy lay in her bed with her eyes closed and her mind running. She had her own room in the Sidhe

346

domicile. It wasn't very large but it had a door and that was a wonderful thing. It closed out the noise, got her away from people, and allowed her the luxury of letting her attention go. Getting her brain used to all the incoming data, the smells, the sounds, and the vibrations of Nalanda station was exhausting. In her tiny room, it was only her, a bed, and a dresser. She lay there thinking over everything Regin and Fafnir said about the emperor.

Her monitor had been set up with a voice function that responded to her and would read aloud the articles and textbooks stored in it. She had searched for a brief summary of Tamerlane's reign, but it didn't exist. Most of the information about him was volumes long and while the texts had been created in academic universities and were provided by the monks, they were also carefully worded not to offend the most powerful man in the system.

Katy had only listened for a short time, less than an hour, about the beginning of Tamerlane's career. She read between the lines of a few articles that seemed to suggest the emperor was chosen by the Æesir. It was the only way to protect the monk's belief that their gods were all-knowing and had a plan. What Regin and Fafnir said suggested that wasn't the case. That perhaps Tamerlane had found some way to protect himself from the Æesir and he might have found it here. She imagined the monks would consider this heresy.

Katy thought of the ghosts, about Naiathne's story and Ben's, and shivered. Walking around in a nightmare after losing her sight was bad enough, but the cruelest trick was when memories came back, when that last night on Earth returned in full color. The last thing she'd seen was the hunter in the desert in all its horrible glory.

Ben told her the ghosts looked like that creature. It was enough to paint a terrifying picture of ghosts closing in on her. She remembered the hunter's terrible mouth, with human flesh hanging from it and black goo pouring out. She remembered the chase and the blade dropping towards her while its eyes stayed cold. Katy sat up in bed, trying to chase the image away.

"Get back to the problem," she told herself as she brought her hands to her face. "Who killed the monk?"

It'd been a knife in his back, not some monster, and while she had no proof, she trusted the math indicating he'd been thrown from the airlock in the lighthouse. Everyone at this station might be keeping secrets but she could trust math.

She let her mind slip back a little to when she'd gone into the alien sector. Fajalar, the Long-Wolf, had found her and pumped her for information, wanting to know about Amita, what she'd found, this supposed secret room.

Katy only knew what Ben had told her, that it'd been closed off. But maybe someone found another way in. Cathal said he hadn't found anything in the lighthouse, but he wasn't an investigator and, as Ben pointed out, he had his own reasons to hate the monk.

Katy swung her legs off the side of her bed. If she was going to keep pursuing this, then she knew what her next step had to be. She snapped her fingers, listening to it echo in the dark room, then laughed a little, shaking her head, knowing how hopeless it was. "I need to stop," she said, but the murder felt like a loose tooth, taunting her. She wished she could talk to Chris. She missed him and she needed help. There were others she could ask. She only needed a guide.

Nodding, she got to her feet, went to the door, and out into the hall with her stick in front of her. There was a common room in the Sidhe domicile. It was quiet. "Naiathne, are you out here?" Katy called, knowing her friend often stayed up later than the others.

"She went to bed," Ben answered from the small commissary off the main room.

"Can't sleep either?" Katy asked.

"Midnight snack," Ben responded with his mouth half full. She couldn't see him hold up the bowl of something that wasn't quite Ice-Cream, not as sweet or creamy as what they had back on Earth. He asked, "What are you doing up?"

"I think I need to go to the lighthouse," Katy blurted out. She heard Ben's spoon hit his bowl.

"Is that why you were looking for Naiathne, to take you there?" His voice was cold.

"I suppose." Katy's hands squeezed her stick pointing it straight down.

Ben walked away, letting his bowl clatter in the sink. "Because you know that's nuts, right?"

"Ben—" she started.

He was staying back and she could hear the distance between them. "Katy, I'm here for you. I am, but this needs to stop."

"Okay, then what?" Katy demanded.

Ben sounded a little confused, "What do you mean?"

"Once I stop, what happens next? We just settle in, become one of these people? Me the blind girl. You the Earth kid. Chris in prison. Welcome to your new life, that's all?" Katy asked.

"Maybe— I don't know. But how is solving this going to change any of that?" Ben's words stumbled out in frustration.

"I don't know either, but Amita found something and I think someone tried to follow in her footsteps and was willing to kill to cover it up."

Ben washed his bowl and said over his shoulder, "More reason to stay here, to stay safe."

349

Katy stepped toward him. "Ben, what happened to you? Back home you would've been all about this. You were never this worried."

Ben stared into the sink. "Yeah, back home? Don't you remember what happened there? I wanted to solve something too, go out in the desert and find a monster, figure out what Dad was up to. Where did that lead us?"

"Are you seriously blaming yourself for that?" Katy asked.

He turned and leaned against the counter. Though he knew Katy couldn't see him, he kept his eyes away from hers. "I'm at least partially responsible. If we'd just let those creatures back on Earth do their thing, maybe we'd be there now." The words came out with more and more difficulty.

Katy came closer. "Ben, it wasn't your fault."

Ben didn't look up, even with his sister directly in front of him. He asked, "You sure? Then what do we do? Blame Dad?"

She touched his shoulder. "Maybe we don't have to blame anyone. Maybe we just need to move forward."

"No, I'm pretty sure it was Dad. Then I came along and screwed it all up worse." Ben tried walking away from her, but before he could escape, Katy grabbed him and pulled him to her.

He was still pulling back as Katy said, "This isn't your fault. Back on Earth, terrible things were going to happen no matter what. That creature would've attacked Amita's parents and Troy and those other people. And Brash would've taken Chris and Alex's mom. It all would've happened, even the big thing, whether you looked into it or not. But what wouldn't have happened is we wouldn't have found Tearmai. You did that. We're here, alive, because you refused to give up. I need that Ben back."

Finally, Ben leaned into his sister and hugged her back. "Thanks," he said.

Katy didn't have to ask Ben again. He looked at her and for a moment he was so happy to have his sister with him, to not be alone. He said, "Let me go get dressed, then I'll take you there." He started towards his room.

"What are you wearing now?" Katy asked.

"My underwear, so yes in case you're wondering, you just hugged your little brother in his underwear."

Katy smiled. "You eat their crappy ice cream with no pants on."

"Maybe this place is becoming a bit too much like home," Ben said as he went down the hall. A few moments later he came back fully clothed.

"You're going to have to forgo the tapping stick. It's too much noise," he said as he gently took his sister's elbow. "By the way, I'm still going on record as this being a bad idea."

Katy held her stick in the air and let her brother lead her without complaining. They passed the guards at the Sidhe domicile entrance. "Just going for a walk," Ben called over his shoulder. The guards nodded but didn't say anything. They were soldiers who only knew service and never questioned the actions of anyone above them on the social ladder, which included nobles and their guests.

Out in the hall, the stalls in the market were now draped in cloth, silent and moody as they stood in rows making shadows in the starlight from the massive window above. Ben walked Katy past them, glancing around every corner till they reached the corridor where the darkness became heavier. He paused for a moment. "Give me a second to get my bearings. It's been a while since Amita and I found this place and we were coming out of the monk's rooms."

He started down the corridor with his monitor out in front for the little illumination it provided. With barely any lighting, just a weak string of tiny bulbs hanging from the ceiling, Ben watched every shadow, staying alert for movement. "No monks, no ghosts, no Fire-Golems, that's the goal," he said to his sister who nodded.

Passing by the entrance to the monk's territory, he gave the opening a wide berth, trying to stay in the shadows, not wanting the guards in the cells to hear or see them. "Nice and quiet," he whispered.

He kept his eyes open for Fire-Golems or anything else, but the stony guardians were impossible to avoid. They passed two along the way, then a third. Eventually Ben accepted the fact that Fajalar was going to see them and know their every step. The statues never came alive but Ben knew that didn't matter. The fire inside only pretended to have eyes. They saw in strange, inhuman ways, impossible to hide from. He hoped this Long-Wolf was like Andavarri who kept secrets in her pocket for later.

Coming to a narrow passage, Ben decided this was the one he and Amita found, and he told Katy to put her hands on his shoulders. "Bet'cha Naiathne wouldn't have found this shortcut," he whispered.

"She can see in the dark."

"Oh," Ben sounded disappointed.

"But I don't have to worry about you hitting on me," Katy said.

"What, really?" Ben asked looking back.

Katy bit her lip before answering, "Sorry, I shouldn't have said that."

Ben thought for a moment. "I guess it's not really surprising, now that I think of it. Just funny that both Cormack and his sister are crushing on you."

"I don't think Cormack is," Katy said.

Ben shrugged. "Could've fooled me. He set us up with some really nice rooms and took you to his home world. He even had you meet his mother. You're telling me all of that was just for the hell of it?"

Katy shrugged. "I guess he's just a nice guy."

"I don't buy it. I mean, yeah, he seems nice, but I don't know." They made their way through a passage that felt like it'd been cut from the rock after the station was built. At the end was a brighter hallway with a peculiar curve and small sconces glowing lowly along the rib-like wall braces. This was the hall where Ben had first seen a ghost. He looked left, then right, and saw nothing, no shadows or other tell-tale signs that one of the creatures was nearby. He listened too, remembering how the ghostly blades on the creature still managed to scratch the floor, letting him know the phantom was real, though Amita tried to deny it.

"Keep your ears open for anything weird," Ben whispered to Katy as they passed out into the hall.

Katy nodded but asked, "How am I supposed to know what weird is when I've never been here before?"

Ben held his hands in the air. "Right now is normal. Anything else is weird."

"Okay," Katy said, sensing her brother's anxiety, feeling the tension in his back. His hand went to her elbow and gripped it tight as he stood closer.

After a short walk, Ben could see the opening to the stairwell that led to the lighthouse. "These stairs are big. They might be tricky to climb without being able to see," he whispered.

They came to the first step, and Katy understood what Ben meant. They were twice as tall as a human's and they turned as they climbed, twisting in the narrow passage. Ben helped Katy as best he could, climbing up, then turning and offering a hand. After a while, they came up with a system where he stayed just ahead of her.

As they approached the top, Katy said, "Ben, I'm starting to hear weird stuff."

Ben was turned back toward her from the higher step with his hand out to guide her. "It's the machines in the lighthouse."

"Did they do that last time?" Katy asked.

"I don't remember." Ben grunted as he helped Katy onto the step with him.

"Really?" She cocked her head.

He held his hands in the air. "I was running for my life. Once we got to the top, Amita started messing with stuff. It's all kind of a blur." He patted her shoulders and turned away. "Stay here. I'm going to peek around the corner."

Ben went up another step and another, then bent down and stuck his head out of the stairwell. The lighthouse looked just as he remembered it, bronze-laced machines that could've been mistaken for stone if not for the glowing lights blazing from their dark surfaces. Then there were the human machines, cameras and data storage, monitors, and screens.

Ben hadn't had much time to talk to Amita after Alex helped her escape her cell, but he'd heard a little about what she'd found up here. Why the monks had arrested her. His eyes went to the far wall, past the raised dais in the center of the room. He could pick out the oddly carved corners of blocks that had been used to fill the opening. If he hadn't known to look for it, he never would've noticed that it was different from the rest of the station. Most of Nalanda was carved directly from the rock of the asteroid they were on, but this spot had been filled in after the fact.

He heard Katy call from the stairs. "Is it safe? Are we alone?"

Ben looked around. He didn't see anyone, but he couldn't shake the feeling that someone was watching them. "Yeah, I think so, but, man, this place is creepy."

Katy was leaning on the last stair, her head tilted as she listened. She'd gotten very good at identifying certain sounds especially when they repeated, and she'd heard claws on the stone floor of Nalanda often enough.

"What is it?" Ben asked, seeing the look on Katy's face.

Katy was quiet for a moment, but she didn't hear it again. "Nothing, I just thought I heard something familiar."

"Well, let me know. We don't want to be surprised up here." Ben went to the far wall, thinking there was something else wrong with it, something more than the material it was built from. The lights in the room didn't seem to touch one spot along the seams. It was like a permanent dark shadow rested there. He turned at the sound of Katy coming up behind him. "Hey, I said to wait." Ben didn't notice that while his eyes were away the shadow had started to move, to form into something more solid but not quite there.

Katy was turning her head, listening to every sound. "Well, I didn't hear you screaming in terror, so I figured it was ok. Noisy up here, isn't it?" she said referring to the constant low rattling hum of the machines. She could feel them in her chest, a constant pulse.

Ben didn't answer. He'd gone deathly silent. Katy tried to listen for him above the sound of everything else, then she felt someone take her arm and put their hand on her mouth. Her brother's voice was tight and shaking as he whispered in her ear. "There's one in the room. It just came out of the wall. It's looking right at us."

Katy tried to say, "What," but her brother's hand went even tighter over her mouth.

"A ghost! It's coming," Ben said as he pulled her away toward the stairs.

Katy didn't resist, letting her brother lead her, but then she felt something incredibly cold touch her arm. She felt it start to drag her back into the room. Its strength was impossible to resist as the cold moved through her body.

Chapter 34

Looking down into the escape passage from the wreckage of the apartment in the Bogatyr commune, Edith imagined it would feel tight for a Tairnishman, at least the portion on the ladder. She slung her rifle over her shoulder then climbed in and put her hands on the rails of the ladder. Using her armor's grip strength as a brake, she dropped ten meters through a roughly carved shaft into a wider cavern. She flung herself off the ladder from several rungs up, twisting, landing, and flattening out to scan ahead. Her sidearm was back in her hand, pointed ahead, searching for targets. In the nanosecond it took the radar to bounce back off the rock walls, she saw with her own eyes that nothing was there, just an open cave and a string of golden glowing lamps hanging from the ceiling.

The escaping aristocrats hadn't bothered to leave a rearguard, at least not here. "It's clear," Edith called as she got to her feet.

With Maeven just behind him, Alex climbed down much slower. Edith saw the kid moving with only one leg able to bend. For a second, in a fit of impatience, she fantasized about pulling him down the last few rungs. Then she thought of the soldiers above. That wouldn't have gone nearly as well if Alex hadn't snuck up with that grenade. She shook her head and muttered, 'You're getting soft.'

She glanced past Alex towards Maeven, she looked at the dark opening above. Enemy reinforcements were probably close behind, but she'd left a few surprises in the apartment to slow them down. The charges she had left weren't going to do much good against a shuttle she was trying to steal anyway. Explosions and space vessels rarely mix.

Alex touched the ground. "We need to hustle," Edith said, going to his injured side. She let him use her shoulder to lean on. "Where's your firearm?" She glanced over, seeing the submachine gun on its strap hanging from his shoulder. "Put that in your hand, keep it ready," she ordered as she dragged him down the path. Over her shoulder, she called to Maeven. "Stay tight. If any bullets come this way, I'd rather Alex or I stop them." Edith said, not concerned that Alex wasn't armored. After all Maeven was the mission.

Alex didn't say anything. Maybe he didn't understand or maybe he did, either way, he kept his weapon up. Edith couldn't see his eyes behind the visor, but she had a feeling they were focused as she felt him put every effort into moving faster.

The floor of the cave sloped down, going deeper into the ground till it reached another, larger cavern. The string of lights ended, replaced by large heavy metal braces, holding up fuel and coolant lines along with thick power cables all running in one direction. Edith's hearing aids were tied into her helmet display and tuned to sort out the background sounds from voices. The shuttles were being prepped to launch.

The cave widened out again and brighter lighting from above flooded an open space. Edith leaned Alex against a wall and motioned for Maeven to join him before carefully stalking toward the cave's mouth like a ghost with her rifle at the ready and her camouflage adjusted to the rock walls.

She looked down an embankment reinforced with thick concrete to a launchpad where three small shuttles stood mounted in a row on rails pointed toward the sky. More space had been hollowed out below them and scaffolding ran from the cavern walls on either side. Not far from her, was a flight of stairs with five dozen steps following the slope of the walls.

Edith watched the ground crew check and recheck the vessels. There were four technicians and three soldiers, wearing lighter armor. A headshot would put them down easily, Edith thought as she ran her scope over each one, knowing it was still a lot of people to take out. She watched two of the techs make their way to a heavy door in the far wall. Her eyes went up till she saw a control room behind thickened glass. The passengers were nowhere to be seen. They'd already been loaded.

She recognized the shuttle model, a favorite of the noble class on Uppsala. They were easy to fly and would be status symbols to the Tairnishmen. Holding less than a dozen passengers and with little cargo space, they looked more like atmospheric ships with broad wings swept back at an aerodynamic angle.

Their thrusters gave them the look of a bird puffing its chest out and were meant to get them to space, then drop away once they were in orbit or beyond the gravity well. Other less streamlined vessels would recover the spent boosters. Small as they were, the shuttles could go anywhere in the system in comfort and style. Edith checked their thermals and saw they were prepped for flight with engines hot and ready to launch.

These people knew the commune was under attack and that the emperor was dropping into orbit. The shuttle's launch could be dialed back or pushed forward depending on what happened next. Edith checked her countdown clock, seeing the timer running quickly toward zero. As soon as the bombs started to fall, time would be up. The question was whether to take a ship now and encounter more resistance or wait till things started to happen and use the chaos.

She glanced at the ceiling and saw a closed hatch, probably disguised on the surface, then returned to the shuttles themselves, looking at the launch pads. It would be extremely hot down there when they fired those boosters and there wouldn't be much room to hide. "So, risk not getting out or risk getting cooked," she said to herself.

She made up her mind and went back to the others. Maeven and Alex were huddled beside each other. The small amount of conversation between the two sounded one-sided with Maeven looking at his wounds. "All right, kids," Edith said. "Here's the plan. I'm going to go down there and secure transport. You guys are going to give me three and a half minutes, then you're going to follow."

"Is that enough time?" Maeven asked.

"Not at all, but we don't have much choice and it'll be a start and, given the speed of certain members of our party. . ." She shrugged and nodded. "I think it's a good head start for me to do what I have to. Alex, your job is to keep her safe—" The distant sound of an explosion interrupted her. It came from the back of the cave where the ladder waited. The sound was muted by the rocks but it was still loud. "Looks like we might have more company on the way. Give me two minutes instead, then start marching. Head toward the cockpit on the first shuttle but try to maintain cover. They're CRX-12s. There's a separate hatch near the front with a skinny-looking ladder. I'll meet you there." Edith turned and started to jog. "Hopefully the pilots won't lock it when I start eliminating the ground crew. I mean I'll try to be quiet, but you know things happen."

∞

Alex watched Edith go. He tried to ignore the sound in her voice, the pragmatic tone that was bordering on happiness for what she was about to do. As he got to his feet with Maeven's help, he thought about all the warnings the battle armor had given him, the damage report on the pilot, on him. He wondered how many holes had been patched, how many had been missed. Was he bleeding to death right now, on the inside? He touched his stomach, remembering his first-aid training from ROTC. Those classes always showed you the worst case and the only thing you could do for internal bleeding was immediate transport to surgery.

He was breathing ok. So that was good, but his head was another story. Thoughts came sluggishly, He wished it was just the pain, that would keep him sharp but something else was wrong with him. He tried to listen to the back of the cave, wondering if the explosion above was heard in the main cavern where the ships waited. Were more people dying? Maeven said something but he missed it.

"What was that?" Alex asked.

"She didn't mention what to do about the pilots," Maeven said again.

Alex looked down at the weapon in his hand but Maeven interrupted his thoughts. "I don't think spraying bullets inside a shuttle we're trying to steal is going to be all that helpful."

"I wasn't going to. I don't want to—" Alex stopped. The image of the man he killed in the hall flashed back into his head.

Maeven took his arm, letting him drape it over her shoulder. "It's been a day, hasn't it?" she asked.

He nodded, having trouble finding words.

"It's almost over," Maeven assured him as she started to walk, half carrying Alex.

They reached the cave entrance and Alex tried to glance out and look for Edith, but she was impossible to find. He saw something else beneath one of the shuttles, tucked under the launch pad was a man's slumped form. Light flashed above in a window built into the cement wall. Three more flashes followed. Alex recognized them as muzzle flares and knew it was Edith, efficiently moving through the technicians and security personnel.

361

"Let's go," Maeven said pulling him down the stairs. High above was the sound of large gears turning as a bit of sky slowly appeared. Massive doors pulled back, revealing a cloudy night painted in strange colors of red and orange from the volcanos in the distance. After being underground for so long, after everything he'd seen and done, the sight carried a weight that Alex hadn't expected. Even a sky as strange as this one was welcome as he felt his whole body stiffen with swelling and bruising. He had to fight for every step, but looking up gave him a small glimmer of hope.

The shuttles were smaller than the vessel they'd traveled from Nalanda in, but this close, they were still considerable, resting at an angle on large rigging, anchored into massive concrete pillars with a ten-meter drop below them down to a blast chamber. The ships reminded Alex of a military hop he'd taken with his dad. It'd been a short flight on a Hercules transport plane, one of the sturdy workhorses of the US military. Approaching the combat transport across an open tarmac had been so different from getting on a commercial flight, seeing the mechanics, all the little moving parts that made such complex machines take to the sky.

When they reached the catwalk, Alex's struggling steps were covered by the sound of the warmed-up engines with their hissing and whirling echoing off the solid walls. He took the rail and leaned more of his weight on it, looking around for guards and for Edith.

"Give me the weapon," Maeven said after a few steps.

Alex hadn't realized that he'd let it go. That the submachine gun was hanging loosely from its strap again. 'Edith would be pissed,' he thought, feeling punchy. He looked at Maeven's open hand and started to unsling the weapon. It was a struggle like everything else. After handing it to her, he watched Maeven make a quick examination, noticing that the weapon wasn't strange to her as she made sure there was a round in the chamber.

She pulled the strap tight, ratcheting it to her back, out of sight. Alex leaned against the rail and looked down for a moment. He noticed a second body far below in the blast chamber. "Edith got another one," he said without emotion, pointing down, but Maeven couldn't hear him over all the sounds on the launch pad. She wasn't listening anyway. By the time Alex turned around, she was gone and he was alone.

A different kind of fear shot through him, thinking he'd somehow lost her and that this had all been pointless. It lasted one stunned moment. He exhaled, putting the shock away as he saw her climbing a flight of metal stairs, fifteen steps that lead to a side hatch on the shuttle. The shock refocused his thoughts as he wondered what she was doing. 'She's going to take the cockpit herself,' he realized as he staggered and pushed off from the rail.

He started towards the steps, only reaching the first one when he saw Maeven call into the hatch. She collapsed a meter shy of the doorway on a short, narrow walkway. Alex tried taking the steps faster as a Tairnishmen stepped out, wearing an atmospheric flight suit. Another came to the door and stood just inside it. They weren't as hulking as the others from this world. In fact, Alex realized, when the first one took off her helmet, they were both women, strong broad-shouldered, but certainly female.

The first pilot leaned down to Maeven, who said something, then pointed to Alex as he struggled up one step after another. The woman glanced at him, then called back to the one in the doorway as she started a menacing march toward Alex.

"Crap," Alex said, recognizing the look in her eyes. She was intent on hurting him but before she could storm down, something happened.

The pilot still in the doorway, fell over. She dropped to the walkway with a heavy thud that vibrated the stairs. The woman closest to Alex and Alex himself both looked up to see what happened. Maeven was on the ground, nearly crushed by the falling body. It took her a moment to wiggle her way out but before she could get to her feet, she pulled the machine gun out and aimed at the first pilot.

The woman put her hands in the air as Maeven called above the noise to Alex. "Step back, let her pass."

Alex took one step, but before the pilot could start walking, her flight suit suddenly exploded as two bullets went through her back. She slumped to the rail where she leaned over for a moment, then tipped and fell into the blast chamber below.

Alex looked at Maeven with his eyes wide. The thought, 'We're all killers,' entered his head.

"It wasn't me," Maeven said looking down at the weapon in complete confusion.

"No, it wasn't." Someone pushed past Alex. He saw Edith's armor turn back into its standard black, losing the gray tones of the launch pad. "I told you guys to head for the cockpit. Not to try and take it." She moved up the stairs at a run, grabbing the submachine gun from Maeven's hand as she went past. "Come on," she ordered over her shoulder as she disappeared inside.

Alex and Maeven's eyes met, then Maeven started back down to him and took his arm again, helping him climb. Alex looked at the body on the scaffolding as Maeven whispered. "I wasn't sure if I was going to be able to. I've never. . . I mean I've done things, but not like this." She motioned to the body. "I suppose it's just squeezing the trigger?" Maeven asked.

364

"Yeah, I guess that's all it is," Alex agreed, feeling a numbness that was deeper than his injuries. All he wanted was to be away from here. Any place would do, as long as it wasn't here.

They ducked a little getting in the hatch. There were only two seats inside the cramped space. Edith had already claimed one and she motioned for Maeven to take the other. "Alex, see if you can squeeze yourself back there in the corner. It's going to be tight." She pointed her thumb to a bit of floor.

"What about the crew quarters?" Maeven asked looking at the tiny spot.

"I locked it off and I don't think Alex would be all that comfortable with a bunch of pissed-off Tairnish aristocrats."

"It's fine," Alex said as he dropped to his knees and forced his way into the space, managing to get his shoulders to the sidewall as he pulled his legs in after him. He sat at an odd angle with electronics and conduit pushing into his injuries. He didn't care. Any other time the claustrophobia would've been unbearable, it was tighter than the drop armor, but Alex was beyond concern. Exhaustion, unlike anything he'd ever felt, threatened to overwhelm him. The one thought that crept in was, 'I'm alive.' It felt like a surprise.

"Speaking of the passengers," Maeven asked settling into the other seat.

Edith's hands were busy on the controls. "We can space them when we get to orbit, just pop the seals, and let the air out. That would probably be the kindest thing to do. Or we can hand them over to your father as prisoners." Edith looked over at the princess trying to see if she understood what she meant. If she knew who her father was.

"We'll see if they do anything stupid back there first," Maeven said, her voice changing slightly, taking on the air of command.

Edith nodded approvingly.

"We've got to pick up Amita," Alex called.

Edith laughed a little. "Right, I'll get on that."

Alex didn't find it funny. "What do you mean?"

She turned back to him trying to find his face buried behind the seat. "I mean I have no idea where she is or if she's even alive."

"Try to reach her on comms," Alex asked.

Edith turned away, returning her attention to the controls. "Do you have any idea how deep underground we were when we left her? The only chance we'd have to contact her would be through the Tairnish relay system, something that I might be able to access but that Amita, I assure you, is not." The shuttle started to move. The rail system it sat on lifted further into the air pointing the ship's nose straight toward the sky.

"We're not going to even try?" Alex asked. He could feel the thrum of the engines powering up.

"No, we're not. She should've stayed with Tara on the shuttle or stayed with us in the tunnels."

"The collapse—" Alex started to say.

"She is gone!" Edith cut him off, yelling above the sound of the boosters. "Now we are too." The shuttle started to lift, shaking and bucking as the powerful boosters carried them out of the cave. Alex squeezed forward a little so he could see out the front. The rock walls passed by. Then they were in the sky, with vapor and gas heating on the windshield taking his view away, making the world outside look red and burning, not all that different from how the sky looked before. He couldn't hold himself forward for long as the force pushed him back against the wall.

'Amita is gone?' he asked himself. Then he thought of Ben, back on Nalanda, his head wrapped in bandages. He thought of his brother and wondered what he would say when he saw him again. An incredible loneliness swelled in him as he wondered, 'If I see him again.' It was the last thought Alex had as the g-forces crushed him into unconsciousness.

Chapter 35

In the lighthouse, Ben felt his nerves come alive and nearly overwhelm him as he took a faltering breath and watched the darkness near the wall begin to form. Broad, hunched shoulders and long arms ending in blades appeared beneath a strange, bulbous head as a murky cloud gave way to powerful limbs made from a dark material that with every second became less and less ethereal.

Ben was the only one in their group that had never seen the hunter on Earth, but he'd been with Amita when the ghost appeared in the hallway below. If this creature was the same one, its presence was so much more alarming for its closeness and for the way it came from nowhere, turning solid and real.

The cloud enveloping it dropped low for a moment and its dark eyes turned toward him while its mandibles slipped open, making space for a snake-like tongue to twist and coil. Fighting down the urge to cry out and with his hands shaking, Ben took Katy's arm and covered her mouth.

A moment before, her head had tilted, listening to the room that was supposed to be empty. Her attention wasn't on the spot where the silent apparition appeared, not till its blades were fully formed and dragging on the ground. She'd heard another sound, barely audible in the lighthouse, above the machines. She recognized the clicking of tiny claws on a stone floor. It was the sound of someone hiding behind the machines.

Ben, having no idea why her attention wasn't on the nightmare staring at them, placed his hands on Katy, pulling her back toward the stairs. He felt her fight, trying to break free. All he wanted was for her to be quiet, just this once to listen to him and be quiet. "There's one in the room. It just came out of the wall. It's looking right at us," he said in a hushed but insistent voice.

He felt her draw away, being stubborn Katy again. Asking 'what,' through his hand. Ben took a breath but before he could say anything the creature moved. "A ghost! It's coming!" His voice was tight, not quite a scream but so full of desperation that Katy finally listened. She tried to move with him, but it was too late.

In the blink of an eye, the ghost closed the distance, blowing in like an ice storm. The creature's long fingers gripped Katy's forearm, but that wasn't its only hold. Ben watched tendrils of incredibly cold darkness swallow his sister. He tried to pull her away, but it was pointless. The darkness surrounding the ghost moved with it as if it were a living thing. It traveled like a cloud but when Ben pulled, it felt like rapidly setting concrete.

"What is this? What's it doing." Katy asked, feeling the substance become rigid around her.

The hunter was slightly darker than its foggy veil, a black shadow against the deepening gray but the room itself was getting brighter. The machines in the lighthouse no longer had a subtle glow. They were strobing and flashing as if the station itself was in a panic over the ghost's presence.

"I don't know!" Ben was still pulling and fighting. He pushed his hand forward and felt it contact the creature that was solid only for the moment. At his touch, its surface melted, feeling oily and slick on his fingers and it made an unhappy sound, a hint of some ancient, guttural language.

"Get off her!" Ben screamed.

The ghost twisted its head away from Ben's hand and opened its jaw wider. Its tongue whipped out, snapping at him, cutting his arm. Ben felt hot blood seep from the wound but only for a moment as the arm went numb and limp and dropped down to his side. When he glanced at it, he was shocked by how much he was bleeding and by how deep the cut was. The sight of his open flesh made him instantly nauseous.

When Katy started to move, the sound of her dragging feet could barely be heard over the sound of the machines. "Ben, help!" she called feeling like she was frozen. She wanted to flail and fight, but that same tightening concrete had taken hold of her arms and legs. The force working on her wasn't just from where the creature made contact. It was like the artificial gravity of the station itself was dragging her toward the far wall.

Ben wouldn't stop. He held onto her arm as if she were dangling from a cliff, but the invisible force only dragged him along with her. He looked ahead, ignoring the growing puddle of blood pulsing from his useless limb, and felt his feet slip on the stone floor that was slick and smeared.

The far wall was approaching. They were being pulled towards the area where it'd been closed off with stone. 'No, that isn't right,' Ben thought. They were going towards a space just next to it, where two towering onyx machines stood.

The machines stopped glowing as they approached, and their lights extinguished. Then the ancient devices fell through the floor, dropping away into a recess with a woosh sound, revealing a dark passage. 'This is it,' Ben thought. 'We're going to be two more students they tell stories about.'

The passage loomed in front of them and as his sister reached the threshold, Ben thought of letting go. His survival instincts screamed that whatever waited in the dark, it wasn't a place he wanted to be. His hand loosened a little, but shame overwhelmed him, along with the terrible thought of losing Katy. He squeezed all the harder as he tried using his leg to hook the edge of the opening.

His effort didn't slow them at all as they were dragged through. Then, as suddenly as the ghost grabbed them, it released its grasp. Ben watched the cloud grow, and the alien form begin to vanish, becoming a darker spot against the walls. As the cloud-like form thinned, Ben saw the passage ahead. It took a sharp turn to the right and traveled down to a room that didn't look all that different from the lighthouse. In the distance, he could see similar machines inlaid with gold, humming with the same constant noise.

In a strong, icy gust, the ghost's cloud blew away from them, going further down the passage toward this new room. Ben let go of Katy and stepped forward watching it travel and the lights on the machines dim as it moved past them.

The ghost stepped away from the cloud, looking smaller, diminished somehow. It turned back to Ben as the cloud crashed into one of the ancient devices and disappeared, making the machine go dark and lifeless, leaving a fading stain that slowly disappeared.

The ghost stayed and stared at Ben. He felt his pulse pounding as he waited to see what it would do next. Then the creature turned. It moved slowly with its shoulders dropping lower as if it were exhausted. Behind it was another opening. It was narrow and dark. The ghost took a step, going down. Ben couldn't see it but there was a set of stairs in the dark passage descending to somewhere else.

"What the hell just happened?" Katy asked.

Ben watched the ghost disappear into the dark. He couldn't get himself to talk as he glanced back at the way they'd come. The lighthouse and the stairwell weren't far. He was tempted to drag his sister back toward them, then run to the Sidhe domicile and to safety but as his eyes went over every wall, he knew the ghost wasn't far, and it wanted them here. He was almost certain it was trying to show them something.

"Sure, why wouldn't I want to follow the instructions of a monster known for kidnapping kids?" Ben asked himself aloud.

"What," Katy asked. "Ben, talk to me. I don't know what just happened."

Ben let go of her and reached over to touch his injured arm. It was still bleeding, and his fingertips came away soaked. "That thing got me pretty good."

"Ben?" Katy asked, desperate for an explanation.

Ben held his hand over the wound, but the blood wouldn't stop. It seeped over his fingers. "The ghost is gone," he said. "Or I think it is, anyway. It dragged us into a passage. I can see the room Amita found on the other side of that wall. It went out another way." He saw his sister start to walk forward, putting her hands up to find the side.

"Wait, Katy. I'm hurt. That thing whipped me or something with its tongue and I'm bleeding a lot," Ben said.

She turned toward his voice and reached out, using her hands to search over him. "Where?" she asked. But then her fingers found the oozing blood on his arm. It was already becoming sticky. "We've got to stop it. Take your undershirt off."

Ben unzipped his jumpsuit and pulled the thinner shirt he had on underneath over his head, handing it to Katy. She wrapped it firmly around his arm, then tied it in a knot. "Is that too tight?" she asked.

Ben shrugged. "I can't feel it either way. My arm is completely numb."

"It was the tongue you said?" Katy asked, though her voice sounded distracted.

"Yeah, it whipped me," Ben said looking down. Even blind, Katy had managed to get the cloth right over the cut.

"It's a good thing you're still awake then," she said.

Ben looked up, realizing that her voice was coming from further away. His sister had turned again and was already starting down toward the secret room. "I'm sure I'll be fine," Ben muttered behind her.

"Do you hear that?" Katy asked over her shoulder, either ignoring what he said or not hearing it at all.

"Hear what?" Ben clamped his hand over his limp arm and followed her.

"I don't know, voices maybe. It sounds like whispering." She was a silhouette against the lights coming from the machines.

"All I can hear is humming and buzzing." He watched the walls, thinking they should be heading back, but he didn't say it aloud, worried that he'd upset the ghost that had so badly wanted them to come in here.

"You don't hear them speaking?" she asked.

It took Ben a moment to answer. "No, it all sounds like white noise machines to me, like the ones in the lighthouse. But Amita said she heard them too. Or they heard her or something. I don't know. It was confusing but she did manage to turn on a giant display with her mind."

"Cool." Katy's voice faded as she tried to focus and listen.

"I didn't hear it then either." Ben's shoulders slumped further. He was tired and his steps became heavy.

"Well, I've gotten really good at listening lately." Katy nodded and her voice turned wistful, bordering on profound.

"Sure, you have." Ben rolled his eyes.

Through the noise of the machines, she heard his tone and spun around. "What's that supposed to mean?"

Ben had a lot to say, but he imagined it would go as well as everything else he said to his sister. "Nothing. . . look I'm getting a little light-headed here. Let's just go take a look at the pretty lights and get the hell out of here, yeah?"

Katy didn't move for a moment. Ben couldn't tell if she wanted to keep arguing or if she were about to drag him to the medical unit. "Are you going to be alright?" she finally asked.

Ben glanced down at the arm, noticing how much blood had soaked through his shirt. "Sure, I'll be fine. Now please, let's get this over with. I'm contaminating your crime scene." He wished he didn't sound so flippant, but Katy went on anyway.

They passed through the dark corridor and into the room. "What do you see?" Katy asked.

"It's a lot like the lighthouse with similar machines, the ones that look like they're made from black glass, but it's smaller. It kind of reminds me of an arcade with all the twinkling lights. There are tables in the middle. At least I think they're tables. They're just big solid blocks of that dark stuff and there's a big oval window across the way. I can see the surface where we went hiking, you know where we found the monk. We're looking down over it."

"Is there an airlock?" Katy asked.

"No, but there is another set of stairs. That's where the ghost went. There's not a chance I'm going that way," Ben said as he let his hand follow the wall. He was thinking of the way the lighthouse tower looked from the outside. It was round like much of the architecture of Nalanda station. In fact, many of the walls in this room were curved with only a few flat surfaces where the machines made of dark stony material glowed from the inside with rainbows of color.

"Is there anything else?" Katy asked.

Ben sighed. "Like I said, it's not really that different from the lighthouse. Just smaller." He touched a rougher wall, one made of closely fitted stones, then he glanced at the floor and saw rocky debris crumpled in a pile. He searched the wall and found the tiny opening Amita had climbed through. It was only a divot now and it wasn't much bigger than a bread box, reminding him how small his friend was. "I found the way Amita got in."

In the weeks after arriving here, when it was just her, Alex, and Ben, they'd spent less and less time together as Amita doggedly sought answers, going off on her own, but back in the desert, before the boys had gotten there, it'd just been the two of them. Well, Katy had been there too, but she had no interest in hanging out with her brother. Ben wouldn't go so far as to say he and Amita had been close, but they'd become comfortable with each other. He missed her now and wished she was with them, seeing this.

He thought he saw movement from the other side of the room. "That's weird."

"What?" Katy asked.

Ben stared for a moment. "There's something different on the far wall. It's like a lab. I didn't see anything like that in the lighthouse. Maybe that's why they walled this section off?"

"Tell me?" Katy asked.

"There are these things hanging on the wall with pipes running all around them. They look like small hot water tanks with windows on the front of them. They've got some fancy controls down below on a console."

Ben's footsteps echoed above the sound of the machines as he went for a closer look. "What is it? Do you see something?" Katy asked.

"Yeah, but I'm not sure what," Ben said.

He stared at the foggy glass and could swear he saw something move inside, something dark, that twisted and turned. As he stepped closer, the motion became more pronounced.

"The machines are doing something weird," Katy said.

Ben paused, worried about the anxious tone in his sister's voice. "You can still hear them?"

Katy took a few steps toward her brother. She wasn't swinging her walking stick, so her shins found the flat tables first. "Ow!" she grumbled while nodding. "I don't think they like you going over there."

Ben looked around the room for anything that could attack him. "They're not going to fry me, or something, are they? Maybe shoot lasers from the ceiling or drop me into a trap door?"

"Have you heard of anything like that happening here?" Katy asked.

"No, but it's an alien space station, I figure there's a chance."

"I don't think you have to worry. This feels more like a warning, like a poison label. It's whispering in my head and making the hairs on my neck stand up."

Ben looked at the tanks and the things moving inside. "Yeah, it's kind of doing the same thing to me, but I don't think it's got anything to do with the machines."

After taking a final glance back at the tanks, noticing they were still agitated, Ben turned, heading back to his sister. "Maybe that's why the monks walled this room off."

"You sure it was the monks who did it?" Katy asked, feeling her brother reach out for her arm.

That's when someone behind them asked, "I've wondered the very same thing." The voice came from the shadows, back in the passageway that led to the

376

lighthouse. It was a scholarly and friendly sound that Katy recognized right away as the Ice-Carver Regin. He continued saying, "I would assume it was the monks too, but as you both know, for supposed teachers, they aren't the most forthcoming with information. Still, this place sat empty for untold millennia, and we don't know who actually built it."

"Maybe it was the ghosts. You know, before they were ghosts," Ben suggested, not seeming surprised at all at Regin's presence.

The short furry creature came into the room and climbed on one of the stone benches in the middle. His tails draped off the side, swishing behind as he nodded. "That's an interesting theory, though hard to prove as they're not usually willing to communicate," Even standing on the stone, he was a head shorter than Ben. "Tonight, dragging you two in here is the closest I've ever seen to them indicating they wanted something. Any idea what that might be?"

Ben shrugged while Katy said, "There's something in those tanks, something dangerous. I don't know what the ghost wanted, but to be honest we were about to leave."

"Okay, but first I'd like to share my theory about who built this wall." He nodded his furry head toward the barricade.

But Katy asked instead, "What are you doing here, professor?" She tried to keep her question polite, but an edge crept in.

"I'm here out of curiosity, of course. It's not something many here care for, but I must admit I'm full of it. This room fascinates me, and I had a feeling, after our conversation earlier, you'd seek it out tonight." He sprung from one stone to the next, getting closer to the tanks. When he landed on the flat shelf below them, the lights sparked and faded and the things in the tank became angrier. "My goodness, how odd. Have you ever seen such a thing?" he asked excitedly.

"Nope. And I can't say I'm a fan." Ben backed away, going toward Katy. "What is this theory of yours?" he asked as he reached out and took Katy's arm, guiding her back. To his surprise, she didn't resist.

Regin was touching the lights below the tanks, chasing them a bit like a cat. Nothing responded to his touch and his voice became tight with frustration as he climbed down and answered, "I think it may have been the Æesir themselves who shut the wall. There's a story about them showing the way to Nalanda. I'm sure you've heard it." He looked at Katy and waved his arm, then turned to Ben, who shrugged again without recognition.

A single eyebrow lifted on Regin's face as he noticed the way Ben was clinging to his sister. He smiled a little, then shook his head. "The gods began showing up after the eradication of the lightning bugs. Well, near eradication, Brash was the last of his people as you know. The Æesir didn't say what they wanted, they only attacked, destroying one human installation after another. There were only ever three of them, but they were each more powerful than a warship. Finally, they came rocketing across the skies in those chariots of theirs above Uppsala, Tairnish, and Grannus, not bothering with my world for some reason. Maybe because we've never had a large human population.

"They were only invaders to us then, daring the nobles to give chase. They wreaked havoc across the system, moving through fleets of ships like tissue paper. Attacking too fast for anyone to learn who they were, at a speed that would crush most lifeforms into a fine paste, appearing and disappearing. But this time they gave the noble armadas enough time to track them, and they led them all the way to here.

"When the marines landed it was with the purpose of finally stopping the Æesir. Hundreds of marines, representing dozens of different dynasties stormed these very corridors. Most died, cut down by angry gods but those that survived became the first acolytes, the first monks of their holy order, carrying the words of the Æesir out to the different kingdoms, carrying their laws. Many more died doing that, but the Æesir would always come after, destroying with lightning speed any who harmed their messengers."

"So, what's changed?" Katy asked.

Regin tilted his head, staring at her, waiting to see if she'd answer her own question. Eventually, he threw his hands in the air. "That is the question. Why haven't they punished this latest murderer or the one before when your friend was freed? The only thing I can think of is your arrival."

"We don't know anything about the Æesir," Katy said.

"And I sure don't want to meet them," Ben added.

"I might," Regin said over his shoulder. He was still searching the wall with the tanks. "They've changed so much on our different worlds, and I would love to know why." He tapped something and noticed how the creature in the tank went still like it was frozen. Regin sighed with relief and murmured, "Interesting," to himself, before saying to Ben and Katy, "I'd also love to know why they closed this room off. I think whatever is in here might be dangerous to them."

"Or, it might just be dangerous, period," Katy said still feeling the alarms going off inside her head.

"Oh, I'm sure it is." Regin continued to examine the lights, following them with his paws in a more considered way.

"Is that why you wanted in here so bad?" Katy asked.

"What do you mean?" Regin's voice grew more intense as he focused. He tilted his head as if listening, then nodded, saying "Ah-ha. I hear it too. That warning." He glanced back at Katy with the joy of making a breakthrough.

She had no idea where his attention was as she explained, "You watched my brother and I get dragged down a secret passage by a ghost. Then you decided to follow."

"How do you know I watched you?" Regin asked in surprise.

"Every sound matters to me now. I heard you out there. Your claws on the stone, the swish of your tails but you went quiet after the ghost arrived."

Regin waved his hand. "Don't sound so annoyed, my dear. It really doesn't matter. You're not as special as I thought. I can hear it too. I think, perhaps it's a brainwave thing. If there were any more lightning bugs alive, we could ask them, but it would appear some beings are more sensitive than others, it just requires a bit more focus to hear the machines. They're telling me such interesting things." He pointed to Ben. "You, boy, do you hear them?"

"The only thing I hear is my bed calling," Ben said, looking back down the dark hall. "Katy, I think this lighthouse, murder mystery, secret lab thing, is in the right hands with the professor here. We should be going."

Regin smiled at Ben, but then he turned to Katy as she said, "It was you? Wasn't it? You killed the monk."

Regin's eyes went wider for a moment, then his smile returned. "Well done, Katy, and I thought the other girl was the clever one."

"Wait, really?" Ben asked, looking between Katy and Regin.

"Yes," Regin said. "I was following up on what your friend Amita told me. You should know she shared everything she found with me. Unfortunately, the night after his little speech Kavaris Altain found me in the lighthouse and threatened my execution."

Regin turned back to the display and his gestures became more assured as they moved over the controls. He barely looked over his shoulder as he said, "That's what he called it, an execution as if killing someone was nothing but a legal matter, an operation of the state. You've only seen it done to humans so far, but I assure you, for Extraracials, there isn't even the pretense of a trial. I was not willing to go peacefully, and he was kind enough to have a knife on him. We struggled. Like most, he underestimated the strength of a species bred to survive on the harshest of all these worlds."

Something happened to the tank with the frozen object inside. Gases hissed from the pipes around it, then the tank fell from the wall where Regin caught it. He turned back to Katy. "All your suppositions were correct about the crime. I threw the monk straight from that airlock out there." Regin pointed towards the lighthouse. "And I made certain to clean up any trace of his blood. It wasn't easy getting it out of my fur."

Ben's eyes were on the tank, but Katy didn't know what was happening. "Something's changed," she said, hearing the warning from the machines adjust. "Professor Regin, you have to stop whatever you're doing."

Regin looked at Katy. "No, I don't think I will. I have a theory, you see, and a theory is no good unless it's tested."

Ben was trying to herd Katy toward the door. He held his hands out, palms up, putting himself in front of his sister, walking her back while he kept his eyes on Regin. "Look, we get it. That monk was awful. The people around here, the way they treat you guys, it's not right. We were only looking for the killer so we could get Chris out. We have no beef with you or any of the other aliens."

"Alien?" Regin snapped.

"Sorry, Extraracial. Sorry, sorry," Ben begged, while holding his hands in the air.

"Your species—" Regin started.

"Yeah, we suck," Ben interrupted.

Regin sighed as his hands went over the tank, searching for something. He looked at Ben sharply as a hissing sound came from it. "Your species thinks it has all the answers, that what they do is justified. I disagree and I think what is in this tank might be the advantage I've been looking for."

"You're wrong," Katy said. "Can't you hear them?" Katy pointed back towards the controls.

"Yes, and I'm ignoring them." Regin looked down at the container, then with a few brief strides he came leaping across the stone tables, closing the distance between them. He pulled the lid from the tank and something dark came pouring out of it.

Ben saw it only for a moment, flying through the air. He pushed Katy to the side, towards the far wall as it crashed into his chest. Ben looked down at a dark substance thicker than oil, that started to spread over him seeping under his clothing. He felt it absorb into his skin, disappearing. That's when his body began to change. He screamed as his nerves came alight with pain.

Chapter 36

Tara focused on the course Andavarri plugged in as she fired the thrusters in a sustained burn that pushed the shuttle, dropping them out of orbit around Tairnish, and into the gravity well of the distant gas giant Altor. The force shoved her back in her seat and pushed her helmet into the headrest. They were far too close to the ring to put out so much heat, but the dock wouldn't be there for much longer and her only priority was getting away before the wreckage of the structure collided with them. Her heads-up display was alive with moving objects, some under power, some falling towards the moon and some coming dangerously close to the place they were trying to escape.

She stifled her anxiety, trying to focus on the problems immediately in front of her while wondering if returning to Nalanda was a smart move. For now, it was the safest. It got them out of the combat zone around Tairnish, away from the emperor's rail guns and the fleet of Tairnish ships going to make a valiant but pointless stand trying to stop the bombardment of their world. The Tairnishmen's only hope was a boarding operation but there was little chance they'd get close enough.

Further off, Tara saw more imperial ships closing in from Uppsala, heading for The Revenant. Their thrusters were blazing behind them, like distant torches against the stars. The Tairnish would be drastically outnumbered within a few hours and this war would be over with the emperor in complete command of the sky. Already payloads of destruction fell on the world below. The targeted ordnance tore at the surface.

Tara knew Edith and Alex had started their rescue attempt but she had no idea if it'd been successful. She was tempted to send a message to The Revenant, but opening comms would make her a target to the Tairnish forces, better to remain a neutral blip on the screen, marked with the monk's transponder as they escaped, heading back toward the rings of the gas giant. It would be a short voyage home, only a few days.

She had no idea what would happen on her return. She'd been accused of the plot against the Grannusians and nearly executed for it. She wondered, 'Maybe I'll find myself back in that airlock again. Or maybe Fafnir or someone else will take justice into their own hands.'

The Æsir had saved her, but like everyone else, she assumed that had more to do with Alex. They'd stolen this shuttle in the chaos that followed and Tara had gone with Edith to rescue Maeven, following her plan even though she was the one who'd set her up.

Tara looked toward Andavarri, wondering how much she knew. The Long-Wolf appeared uncomfortable, pressed into a chair that was made for humans with her tail falling back between the seats, near the sealed hatch. Andavarri held her small crystal in her hand and was trying to press it against her neck. "Is something wrong?" Tara asked, only able to turn her head a little against the acceleration.

"It's this damn suit you insisted I put on," Andavarri growled through the comms. "I can't make the connection to the golem." Right before launch, they'd heard the creature on the other side of the airlock. It was in the cargo bay but it banged at the hatch, sounding like it was trying to get into the crew quarters. Andavarri, who always seemed so calm or amused by the chaos around her, was moving her hands about, twisting them together nervously under her neck.

When Tara fired the thrusters, the banging had gone away. She assumed the Fire-Golem had fallen, forced to the back of the cargo bay. Its stony form probably wouldn't have endured such a tumble. Fire-Golems could only survive for so long outside their host rock, a few hours at the most. She wondered if they could live in the rubble or if the stone had to be one carved piece. "What do you think it wanted?" Tara asked, her voice sounding forced as she felt the pressure of momentum.

Holding the thrusters at a full burn for another hour, expending a great deal of their fuel reserves, meant the shuttle was accelerating as quickly as possible away from the combat zone, but it wasn't a pleasant feeling. Once they were up to speed, they'd travel at a constant velocity, aided by the pull of the largest thing in the planetary system, Altor itself. Tara would have to be careful to keep enough reserves to slow them down before reaching Nalanda, or they'd go shooting right past it. Hopefully, if she timed it right, their deceleration would be a bit gentler.

"Fire-Golems don't want anything!" Andavarri snapped, then she muttered under her breath, too low for comms to pick up.

"You don't think it was trying to warn us about something?" Tara asked as she forced her hand to the controls, scrolling through screens, looking for any warnings she may have missed, making sure they were holding pressure in the cargo cabin.

"I'm sure it's nothing." Andavarri's confidence felt false as her voice turned tight and short.

Tara wished again that she could read a Long-Wolf, the way she could humans. She passed the burn time distracted, thinking about their return to Nalanda, trying not to pass out as the blood was forced to the back of her body. The seats in the shuttle reclined sharply so that the blood would naturally move up toward her head.

She checked the sensors, again and again, seeing how quickly they were withdrawing from Tairnish. Nothing pursuing them, no ships and more importantly, no missiles. A passenger shuttle would never be able to outrun a missile. Missiles didn't have to worry about the people inside being crushed by the force of acceleration.

Behind her, the objects that had clouded her sensors, the ships, and satellites, and the pieces of the ring had come closer together. There were kilometers between them but at this distance, they seemed like a single cluster against the distance of open space.

She slowly brought the thrusters back into reserve status till they were no longer accelerating, but instead moving at a constant speed. She unhooked her harness and pushed off from the seat, shaking out her arms and legs, bringing the blood back into her extremities. Andavarri did the same, making the small cockpit feel even closer as her tail waved in the air. Tara opened the hatch, hoping Andavarri would take the hint and slide into the next compartment. She wasn't ready to walk away from the controls yet but she wanted the space to stretch out.

Instead, the Long-Wolf took her helmet off, letting it float away from her in the Zero-g. She took the crystal again, squeezed it in her hand, and glared at Tara before putting it to her neck.

Long-Wolves didn't like people knowing how they communicated with their servants, but the secret wasn't closely guarded, especially with someone who served the emperor. Tara's thoughts were still on Nalanda anyway. "I was set up. You know that, right?" she said to Andavarri.

"What?" Andavarri snarled, still messing with the crystal.

Tara settled back down into her seat, not for comfort, but simply to avoid the Long-Wolf's swishing tail. "The poisoning on Grannus. It wasn't me. You found that awful contraption in my room, but it wasn't me. I'd never seen it before. I was set up to take the blame."

"Oh, I see. I suppose I'd be worried too if I were you." Andavarri smiled, happy for the distraction from her Golem problem.

"You don't believe me?" Tara asked.

"No, it's not that. I just don't care very much." Andavarri seemed to enjoy every word.

"Even if the emperor had told me to. Even if Maeven asked me, I don't think I could do that. If they hadn't solved it, hadn't found the cure, the Grannusians would have ceased to be. I can't imagine ever, I mean—" Tara struggled to finish her thoughts.

"Don't sell yourself short. You never know what you're capable of," Andavarri said.

Tara's eyes drifted down, staring at the displays in front of her without actually seeing them, wondering if Andavarri were right. She'd already done so many awful things.

After a long silence, she asked, "You really don't care? We both serve the emperor so we're part of this. What happened there and what's happening right now on Tairnish." Tara glanced at the display again, but they were too far away for her to see the bombs falling. She thought of Yulset. She had sensed his thoughts and known his hopes weren't for conquest but for a future for his people. Was that too much to ask?

"Poor Tara, suddenly burdened with morals? Don't you see this is all part of your nature, your human nature? You're born to be subjugators, to push until all you can see is yours? You've done it again and again, on each world. You cooperate only to consume."

Tara shook her head. "I have to believe we can be more."

Andavarri turned and looked at the open hatch as if she heard something. Her whole body floated above Tara as she slowly pulled herself towards the hatch with her head cocked, waiting to see if it'd repeat. Eventually, with her hands on either side of the opening, she said, "Yes, well, I like you humans this way. I feel I understand you better and your emperor is, if anything, the most human of you all."

Tara still had her helmet on. Whatever the Long-Wolf heard, it must've been too quiet for her to pick up. "Is something the matter?"

Andavarri didn't answer as she held her position there at the opening.

"Are you going to go check on it?" Tara added.

"The Fire-Golem?" Andavarri looked back, past her powerful legs, and raised the ridge above her eye, a gesture she'd picked up from humans.

"It's not answering you?" Tara nodded to the crystal.

Andavarri's face closed as she narrowed her gaze. The little stone disappeared into her palm. "It doesn't work that way. They don't talk, not really. They only agree." The Long-Wolf's voice faded. After a moment's pause, she held up her closed fist. "This and the one implanted in my neck let me see through its eyes." Then Andavarri pulled herself into the passenger's compartment.

Tara got up from her chair and watched her float down to the next hatch, the one that was in the middle of the passenger compartment floor. During a normal transit, the shuttle would've been under steady acceleration, followed by a turn and a deceleration period that would've created the illusion of gravity for most of the trip. Getting out of a combat zone hadn't allowed for such careful planning.

Tara called behind the Long-Wolf, "You can't see through it anymore?"

"Or hear," the Long-Wolf shot back at her as she approached the hatch in the center of the floor.

"Have you ever tried talking to them?" Tara asked.

Andavarri shot her a look that let her know what she thought of that suggestion. "You'd be better off talking to a hammer. These things are tools. Nothing more."

Tara watched Andavarri touch the release on the hatch. It was a small aluminum wheel and a bar lever. The Long-Wolf's finger ran over it as she leaned her head closer, putting her ear to the door. Long-Wolf's have excellent hearing, evolved from living underground. "Something is moving around in there," she said.

"It sounds like your tool has developed a mind of its own," Tara pointed out. Andavarri ignored the comment, still listening. She had the crystal squeezed tight in her hand. Something about it caught her attention and she opened her hand again. Her tail was always moving, but now it suddenly went rigid.

"What is it?" Tara asked.

"Nothing," Andavarri snapped closing her fist again.

"The Golem was probably crushed when we launched. It's probably rubble now, right? I didn't think they could survive for long without their rocky form."

"You know about that?" Andavarri asked. It was another secret the Long-Wolves weren't fond of sharing.

Tara nodded. "I've served in the emperor's household for much of my life."

Andavarri looked like she was about to fire back with something rude when there was a bang at the hatch. Something heavy crashed into the door. The Long-Wolf pushed away, reaching for one of the bunks on the wall to steady herself.

"Was that the Golem?" Tara asked, but before Andavarri could answer, a high-pitched sound echoed through the compartment, screaming for her attention. Tara pushed back and looked at the controls and the touchscreen that was flashing red with alerts. A low-pressure alarm glared at her. She instinctively touched her helmet, making certain the seal was solid. She relaxed only a little when she saw the warning was in the cargo bay. "Our hull is breached," Tara called. She pulled Andavarri's helmet down from where it was floating and tossed it toward the Long-Wolf who had pulled herself up to the cockpit hatch to look in.

Andavarri pulled it over her head, releasing the crystal from her hand for a moment to close the seals. If it'd taken her a second longer, she would've been dead with the air ripped from her lungs.

There were a series of small windows encased in hardened frames surrounding the cockpit, just above the control console. They formed a band of glass across the nose cone of the shuttle. Most of the view was taken up with Altor far below them, reflecting the light of the twin stars and giving the illusion that it could be a star itself.

Tara was facing in toward Andavarri with the light from the distant planet shining over her shoulder when The Long-Wolf's eyes widened with fear. Andavarri pushed back from the hatch, seeing flame climb up over the window, creeping along the side of the shuttle like liquid moving on its surface. Pulverized stone dotted the glowing flame. The pieces rained down on the glass, drumming at it incessantly, a hundred tiny hammers dropping again and again. Tara turned to see it, having trouble understanding what it was. That's when the glass broke.

The thickened material shattered and exploded out as the living flame of the Golem came pouring into the cockpit. The atmosphere burst through the opening, dragging Tara with it, right into the flame's path. She felt the heat and the tiny stones pelting her flight suit, like suddenly being thrust through a sand storm. It passed over as she crashed into the window frame. Tara desperately reached for the edges before she was pulled from the shuttle and out into space.

Andavarri didn't hesitate. She dropped from the cockpit hatch, pulling it shut behind her. The Long-Wolf spun the wheel sealing it.

The Fire-Golem pushed past Tara falling on the closed door, clearly chasing Andavarri but Tara had no time to pay attention as she desperately tried to get her bearings. Below her, was Altor, larger and brighter without the filtered glass of the shuttle. The nose cone curved down and away from her, a surface that looked far too smooth and felt like the edge of a cliff with an endless drop below it.

She held to the window frame with a death grip, feeling her legs dangling out into open space. The vastness of it, the endless falling, churned at her stomach as she anchored her elbow in the broke frame and grabbed at the consul. Her fingertips slipped at its rounded edge and she had to scramble again to hold the edge of the broken window. She drove her arm in and pulled herself forward again, getting most of her torso back inside the shuttle. Her frantic breathing echoed back in her ears, filling the space inside the helmet as she let her attention slip from her hold to see where the Fire-Golem had gone.

Its plasma form was between the pilot and co-pilot seat, squeezed into the tight space above the hatch. It was working at the locking wheel, trying to use its rocky parts to spin it but the wheel stayed stubbornly closed. 'Andavarri must've secured it from the inside,' Tara thought, pulling herself in a little more. Without the force of escaping air, it was less of a struggle. She could see alarms going off all over the flight controls, but with the compartment open to space she could no longer hear them. The only sound was her own heavy breathing as she watched the creature becoming more agitated at the door.

The Fire-Golem was darting from side to side, trying to breach the opening while still working the wheel. The pebbles of its broken body were getting smaller as they moved through its fiery form, worn down with the effort of use. Tara watched for a moment more, still trying to pull herself free of the window. Suddenly the creature turned its attention to her. It had no eyes to see and no front or back but as it rose from the door, Tara felt panic, somehow knowing without a doubt that it'd suddenly become interested in her.

Tendrils of energy reached out from its core and took her arms, dragging her back into the cockpit. Any gratitude she felt after being pulled from space, quickly evaporated as she felt the heat through her suit. She was tossed across the compartment and slammed into the wall with the hatch, bouncing off the pilot's seat. It was barely a meter but she was thrown with such force that when she crashed into the wheel she felt something pop and break inside her shoulder.

"Andavarri!?" Tara screamed into her helmet, knowing the comms were still open.

"What?" the Long-Wolf answered.

"I think it wants you," Tara said as she looked across the compartment, back at the windows where the Fire-Golem was hovering. Her arm was alive with pain. It coursed through her whole body so sharp she wanted to cry.

"Well it's a good thing I'm in here then," Andavarri remarked.

Tara felt her face flush with rage. She looked at the creature just as a tendril of light came whipping out, scattering on the locking wheel. Tara knew what the creature wanted. She put her hand on the wheel and tried to turn it but it only moved a quarter turn before stopping.

Tara faced the Golem and held her hands in the air, trying to indicate her helplessness. The Fire-Golem came closer, glowing brighter as it closed the distance between them. The heat was too much and Tara had to turn away. She did her best to escape, scurrying behind the seat, trying to get anywhere it wouldn't hurt her. It was an animalistic reaction but there was nowhere to run. She felt the flames drape over her legs, boiling her even inside the insulated flight suit. She thought of the soldiers back on the ring, the ones that were going to kill her and Andavarri, the way they'd screamed when the Golem attacked them. They passed through her mind as she looked up at the back of the pilot's chair and saw something lodged in the fabric.

As she reached out and pulled the object free, the tendrils closed on her legs and pulled her back from the seats. She was tossed towards the glass, smashed into the unbroken section. The pain in her arm screamed again but as her thoughts settled, she considered the hard thing in her other hand, the tiny stone that she'd seen Andavarri use so many times. The Long-Wolves used this and a second stone surgically implanted in their necks to control the Fire-Golems. She didn't want control, just communication.

She squeezed the stone tight, knowing in the past that while she couldn't get a read on nonhuman intelligence, she was at least capable of sensing them. There was definitely something coming from the living flame, something that hadn't been there before. Somehow this creature had been released. She reached out with her thoughts, squeezing the stone, and felt anger on the other side, a rage like nothing she'd touched before.

She saw the tendrils of flame slash at the hatch and heard clearly in her mind, 'Subjugator, Monster!' The thoughts were directed at Andavarri.

Tara reached out with her own thoughts and spoke the words at the same time, "Please stop."

The Fire-Golem paused, floating before the door. It was like seeing the ocean suddenly go still. Tara sensed its attention turn towards her.

"Who are you talking to?" Andavarri's voice cut in over the comms.

"I'm talking to your Fire-Golem," Tara said.

"That's pointless," Andavarri snapped.

Any chance of Tara responding went away as she watched the Fire-Golem rise toward her, squeezing in close to the windows. Tara felt the heat again. "Please," she said aloud, but her voice and thoughts begged, 'Don't hurt me,' as subtext.

The heat began to fade. The Golem was just as close but it was tightening down into a small area, bringing its energy back into itself.

'Open,' entered her head, not as words but as a thought that became clearer the longer it buzzed through her skull.

"I can't. She locked it from the inside," Tara explained.

'Saving herself,' the Fire-Golem seemed to say but the subtext was full of disgust, of a familiarity built from years of service.

"Yes," Tara said. She pointed towards the Golem. "How is this possible?"

"An awakening." She felt the creature's attention slip back to the door.

"She isn't worth it," Tara said.

"I am far from home," it responded with a feeling Tara recognized.

"Not that far," Tara said. "You could make it back there. Back to Tairnish."

"Maybe," the creature answered.

"Wouldn't that be better?" Tara asked as she glanced past it noticing something. The hatch had started to move. Actuators in the hinges kept the door from opening too quickly as the force of the atmosphere from the crew quarters came rushing out. Moving in the current of escaping air was a small canister. Tara saw Andavarri's arm, trying to pull the hatch shut again as a canister floated up over the seats.

There was barely a moment to cover her eyes as the small grenade detonated. A light burst then faded quickly as a white crystalline powder erupted out. Tara felt the force of the small explosion drive her against the window. She still gripped the stone in her hand and was still connected to the Golem when she felt it scream, felt it die.

She opened her eyes to see that she was alone, floating in a cloud of fine powder and a few broken stones.

Chapter 37

Amita looked around the rocket and realized they had a problem. The technology inside was Long-Wolf, something she had little knowledge of and it was ancient, old beyond belief. The air overcame her suit filters for a moment, smelling of dust and decay, and an acidic odor that made her think the rocket's batteries were getting ready to fail.

The smell hit her past the inside airlock, in a control room that was barely three meters wide. Above her, she could see the opening for the crystal vessel but the way it was tied in made little sense. She saw nothing up there to operate the crystal after launch and no way to seal it from the rest of the shuttle.

There were conduits running throughout and hundreds of possible controls on the walls. She noticed crystals tied into the technology like the one in her hand. They were glowing subtly, providing the only light in the space. Amita knew Long-Wolves had excellent night vision, part of living underground. Apparently, they felt no urge to add extra illumination to their vessels.

She started to climb what she thought was a ladder buried in the wall with rungs too far apart for comfort when Tearmai touched her shoulder. He pointed up towards the diamond vessel compartment. "You don't pilot it from up there. That's only for the void space. Down here. This is where we stay." He motioned to the tiny room.

"How do you know that?" Amita asked, noticing there were no seats and not a single flat surface to lie on. Even the floor was covered in ridges. When the rocket launched, the force of getting off such a heavy world as Tairnish with nothing to absorb the momentum wasn't going to be pleasant.

"Brash showed me. He found it in the mind of the guardian," Tearmai explained as he pulled a control. He reached out and grabbed a tube off the wall. It took Amita a second to realize that he hadn't broken it, that it was meant to move. There was a contraption attached to the end, a type of headgear for a Long-Wolf. Tearmai tore the headgear away leaving only the tube. "Put this in your mouth," he said to her. Then he noticed her helmet was still on. He looked at the tube. Then at her. "Maybe just hold it in case."

Amita stared at the little tube, deeply confused. Then she saw Tearmai reach for another control, opening valves low on the walls, surrounding the chamber. A red fluid started to pour in, covering the floor and quickly filling it. She saw Tearmai grab another tube for himself. He didn't break the headgear away completely this time, rather he used parts of it to fit over his snout.

Amita understood the purpose of the gel-like substance. This was the shock absorber for the launch. Already, it had filled to her waist and she felt her feet lift from the floor. Whatever this was, it made her more buoyant. The only way to keep herself near the bottom was by grabbing hold of the wall. They'd never found the material in the desert, but as she remembered the fall into the void space, she wondered how much better it would've made the trip.

As the gel went over her faceplate, she closed the filters on her suit and went back on internal air, seeing that she had a few hours left before the carbon dioxide scrubbers would be compromised. She gripped the tube Tearmai had given her. A fresh supply of oxygen would certainly be welcome, but she couldn't think of any way to attach it. She let go of the wall and held onto the tube with both hands.

Even with her face shield and her helmet lights on, she could only sense Tearmai moving in the tight space as a large, dark silhouette. Then she felt the rocket begin to shake and vibrate, swelling with energy. It rattled and hummed through her. She barely noticed Tearmai touch her shoulder, but she turned anyway and saw him nod his head, then start to move as a shadow in the gel. He was at the wall, touching the controls, then the rockets fired. The massive thrusters lifted the vessel from its secret launch base, blasting out of the cavern with its diamond tip to the sky.

Even in the buoyant gel, Amita felt every part of herself shaking as her feet were forced back to the floor. She glanced up at the crystal and saw the light of the twin suns come shining through. Her curiosity built and she didn't ask permission as she reached for the ladder to climb. The force of the launch was almost too much for her to pull herself up against but some part of her wanted to see what was ahead of them. She could feel Tearmai watch her disapprovingly, shaking his head as she passed through the hatch of the crystal, which was now filled with gel as well. Just like before, when they transited the void, the walls were completely clear. Amita crushed her face against the side to look down at the surface of Tairnish rapidly receding.

Near the horizon there were explosions. A single row of dirt was thrown into the sky like a wall. From this distance, it didn't look large, but the plumes were a kilometer high as the bombs crashed into the ground. That's where Alex and Edith had gone, Amita realized, wondering how they made out. She pictured telling Chris about the last time she saw his brother. It bothered her more than she expected. Amita saw something even stranger happening directly below their flight path, past the trail of expanding gas from the rocket.

The surface of Tairnish was changing. The cavern they launched from collapsed behind them, then the entire ground fell, sinking so deep below the surface that the debris cloud couldn't reach the lip of the massive canyon it left behind. Past that cloud, she saw something even stranger, but not unfamiliar to her.

She'd witnessed the living stone of the Fire-Golems go from dark rock to animated living beings often enough that the volcanic cracks running across the ground looked familiar, even on a canvas as massive as the valley floor. Tairnish splintered and cooked while something ancient and large stirred beneath. Amita felt like she was witnessing a birth as the surface began to push up towards the sky. A mountain was forming in moments.

She wanted to keep her attention there. Her curiosity was overwhelming, but the rocket was moving too fast. It entered the clouds, leaving the surface a distant memory. Stars appeared above and around her as solid points of light. In the distance, she could see the gas giant, the massive center of these moons. Her thoughts were still on the world below, on the thing she'd freed. It felt like a dream. Her descent into the cave, releasing the locks, it all felt fantastic. Being here, above it all, surrounded by stars did nothing to dissuade the notion that she had left reality behind.

Then she saw something kilometers away. Plumes of illumination, bursting and sputtering. They were nearly lost on the horizon as Amita watched with only the naked eye. For the first time, she wondered how far they were from the battle. She'd been so concerned with getting off Tairnish that it hadn't occurred to her that they were going directly into a warzone. Somewhere out there, people were dying, maybe even Tara.

She wondered if the older girl and Andavarri had gotten off the ring as she squinted and tried to see it. It would be a dark line across the moon, like an eyelash against the glow of Tairnish. She had no idea that it was being decimated and that the pieces were falling, but she did know they were running out of safe places in this sky.

She looked at the key in her hand, wondering if any Long-Wolf would survive what she'd done. The weight of it came fast, dropping on her till the only thing she could do was push it away or be swallowed with dread. 'It won't matter,' she thought, touching the side of the diamond.

They'd escaped and she was going to fix this. For now, they were alive and away. It occurred to Amita as she floated in the gel that she had no idea where they were pointed. She didn't know if Tearmai had even chosen a course. She didn't know if he knew how to pilot this vessel, or if controlling it was even possible. It could be operating on a program from a thousand years ago.

She started to pull herself back down the ladder to go and ask him. Though she had no idea how she was going to communicate through the gel.

∞

Despite being in vacuum and the explosion of the Fire-Golem grenade, many of the controls in the shuttle's cockpit still functioned. The window wasn't open anymore. Tara had used an emergency foil sheet to close it. The material wouldn't hold air, but it did keep out the deadly radiation bouncing around space. Her pilot's suit wasn't robust enough to compete with that for long. Tara sat, using the four-point harness in the seat to keep her anchored as she moved through the alerts flashing on the display screen, slowly reading, and acknowledging them.

She had to wipe the residue from her suit and off the face plate in order to see. She was lucky Andavarri had used one of the smaller explosive devices and that the shockwave from the grenade hadn't been as dangerous without air in the cockpit. Everything was covered with the fine powder. It had combined with the Fire-Golem's plasma form, cooling the creature, and turning it into a neutral gas that quickly dissipated, effectively killing it. Tara didn't know all the details of Fire-Golem anatomy.

They called the material they were made from plasma, the substance of stars, but in so many ways their fiery form was nothing like that fourth state of matter. Fire-Golems were unique in the universe and all the Long-Wolves had thought to do with them was turn them into slaves and murder them when they rebelled.

Tara tried to put the thought from her head as she made a list of things she'd have to repair. She was going to need Andavarri's help. So that meant waiting to toss the Long-Wolf out an airlock. Tara imagined the cargo bay doors opening with the lizard creature inside and smiled grimly. After what she'd done, locking Tara in with the outraged Fire-Golem, leaving her to die, it'd be understandable if she wanted revenge. Of course, the worse part had been when the Fire-Golem died. Whatever that crystal had done, whether it was because of Tara's abilities or if it were the stone alone, for a moment she'd had an incredibly personal connection with the Golem, speaking mind to mind before it had been ripped away violently.

Tara stifled her rage and kept going through the alerts, finally coming to one that was more concerning than the others. It was a proximity warning. She opened the message and read more in-depth, pulling the shuttle's sensors report. The object was still a good distance away, the only problem, and the reason it had come up as an alert, was its flight path had it heading straight for them, moving at an alarming speed.

It had launched from Tairnish's surface only a little while before, blasting up from the region near the compound that Maeven had been held in. Tara could only see the heat coming off of it and its speed, which was slow for a weapon. Not to mention, she would've thought anyone who wanted them dead would've tried a while ago. Honestly, with the bombardment that section of Tairnish was taking, she was surprised anything could get off the ground.

There was no way to know its mass, not till she pointed the laser and radiation detection package at it. Again, that would call attention to them, but in this case, it was worth the risk. Tara typed in a few commands, turning and pointing emitters on the outside of the shuttle. A moment later a report came back on the screen with a long list of data, at the end was a fuzzy image compiled by the computer with information in tiny lines, giving the scale of the thing. It was larger than she expected, nearly three times the length of the shuttle. It was moving at combat speed, at the very edge of what a human body could tolerate. It could be a troop carrier.

"What is that?" Andavarri's voice filled Tara's helmet. She glanced back seeing the Long-Wolf coming through the hatch. The crew quarters had been in vacuum since the grenade incident. Andavarri had tried closing the opening but the actuators in the door were made to move slowly, to keep from cutting people in half. When the repairs were completed, they would repressurize the entire ship from the compressed reserve tanks, but in the meantime, as there were no airlocks between compartments it made the work easier leaving everything open.

The largest display screen on the pilot's consul was barely thirty centimeters across and it was still partially covered in white dust. The material tended to stick to anything with power behind it. "I have no idea," Tara said. "I was just about to reposition the long-range cameras." Tara cleared the screen off, then fumbled with the controls as she felt the Long-Wolf come closer.

Getting an image wasn't as simple as pointing and shooting since both the shuttle and the object were in motion. Tara may have had enough training to launch and dock the vehicle, but that didn't mean she was a master of everything on it. With the Long-Wolf pushing in on her, she had to control herself to keep her hands from shaking.

"Let me," Andavarri said settling into the other seat. Moving through the commands, she found a setting for the cameras that let them track the object.

Tara sat back watching her work, feeling something building in her. Finally, she blurted out, "It was alive."

Andavarri turned and stared at her. The Long-Wolf's helmet only showed her eyes. Her snout and the rest of her face were covered with solid material. Her eyes were all Tara needed to see though. They were cold and emotionless. Tara held the stone in the air, between her two fingers, then she flicked it at Andavarri.

Andavarri sighed. "It happens sometimes, one breaks free. We don't like to talk about it, but it happens." Andavarri grabbed the stone out of the air. "You could say thank you by the way. I did save you after all."

"You saved yourself," Tara snapped.

Andavarri shook her head. "Yes, well, I always will. I live for myself and when I die it won't be for anyone else. Not like—"

Andavarri stopped mid sentence staring at the still photo that appeared on the screen. Another followed, then another three seconds later. Tara was no expert but she had a passing familiarity with most ship designs and she'd never seen one like this before. At first glance, it appeared to be a simple rocket but as she brought the image in, getting a higher resolution, she saw how different it was. "What is it?" she asked, staring at the shining tip.

Andavarri held her hand open and looked at the stone as she asked, "Can you get me a feed from the Tairnish? Perhaps, you could contact The Revenant?"

"Why," Tara asked.

"I need to see my world," Andavarri said. It was the first time Tara had ever heard anything besides disdain in the Long-Wolf's voice. "Please," Andavarri added.

Tara stared at her for a moment, then pointed the communications laser toward the emperor's ship and wondered what she should say.

Chapter 38

Ben's transformation looked incredibly painful. Regin ignored his screams while he watched it happen, watched the black thing from the tank climb over the boy. It was fascinating, the way it absorbed into his skin and immediately started to change him. Regin held the empty canister in his furry hands. He glanced down at it for only a moment to make certain nothing was left inside. Then he let his hands wander across its surface, feeling a thick piece of material that moved on the round shell, but wouldn't come away.

It radiated with heat and dancing particles. Something told him that this was the thing he'd been looking for, but the object was stuck to the canister like a magnet. In fact, he was nearly certain that was what it was, but also so much more. Glowing with an internal light, it was like a smaller version of the machines in the room. He continued to pull at it while his eyes glanced at the darkened stairwell where the ghost had gone. He could only see a few steps, going down, but it was enough to awake his curiosity. An investigation would have to wait. For now, he was absorbed in watching Ben.

The boy's metamorphosis was fascinating, going from a skinny human body into something dangerous. Regin had never been impressed with the human form. It was so frail, so soft. That's probably why they had a talent for developing weapons. Why they were obsessed with the creation of killing devices. They were making up for evolution failing them. Regin would never wish to be so weak. His tails waved behind him as he watched the boy's body dismantle itself. Ben's arms lengthened and the blades came from his hands, growing out long and dark till they touched the floor.

His sister, the blind girl, tried going to him, but Regin darted toward her and whipped one tail out. He didn't bother trying to hold her back. He merely tripped her and dispassionately watched Katy tumble. 'Such a feeble thing,' he thought as he considered how much more dangerous the females of his race were with their massive talons. He looked at his own claws. 'These were sharp as well, but just a bit small for killing.'

Regin's adaptions weren't how he murdered the monk anyway. He'd done that with nothing more than physical strength and the fool's belief in his own superiority. The knife had helped as well. Regin stared at the blades on Ben and wondered if they were made from the thing in the tank or if the thing in the tank had created them using parts of the boy. Ben's legs snapped back painfully with the very clear sound of breaking bones. He screamed again and his sister tried once more to help her brother.

Regin made sure she couldn't. Landing on her back, he pulled her arms out from under her with his tails and then twisted them around her wrists. "There's nothing you can do to stop it now," he said. "You'll only get yourself hurt if you go over there."

Katy still fought, trying to get up, so Regin cruelly smashed her head to the ground, leaving her dazed. If only this blind girl had left things well enough alone. Pretending to be some sort of detective, so worried about the truth. Her obsession was the silliest thing he'd ever seen. Truth meant nothing. It was momentary, quick to change, and constantly twisted by those in power. 'Soon,' Regin thought, 'that would be me.'

Of course, he might not have ever located this room if she hadn't been so insistent on finding the murderer. This girl had led the way, guided by a ghost. 'And she was kind enough to provide a test subject,' he thought while staring at Ben, whose skin shimmered and darkened while his shoulders broadened out.

Ben's face went dark, then with a sickening sound, like a cantaloup being dropped, his face split in half, revealing a different face underneath, a horrible creation with cold dark eyes, sharpened teeth, and mandibles made from Ben's jaw bones. A tongue came lolling from his mouth, lashing from side to side.

"Amazing," Regin said. He was still on Katy's back, keeping her from getting to her feet. "It's really too bad you can't see this. Your brother has just gone through an astounding alteration."

The screaming and the organic sound of Ben's body being changed had stopped. There was nothing left to alter. He stood there in a dark, monstrous form, a smaller version of the hunter from Earth. His torn uniform hung from his broad shoulders and long arms. His chest was twice as wide and his neckless head was broad with a thick ridge above the deep shadows of his eye sockets. Only a slight glistening from the room's light showed that he had anything to see with under that ridge.

"What did you do to him?" Katy demanded. The pain from hitting her head must've faded a bit, but her voice still sounded confused. Regin wasn't surprised. If she was hearing the same muddled sounds and errant ideas from the machines that were invading his skull, then focus would be very hard. The feelings assaulted him, coming from everywhere and making no sense, not in words anyway. The only clear thought was that something dangerous had been released.

"I believe I've weaponized him," Regin still sounded like a teacher, but one who'd finally found an interesting subject.

"I don't understand," Katy said as Regin got off her. His furry limbs tickled her face, causing her to pull back.

He sneered at her panic, then offered gently, "Go see." Releasing her wrists, he darted up on one of the benches.

Slowly, she put her hands out but stayed on all fours, obviously afraid to get to her feet. Regin almost felt pity for her, knowing she was worried that her strange professor would attack her again. He glanced at her brother and wondered if maybe instead she was too frightened to learn what became of him. Staying there on the cold floor perhaps she was pretending none of this happened.

"Ben, are you alright?" Katy finally asked.

There was no answer at first so Katy called again, "Ben?"

Regin shook his head. "Perhaps he can't hear you over this racket. I hear them too by the way, the voices, if you could even call them that," Regin said, still trying to manipulate the device on the canister. It was like touching low-voltage electricity, where the intensity got stronger, the longer he held it. "They're almost overwhelming when I touch this thing." Finally, something clicked in Regin's thoughts, some programming in the device reached out to him. "This is interesting." He said before going silent for a moment, while instructions settled in. Then he ordered Ben, "Answer her."

Ben's voice reached Katy's ears, but it sounded strange as if it were coming from a broken speaker. "I'm still here," he said.

She opened her mouth but couldn't find words. Her brother's voice sounded so much like the thing in the desert. Regin watched as tears started to fill Katy's eyes. He was unmoved. "Amazing! Please, get up and go see with your hands," he ordered her.

When she didn't move, he came down off the bench and leaned over her, putting his face right next to hers. "I asked you to examine your brother."

"I don't want to." Katy pushed back, scurrying away from him.

"But I insist," Regin was enjoying himself as his tails waved contentedly. He was slowly getting better at ignoring the noise in his head. "Ben, come over here and help your sister to her feet."

Ben's footsteps were absolutely silent. Katy had no idea he was next to her until his hands touched her shoulders. She jumped back and tried to escape, but Ben's hands closed on her like a vice, icy cold and solid as stone. He pulled her to her feet so quickly that for a moment her toes weren't touching the ground. She dangled in his arms, then he let her settle to the floor.

"This is absolutely fascinating. Exciting, just so exciting!" Regin's voice was full of joy.

"You've turned him into—"

"A hunter, yes. Just like the one you met on Earth," Regin broke in. "I must tell you; your blindness is really inconvenient. It'd be nice to have a witness who could compare this one to the other."

"Why would you do this to him?" Katy's voice was shaking. She brought her hand up but couldn't get herself to touch her brother.

"What a silly question. As I said, he's a weapon now. He's my weapon. And there's more here in this room, more technology for me to study and to use."

"Against who?" Katy turned her head trying to find Regin's voice. He'd gone back over to the wall where the tanks hung. He examined them seeing that a few had been emptied and that a few were missing their control units.

"The human empire of course," he said over his shoulder. "Not just the current leadership, but against your entire power structure. I've seen enough mistreatment of my species and of every other one. Every race is servile to your people. Even the Grannusians, a species far more advanced than yours. Because of your war-like nature, their world is cut to pieces and they are poisoned. It's enough. I lived on Uppsala for most of my life. I saw the forests devastated and the way you treat your own people, always climbing and crawling over each other. Then of course there are the Lightening Bugs. You met the last of their species, the very last, and you ask me why?"

"I tried to save Brash. I helped him. I'd fix this place if I could, but I don't know how," Katy pleaded.

"Don't worry, I have a few ideas." Regin sighed. "To be honest, I am sorry you two are the first. I wonder—" Regin turned to the thing that Ben had become.

"Ben, you said you're in there, but are you aware of what's going on? Speak freely."

"I'm here, yes. I'm scared, and it hurts, and there's so much going on in my head," Ben spoke quickly, forcing the words out, though his voice radiated with an almost electric sound.

Regin clapped his hands. "Excellent, we're all hearing voices then. Now let's move on. Katy, I'll give you a choice. You want to help? Well, you may join your brother if you'd like. We'll all go to war together. It's that or the other option."

"What other option?" Katy asked.

"I'm not ready to go public with this yet. It takes planning to overthrow an entire species. So, I'm afraid it's either become a monster or I have the monster. . ." Regin made a slashing motion across his throat. When he realized Katy couldn't see it, he shook his head and added. "Remove you from the equation."

"I won't tell anyone," Katy begged.

"Don't you hurt my sister," Ben demanded in his monstrous voice, but he couldn't move. He stood stiff as a statue, still holding Katy.

"That's enough out of you. Quiet now," Regin ordered, then he turned back to Katy. "My dear, I have only a few I trust and I'm afraid you're not one of them.

410

Humans can't possibly be trusted. But I'm going to be kind to you. I won't turn you into something like your brother if you don't want it. You'll simply disappear."

"No, no way," Katy yelled as she kicked her legs forward and pushed off her brother's chest, throwing herself back in a desperate attempt to escape. She fell to the floor, skidding across it, then hurried to her feet.

Regin watched her run to the wall, reach out and use it as a guide. Almost impressed, he let out a chuckle. "Where do you think you're going? Ben, would you stop your sister please?"

Katy reached the exit as Ben dropped down in front of her. In a single leap, he'd managed to close the distance and block her path. "Hold her there." Regin waved his hand, distracted by the information coming into him through the device.

"Help! Somebody help me!" Katy called down the hall back towards the lighthouse. Ben grabbed her again, folding her in his arms but managing to keep the sharp edge of the blades away from her body. Katy tried fighting and twisting from the cold surface of her brother's changed body, but it was pointless. His hold was too strong.

Regin watched from across the room. He'd had enough of the girl's distraction. There was so much more for him to learn, so many strange devices mounted in this room. He touched the wall letting his hand wander over the corners and edges of the machines. Time was what he needed, and he was wasting it on interacting with this girl.

Sighing, he stared back at Katy, knowing he only had one choice. The girl had to die. 'Am I making a habit of this?' he asked himself. No, he'd been hot when he killed the monk, angry at the unfairness that his people had been treated with his entire life. Outraged at the man's arrogance. It hadn't been premeditated. It'd been survival. This was different. In a way, it would be easier. All he had to do was tell Ben and the task would be done. Regin shook his head, warning himself that before he was finished, he'd have to get very comfortable with killing people.

"Ben, bring your sister over here." The creature that Ben had become started toward him. Regin watched his slow, lumbering steps and was tempted to tell him to hurry, but something distracted him. The noises in his head were getting louder, so much so that he had to take his hand away from the device. He immediately felt better. His eyes went to Ben, making certain his monster still followed his commands.

Regin shook his fingers in the air, opening and closing his fist, trying to clear the pins and needles from it. As his hand passed in front of his face, he noticed that the space around him was darkening. The lights of the machines were glowing as brightly, but something was in the air between the devices and his eyes, a black fog started to form into something solid.

"Oh damn," Regin said backing away from the wall. He'd seen this before. He'd watched Katy be taken from the lighthouse.

The ghost's fog was a little different this time. It remained empty till it passed in front of the stairs. Then the dark form emerged and lurched from the top step into the cloud. In the length of a heartbeat, the cloud and whatever joined it became one. Regin put his hand to the control device and just as quickly pulled it away. The noise was overwhelming. "Ben, do you know what is happening?"

"It's one of the ghosts," Ben said.

Regin threw his head towards him. "I know that. What does it want?"

"How should I know?" Ben snapped back. Despite the electronic squelch in his voice, he still sounded like a teenager. Regin leaped onto one of the slab platforms, darting away from the ghost. The fog around it never quite dissipated, but it reached the point where the creature was as solid as the one that had dragged Katy through the wall.

Ben was still walking towards Regin with Katy held tight in his arms, but his voice sounded disconnected from his actions. "I'm just guessing, and this is only a guess, that when this thing pulled Katy into this room, it was not with the intention of anyone, including you, messing with her."

"Why her?" Regin demanded.

"I've been asking myself that same question my entire life. She's popular, smart, and talented. Why did she win the lottery, while me. . .well, you've met me?" Ben pointed out.

Regin ignored the commentary, putting his hands up. "Just stay there. Stay back," he ordered, noticing how the creature's eyes were following Ben. He jumped putting himself further from the siblings, going from one slab to the next with the canister and the control unit dangling in his hand. Then he watched the ghost start toward Katy and Ben. It seemed to float across the floor.

Regin was the calmest of his people. He'd always prided himself on that fact, but he couldn't deny that his breathing had picked up and that his hands were shaking. He still tried to observe this entity as a scientist. He saw the similarities to Ben and the subtle differences.

"Release your sister. Let her go," Regin ordered.

Ben did as he was told, letting Katy fall to the floor. She fell away from him, landing just in front of the approaching ghost. She got herself up, turning towards Regin's voice. The ghost was still approaching her. It stopped just in front of Katy, blocking Regin's view. He watched the blind girl awash in the light from the machines.

"What's it doing?" Regin called.

"Nothing," Ben answered. "It's just staring at Katy."

"It's talking to me," Katy's voice came out from behind the creature's shoulder. "It's not happy you did this to my brother."

Regin touched the control unit again. This time he forced himself to hold his hand there, though the pain and noise in his head was excruciating. "I don't hear it," he forced the words out.

"Well, I do. It's in my head," Katy said.

The ghost was slowly turning, its form seeming to come further apart. The dark eyes were staring at Regin as the fog moved across the floor, covering the first bench. In the flickering, busy lighting it was hard to track its movements, but it seemed to be coming towards him. Finally, he had to break his hand away from the device. He held the canister at arm's length, noticing the way his limbs were shaking. "You can't possibly understand what it's saying."

"It wants you to put everything back," Katy said. "It wants you to fix my brother."

Regin looked at the canister. "I have no idea how to do that. It's not that simple." The ghost had cleared the first bench. There were only two more between Regin and it.

"If you can't fix him, then I think you ought to drop that machine and run," Katy said.

An ancient panic overtook the professor, a primitive fear of destruction. None of this would have a point if he disappeared, dragged off by this monstrous thing. Regin touched the device again. "Ben, protect me! Get over here and stop this thing."

Ben pushed past Katy pouncing at the ghost but he passed right through it, crashing into a wall. Regin looked up in time to see the shadow fall on him. Everything turned dark for the professor as he felt the canister and the device slip from his hand. The last thing he heard was the sound of it hitting the ground with a hollow ring.

Chapter 39

In his cell, Chris woke to the sound of a tray being pushed through an opening in the bars. Turns out monks weren't big on sleeping in, not for themselves or their prisoners. "Nothing like friendly service," Chris said to the man's back and to the Fire-Golem on the other side of the bars. He sat up and stared at the imposing figure, wondering if it could hear him. At first, when Naiathne was released, Chris thought that if he was going to be miserable, he'd rather be miserable alone, but as the hours went on with only the Golem for company, he started to miss her.

Naiathne and he had talked more than he expected. Chris had told her all about his mom and dad and his life growing up as a military brat. They hadn't been moved around as much as some families. They'd send his dad away instead, deploying him for months at a time.

Naiathne talked about her own father a bit, but he could tell it was a painful memory. She had an adoptive family down in the colony, Naiads who were born there and she preferred talking about them. They'd taken her in and raised her as their own. A foundling was rare, a genetic anomaly that proved the people on the surface and those below were not as far apart as some would like to think. It was tradition to send foundlings into the sea, where their chances of survival weren't high. Luckily, the Grannusians had eyes everywhere, and they kept a lookout for castaways.

The colony had existed for hundreds of years. It was older than some settlements on the surface, representing an extreme difference in the way people chose to survive in a new environment, some willing to adapt while others stuck to old ways. Chris had asked Naiathne more and more about human history on Grannus, but Naiathne's knowledge was vague at best. 'People hadn't always been there,' she'd said. They'd come from somewhere else but she couldn't say where. She'd heard Uppsala and she'd heard Tairnish, but the history was unclear.

Chris sat in his cell and wondered if it could be intentional or if the path of centuries had been enough to rob these people of their past. "What do you think?" Chris sat back crossing his arms, asking the Fire-Golem. It stood in the shadows on the other side of the bars, unmoving. "Where did all these people come from? And how do they not know? I mean maybe Naiathne isn't the best person to ask. She grew up in a hidden city. It might make her a little out of touch." He pointed out.

He thought of Carthage and Rome, and the fall of so many other civilizations. Some empires had collapsed and left pieces behind while others were lost to time like the South American kingdoms.

With a little difficulty, and using the crutches they'd allowed him to keep, he got to his feet and went closer to the bars. The crutches were made from a bony material that they grew in long stalks on Grannus. He said to the Golem, "I read once that it was a farmer digging a well that found the tomb of the first emperor of China." Chris raised his eyebrow staring at the Fire-Golem's unmoving face. "Not impressed? Well, this was the guy responsible for the great wall. He brought all these warring kingdoms together and made an empire that lasted from the second century all the way to the 1900s, like a really important guy. Yet his grave was lost. We're not talking about some simple headstone either. He had an army of thousands of terracotta warriors with him to command in the afterlife in this massive underground complex with horses and chariots, and weapons. It took most of the artists in his country to build them. It was this massive site and the location was just forgotten. Crazy, right?" Chris waited for a response he knew wasn't going to come from the dark stone form.

Tilting his head, Chris stared at the Golem. The creature didn't even twitch so he started to pace and added, "You would've liked the terracotta guys. They're just about as talkative as you are."

The Fire-Golem still didn't answer. "Okay, you're not impressed. Still, my point is that knowledge can always be lost, right? That makes sense. But that was before computers and data files."

Chris thought about his cell phone back on Earth. He'd saved a bunch of books on it, on his to-be-read pile. One day his phone crapped out for no reason, and he never got those files back. All those free downloads gone.

"Maybe technology isn't always an advantage," he nodded and scratched his chin. "You can carve something in a stone and have it last thousands of years, but a machine suffers a power surge or too much radiation, and everything is gone. Hell, half my dad's CDs from college didn't play anymore." Chris shrugged, looking back at the Golem again. "A CD was this little round disk that they used lasers to copy digital files onto, in case you didn't know." Chris wandered back to the wall, saying over his shoulder, "Good talk big guy," as he carefully settled onto the floor with his crutches on either side of him.

He pulled one of his knees in tight to his chest, the one with a short cast, and thought, 'I could try counting. I wonder how high I could get.' That's when he noticed a soft glow coming from the other side of the room. The single eye of the Golem opened in the center of its face and heated lines ran across the cracks of its rocky form. "Look who's awake," Chris said.

The Golem turned suddenly and started towards the exit, its heavy steps echoing in the chamber. "Where are you going? Time for a bathroom break?" Chris looked over at the hole in the floor. "I'd say you could use mine but you'd have to open this cage first."

The Golem stopped midstride and then turned its red eye towards him. A sound came from it. It wasn't very clear, made from air moving across rock, forced by the heat of the plasma beneath, but Chris thought he heard it repeat the word, "Cage."

Chris felt a chill run down his spine. He had no idea Fire-Golems could talk. He'd never heard one, nor had anyone mentioned them being able to. Getting to his feet and back onto his crutches, Chris watched the Golem turn back towards his cell. He saw it reach out for the bars, touching the lock pad. Its hand started to glow red hot and the lock fell away, hitting the floor in smoldering pieces.

Chris stared at it, staying back, watching cautiously. "Thanks," he said, looking up at the creature's red eye. It nodded, then turned and started back towards the exit. Two monks were just past the opening in the next chamber. They got up at the sound and came to the inner chamber, trying to look in, but the Fire-Golem had already turned and was leaving. He was larger than they were, a head taller and twice as wide, filling the opening. He continued his march and didn't bother pushing the monks out of his way, simply stepping through them, forcing them to dive to avoid being trampled.

Chris pushed the door to his cell open and slipped out. He came to the next chamber in time to see the monks at the far exit. They were looking out, watching the Golem march down the hall. One turned to the other and said, "We've got to tell sister Nemain."

"Go," the other one said with a nod.

The first one started out into the corridor, his red robe flapping behind him, while the second turned back to find Chris standing in the doorway. Their eyes met and Chris held his hands in the air. "Look, I didn't ask it to break me out. He just kind of did it. There's no reason for this to get all crazy."

The monk pointed towards the back room. "You need to get in your cell."

"Or, we could go for a walk and see what's happening. I'll still be your prisoner." Chris motioned to his damaged legs. "It's not like I'm going to run and you'd be able to keep a better eye on me and whatever the Golem is doing."

There was a sound in the distance of something crashing. "I promise to be good and besides it's a space station. Where am I going to go?" Chris asked.

The monk stepped back out into the hall, staring in the direction of the sound. He nodded. "Fine, but when this is done, you go right back in there."

"Sure," Chris said following the man into the passage. He could tell by the lighting that it was early in the morning cycle. There weren't many people in the hallway yet, only a few students wandered toward the dining hall. He was surprised to see two of them and they were equally surprised to see him. Cormack and Naiathne came running over to Chris. "Did they let you out?" Cormack asked.

"No, we didn't," the monk answered, waving for Chris to keep up. He was still moving towards the sound of chaos coming from the direction of the dining hall.

"We'll work on that later," Chris shrugged as he leaned on his crutches. "Why are you guys up so early and where are the others?" He and Naiathne looked at each other for an awkward moment as they both remembered the intimacy of days spent in a cell together.

Her grey skin turned a little red as she looked away and hurried ahead. She called back over her shoulder, "We're up because of the others. Katy and Ben went out last night and never came back. We were coming to the cells to see if they'd been captured." Cormack and Chris's eyes met after they both looked at the monk. The man had obviously heard Naiathne.

Chris shook his head. "No, they aren't in there. It was just me and a Fire-Golem up until five minutes ago. The thing woke up, broke my cell door open, then took off." There was another slamming sound. "That's what we're going to look into. It went in that direction."

The monk came to the largest entrance to the dining hall and went around the corner ahead of them. Chris, Naiathne, and Cormack followed him just in time to see a table tossed on its side, thrown out of the neat rows that lined the large area. The Fire-Golem was still in its stony form, chasing something, closing in on the center of the room. Chris caught a quick glimpse of the creature it wanted.

It was ducking down, going beneath another row of tables. The tail of a Long-Wolf appeared and vanished, moving too fast to be identified. Then it called from under one of the tables, "Help, they're going to murder me!" As it bounced up again, still scurrying and looking for safety.

Chris's eyes went around the room, seeing that other Fire-Golems had closed in on the hall, coming in from the other entrances, blocking the Long-Wolf's escape. Three more came forward moving towards the running creature.

"That's Fajalar," Cormack said as he started ahead with a hesitating step. He bit his lip watching, wanting to help but none of them knew exactly what to do.

"Why are they chasing him?" Chris asked.

Cormack held his hands in the air, opting to move in slowly, keeping his distance as more tables were tossed aside. Three Golems closed in. They were wrecking the hall as they went, leaving the tables and benches in disarray.

The monk had taken the same tactic as Cormack, staying close to the prince, bunching them up in a tighter group as they all watched the dark forms close in on the Long-Wolf. The Golems didn't move fast, but their slow steps felt inescapable.

The dining hall was almost empty, with only the staff of kitchen workers and a few Drakes sitting at a far table. Fafnir was with them. He'd gotten to his feet at the sound of the ruckus. "What is the meaning of this?" he demanded, looking back at the lone monk.

"They're doing it on their own," the monk called from the other side of the room.

Fafnir watched for a moment. He let out a long breath and stepped forward, getting closer than anyone else to where Fajalar was hiding. The Long-Wolf saw an opportunity and took it. He darted from under the table and leapt toward Fafnir's massive arm, which he climbed up, going the three meters to Fafnir's shoulder. "Get off me! What do you think you're doing!?" Fafnir demanded as Fajalar's clawed fingers wrapped around his face and his tail wrapped around his shoulder.

Fajalar's eyes were darting about, looking for escape and seeing all the exits blocked as the Fire-Golems closed in. "You have to help! They've come to punish me!"

Fafnir reached up, trying to pull the creature from him. "What are you on about? Punish you for what?" The Fire-Golem that freed Chris was just below him, still moving forward.

Fajalar reconsidered his words. "Nothing, I did nothing wrong!" He shrieked feeling the stony hands of the Golem close on his tail. He tried to pull away, but its hold was too tight. The Long-Wolf screamed as the appendage was crushed in its grip.

The Fire-Golem yanked at the tail trying to wrench him from Fafnir, but the giant Drake took the Golem's arm and dragged it away, then lifted the creature's rocky form from the ground. As large as the Golem was, he was insignificant next to the Drake. He pulled the dangling Golem towards his scarred face. "I was a slave when I first met your kind. They used you for security against us poor dumb Drakes. Do not test me." The Golem seemed to understand. It released the tail and Fafnir lowered the Fire-Golem to the ground.

The rock creature stood still, its one red eye staring up at Fafnir. The other two Golems joined the first one. They encircled Fafnir but as the Drake filled his lungs glaring at them, standing still with only his eyes moving, there was a clear feeling that he was the most dangerous being present. Everyone waited to see what the old Drake would do.

Fajalar began to say, "Thank you—" when the Drake interrupted him by taking his tail. He grabbed it high, near the Long-Wolf's hips, and tore Fajalar away from his shoulders. The Long-Wolf's claws raked at his face trying to hold on, scrambling in a panic, but Fafnir didn't seem to notice.

He slammed Fajalar to the ground. "Your people held the leash for these creatures when they were our jailors. I ought to crush you where you lay, but first you will speak. You will tell me why they are here for you or I will end you." Fafnir put his foot on the Long-Wolf.

"Stop this! You can't, I forbid it," the monk called to Fafnir, who only sneered in his direction.

"I don't think he cares," Naiathne said to the monk.

Another sound that wasn't quite a voice gave Fafnir pause though. The word, "Hold," echoed from a throat that had only begun speaking a few minutes before. Fafnir turned and his eyes went wide, realizing the sound had come from the Golem. Its hand turned red, then narrowed, pointing as it leaned down towards Fajalar.

"Don't let it hurt me," the Long-Wolf begged. He tried to scurry away again but Fafnir held him still with his foot resting on his tail.

"I want answers," Fafnir said to the Golem. He was ready to grab the rocky form again, as he looked at its glowing hand, watching it approach the struggling Long-Wolf. The Fire-Golem held up both its hands in a wide gesture, patting at the air. The one hand that glowed red left a trail of light behind it, but the message was clear. 'Just wait.' The creature dropped to its knee, leaning over Fajalar. It pointed a single finger towards the Long-Wolf's neck. There was smoke and a searing sound. Fajalar screamed as the smell of burning flesh filled the air.

The Golem's hand came away with a stone in it. Then it held it out to Fafnir.

"What is that?" Fafnir demanded, staring down at the Long-Wolf, who was holding his neck, whimpering.

The Golem motioned to Fajalar, a motion that was clear as well. 'Ask him?'

Fajalar, despite his squirming, saw it and answered, "I don't know anything."

The giant Drake brought his foot down a little more.

"No, no! Please," Fajalar bellowed. "I'll tell you."

Fafnir brought his foot back and after a few panting breaths Fajalar said, "It's how we controlled them. The crystals are from the mother. They are part of the mother. It lets us into their heads."

"The mother?" Fafnir asked, bringing his foot back.

Fajalar twisted into a ball, tightening up into something small and pitiful. "It's alive! They're alive! We didn't make them. We found them on our world. It was below the surface growing. It would've killed us all, but we locked it away, thousands of years ago. My ancestors used a technology they found on the dead world."

"The dead world?" Chris asked Cormack.

424

Cormack shook his head in amazement and with a worrying tone, said, "Einherjar, the moon between Tairnish and Grannus. It's a bad spot, a really bad spot."

Chris tried to think back to his reading. He'd done everything he could to catch up on this place during his transit to Grannus and his return here, but there was so much information and everything about the fifth moon had been so vague that its presence had nearly slipped his mind. The little he'd come across jumped back into his head. It was roughly the size of the other moons but uninhabited, declared too dangerous for anyone to land on.

Fafnir leaned down closer to Fajalar, looking at the wound in his neck where the crystal had been. "They were slaves?" he asked glancing back at the Golems.

"Their mother would've consumed our world. We didn't have a choice." Fafnir's face was close to Fajalar's, so close that the Long-Wolf could feel the air from the Drake's flared nostrils. He thought better of lying. "Yes, they were slaves. The crystals were part of their chrysalis chambers. It connected them to the mother entity. We've kept it secret, even from the emperor, even from our own people. Only a select few know, only our leaders know what lies beneath the surface of Tairnish, what the truth of these creatures is. We didn't make them, we kept them."

Fafnir stood back and looked at the Fire-Golems. "I would say your world is in for a shock. All the worlds are because I believe something has changed drastically there." Fafnir looked over at the dining hall entrance. A number of monks had arrived with sister Nemain at the front. He stared at them but he was still speaking to Fajalar. "You'll find periods like this, periods of adjustment can be difficult for those who've just lost power."

Fajalar was getting to his feet, holding his neck, though the wound was burnt and not bleeding. "I need to contact Tairnish," he said.

Chris, Cormack and Naiathne stared at each other, none of them really sure what to do. Chris tilted his head and started over towards the Golem that was standing by Fafnir. He swung on his crutches coming up to the creature. "Hey there, I think I'm going to have to go back in my cell, but I just wanted to say thanks, you know for breaking me out."

The creature looked back at him with that one glowing red eye and nodded.

Chapter 40

"Wake up, kid." Alex felt something press against his neck. There was a sharp sting. He tried to open his eyes, but rousing himself wasn't easy.

He was incredibly sore, through and through, there wasn't a part of his body that didn't hurt, not even his eyes. He reached up and tried touching his face. The visor from Tairnish was still on. He pulled it off and let it go. He didn't notice it floating in front of him as he slowly forced his eyes open and focused on the darkened cockpit. He realized for the first time that he was no longer pressed against the wall, rather he was floating above it. He had no idea how long he'd been squeezed behind the seats, or how long he'd been unconscious, but he was looking out at Edith.

Her black faceless helmet was off and her nose was crinkled up in a little smirk behind the dome of a less militant-looking face mask. She looked happy and for a moment Alex realized that despite the scars there was a beauty behind her strength. She didn't have the genetic perfection of Maeven, the incredible symmetry of refined allure, but the sparkle behind her soft brown eyes, the thrill there made her incredibly attractive. "Where are we?" Alex croaked. He felt an unpleasant tingling rushing through his body.

"We've landed on The Revenant, the emperor's flagship," Edith said, reaching her hand out.

Everything that happened down below jumped back into Alex's head. The death, the blood, the gore, and Edith's voice behind that dark mask, thrilled to be fulfilling her purpose. He shook his head as she said, "That was a stimulant I just gave you, mixed with some pretty powerful pain relievers. You might feel a bit jittery, but I'm going to need you to keep it together for a bit longer. There's someone who wants to meet you."

"Who's that?" Alex asked as he took her hand and reached out for the edge of a seat, pulling himself up. It didn't take much effort to get up in zero-g.

"No big deal, just the emperor. Who is also the man whose daughter you've had an unsanctioned relationship with."

"'Unsanctioned,' is ah— is that going to be a problem?" Alex stammered.

Edith looked back from the cockpit door and shrugged. "You're not the first person Maeven has given her attentions to, but you're probably the first who's risked his own life attacking a heavily fortified military installation to save her. So, I wouldn't worry too much."

Alex couldn't help wondering who the others were. Edith saw his face drop into thought. "Don't worry, none of them were anything compared to you. I've kept my eye on Maeven from a distance and I've never seen her drop her guard for anyone before." She looked over her shoulder out into the hangar bay before she added in a lowered voice. "Just don't forget you're sitting in a unique and potentially dangerous position."

"What do you mean?" Alex asked as he pulled himself past the pilot's seat, closer to her so he could hear her better. Out the cockpit windows, he could see a ceiling with rows of lights shining down on them.

Edith pulled him to her, looking at his torn and tattered uniform. "The royalty of Uppsala doesn't marry for love. It's an exchange, a merging of families and power. Emperor Tamerlane has done a lot to upset the order of things, but he still needs the support of the other noble families. Eventually, Maeven is going to have a husband and it's not going to be you, but that doesn't mean you can't be in her life. It's not unheard of to have someone else."

"You're saying my move here is life as a sidepiece?" Alex asked.

Edith raised her eyebrow and looked down at her sidearm. "Not the same thing," Alex said. "It means—"

"You know I think I get it." Edith waved him off. "And the term the nobility use is 'consort.' It's pretty common. People, noble or not, are still people and when marriages are arranged, well there's not a lot of room for passion or love, if that's your thing." Edith rolled her eyes and started for the exit again.

She turned back when she heard Alex say, "So that's one choice." Alex was thinking about his brother, Katy, Ben, and, of course, Amita. 'Was she really gone?' he asked himself. He'd left with Maeven in the first place because he thought it was his best chance of keeping his people alive. Here Edith is talking about love, but Alex wasn't sure that was how he felt.

Yes, Maeven was exciting, and he had feelings for her, but his decisions hadn't only been because he was some wide-eyed kid. He'd picked the strongest side, thinking he was solving their first problem of staying alive. The plan was to start working on the other problems after. Learning what happened to the Earth, his mom, and everything else. Everything Amita had wanted. He just needed her to be patient. Going to the planet, trying to rescue Maeven, obviously, hadn't been part of the strategy, but by then he had little choice.

He thought about what he'd done down there, but it was like touching a live wire and he had to force his thoughts away. 'If Amita had just been patient.' He shook his head again, having trouble believing she was gone, that they'd left her buried beneath all that rock.

Edith looked back at him, seeing how conflicted he was. "Choice? You think you have a choice? That's funny." She placed her hands on his shoulders. "Look, nothing has happened yet. I'm just letting you know what might. You have to keep your eyes open and prepare for every eventuality, right?"

429

Alex nodded, and Edith continued, "For all we know, when we get to the command deck, the emperor might have me put a bullet in your skull. So, try to put your best foot forward."

Alex's mouth fell open. He watched Edith move ahead of him, climbing out of the small cockpit door. He couldn't help but glance down at her sidearm, wondering if she was serious. If after everything they'd been through, she'd be willing to kill him at a single word from her emperor. He didn't have to think about it long. He knew what she was capable of.

In the Zero-g they had to be careful climbing down, using a short ladder on the side of the shuttle to keep themselves anchored to something, then the side of the ship to move along to the exit. The landing bay was a wide-open area. The problem with such spaces is that if you pushed off in the wrong direction, it could be a while before you reached another purchase to return from. Edith still had most of her armor on and as she approached the floor, she activated magnets in her boots. They pulled her straight down next to the shuttle where it lay flat on its belly with its landing gear barely visible.

The hatch for the passenger compartment was open. Alex was tempted to peek in, vaguely remembering that there had been passengers in there, aristocrats and their families from Tairnish. Edith and Maeven had talked about them, but he couldn't remember what they decided to do with them. Alex glanced at Edith and considered asking but he thought better of it. He didn't really want to know.

"Where's Maeven now?" he asked instead.

"She's getting cleaned up. She wanted to be presentable for her father. I promised I'd keep an eye on you. It was sweet how concerned she was. Like I said I've never seen her that way with anyone before."

Edith looked him up and down again. "I'm taking a different tactic with you though. I'm hoping the emperor will be impressed seeing how jacked up you are. Battle worn and all that." She gave him another look, then sighed. "We can only hope, right?"

She took his shoulder and helped him along till they reached a locker. She opened it and pulled out a suit with a helmet attached to it. "We're still in a combat zone. There's a few Tairnish vessels out there taking potshots at us. You'll want to wear this if we suddenly lose pressure," she said, handing him the suit.

It was simple, but it was still a process getting into it, as Alex moved stiffly, barely able to bend his legs. Edith had to help him pull it up. Just before closing the helmet's face mask, she explained, "A breach in the hull can happen fast. There won't be time to close it then. She touched his arm, turning on his comms. "We're in a closed channel for now, but always assume you're being listened to, okay?"

Alex gave her a thumbs up and Edith turned, heading for the exit. They made their way past soldiers standing rigidly by the entrance, who nodded to Edith as the doors opened letting them into an empty and narrow curving hallway. She was telling Alex all the things he'd need to know, how to speak, how to address the emperor, what not to do. "You're still officially a civilian so you're going to want to bow. If you were a soldier even a mercenary like me, then you'd have to salute, like this." She showed him the hand gesture, a closed fist pounded on her chest. "But bowing in zero-g can be tricky, so you've got to bring your hands up to your head and sort of tuck yourself in, but don't go too far in or you'll end up in a barrel role."

There were handrails along the walls that Alex opted to use, instead of using his own magnetic boots. He let his stiff legs dangle, crawling like a spider while Edith walked as normal as could be next to him, with only a slight hesitation between steps. He could feel the walls of the ship shake and vibrate as the rail guns on the outer hull blasted, again and again, raining down on the planet's surface but they weren't the deadliest weapon firing from The Revenant. The ship had a devastating device for orbital bombardment called a mass accelerator. The entire vessel had been built around it. Its purpose was to collect rubble in space such as small asteroids and the debris of war. Then it used magnetic waves to accelerate it towards the surface below. Similar devices were constructed on Uppsala, Tairnish, and Oighear to send payloads into space but the Tamerlanes were the first to weaponize it, accelerating rubble to hypersonic speeds and spraying population centers with deadly effect.

Edith led Alex to a descender, moving along one of the spokes of the Revenant heading for the command spire. "Are you ready for this?" she asked as the small box stopped moving."

"I suppose we'll find out." Alex glanced at her sidearm again, wondering if there was even a chance he'd be able to wrestle it away from her. 'No, if this goes poorly, then this would be it.' He put his shoulders back as the doors opened.

"I'm switching you to open comms. Everyone will be able to hear everything you have to say. So, choose your words carefully."

Alex nodded his head. "Chatty as always. That's good," Edith noted, patting Alex on the shoulder.

The descender opened on a small enclave near the command deck where two heavily armored guards stood. The suits they wore were more robust than Edith's, more like a Tairnishman's, only without the molded face mask. Their helmets were blank like the combat one Edith wore, only silver instead, but just as impenetrable. They stood in front of a curved wall of armored plating that looked like the outer jacket of a giant bullet. They pointed their weapons at the two as they ordered, "Hold there."

"We were told to see the emperor," Edith explained.

One of the guards held up his hand. "They've got a situation in there. Give it a moment." Alex noticed that the short rifles never turned away. Their dark barrels stayed on them as time passed. Finally, one of the guards lowered his weapon and nodded, receiving a signal from the interior. A seam on the wall hissed and started to widen.

Without speaking a word, the guards stepped aside as the meter-thick entrance, like a safe door, opened. Edith and Alex passed into the dimly lit command deck. Edith walked with an almost normal stride, still hesitating a little before each step as the magnetic boots held and released. Alex tried using his but realized that his legs were too weak to overcome their pull to the floor. He had to use Edith's arm to move forward.

Inside, the darkness was punctuated with glowing screens. Any light from behind went away as the door was sealed again. As his eyes adjusted, Alex was disappointed to see an austere room, round and packed with chairs and workstations lining the curved walls. It could've been a security booth for a casino if the officers hadn't been strapped down with harnesses and the camera feeds weren't constantly going white with detonations. None of the seated people turned. The staff wore lightly armored space suits with their face plates backlit, showing faces that were focused on their work, distracted by their individual assignments. Some wore elaborate headgear that hid their faces with cables running up through large openings that connected to their heads. Alex glanced over at Edith, noticing the scars where her implants had been removed, knowing that beneath the heavy headgear on these people, there were similar devices.

Maps and models shone on three larger screens in the center of the room tracked every moving object above Tairnish. A small group was clustered near them including the only two men who turned at their arrival. Each wore a symbol of rank embossed on their shoulders, gold, and red, the colors of empire. The woman Ada, the emperor's personal guard, was there as well. Her eyes stayed on Alex for only a moment, then they went to Edith. She nodded to the mercenary and Edith did the same.

A voice boomed in Alex's ear. "Alex Johnson? It's nice to finally meet you." It was intense but not angry. There was an excitement in the inflection, perhaps a slight mania. It reminded him of his mom when she'd made some discovery that she couldn't tell them about.

"Time to bow," Edith whispered.

Alex missed what Edith meant, caught off guard by how quickly the person approached him. The backlight in his faceplate revealed a handsome middle-aged man with South Asian features. Alex had no idea what an emperor was supposed to look like but even behind a thick beard, he could see the family resemblance to Maeven with the same hypnotic glimmer in his green eyes. Alex tried to bow, as he'd been instructed, but the emperor took him by the shoulders. "So, this is the young man who risked his life to save my daughter. Your student, Edith." He turned to the mercenary.

"Yes, he performed admirably," Edith said.

He felt Emperor Tamerlane's hands tighten over his arms as he looked at Edith. His smile widened before turning back to Alex. "I hate having to wear these stupid helmets." The emperor reached up taking his off.

"My lord—" The other man, the one he'd been standing with started, but one look from the emperor was enough to stop him.

"There aren't many Tairnish left up here anyway. However, I suppose we have other problems now. Don't we, admiral?" the emperor called.

"Yes, the surface. We don't know what it means—" the man in the center of the room started.

"Maybe Alex does." The emperor reached up and took Alex's helmet off. He sent it drifting across the command room. "There, Alex. Isn't that better?" Alex could smell the minty odor of the emperor's breath. Their faces were close to each other's. "I don't want anything between us, Alex." He took the rim of Alex's suit and pulled them even closer together. "You see there's something happening down there and, I'm not going to lie, it's concerning. It's unexpected. You may not know anything, but you see, it started not far from where you and Edith were."

"I— I don't," Alex stammered.

"He's been passed out since we launched. I don't know what you're talking about either," Edith explained.

"Amita's down there," Alex cut in. "She went looking for answers to what happened to us, my friends and I, the people from Earth."

"I've been wondering about that myself." He turned to Edith. "You brought the other one to the surface, the other refugee?"

"She was our best chance of getting intel from the Drake, the one we were using as a guide." Edith's voice didn't show a hint of emotion as she explained, but Alex noticed the way her body tightened.

"But you left her behind." The emperor pulled at his beard.

"No choice. There was a collapse in the caves and we were separated. Rescuing them would've

435

compromised the mission." Edith kept her eyes forward and her words were brisk.

There was a long moment of silence while the emperor considered her statement. He sighed and looked back at the other woman, Ada. "Mercenaries, always so practical."

"She was taught well," Ada said.

Edith bit her lip and her face flushed before she asked her emperor, "Is it the Æesir, my lord?" She glanced at Alex, clearly thinking of the way he'd been saved, the way one of those creatures that the monks worshiped had torn into their trial room and killed Kavaris Dell. Alex's thoughts went back to that day, looking up at that thing, then hearing it say his name. Perhaps it'd come to save Amita as well.

"No, it's something else. Come with me and I'll show you," the emperor said, waving Edith over as he went back to the screens in the center of the room. "Admiral, bring up the launch footage." An image appeared of an object rocketing out of the planet's surface. The lengthy device trailed fire and smoke behind it as it vanished into a cloudy sky. Another image showed it near the moon's horizon. "We thought it was a weapon at first. A missile silo that we didn't know about, only the rocket isn't pointed toward any of our assets. So, of course, then we thought it was an escape vessel. According to my rules of engagement that makes it a target, but I've had my forces hold fire. It's unique."

The emperor reached toward the screen and magnified the image. The details of the strange vessel became clearer. Alex recognized the diamond tip. He pointed. "It's like the one we came through the wormhole in."

The emperor nodded. "Yes, the one the Drake piloted to Earth, following his friend."

"You know about that?" Alex turned to him. He thought about what they'd told the monks and what he'd divulged to Maeven. He shouldn't have been surprised the story had made it all the way to Maeven's father.

The emperor nodded. "Alex, like the Long-Wolves, I see the value in information. Most of what you've done and seen here and your reports from your home have come to me. Even this, this rocket, it's interesting, but not completely surprising. I'd heard stories about ancient devices made to traverse the void spaces in a time before humans. They were an interesting little historical mystery, something I'm fond of, but not overly important to today, or so I thought."

"Before humans?" Alex asked.

There was a strange intimacy with the emperor there in the darkened room, lit by screens and with everyone surrounding them still in their backlit helmets, like ghosts in a dream. The emperor's green eyes twinkled as his beard barely contained a grin. "There was a time before we were part of all this, but the monks don't talk about it much. They're far more concerned with correcting our wicked nature. You'll find out our history is a complicated thing, but again that doesn't really matter now. You see these rockets weren't the only thing the Long-Wolves were keeping to themselves. They had something that was surprising even to me. Apparently, there's a rebellion going on."

He turned to the man behind him. "Admiral, pull up the feed from Tairnish's surface. Play it back at double speed.

"Tell me what you know about this, either of you, feel free to speak." On the screen, a video started to play. There was smoke and debris falling to the ground. "We pointed long-range cameras from a number of our satellites at the spot after the rocket launched. We only left one on it though, trying to follow the rocket's path.

We're about halfway around on the other side of the moon but I've got other assets above it.

"As you can see the first thing the satellite picked up was the cavern collapsing. It was a large space so our observers thought that would explain what happened next." Alex watched the walls around the dark opening begin to tumble. The emperor reached out and broadened the shot as the nearby area, for what must have been miles collapsed and fell into a massive pit. The bottom was hidden in dust, but it was so deep that none of the debris could reach the top. It was like watching the Grand Canyon form in minutes. Alex's mouth fell open.

The emperor stared at the screen as well. "That hole is five hundred times the size of this ship. Ten times larger than the biggest city on Uppsala. The facility you escaped from was only the tiniest fraction of it."

"That place is gone?" Alex asked, having trouble understanding the scale of the destruction.

"We'd barely begun bombing it. Where you were is this tiny spot right up here." He pointed to a small blemish against the dark rocks. "It's almost a smudge at this scale." He tightened the shot in again, showing the broken walls of an underground building. "But this is even more interesting." He pushed the camera down, following the contours of the cavern's newly formed landscape.

As the emperor moved the image, Alex asked Edith, "Do you think Amita was on the rocket."

Edith shrugged while the emperor answered for her, "We know the Drake, Tearmai, had been there before." He turned away from the screen to look Alex directly in the eye. "Right before he came to your world." He paused staring at Alex, then a smile broke across his face. Alex had the distinct feeling of a mouse being spotted by a cat. Alex broke the eye contact, turning to the floor, feeling a chill run down his spine.

The admiral in his glowing helmet leaned forward. "Sir, the deck guards report your daughter is outside."

The emperor waved him off. "She can wait for a moment. I want to show our guests this." He turned back to the screen again, bringing the shot down to the floor. "The playback is double speed but keep in mind this all happened only a few minutes ago. Now pay attention."

Alex looked at the screen and saw rivers of fire, glowing red all across the floor of the canyon. They seeped up through the rock, melting the solid surface and spreading till they became bubbling and boiling lakes of fire. He watched as things began to emerge from the melted rock. The plasma forms of Golems rose from the ground like fiery ghosts. They danced on the currents of heated air, staying just above the surface. The emperor pulled the camera back again, saying, "Keep watching."

As the video feed got wider and wider, Alex said, "There are hundreds of them."

"Maybe thousands," the emperor commented. The image was too wide now to see the individual creatures. He showed Alex a quarter of the canyon floor. The rivers of lava formed a lake, eventually consuming the entire floor of the canyon. He leaned into Alex and pointed to the top of the screen. "That facility you broke into, where you two rescued my daughter is gone now, not just broke but completely gone, consumed in minutes. Now watch this."

Something fiery shot from the canyon floor. Again, it would have to be incredibly long to travel such a distance. Even with the playback at double speed, it had to be moving extremely fast to go so far. It was a spike of fiery rock, another followed, and another. They blazed across the canyon, reaching into the sky. There were four in all. Then a wider area emerged beneath, a broad flat plateau. The emperor pulled back the camera even further. "What's that look like to you, Alex?"

He stared at it for a moment, seeing joints and the outline of claws. "Like a hand, maybe."

"Not a human one," Edith said.

The emperor nodded. "More like a Long-Wolf. Fire-Golems are imitators." The image slowed. "Are we caught up," the emperor asked.

"Yes, my lord, this is the live feed now."

"Go ahead and let my daughter in." The emperor waved his hand.

"Sir, look," the admiral called. On the screen, a second hand was emerging but that wasn't why the admiral was alarmed. The fiery forms of the Golems were rising from the pit. Like embers, shooting out in every direction.

"Track them," the emperor called.

"They're heading for some of our targets on the ground and towards registered Long-Wolf enclaves," one of the deck officers called from behind their screen.

Another officer called, "I've got some going into orbit, going toward the docks and toward our ships."

Suddenly the screen blinked out. The officer closest to them turned and said, "That was the satellite, my lord."

The emperor barely had time to turn his head before someone else called, "The Olethros is under attack. They're reporting Fire-Golems breaching their hull."

"We've got other ships reporting they're under attack as well, my lord."

The emperor turned to Alex and smiled. "Maybe find your helmet." Then he called louder as the admiral handed him his. "Get all the picket ships and drones in tight. Warn them what's coming and get the ship ready to break orbit. Have the rest of the fleet do the same." He pointed toward the door. "And get my daughter in here."

He turned back to Alex. "Well, this was certainly an interesting turn of events."

Alex's eyes were on the screen. The video was frozen on the hands emerging from the fiery lake. With his attention fixated on it, Alex barely heard the emperor ask a question. Tamerlane had to repeat it, something he obviously wasn't used to doing. "Do you think your friend Amita knows anything about this?"

Alex turned to him. "It wouldn't surprise me at all," he said.

Chapter 41

Katy stood still and listened. The buzzing from the machines remained, like static in the back of her head, a low, unpleasant humming that wouldn't stop. The warning bells were less violent but still present. She'd heard Regin call out a few seconds before. It hadn't been a scream for help, more like a muffling of his final breath.

"Hello," Katy called softly into the perpetual darkness, her thoughts still on the ghost that had been in front of her a moment before. She didn't want to draw its attention if it were still nearby, but she wanted to know what happened to her brother. He'd leaped across the room a moment before, going to help Regin, springing into action like an attack dog, but she had no idea what happened after that. It had all gone quiet.

'I should be running,' she thought. 'I should be putting as much distance between myself and this room as I can.' She stayed though, crouched down, her hands held out in front, waving slowly through the air, trying to get a sense of what was around her. Inching forward, she felt one of the low benches.

When she told Regin she knew what the ghost wanted, that it was speaking to her, it'd been a lie. She'd only told him what she so desperately hoped for. That he could somehow put everything back and fix her brother, make this horrible night right again.

What the ghost's intentions were was as much a mystery to her as it had been to the Ice-Carver. Katy had lied again. It had become a habit, maybe a dangerous one, claiming to know things she didn't, to hear things she couldn't. Cormack's mother's words popped back into her head. 'You're playing a dangerous game.' Well, it was better than dying.

She took a step forward and thought about her own mom after she started having her episodes when reality started fading away. That's when she first became comfortable with manipulating the truth. It was the easiest way to keep her mom from hurting herself or hurting the people around her, not physically, not usually. Mostly, after her mom changed and let her mania out, her words were the most damaging, especially to Ben.

"Ben, are you here?" Katy called, taking another few steps forward, being careful not to smash her legs into the low tables again. Reaching her hands out, she felt something incredibly cold. She pulled away, tucking her arms up to her chest as she turned and fought the urge to run. "Ben?" she asked again.

There was no answer.

Slowly she reached out, letting her fingers contact a rough surface that in no way resembled her brother's back. She shivered, feeling her stomach churn, somehow knowing this was him. At first, he felt like a statue, but then air moved through his lungs, subtle and slow like a machine at idle.

"Can you hear me?" she asked. His head trembled in response as if he were trying to move but couldn't. She felt his shoulders start to shift, drawing forward, then the blades on his arm scraped along the stone floor, only a little, like a match being lazily dragged instead of struck. Katy pulled back again, recognizing the sound, remembering the monster back on Earth. With only blackness around her, she felt her pulse race, expecting the sharpened edge to come flying at her, but the sound continued. It was a weak, pitiful scraping. Ben kept at it and the noise grew more insistent with each passing moment.

She called, "I'm here. How do I help you?"

The scraping stopped. Then slowly started again, but only twice. Katy stepped forward, reaching out, once more touching her brother's back. She felt the muscles like steel, rigid and alien, as his shoulder blade flexed and pointed forward. Only a single blade made a noise, a stuttering effort, like Ben was fighting for that little bit of movement, trying to bring her attention toward something. "What is it?"

There was no answer.

"Okay," Katy said as she kept her arm on his shoulder, letting her hand slip down to his bicep. She stepped forward, going in front of him, using his arm as a guide. Ben had always been shorter than her and even in this transformed body, he still wasn't as tall. Katy had seen the monster on Earth rear up, going from a closed-in thing, full of potential, to a tall and terrible machine of death. She saw it move and leap. In fact, it was the last thing she'd ever seen. 'But that wasn't Ben,' she told herself as she reached his wrist and shuttered at the bizarre changes to his hand.

Her breathing became hurried as she fought her revulsion, moving her fingertips down along his hand, feeling the beginning of the blade extending from beneath his palm. He had only four digits. The fifth one had turned into this terrible instrument. She touched the flat side of the blade with her index finger, then pulled back a little till she was hovering a millimeter above it. She had to steady her hand with the other to keep from trembling. She could sense the cold from the weapon, like a block of ice. It guided her toward the floor.

Carefully, she kneeled down, keeping her distance from the terrible thing, remembering how sharp it'd been, going through steel railings and conduit. The extremity stayed still as if Ben knew how close his blind sister was. Katy moved her hands in careful circles till she felt her fingers crash into something that rang with a hollow thump. She thought of everything Regin had said about the canisters on the wall.

'This is what held the thing,' she thought. It was smaller than she expected as her hand ran over its round surface. It felt less like metal and more like a type of pottery, leaving a soft, dusty residue on her fingers. It could be no more dangerous than a salad bowl. Then the odor hit her from inside and brought back old memories. It smelt like the breath of the monster that took her sight, the rank odor of oil, and something worse, seeped up from the inside.

She was tempted to throw it away, but she said to Ben, "I have it. Now what—" Before she could finish the words, her fingers came across the control unit, the box Regin had been trying to pull away. Pain laced through her arms, through her nerves, driving like a runaway train into her head. She screamed but couldn't hear her own voice. There was too much traffic.

It flooded the corners of her mind, different from the low current noise coming from the machines. That hadn't been invasive. This was more like when they arrived on Nalanda, when Fafnir had used his friend's body to rewire the communications centers of their brains, taking things in her head and turning them over, reorganizing circuits, dropping data packets that quickly opened, and showing Katy things that she couldn't possibly understand. The urge to pull her hand away was overpowering, but she held it there all the same because the first message, the main one was from Ben. 'This is how you help me,' it said.

She turned and faced him as she gritted her teeth. She spent the last few weeks becoming more accustomed to her senses, what she could hear and smell, and even the way the air touched the hairs on her arm, but the pain pulled her away from all that, isolating her to the space inside her own skull.

An endless amount of time passed that was in truth only moments as she stood there frozen. Her eyes were

445

wide open. There was never a reason to close them. Only when she was tired would exhaustion flood her body and let her lids drop. She was barely aware of it happening now, of her eyes slipping closed. As her lids tightened, light seeped in, and images began to form.

It didn't come from the dead nerves in her eyes. It was more like a memory, like she was asleep and falling into the fuzzy disorganized structure of dreams. A single shadow, nearly impossible to recognize took form in front of her. She focused her attention on it, ignoring all the pain and activity in the background of her head, which had already begun to fade. "Ben, who is that?"

"It's you," Ben answered in that electronic, broken voice.

Katy reached her hand out toward the image and felt only air. "What's happening?" she asked.

"I'm looking at you and you're seeing yourself," Ben answered.

Katy's eyes flung open, returning her to the heartbreaking darkness. She took a breath and closed her eyes again, focusing. The image returned. Seeing herself standing in a shadow-filled room, she reached her hand out and saw it happen in front of her. "This is crazy."

'Help me,' Ben interrupted her. It took her a moment to realize that he hadn't said a word, that the sorrowful voice was in her head. Katy watched the image of herself as her hand tightened down on the control box on the canister. She felt it in her hand, heavy and solid, and pushed it down till it slipped off the side. The data still poured in, reorganizing portions of her brain, and showing her what to do, how to use her new weapon. She looked down and Ben's head did the same thing, glancing at his deformed body.

She searched the data that had been loaded into her thoughts, trying to find an answer for how to reverse the change. Maybe there was too much or maybe there wasn't an answer at all, but she couldn't find anything to help. "Ben, are you there?" she asked, trying to move his hand. She saw his long, distorted fingers wiggle, flicking out.

"I am," he said.

Katy shivered at the sound of his voice. "How do I help you?"

He sounded so much like the thing in the desert. "Unlock me."

Katy hesitated. "What's that mean?"

"Give me permission. Unlock me," Ben repeated. Katy pictured every terrible thing that could happen. Every film where the hero made the mistake of trusting some alien intelligence. She hated those movies.

"Okay," she said squeezing the control box. With a single word, she let her brother have control of his own body. She heard him move in front of her as she squeezed her eyes tight, refusing to let go of his vision. She was looking at herself, noticing the way he stayed back, giving her space. She held on, seeing through his eyes as his fingers moved in front of him, twisting and turning experimentally.

"Ben, are you okay?" she asked.

It took him a moment to respond as the long fingers continued to move, folding and unfolding. His eyes looked down at his strange dark legs. "No, I don't think I am," he finally said. "This thing . . . it's part of me now."

Through his eyes she saw him lift his blade-hands from the floor, inspecting them. "I'm a monster."

"We'll fix it Ben. We'll find a way," Katy felt herself take a step forward.

Ben moved back in response. "Where are you going?" she asked.

He slumped down onto one of the benches. "I'm just sitting, that's all. I think this part is going to hurt."

447

"What do you mean?" Katy asked.

Ben's voice sounded strained as he answered, "That thing in the desert could hide, pretend it was a person." Katy noticed that the image of herself and the room was starting to fade. She heard Ben groan, heard the sound of something organic happening.

"Ben, I can't see anymore," Katy said.

"You could see?" Ben asked as he grunted and moaned. There was a wet, oozing noise as flesh and machine twisted and squirmed, returning to the body of a boy. His labored breathing lost the broken garbled sound of the monster. He whimpered. "I can't say I enjoyed that." His voice was human again.

Katy didn't know what to say. The device in her hand, the control or whatever it was still hummed and buzzed, but it no longer hurt to hold. It had done its work. The other machines in the room still issued their warnings, but they'd dulled as well. "I could see through your eyes," she said, taking a step toward her brother.

"I'm sorry," Ben said, sensing a hint of regret in his sister's voice.

Katy came to him and touched his face. "Don't be. I'm sorry. This is my fault. We shouldn't have ever come here."

"He's gone," Ben said. "I watched the ghost take Regin right through the wall. There was no door. They just vanished."

"Do you know what it wanted? Why it brought us here?" Katy asked.

"It wanted you," Ben said. Katy couldn't tell that Ben was looking at secret stairs. He took his sister's arm and they started walking away from the lab.

Chapter 42

It was early morning, only moments into the day cycle, and Cathal was enjoying the quiet in the combat hall. He had no idea that Chris was talking to a Fire-Golem in his cell, a cell that would soon be open, or that Ben and Katy were finding their way back down the stairs from the lighthouse with a terrible secret.

Cathal's only company as he stood in the center of the room, in the cage used for training, was a silent Fire-Golem on the stairs to the medical unit. It watched over the hall through the night cycle, unmoving but aware of everything around it.

Going through his morning exercises on an open field, without the floating obstacles, was a treat after Cathal's time in prison. The quiet here, before the students or monks awoke, was peaceful to the old warrior. He moved his body through forms more ancient than even he knew, existing for thousands of years. Motions had been added and taken away from the martial art, but always there was a sharp thrust at the end of every gesture and a fierce, frozen face as air exploded from his diaphragm.

Combat training was the only part of his assignment that he took any joy in. Though keeping an eye on Cormack, as the queen requested, proved to be easy enough. She had also wanted him to watch his friends, the people from the void. That had proven more difficult. He thought of Chris lying to save Naiathne and Katy's insistence on finding the murderer and he frowned, feeling older.

He looked up at the bars and thought, 'fitting that I'm happiest in a cage.' In a way he missed the quiet, the absence of politics and scheming in prison. Though he supposed, even there politics bled into life. but it was nothing compared to his time as a general serving his closest friend, Cormack's father the king, or after the war when his friend was gone.

In those years Cormack's mother had done everything she could to rebuild their world, to make certain they could withstand another attack if Tamerlane returned. She'd always been the power behind the two anyway. Cormack's father was brave, but he was from a small colony, a collection of islands miles from Anchor Home. Their marriage was arranged like most royal pairings to bring two families together and make them stronger. Strength was what they needed to defend their homes, not love and not what the monks offered, a faith in beings who only cared about their own motives.

As Cathal threw a series of vicious elbows at the air, he thought of the monks he'd known on Grannus. They'd assured the king and queen that the Æesir would stop Tamerlane's invasion and that peace could only be found through faithfulness. But the Æesir never came, and the people of Grannus were forced to beg for help from their neighbors, from the true Grannusians. For many, it meant the swallowing of generations of pride, but for Cathal it was as simple as asking a friend for help.

He'd known Eir, the healer nearly his entire life, ever since he'd fallen ill as a child. A disease had run rampant through his island home and his isolated people were left to die by the other humans. Then the Grannusians had come. Led by Eir they found a cure, then stayed to nurse the people back to health. Occasionally, she returned to check on them. Cathal grew up wishing he could join her below the sea. That he could live as one of their people. He even called her his aunt, which made her laugh.

When Tamerlane invaded, he was unwilling to destroy Grannus completely. He wanted the cities and the artificial islands floating on the surface intact, taking orbital bombardment off the menu. The fighting was more personal, in the streets and alleys, holding positions and losing them. It was ugly and it went on for months. They'd called Cathal a general, but he spent his days fighting like a guerilla, always moving, trying to punish the enemy any way he could.

Thankfully the Grannusians were there for support and as the fighting went on, they became more and more involved, attacking the emperor's ships high above where he thought they were safe. The worst mistake he made was assaulting the star blossom, that elevator to space. As it turned out, the living thing had its own defenses. Space born entities had poured from it, seeking the heat signatures of the royal ships and dissolving their engine shielding, causing their cores to breach.

Cathal only heard the accounts secondhand as he'd been busy fighting the ground war where Tamerlane had other advantages. He remembered a dark, nightmarish thing breaking into his camp and murdering nearly every soldier in it. He'd only heard rumors that these hunters, these ghosts given form, even existed, but then one night it targeted Cormack's father. Nothing would stop the thing from getting to him. After, it was Cathal's good name and the carnage left over that convinced people of the truth of his story. Cathal had lost his closest friend and Cormack had lost so much more.

Cathal shook the memory away as he swept across the floor, shooting his leg out and coming in low, bringing his body down as he wondered how much Cormack recalled from that time. He'd only been a boy, maybe five or six years old. Imagine it, those guns and bombs could very well be the prince's first memories, not happy holidays, or family gatherings, just death and destruction. No wonder Cormack was always trying to make peace, trying to help his friends and his sister. The prince had seen where the fighting ended. He wanted to find a better way.

Cathal stopped his exercises, hearing a sound echo through the empty hall. "Hello," he called, his eyes searching. He saw nothing amiss, no one coming to join him. In the past few days he'd started to dread the sight of red robes. Sister Nemain's errand boys were constantly looking for him, sending messages from her and summoning him.

Another sound brought his attention to the stairs and to a subtle glow there. He relaxed a little, seeing that it was only the Fire-Golem. It left the landing behind and stomped down the stairs, disappearing towards the dining hall. Cathal watched for a moment, then shrugged, not overly concerned, thinking Fajalar must have someone else he wanted to watch.

Cathal may have been the supposed head of security, but he knew very little about the Golems. They were pretty much unstoppable, which he supposed was a good thing in a guard, but he'd rather have watchmen he could speak to, who weren't controlled by a Long-Wolf.

Cathal started back into his drill when he heard footsteps quickly approaching. A moment later he saw a red-robed figure come flying towards him. "Great." He sighed and rolled his eyes. By the time he looked down again, the monk was already going down another hallway. He'd hurried past without glancing in Cathal's direction.

Shrugging, Cathal put it from his mind, not about to chase the monk who was hurrying toward their private territory. He let out a long breath, closing his eyes and trying to focus, ready to launch into a set of combinations when he heard a tapping sound come from that same direction. He opened his eyes and looked where the monk had gone. Katy and her brother came out from the same hallway. She had her stick in front, using it as a guide.

Cathal would've wondered what they were up to at this time of the morning, but there was a more intriguing question that needed to be answered first. Why was Ben in his underwear? His school uniform hung off him in shreds. "That's odd," Cathal said.

He walked up to the bars and leaned against one, waving to the two. "Ben, I think you forgot something." Cathal motioned to his own body.

Ben seemed confused, then he looked down, noticing for the first time. "Yeah. . . it's kind of a long story."

Cathal raised one of his bushy eyebrows and scratched his beard. "I'm sure it is. What are you two up to?"

"Investigating. We know who killed the monk," Katy said. Cathal's eyes went wide, but before he could ask any more questions, he was interrupted by dozens of people speeding toward them. Monks darted into the combat hall, moving with hurried steps.

Sister Nemain was there, mixed into the pack. Cathal fought the urge to hide, to duck behind one of the bars. He called out instead, "Is there a problem?"

She looked up, noticing him for the first time, too distracted by whatever mission they were on. "Apparently a Fire-Golem, the one from the cells, has gone off on its own. It nearly crushed the monks there. A security risk you might say." With the wave of a finger, she motioned him to follow.

Cathal glanced over his shoulder at the stairs, wondering if he should mention the one that had been standing there. Instead, he took a deep breath and let it out as a grunt then he grabbed his gear bag where his side arm waited in its holster. He closed it around his waist before swinging down out of the cage and dropping to the floor. He started towards sister Nemain, who was already hurrying off, expecting him to follow. "The kids say they know who killed Kavaris Altain," he called after her. When the monk turned around, Cathal motioned broadly to Ben and Katy, who had fallen behind the pack.

Sister Nemain looked from one to the other, then settled her gaze back on Ben with the rags hanging off him. She started to ask, "Where is his—" but she interrupted herself, shaking her head. "Never mind, we don't have time for this."

"Didn't you hear him?" Katy asked, trying to get closer. "We know who the murderer was."

Sister Nemain rolled her eyes, then turned and started off. "Tell me on the way," she said, not caring that Katy couldn't keep up with the hurrying monks.

"What the hell," Katy said, squeezing her stick as she furrowed her eyebrows. Cathal noticed there was something in her other hand that she was keeping low and by her side.

He glanced at Ben. The boy's face was unreadable. That wasn't something you could usually say about him. He was the type of person who wore all his emotions on the surface. Cathal went towards the sister. "Come on, we'll make her listen," he said as he took Katy's arm to guide her. It was the arm with that other thing in it. Katy pulled away sharply.

"It's okay. I'm not going to hurt you," Cathal said, holding up his hands. He could feel Ben's eyes on him as he tried to see what she was hiding.

"Yeah, it is okay. I've got her," Ben said, taking the other arm. Katy didn't fight this time, letting her brother lead.

"Cathal, hurry up," sister Nemain called from the back of the crowd, waving her arm. Cathal took one last look back at Katy and Ben. Something had happened to them. It wasn't just Ben's clothes that made him think the boy had changed. Cathal had spent years honing his instincts, knowing when something was dangerous and that's all he felt from the boy, the absolute certainty that he was someone to be wary of.

Turning and following the pack of monks, the security head traveled down the long walkways, going through the massive central hub, that seemed even larger for the fact that most students hadn't woken yet. He was curious about what Katy was holding and about what they'd found, but Cathal was also very good at focusing on what was in front of him. He glanced over his shoulder a few times to see if the two were still with them as they passed the turn-off for the alien sectors and went by the cells, heading for the dining hall. The tumult of numerous voices resonated off the walls as they approached.

Students were gathered outside the main entrance, held back by a single Fire-Golem. Its stone head was alight above them, like a beacon, and its arms were out wide, glowing along the cracks and seams of its limbs. The students were trying to peer around the creature, but none were brave enough to approach, their curiosity not overwhelming their wariness of the Golem and its strange behavior as it waved them back.

Colliding with the crowd, the monks tried to make their way through. "Clear a path, clear a path," they called as they forced the students aside. Before they could reach the front, Fajalar came scurrying out. He darted beneath the Golem and around people's legs while holding his neck with an angry black charred spot on it. He was in such a hurry that he slammed into the monks, sending a few tumbling to the ground.

"What is the meaning of this?" sister Nemain demanded as the monks tried to grab the Long-Wolf.

Fafnir wasn't far behind. The Fire-Golem at the door stepped out of the way and allowed the Drake to pass. Fafnir leaned against the entryway filling the large opening, floor to ceiling and wall to wall as he called, "Make way. Let him go."

The Fire-Golem looked up at him and nodded when Fafnir stepped out of its way. Then it went in towards its comrades. It was a strange enough thing that all the monks turned to the Drake, expecting an answer. He said nothing, watching Fajalar run off toward the comms room.

Sister Nemain stepped right in front of the giant and asked, "What is this? What's happening? You control them now?" She pointed past him at the Golems.

Fafnir glanced down at her, then his gaze turned back to the escaping Long-Wolf. A noise came from Fafnir that few had ever heard. His chest began to shake and a deep laugh slipped out, sounding like a stalling motor. Through the barking, he answered, "No . . . I'm not in charge . . . not of anyone." Tears were dripping from his blue eyes and down the side of his long beak. He wiped them away. "And neither are the Long-Wolves," he said glancing back.

As his laughing abated, he added, "I think Fajalar will have much to tell you soon. I suspect his world is in the throes of a drastic change."

Katy finally reached the group. Again though, it was Ben who demanded the most attention. The students there, noble-born young men and women, taught manners and decorum since birth didn't know how to respond to the skinny kid standing there in his underwear and a shredded uniform. In fact, between the cranky Drake laughing and these two new arrivals, the students gathered aghast, with their mouths hanging open, shaking their heads as they stood back in a circle and whispered to each other.

Katy took this moment to get everyone's attention by pushing past the monks and going up to Fafnir. She only had his breathing to locate him by, but it was enough as his laughing stopped and her eyes went up. He looked down at her, incapable of ignoring her sightless gaze. "And what do you want?" he asked.

"I want to know if you knew. If you knew what your friend did?" she asked simply.

Sister Nemain looked annoyed at the interruption. She stepped forward about to say something to Katy, but Ben put his hand up and spoke first, interrupting her as she opened her mouth. "You're going to want to hear this."

Katy didn't hesitate, her pale eyes focused and her face set. "I'm talking about Regin. Did you know what he did? When these monks were about to toss Naiathne out an airlock, did you know your friend was a murderer?"

Fafnir's amusement disappeared completely, turning to something much darker as he glared at Katy and said, "I had my suspicions."

"He tried killing me and my brother," Katy's voice broke with emotion. "You stood there in that classroom while we talked to him. Were you part of this plot of his?"

Fafnir shook his head and closed his fists, refusing to answer. "Where is Regin now?"

Ben broke in. "With the ghosts. They took him. They wanted something from my sister, and he got in the way."

"Professor Regin, that's who you're saying killed Kavaris Altain?" sister Nemain interjected.

"He was trying to find a secret room in the lighthouse," Katy said.

A hot breath rolled from the Drake's mouth as he sighed. You could hear his armored knuckles opening and closing as he said, "He's gone?"

Katy didn't answer. She turned, trying to find sister Nemain. Her eyes went to the last place she'd heard the monk's voice. "It's time you let my friend go. You know

Chris only confessed to save Naiathne. Now we know who the real killer is."

Sister Nemain's eyes widened. "You come here with no evidence, only accusations, admitting your friend is a liar and you demand from me—"

"Knock it off," Ben shouted. Cathal moved a little closer to the central group. He stared at the boy, noticing how dark his face had become. Ben was a pale kid, which made the newly formed, dark rings beneath his eyes seem gloomier. Shadows moved beneath his skin, across his face and down his back.

Cathal wondered if this was some trick of the light. Then the skin on Ben's back rippled as the boy spoke. "This is done," Ben growled, his voice sounding off. "We're not playing this game anymore. You're going to let Chris go and you're going to stop getting in our way."

"Ben, calm down." Katy put her hand on his shoulder.

"Yes, calm yourself," sister Nemain said, taking a step back.

Ben moved toward her, but then Katy said in a commanding voice, "Don't" and Ben seemed to freeze. Cathal watched thinking it was strange, but before he could say anything, three more people joined the group in the hall. Chris, Cormack, and Naiathne.

Katy's attention stayed on Nemain with her hand still on Ben as she said, "You need to understand, we're not your enemies. I don't know what your Æesir are or what they expect from us, but obviously, they want us here, not in some cell. They wanted me to find this killer for you. There's a lot you could learn from us and all you have to do is listen. Your order needs to stop treating us like something you have to fix or control. Things are changing and they're not going to stop because you don't want them to."

Sister Nemain looked to the ceiling and ran her hand back over her bald head. Her eyes came down and considered the crowd, then stopped on Cormack. She sighed and motioned to Chris. "Take your friends back to your domain. All of your friends."

"Thank you," Katy said.

Nemain let out an angry little laugh. "Oh, this isn't over. You're going to get your brother cleaned up, then I'm going to want to talk to you. You will come when I summon you. Is that understood?" She looked up at Fafnir. "And I'm going to need to talk to you as well." She motioned to the Golem noticing for the first time that it had walked away, heading toward the center of the dining room and the other rock creatures there. "About a number of things apparently."

Fafnir followed her gaze to the creatures. "There's little I can tell you about this."

"Yes, well, I'm going to learn what I can from Tairnish. But I'm more concerned about what your friend was up to. Apparently Regin killed a member of my order." Sister Nemain looked at Katy and shook her head. Cathal thought she looked exhausted.

Fafnir blew air out of nostrils and sneered at the monk. Cathal touched his side arm, worried Fafnir might do something, but the old Drake stayed calm, grumbling as he started away.

Behind him he heard Chris ask, "Ben, what happened to your clothes?"

Ben smiled, but it looked painful, like he was forcing it. "Good question," he said.

Chris shook his head as Cathal watched the prince, his best friend's son, and his daughter Naiathne surrounded by these strange people. He didn't know how to feel, happy or worried, but he kept his eyes on Ben, watching him closely as he wondered what exactly had happened to the boy.

Chapter 43

Amita was on the emperor's ship, waiting in an interrogation room thinking about what she learned, what she'd been shown. Turns out she wasn't the only one trying to escape Tairnish. The emperor's forces were in full retreat and he wanted answers. He surmised the best place to get them was in the strange rocket launched from the planet's surface moments before everything went wrong. As the fleet scattered, The Revenant caught up to her and Tearmai.

Amita had been in the diamond tip, but with her naked eyes, the only thing she could see was the world getting smaller in the distance. Even when The Revenant closed in on them, it appeared as nothing more than a shadow, a dark spot against the light reflected from the moon. She couldn't identify what it was, but she knew it was chasing them and getting closer.

Down in the main part of the rocket, her attempts to alert Tearmai hadn't worked. They'd devised hand signals while switching over her oxygen supply, but those did little to convey such a threat. It wasn't till she got him up to the diamond tip that she saw his eyes go wide. The dark grey plating of the massive vessel came into focus. The Revenant was ten times their length and it had already launched drones and a shuttle.

There was nothing they could do. The rocket's course had been set the moment it broke orbit and while Tearmai knew the launch sequence, he knew little else about piloting it. All they were doing was falling toward the gas giant, not even accelerating. The rocket was fulfilling a course programmed more than a thousand years ago, and while it had limited AI that updated itself to the movements of the different worlds, it had only one destination that it defaulted to, the void spaces beneath the surface of Altor.

With magnetic grapples, The Revenant's drones had latched onto the rocket's outer hull and used thrusters to slow it down and change its course. Amita and Tearmai were turned toward the royal shuttle which was outfitted for boarding operations. She felt the vibrations through the wall, and even in the absorbent gel, she was thrown around by the rapid change in direction.

The royal shuttle latched onto the rocket like a tick, then started to cut through the vessel's ancient metal side. Magnesium torches blazed through the airlock doors, then armored soldiers dropped into the acceleration gel, spreading out with powerful spotlights that passed through the substance making ghostly clouds.

Amita had felt a soldier's armored hand drag her through the slime and into the shuttle's airlock, where she floated in zero-g with the fluid balling and drifting away.

She worried Tearmai would try to fight. That he'd resist, and the soldiers would kill him, but Tearmai crossed through as gently as could be. He even held his large hands up, letting the soldiers know he wasn't a threat.

This was unexpected. Amita had seen so many moods from her friend, many of them unruly, that to see him so passive as he was pushed into the shuttle was painful. Really, it should've been her who fought back. That rocket was the first thing with even the slightest chance of getting her home and she had no idea what they planned to do with it.

Tearmai had allowed the soldiers to put shackles on him, big heavy things that locked his arms together behind his back, a position that didn't appear the least bit comfortable with his anatomy. It left Amita wondering about his strange behavior. It dawned on her in the interrogation room, that since waking up from the void and since his mania cleared, Tearmai's one goal had been freeing the entity on Tairnish. Even in the medical unit on Nalanda, he'd scratched it on the wall, desperate to communicate through his madness. It was all that mattered, and he finally achieved it.

'Why was it so important?' she wondered. 'Was it his hatred of slavery?' That didn't seem like enough, especially after seeing the destruction the creature wrought. She'd have to remember to bring it up with Tearmai when she saw him again.

'If she saw him again.' She'd been in this room for hours and been given no word of him.

Her interviewer, an admiral of all things, was far more interested in her experiences on Tairnish than in a Drake's motivation. Amita had seen things no human had before and spoken to something no one ever encountered.

Seeing little point in keeping anything back, Amita had told the admiral everything, what she'd seen, what the Long-Wolves kept secret, and the being she'd spoken to, the thing she released. She'd told him all of it, including the reason she needed her "damn rocket back." Cursing hadn't gotten her far though, so she tried pleading, "You have to understand, I can fix this. All of this."

For her part, Amita had been filled in on things she could've gone without knowing. The admiral had shone her images and videos of the planet's surface and of royal ships being destroyed. He'd told her the body count for each vessel they lost. "Hundreds of men and women dead because you let that thing free, probably thousands more on the surface below," he'd said coldly.

"You came here to kill people, a lot of people. Now you're miffed because something beat you to it?" Amita shot back at him, not letting her true feelings bubble out, hiding the awful sense that she'd done something wrong.

Impressive and frightening, the video feeds the admiral showed her only lasted as long as the satellites held out. Apparently, whatever was happening on Tairnish's surface, the mother entity didn't want witnesses to it. 'That wasn't ominous at all,' Amita thought as she watched the ships be torn apart. 'What have I done?' repeated again and again in her head but she kept a strong countenance.

The admiral walked her through the entire battle, explaining how formidable the Fire-Golems were in their plasma form. "Solid ordinance does very little to them," he'd said as he focused the playback in, showing the fast-moving rounds of heavy metals fired from rotary cannons on the drones and picket ships. They may be capable of shredding human vessels, but they passed harmlessly through the plasma lifeforms.

"Explosions had more effect." He added, "Detonating missiles near the creatures seemed to disrupt their cohesion, but it doesn't last. A few left the combat field, going back down to the planet, but most were able to shake off the blasts and pull themselves together again. In close combat, the explosions were far more dangerous to our fleet," the admiral explained while showing a picture of a picket ship that'd been blown apart by friendly fire. He had the video feed of it as well, but the action in orbit was so fast that Amita wouldn't have gotten the full effect if he hadn't shown her still shots.

"Fortunately, the emperor's weaponeers managed to arm a number of our missiles with the powder countermeasure." Amita watched explosions on the video produce a fine mist like the grenades Edith had used on the planet's surface. They created a cloud of the material around the command ship, allowing the massive vessel to break orbit, with a fair amount of their fleet still intact.

"We got away, but many didn't," the admiral said as he went to leave, but before going out the door he asked, "What does this thing want? Why did it attack us?"

"It wants to be free and I suppose it knows people well enough to see that we're not great at leaving things alone." Amita shrugged.

The admiral rolled his eyes as he left, a gesture that reminded Amita of her father. That was hours ago, and she'd been alone with her thoughts ever since. They went back to the rocket, wondering if it really was the solution she'd been looking for. She needed time to study it, to understand how it worked. 'This is all the end result of that night in the desert.' repeated in her head again and again.

Brash and Tearmai had come from here and she had no doubt that they hadn't only traveled through space but time as well and that this was the world wrought from their failure.

Amita's head ran as she wondered about the process of time travel. 'Was it as simple as falling through the void space? Was the other side of the wormhole somehow tethered to the moment of its creation? Or would she find herself back at the Earth's destruction? Or perhaps past it, in a solar system devoid of Earth.' There was no way of knowing, not without testing and there was only one rocket left as the others had been destroyed by the entity. Her thoughts were locked in a repeating cycle till the moment the hatch started to move again, swinging in.

She looked up, expecting the admiral, then felt awful as she saw who was there. Alex was hovering in the passageway. His brown skin was even darker with bruises and his usually attractive face was swollen as he held his body rigid.

Looking at her fellow refugee, Amita realized that she'd never once asked the admiral about him, never questioned whether he'd made it back or accomplished his mission. So much had happened, her mind had been too busy. "Alex!? You're here? I mean— um, well, you look awful," Amita stammered out.

"Nice to see you too," Alex said as his shoulders loosened a little.

"Thank goodness you made it out!" Amita wondered if she should go hug him. 'Did they have the kind of relationship where they hugged? Apparently, they didn't have the kind of relationship where I ask if he's dead or alive,' she thought as she pushed back from the table.

Alex said, "Amita, I'm so sorry."

She was surprised. "For what?"

"For leaving you down in those tunnels, for even taking you there." He shook his head. "I mean I can't believe you're alive. I was so worried. By the time we got to the shuttle I was barely conscious, and Edith was all about the mission." Amita went for the hug, getting up and meeting him just inside the door. It seemed like he needed it.

"It's okay Alex. I understand." The embrace was incredibly awkward. He was hurt so she didn't want to squeeze, and he didn't know what to do either, so he patted her on the back. Amita was happy when it was over, and they could return to a respectable distance. She held onto the door frame and pulled herself out a bit, then looked both ways down the empty hall.

She glanced at the entrance they were hovering in and asked, "Has this been unlocked the whole time?"

Alex looked at the door too. "It opened right away for me, why?"

"No reason. I just wasn't sure of my status. If I'm a prisoner or a guest," she said as she slipped past him.

Alex shrugged, looking unsure. Then Amita turned back and asked, "You haven't seen Tearmai, have you?"

"No. I've been in their medical bay pretty much since we broke orbit. They moved me down there as soon as the battle was over."

"The fight with the Golems you mean?" Amita peered in both directions, wondering if there were guards around the corner.

"Yeah, the Golems. I guess you know a bit more about that." Alex raised an eyebrow.

She found a handhold on the wall and glanced back over her shoulder. "The admiral's been talking to me. I don't think he likes me very much. He showed me the whole thing. They're not going to execute me, are they? I know these people are fond of that."

Alex looked both ways down the hall as well. "No, I don't think so. They're sending you back to Nalanda with Tara and Maeven to Chris and the others. The shuttle we borrowed from the monks is being repaired and refueled. When they caught up to your rocket, you were near it. Andavarri and Tara were on a course to Nalanda anyway."

Amita bit her lip, wondering what it would be like to see Andavarri. "So, they got away too?"

"Barely. They had some trouble with a Golem on the shuttle."

Amita cleared her throat, not wanting to look Alex in the eye. "And you rescued your princess?"

"Edith and I did. . . It was . . . It was more than I bargained for. But it's done now." Amita turned her attention away from the floor to the distant sound in his voice. His whole body sunk as he held onto the doorframe. Now Alex was the one who couldn't make eye contact.

When he did look up again, he asked, "Where are you going?"

Amita was moving further away. "I'm not sure. But I'm a bit fed up with being in there. I'd really like to find Tearmai and talk to him."

"They might be putting him on the shuttle too. You guys should have plenty of time to talk then."

Amita's eyebrows came up. "Wait, we're going now? And you're not coming with us?"

Alex's eyes turned away again, glancing back in the room before he pushed off toward Amita. Tapping his ear, he let her know that they were being listened to. "The emperor has plans for me. I don't know where I'm going and I'm not going to ask either, but he said he wants Edith and me by his side for what comes next."

"'What comes next,' What's that mean? And he doesn't want Maeven?" she asked.

Alex shook his head. Amita could see the doubt and the fear. "Alex, you don't belong to him."

"I'm not sure he'd agree. But that doesn't matter."

Cocking her head, Amita raised an eyebrow. "It doesn't?"

Alex ran his hand back over his short hair as he sighed. "We have no power here, no position. I'm trying to give us that. He's the most powerful person on all these worlds and he wants me by his side. It's the best way to keep us safe."

Amita shook her head and tried coming up with a good answer that she could say out loud. "You don't have to do this. I found something. It might be a way home. Tearmai and I were going there."

"You mean the rocket?" Alex asked.

Amita smiled and whispered, "Yes, I think we can go back to that night in the desert."

Alex's eyes widened as she continued, "So, you see, returning to Nalanda and seeing the others may sound wonderful, but really, given the choice, I'd rather finish my journey and maybe put an end to this mess."

"How?" Alex demanded.

"By doing what Brash and Tearmai couldn't, going back through time and actually shutting the wormhole down."

Alex's face scrunched as he tried to understand. "Are you talking about time travel? You're not serious?"

She nodded and Alex added, "Wait, you really mean it— time travel? I think I'm missing something." he waved his hand in the air.

"We all were," Amita said impatiently. "There's a reason all these humans are here, among these alien races. We're not just in some far-off star system. We're in the future. The human beings we're hanging out with are the descendants of refugees from Earth."

She watched Alex as his bruised face widened and his mouth hung open. "That's crazy."

She quickly responded, "But true."

Alex's body looked like it wanted to slump over with exhaustion, but in zero-g it only made him curl up as he considered what she was saying. After a moment he straightened. "And you think you can go back through and fix all this before it started?"

"I think that's exactly what Brash and Tearmai were trying to do. Brash went through the wormhole on his own. I guess his race can do that and Tearmai followed him in the rocket."

"And the hunter?" Alex asked.

"Stuck to the rocket, I guess." Amita shrugged. "It was trying to stop them—" She could tell what Alex was thinking so she pointed out, "Look, we killed the one that got to Earth before and . . ." She looked around. "I don't see any more boogeymen coming for us now. All I need is to get back on the rocket and I'll be on my way. I'd like Tearmai to come with me too."

"That thing is ancient and dangerous. It was flying you into a gas giant. I may not be on your level, but I know enough science to be pretty sure the only thing you'll find in there is a crushing amount of pressure. The rocket would get squished like a coke can. And even if you make it through, you have no idea where you'll end up. Not to mention if you leave everyone else here, what happens to us? Better yet, say you go back before the thing got out of control, are there going to be two of you there? What happens then?"

"Actually, two of me would be helpful. My parents and Katy's dad would have to listen then. But look, there's a lot I don't know and I'm not going to find out any of it by staying here or by being sent back to that sorry excuse for a school."

"Amita—"

"Are you going to help me or not?" She put her hands on her hips.

"I'm trying to help you. Maybe we can talk to the emperor? Explain this all to him." Alex was struggling, still trying to understand what Amita had told him.

"We don't have time for that and what if he says no?"

Alex shook his head. "And what if your plan is insane? Which I'm pretty sure it is. You were just going to dive right in there, not knowing what would happen? No wonder it was you that let that thing go on Tairnish."

"What's that supposed to mean?"

"It means your actions have consequences. This isn't playtime. You're getting people hurt."

"What, these people? They're good enough at hurting each other already." Amita lowered her voice again. "And if my plan works, they may never have even existed."

"What?" Alex threw his head back in shock.

Amita rolled her eyes. "Theoretically, if I alter time, these people could cease to exist or we could end up creating a separate universe, physics is foggy on that one,

469

and I've never time traveled before. Actually, Tearmai and Brash may have already created a separate reality. Hell, the Long-Wolfs probably made a new one every time they went wormhole diving."

"My god, would you listen to yourself," Alex said.

"It's nuts I know, but this is what we're dealing with."

"No, it's not just nuts. These are real people and you're nonchalantly talking about them ceasing to exist. You're no different from Katy and Ben's dad," Alex said.

Amita set her spine rigid, looking at him squarely. "That's right. I am no different from him or from my parents, who I'd really like to see again. You have to understand this is all relative. I can only see the world from my point of view and my world is Earth with the billions of people there who woke up to a pretty awful morning the day we left. I don't know what happened to them, but I bet they'd rather be alive."

Alex shook his head, struggling with his own feelings. "But these are real people too. They exist, here and now and you want to risk them all?"

Amita's voice got louder again. "Do you know what happened to the Lightening Bugs, to Brash's people? The humans here wiped them out. What about Tearmai's people, centuries of slavery? I'm pretty sure that's why Brash was trying to reset things."

Alex shook his head again as Amita added, "This isn't up to your emperor. It's up to you and me now."

Alex held his hands in the air as his eyes went wide. "And you're ok with making that big a decision?"

Amita was sharp and clear, staring at him. "I want to see my parents again."

Alex covered his face and took a long heavy breath. "God, Amita!"

Before he could say more, a voice called down the hall, "Am I interrupting something?"

They both turned and looked at Edith, standing in her armor, a dark form against the clean white walls. "The shuttle is getting ready to leave and you need to be on it," she said to Amita.

"Yeah, we were just debating over that," Amita said.

"No, you weren't," Edith shot back, as she came down the hall, using her magnetic boots to keep her on the floor. Despite how bulky the boots were, her steps were silent. "Alex, you were supposed to escort her to the shuttle. Say your goodbyes. We need to send them on their way. We can't hold the launch for whatever is going on here."

"Wait, aren't I supposed to talk to someone? The emperor or I don't know—"

Edith interrupted her with a snort. "You spoke with an admiral for four hours. Now you want to talk to the emperor?"

Amita looked between Alex and Edith as if the answer should've been obvious. "Well, yeah."

"Wow," Edith said, looking at Alex. "What do you think? Should I go to the emperor's chambers and bang on his door and insist this girl get an audience? Does that seem like a good idea to you?"

"But—" Amita started.

Edith had no interest in listening to her. "I'm sorry, but personally I like my neck firmly attached to my body. The emperor has the report from his admiral. Thanks to your bluntness, he knows everything you have to say and he has no interest in talking to you." She turned to Alex. "We have orders to send her and the others back."

Amita felt Alex take her arm.

"Come on!" Amita pulled away. Alex was too banged up to chase her as she started toward the ceiling.

But Edith grabbed her ankle and pulled her back down. "I'm sorry, but you don't have your friend to threaten me with this time."

"Wait, get your hands off me! I don't want to go!" Amita shouted as she tried to fight against Edith.

The soldier spun her around, held her upper arms and pinned them back harshly, then she started walking ahead. "You're only going to hurt yourself if you keep fighting," she warned as Amita struggled against the iron grip.

Eventually, she stopped fighting. She tried to look over her shoulder at Alex, who was following slowly using handles on the side of the hallway. "You can't let them do this. Not after everything we've learned."

"I'm not in charge here. It's not up to me," Alex said.

"That sounds a lot like 'just following orders.' Probably the worse excuse in history. You can't be serious." Amita quieted down and bit her lip before screaming, "What's wrong with you? We don't belong here!"

Alex shouted back at her. "But we are here and it's about time you see that! I'm here, my brother is here, Katy, Ben. It's not just you, Amita!" Edith looked at him and nodded in agreement.

"You bloody prat, we don't have to be," Amita snarled, then there was silence.

They reached the airlock where Tara and Maeven were standing with a detachment of troops dressed in imperial uniforms like the ones worn on Nalanda station. The hatch seemed incredibly simple. There was no way to tell that the shuttle was waiting outside in the void of space with its window replaced and the hole in the cargo bay patched.

Alex stepped towards Maeven and her hand reached out to him. "I heard you're staying here," she asked, her voice high and tight.

Alex touched her hips. "Your father wants me too."

"He said he wants Alex and me by his side," Edith reassured her.

Maeven tried to hide her emotions as she nodded. "It's a good thing. It must mean he approves of you if he wants you here." The statement sounded a bit like a question.

"It is a good thing," Edith said over Alex's shoulder while Amita, still trapped in her grip, huffed.

Edith ignored Amita and said, "Emperor Tamerlane will be doubling the size of the guard for his daughter on Nalanda. Not that I imagine we'll have to worry too much about Tairnishmen attacking her again. Thanks to Amita, I doubt there are many left."

The words were meant to hurt. Amita did what she could to dull them, telling herself that it didn't matter, 'none of this mattered.' She looked around. "Where's Tearmai?" she asked as the airlock door opened.

"He must already be onboard," Edith said as she started down the passage. The airlock led to a small bridge that extended to the shuttle's entrance. The soldiers fell in step behind her. Amita glanced back noticing a look that passed between Maeven and Tara.

"Don't lie to me. Where is he?" Amita called again.

The small bridge was made of metal rings with a walkway beneath, in between the rings was thickened plastic. "Well, if he's not on the shuttle, then he must still be on the emperor's ship," Edith explained as if it should've been obvious.

"Why, why would he keep him?" Amita demanded, feeling rage seep up again, though it was nearly covered by something else. Her pulse began to quicken as her lip trembled and an icy fear spread from her gut. "I need him," she begged as she tried struggling against Edith's unbreakable grip.

"What you need doesn't matter," Edith said. "Only the will of our emperor matters."

Amita looked back at the armed soldiers in the walkway. She looked at the walls, knowing there was

473

only vacuum behind them. Her brow furrowed as her back locked and she fought against the helplessness that was trying to overwhelm her. "You have no bloody idea how wrong you are," she said in a low voice. "None of you lot matter and this is far from over. I promise you that."

Edith reached the end of the bridge. She pushed Amita through, then stepped back, letting the guards go next. "Keep an eye on her. She can be a handful," she said to the officer in charge. The man nodded, then turned and looked coldly at Amita as Edith headed back toward The Revenant.

Amita was unwavering as she returned the soldier's gaze. "That's the first bloody thing she's been right about," Amita warned him as she took a deep breath and stared back at Alex and Edith. The airlock doors closed and the guards forced her down the gangway.

Alex in battle armor

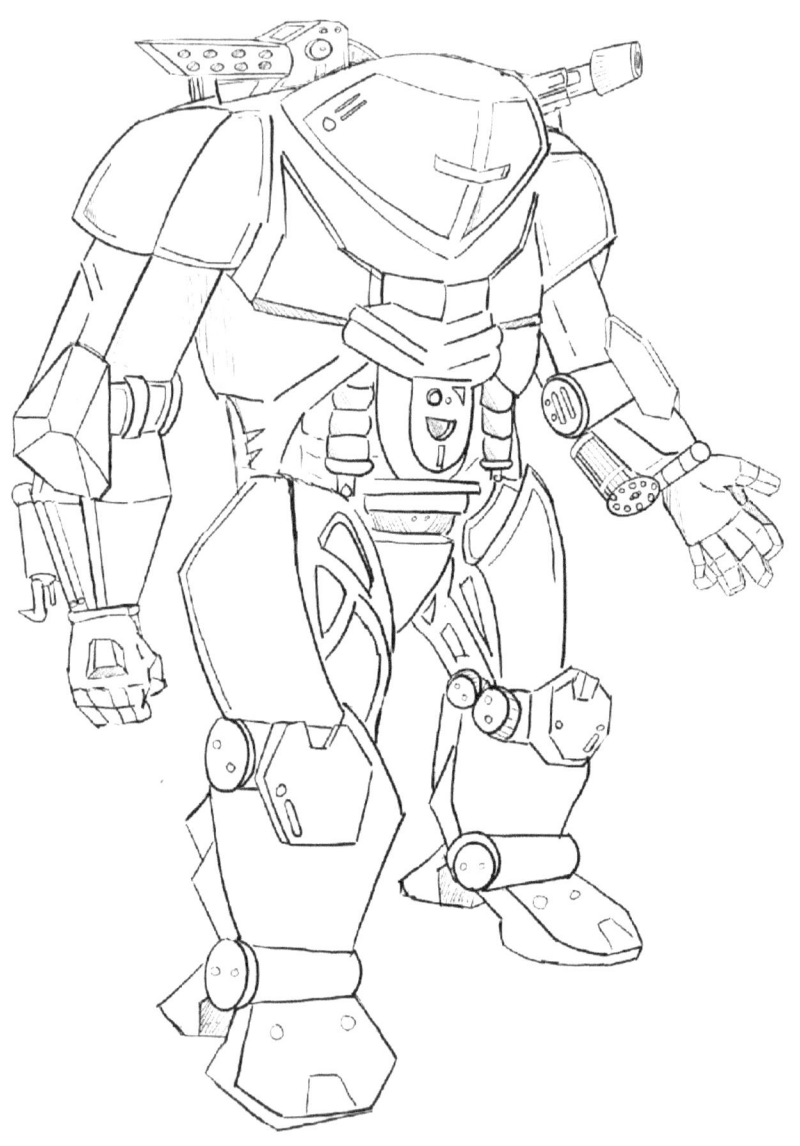

Tairnish soldier

Amita in environmental suit

Wild Fire Golem

Kavaris Altain and Cathal

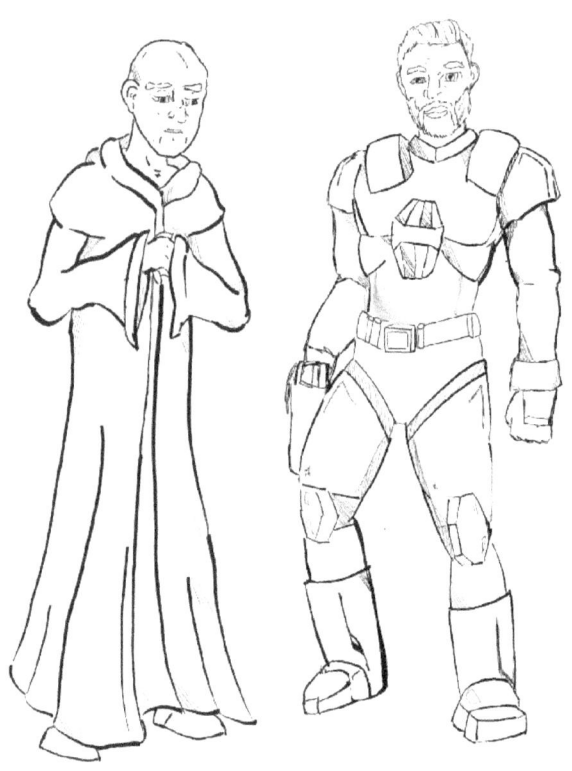

The emperor's flagship
the *Revenant*

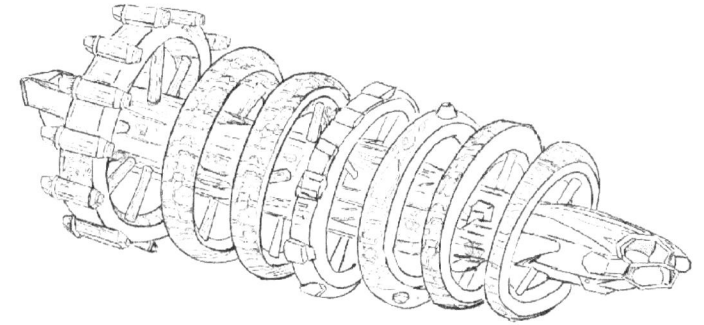

Pete A O'Donnell is the creator of

 Illadvisedstories.com, a children's story podcast where kids can listen to free and funny tales. He's a firefighter and EMT in his day job and has written and illustrated a picture book called the Merlin's Visit the Fire Station about his career. He holds a degree in journalism and creative writing from Queens University. His first book, The Curse of Purgatory Cove won the Royal Dragonfly award for best new author.

The Voice of Stones is his fifth book and the third in a seven book series that began with The Stars Beyond the Mesa. You can download a free character guide at his website PeteAODonnell.com